Mike Willi

The

Cl o

THOROGOOD

Thorogood Publishing Ltd
10-12 Rivington Street
London EC2A 3DU
Telephone: 020 7749 4748
Fax: 020 7729 6110
Email: info@thorogoodpublishing.co.uk
Web: www.thorogoodpublishing.co.uk

A CIP catalogue record for this book is available
from the British Library.

ISBN 978-185418689-8

Book designed and typeset in the UK
by Driftdesign

Printed in the UK by Ashford Colour Press

Dedication

==============

This book is dedicated to all those servicemen and women who, with such selfless courage and professional commitment, keep open the many channels to freedom in today's world…

Author's note

==================

This is the third volume of the fictional trilogy about a naval Special Forces flotilla, which did exist on Tresco in the Isles of Scilly during the Second World War. So secret was this unit that it only became known publicly in 1995, after the fifty-year veil of the Official Secrets Act was lifted.

Volumes 1 and 2 — *The Secret Channel* and *The Channel of Invasion* take the fictional story of this covert unit up to just after D-Day in June 1944.

This book — *The Channel to Freedom* — concludes the saga, from the Allies' Normandy breakout of July/August 1944 to the end of the war in Europe in May 1945 — and the disbandment of the flotilla.

The flotilla base — HMS Godolphin — is a figment of my imagination, included to provide the unit with a focal point and context for its shore-based activities in the UK. To preserve Tresco's strong links to the Royal Navy during both world wars, I have located HMS Godolphin on the site of the First World War Royal Naval Air Service base, of which, even today, some vestiges remain.

Similarly, the characters and events are figments of my imagination, coloured by the influence of personal recall, drawn from my experiences in the Cold War and the impact upon the mainland of the old IRA border campaign. Any similarity between the characters and persons living or dead is purely coincidental.

Other novels by Mike Williams:

The Secret Channel

The Channel of Invasion

Loyalty – or Liberty? (coming soon)

Contents

===============

Principal characters   9

Maps:

    The Isles of Scilly   13

    Crozon Peninsula   14

    Toulon and Les Îles D Hyères   15

    Sweden: The Skagerrak and the Kattegat   16

    Lorient Enclave   17

    County Cork   18

One: Paths To Victory   19

Two: Operation Snatch   35

Three: The Chateau Keeps A Strange Cellar   61

Four: Within A Hair's Breadth   83

Five: Operation Dragoon: The Second
            Channel Of Invasion   99

Six: Channel Of Invasion Cleared
            And Open   117

Seven: A Political Goulash   135

Eight: Bryher – The Island Of Hills   149

Nine: Perhaps A Friend For Life   173

Ten: Blockade Busters   213

Eleven: A Shock For Tremayne   255

Twelve: Mayhem In Parallel   283

Thirteen: Tremayne's Nightmare   323

Fourteen: Heart Of Oak   345

Fifteen: The Final Curtain   385

Epilogue – 2010   395

Glossary of naval and Royal Marine terms   399

Acknowledgements   405

Principal Characters

======================================

In order of seniority of rank.

Royal Navy and Royal Marines

Character:	Referred to as:
Rear Admiral Hembury Director of RN Coastal Forces Operations	*Admiral, The Admiral*
Captain MacPherson Officer commanding HMS Godolphin, Tresco, Isles of Scilly	*The Commanding Officer*
Commander John Enever Senior Naval Intelligence Officer, HMS Godolphin	*Commander, SNIO/SIO*
Lieutenant Commander Richard Tremayne The central figure in this story – an RNVR officer transferred to Coastal Special Forces who commands the Tresco flotilla of MTBs and clandestine fishing vessels	*Flotilla commander/ boat captain*

Character:	Referred to as:
Lieutenant David Willoughby-Brown	*Number One, First*
Tremayne's First Lieutenant (second-in-command) – like Tremayne, an RNVR officer	*Lieutenant, WB*
Lieutenant Hermann Fischer, RNVR	
Tremayne's leading boat captain	
Sub-Lieutenant Pierre Quilghini	*Sub*
Former French naval officer, now with RNVR commission, whose ideas and initiative were fundamental to the setting-up of the secret channels between Tresco and Brittany	
Emma Tremayne	*Intelligence Officer*
Tremayne's wife and formerly Wren Intelligence Officer on Enever's staff at HMS Godolphin, Tresco	*(Navy) SIS,* *'Giselle Trenet'*
Petty Officer Bill Irvine	*Cox'n, 'Swain*
Tremayne's boat coxswain	
Able Seaman Watkins	*Pablo*
A key long-term member of Tremayne's boat crew	
Sergeant Geoff Kane	*Royal*
A key Royal Marine Commando NCO, who has worked closely with the Tresco flotilla	

The Army, SIS and covert Jedburgh team

Character:

Colonel John Farrell
The Rifle Brigade – senior SOE officer

Lieutenant Colonel Tim Galway
'Jed' team leader

Major Mike Black
SAS

Sergeant Paddy Nugent
SAS

US Army of Occupation, Brittany

Character:

Colonel Mark Timmins
US Army local regional CO

French Resistance

Character:

Referred to as:

Capitaine de Vaisseau, Philippe Duvalier
Head of a Breton Resistance Confrèrie

'Lionel'

Philippe
Communist Maquis leader in Lorient

Marc
Local Resistance commander on the Crozon peninsula

Simone
French Resistance courier in Lorient

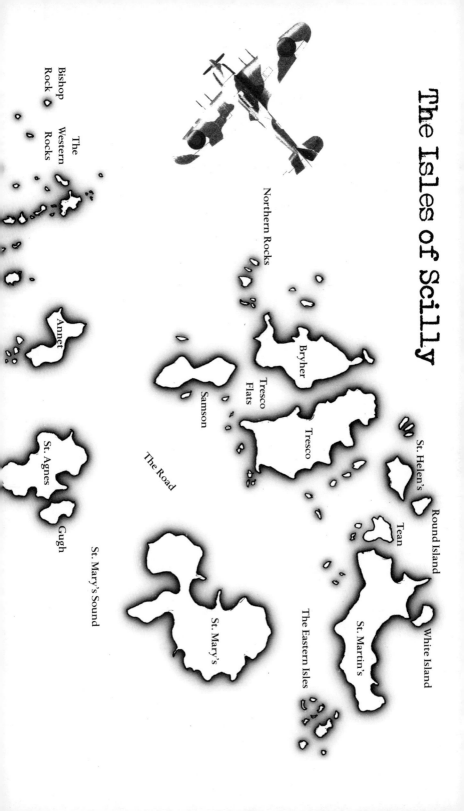

The Isles of Scilly

Bishop Rock

The Western Rocks

Northern Rocks

Annet

Bryher

Tresco Flats

Samson

Tresco

St. Helen's

Round Island

St. Agnes

The Road

Tean

White Island

Gugh

St. Mary's Sound

St. Mary's

The Eastern Isles

St. Martin's

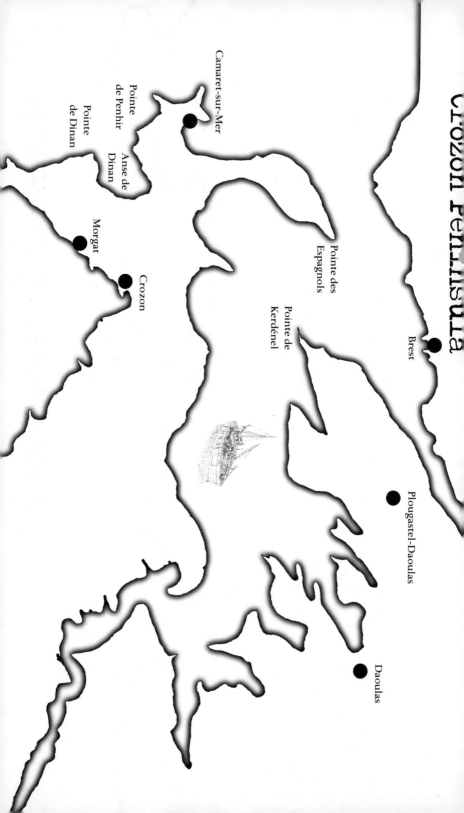

Crozon Peninsula

Camaret-sur-Mer

Pointe
de Penhir

Pointe
de Dinan

Anse de
Dinan

Morgat

Crozon

Pointe des
Espagnols

Pointe de
Kerdénel

Brest

Plougastel-Daoulas

Daoulas

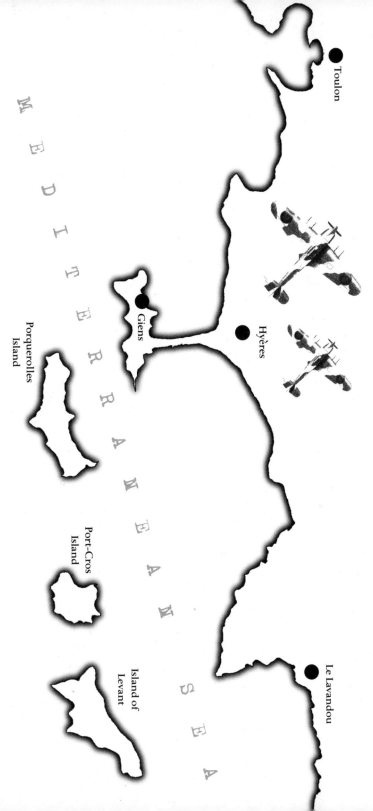

Toulon and Les Îles D'Hyères

Toulon

MEDITERRANEAN SEA

Porquerolles Island

Giens

Hyères

Port-Cros Island

Island of Levant

Le Lavandou

Sweden: The Skagerrak and the Kattegat

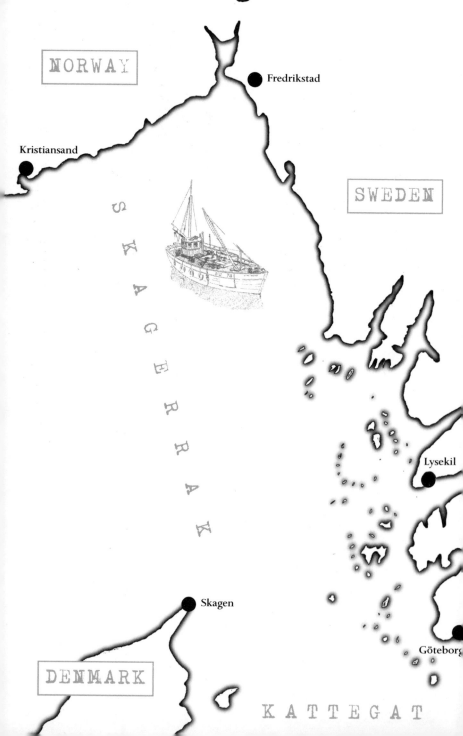

NORWAY

Fredrikstad

Kristiansand

SWEDEN

S K A G E R R A K

Lysekil

Skagen

Göteborg

DENMARK

K A T T E G A T

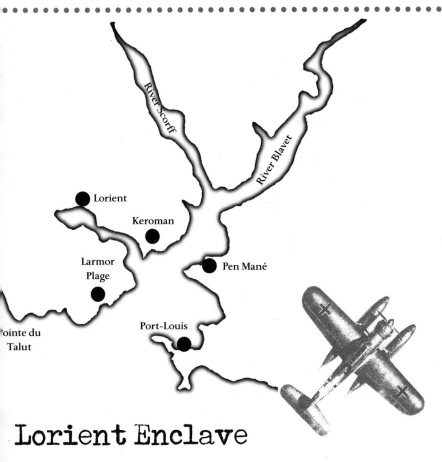

LIBERATED ZONE HELD BY FRENCH AND US

River Scorff

River Blavet

Lorient

Keroman

Larmor
Plage

Pen Mané

Pointe du
Talut

Port-Louis

Lorient Enclave

County Cork

Oysterhaven

Kinure

YOUGHAL BAY

Entrance to
Cork Harbour

To Cobh

One

Paths To Victory

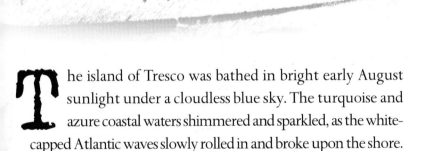

The island of Tresco was bathed in bright early August sunlight under a cloudless blue sky. The turquoise and azure coastal waters shimmered and sparkled, as the white-capped Atlantic waves slowly rolled in and broke upon the shore.

The assembled ship's company stood at ease, in three ranks, lined up on the hard standing that served as HMS Godolphin's small parade ground – typical of a Royal Navy 'stone frigate'. Facing them – and stood on a small dais – was Admiral Hembury DSO, Director of RN Coastal Forces. Either side of him were, respectively, a commodore, RN and a Royal Marine major general. Captain MacPherson, Godolphin's commanding officer, stood behind the Admiral, ready to take over as master of ceremonies when called upon to do so.

Seated on two rows of wooden benches to the right of the dais were a number of VIP guests and visitors. A Royal Marines band added to the relaxed, summery occasion, playing traditional British airs and marches.

In front and to the left of the dais, three officers, one rating and one Royal Marine from HMS Godolphin – immaculately turned out in their best uniforms – stood waiting for the awards investiture to begin. Standing with them was a smartly dressed young woman.

One of the three officers present was Lieutenant Commander Richard Tremayne, RNVR, commander of the Tresco flotilla. Flanking the group were two naval flag lieutenants wearing gold ceremonial aiguillettes on their shoulders.

Immediately to Tremayne's right stood Lieutenant David Willoughby-Brown, his first lieutenant and close friend. To his left stood Commander John Enever, HMS Godolphin's donnish and highly talented Senior Naval Intelligence Officer. Next to them, in order of seniority, stood Royal Marines Sergeant Geoff Kane and then Leading Seaman 'Pablo' Watkins.

Alongside the five, her hands clasped in front of her, proudly stood Sarah McDonald, the widow of Tremayne's engineer – Petty Officer Alistair McDonald – who was so brutally executed when he and Tremayne were taken prisoner in Brittany some eight months previously. Though pale and drawn, she projected an air of great dignity and quiet composure. On the lapel of her new navy blue suit she wore a silver brooch in the shape of a naval Tudor crown.

Today was *their* day and the formal recognition of their courage and professionalism. It was to be a celebration with enough fitting pomp and ceremony to create a memorable sense of occasion for them and those of their loved ones who were present. Acknowledging their own was something that the Royal Navy did well – and today was to be no exception.

Already, Tremayne had found the day to be an intensely moving one, where outstanding service – and sacrifice – were being publicly acknowledged with justifiable pride.

As the strains of the old air *Where Ere You Walk* died away, the substantial figure of Captain MacPherson stepped forward to the front of the dais and, taking command, called the parade to attention. As one, sailors and Marines smartly brought heels together and snapped arms to their sides, as their rifles, with bayonets fixed, were swung into position.

The Royal Marines band, resplendent in white pith helmets and blue parade uniforms, struck up *Rule Britannia*. From the stirring opening bars, Tremayne was delighted that it was the original version they were playing. Mercifully, he thought, it was devoid of any pretentious conductor's tedious, so-called 'arrangements', which too often dilute Arne's inspiring composition.

'Hmmm, patriotism might be the last refuge of the scoundrel,' he mused as his spine tingled, 'but right now, some unashamedly raw jingoism feels pretty good to me!'

Accompanied by his two flag lieutenants, Admiral Hembury moved towards the group of six to begin the investiture and present medals. Starting with the most senior present, he began with Commander John Enever who had earned an OBE for his tireless and crucial contribution to Naval Intelligence. Second was Tremayne, awarded the DSO for his outstanding leadership and gallantry in action on Sword Beach, immediately following the D-Day Normandy landings.

Lieutenant Willoughby-Brown, RNVR, was next in line, also to receive the DSO for his coolness and the example he set, under fire, in rescuing Tremayne off the Brittany coast, following the latter's escape from a German PoW camp.

After Willoughby-Brown, it was Sarah McDonald's turn to receive the posthumous DCM for her husband's courage and devotion to duty in captivity and his persistent refusal to divulge information to his interrogators. To spare Mrs McDonald further distress, no mention was made in the citation of the appalling, brutal treatment that her husband – and Tremayne – had suffered at the hands of the Gestapo before his indefensible execution.

Admiral Hembury spoke to each recipient in turn. A sincere and kindly man, his comments went way beyond trite platitudes and clichéd conversation. It was obvious that he had given considerable thought to what was particularly important and relevant to say to each of those being awarded medals. He spent a little longer with Sarah McDonald than with the others and Tremayne was grateful for that.

Sergeant Kane followed, to receive a Bar to his Military Cross for his bravery, under heavy German fire, with the Combined Operations Pilotage Party shore reconnaissance team at the start of the Normandy landing. Then it was Leading Seaman 'Pablo' Watkins' turn. Watkins, a popular member of Tremayne's own MTB boat crew, was awarded the DCM for outstanding bravery in the face of the enemy when fighting ashore on D-Day as naval infantry.

Following the investiture, MacPherson resumed his role of master of ceremonies. Calling the ship's company to attention, he ordered 'Parade, left turn!' then 'By the left, quick march!' as the band struck up *Heart of Oak*, another telling reminder of the Royal Navy's past deeds — and their most recent successes.

The medal recipients, their families and several VIPs attending the ceremony as guests were then transported in RN three-ton lorries — fitted with temporary seats — to afternoon tea on the large lawn, close to Tresco Abbey and its beautiful gardens.

The band, which had now rejoined the party, began playing light music, maintaining a relaxed garden party atmosphere as a fitting sequel to the earlier, more formal, yet intensely moving celebrations.

Tremayne quickly sought out Mrs McDonald, who was already being well looked after by the attentive, white-clad stewards. He was only too aware of the emptiness of words to the bereaved, yet he wanted to talk with her and, small comfort though it might be, to let her know that he was with her husband when he died.

'Thank you for introducing yourself to me. Alistair often spoke of you with admiration and was so happy that you were his commanding officer.'

'For my part, I was grateful and glad that he was a member of my crew – and such an important one at that. In times of crisis, he was our 'Rock of Gibraltar'. We all relied on Mac – as he was known to us – and on his unfailing dependability. On our last operation together, I was able to get to know him well and was so impressed by his courage and commitment. It was indeed a privilege to have served with your husband, Mrs McDonald.'

Emma Tremayne, herself a former Wren officer from Commander Enever's Intelligence Section, unobtrusively joined her husband and Mrs McDonald. With her gentle sincerity and sensitivity, she added so much empathy and natural warmth to Tremayne's words of comfort. Within seconds, she and Sarah McDonald were fully engaged in conversation, like two old friends who had known each other for many years. Tremayne sensed that it was his cue to move on.

He next found Leading Seaman Watkins who, together with Tremayne, had wiped out a German machine-gun post, firing on troops coming ashore on Sword Beach during the D-Day landings. Watkins – known universally as 'Pablo' because of a sombrero he had insisted on wearing during several runs ashore on his ship's pre-war visit to Panama – smiled self-consciously as Tremayne shook his hand to congratulate him.

Touching the brand new medal with obvious pride, he said wistfully, 'Old Brummie would 'ave laughed like a drain if 'e'd been 'ere today, sir, and seen me get this from the Admiral.'

Brummie Nicholls who, like Watkins, came from Birmingham, had been killed as Tremayne's party came ashore, following the sinking of their MTB early on D-Day.

The two had been inseparable, having known one another long before they joined the Navy together. Almost two months had passed since Nicholls' death, but the pain of the loss of his closest mate was still etched on Watkins' amiable, lived-in face.

They had been chatting for some time when Enever emerged from the guests' refreshments marquee, which had been set up on the lawn, and came over to tell Tremayne that Admiral Hembury wanted to speak with him.

Before he left, he was glad to see that Emma and Sarah McDonald – along with Willoughby-Brown and his fiancée, Lucy Caswell, who, like her friend Emma, was a member of Enever's Intelligence Section – were moving round to converge on Watkins. The Royal Marines major general was engaged in an animated discussion with the recently promoted Sergeant Kane, which was regularly punctuated with bursts of laughter from each of them.

As Tremayne, followed closely by Enever, entered the marquee, Admiral Hembury detached himself from a group of distinguished looking civilians and senior officers from all three Services and came over, his hand outstretched in welcome.

'Tremayne, my dear fellow, do come and join us.' Motioning to one of the hovering stewards, he called for glasses of champagne for both officers.

Hembury quickly introduced Tremayne to those in the VIP party with the words: 'All of you, I believe, will most certainly have heard of Lieutenant Commander Tremayne by reputation and some of you have met him or served with him already.' He looked around the group, noting the number of assenting nods and affirmative responses.

'You will know then, gentlemen, exactly what I mean when I say that he is indisputably a fully paid-up member of the 'by-my-deeds-ye-shall-know-me' school of leadership. You are aware, too, that I am running a major conference on Combined Operations Strategy at the Royal Naval Barracks, Plymouth – the core theme of which is 'The Path to Victory'. The main thrusts of that theme are the urgent need for greater collaboration and shared openness of military intelligence between the three Services and the level of professional leadership essential to create and sustain such cooperative openness.'

The intelligent brown eyes sought Tremayne's. 'I want the lieutenant commander to speak at the conference on what I term 'close-quarter' leadership. That is, the critical importance of a leader to be able to read situations correctly and to make happen, *what* should happen, *when* it should happen. As I believe our American friends say 'If you are in the room, BE in the room.' It is as much that rare skill of *sensing* what is required of the leader, as it is of using logic to intervene and take command.

I have in mind an input of one hour, based upon your experiences and unique practice – with plenty of specific examples.'

Once again, Hembury looked directly at Tremayne to gauge his reaction to being put on the spot and committed so unexpectedly – and so publicly.

With his stomach churning – yet outwardly seeming completely unfazed – and only too conscious of the Admiral's Biblical reference to his leadership style, Tremayne's response was immediate: 'I'm honoured, sir. Thank you. Does a suggested synopsis by next Monday meet your deadline, sir?'

'It does. Indeed it does!' Hembury paused for a moment's reflection. 'A tip, Tremayne. Draw upon what is meant by the 'Nelson touch' – without making the connection glaringly obvious – and then, above all, be yourself and talk from the heart as well as from the head. Concentrate on the 'must-do's – not the 'nice-to's – as I'm sure you will.'

Hembury paused, smiling, clearly delighted with Tremayne's swift and positive reaction.

'Now, keep contact through Lieutenant Armstrong here – he's putting the conference programme together for me and knows exactly what I need from you.'

He indicated the tall, smiling figure of the youthful flag lieutenant, wearing the gold aiguillettes.

Returning to Tremayne, the Admiral concluded with, 'Thank you, Richard – I look forward immensely to your very important contribution to our landmark conference.'

Then to the assembled VIP group: 'Ladies and gentlemen,

the sun is shining, it's a glorious day. Let's go outside and enjoy it!'

Armstrong immediately came across and shook Tremayne's hand.

'Richard, I'm John and here's my phone number. Call me on the blower whenever you need to. As soon as I return to HMS Drake, I will send you synopses of the other speakers' contributions to give you a conference background and context, within which you can pitch your lecture.'

As they left, Enever lightly touched Tremayne's arm. 'Well done dear boy, you've made a big hit. Thank you for such an immediate and positive response. I'm afraid you have me to blame for this!'

'I rather suspected that. I certainly couldn't imagine Captain MacPherson putting my name forward!' grinned Tremayne.

MacPherson, a hostage to procedure, routine and detail, had made it clear from the outset of their relationship that he did not approve of Tremayne's unorthodoxy and preference for the unexpected in the role of flotilla commander. Admiralty Fleet Orders (AFOs) were MacPherson's 'Bible' and, on several occasions, he had sought to block what he saw as Tremayne's maverick operational tactics.

An executive officer of limited imagination – and possessed of a deep-rooted fear of any departure from conventional, copper-bottomed practices – he had often attempted, unsuccessfully, to 'bring Tremayne into line'.

Too often it seemed, his principal motivation for applying

the stifling grip of seniority was to enforce and maintain control – whatever the cost to the outcome of an operation.

Commander Enever, a man of high intelligence and social acuity, frequently acted as a buffer for Tremayne. On more than one occasion, he had simply enlisted the driving support of Admiral Hembury in order to move urgent and critical operations forward. If MacPherson had, in any way, been an impediment to necessary swift and decisive action.

This command was MacPherson's first experience of Special Forces. Their natural, confident resourcefulness and irreverent self-reliance did not sit comfortably with him. Characteristically, he sought to control by fear, stifling authoritarianism – and the rule book – or, at least, *his* literal interpretation of it.

Enever, a highly creative and resourceful thinker, regularly engaged in battles with MacPherson, whose inept and irrelevant orders too often over-complicated and delayed the achievement of operational objectives. On one notable occasion, when utterly frustrated by such mindless interference, he broke protocol, describing MacPherson as someone with an infinite capacity for turning the term 'Naval Intelligence' into a most unfortunate oxymoron.

Teatime refreshments found Tremayne back once more with Emma and Catriona, their two-month-old baby daughter. The glorious August sun continued to shine and the band played more light music, adding to the sense of peace and well-being. So different, reflected Tremayne, from the world he had temporarily left behind, in post-invasion France, just a matter of forty-eight hours ago.

In the confused weeks that followed the first heady and triumphant days of liberation, Tremayne had already experienced the uncertainty and transient stability of the contentious interregnum following the Germans' departure. In those areas liberated by the Allies, the various, competing Resistance groups openly fought and jockeyed for political power and influence.

Attempts to weld the different Resistance groups into a cohesive fighting movement – the Forces Françaises de l'Interieur (FFI) – had created an irregular, as yet uncoordinated, army of impressive potential. The FFI had done much to facilitate the Allies' rapid advance and deployment across France after their beachhead breakout and they continued to pay a terrible price for their courage and initiative. Yet even with their track record of bravery and military success, they acquired the nickname of 'Fifis' amongst some disaffected sections of the population.

In occupied Vichy France especially, French paramilitary units such as the Milice and Groupes Mobiles de Réserve (GMR) regularly operated in conjunction with the German army and SS to wipe out local Maquis groups with savage ferocity. In Vercors alone, in the south of France, some 750 Maquisards were slaughtered by a combined Milice and GMR force, supporting German alpine troops. At Glières, another 150 members of the Maquis were killed and many hundreds were captured when over 1,200 Miliciens and GMR once again joined Gebirgsjäger mountain troop units to crush Resistance groups.

The utter tragedy of Frenchmen killing Frenchmen – and women – had escalated dramatically since D-Day, as many Resistance units prematurely rushed to support the invading forces.

Now, different factions, including the powerful Communist elements and former Vichy unit turncoats, were at loggerheads with one another, fighting for 'territorial' supremacy in the anticipated new order of things. Both, in turn, were opposed to General De Gaulle's rapidly growing influence, as supporters in Paris and the major towns flocked to join the FFI and identify with his very direct brand of French patriotism.

Already, in these early days of newly won freedom, many of those liberated were coming to regard their liberators as another, replacement, army of occupation and were beginning to react against what they termed '*Liberté, à la sauce américaine*'.

In Brittany, Tremayne's area of most frequent operational activity, some Resistance groups were, similarly, at odds with US attempts to assume overall control in those regions where the American army had just ejected the Germans.

After four years of Nazi occupation, the French – understandably – wanted to run France the *French* way, with French customs and practices. Even that seemingly reasonable brand of chauvinism was riven, culturally and politically, by the irreconcilable division of conservatism versus radicalism. As Enever had said, 'We're dealing with a nation of fifty million people – and fifty million different political parties!'

'The territorial imperative can be an all-consuming, all-powerful emotive drive,' mused Tremayne, deep in reflection, as he walked back to rejoin Emma and Catriona.

Emma's burst of happy laughter as she played with their daughter, suddenly broke Tremayne's reverie and brought him back to the relaxed atmosphere of the garden party.

He felt both angry and guilty that his concern with his impending role in France was cutting into his precious and very limited time with Emma and Catriona. These were among tomorrow's most important memories. He recognised, too, that because of Emma's work in Intelligence – both in the Wrens and latterly as a civilian working with the Secret Intelligence Service (SIS) – it was all too easy to take for granted that she would understand and accept his preoccupation. Her unfailing tacit support and lack of reproach only added to his uncomfortable sense of guilt.

To enjoy a more personal celebration of the investiture, Tremayne and Emma, together with Willoughby-Brown and Lucy Caswell, dined that evening at the New Inn. As they laughed and talked animatedly – as they invariably did, ranging over so many shared interests – Tremayne's mood lifted. He was constantly aware of Emma's unconditional love. Expressing it in so many understated ways – by a knowing smile, a concerned look, or by some hilarious but subtle put-down – Emma could quickly put his concerns into perspective.

Whatever her own worries about his role, she invariably managed to cover up her anxiety and not project it onto her husband. That night, at the New Inn, they made love with intense, yet sensitive passion, giving themselves completely to one another in what they termed 'their' room.

The day after the investiture, Enever called a briefing meeting with Tremayne along with members of SOE and Capitaine de Vaisseau Philippe Duvalier, code-named 'Lionel' — formerly of the French Marine Nationale and the leader of the Resistance Confrèrie Bonaparte in Brittany. His priority was to outline the immediate operations he was planning for the Tresco flotilla in France, following the Allies' breakout from Normandy. The war-torn France to which Tremayne would be returning in little more than thirty-six hours' time...

Two

Operation Snatch

In the confused weeks following the delayed US and British hard-fought breakouts from the Normandy beachheads, Tremayne, together with members of SOE, began working closely with the Confrèrie units in Brittany. They had been tasked with helping to bring stability, coherence and direction into the transitional civic administration emerging in the newly liberated areas of the province. Underlying their concern to generate order out of chaos, was their need to speed up the transformation of French Resistance into a unified fighting force to support the Allies' advance.

At times, Tremayne spent upwards of a week in Brittany,

along with his SOE colleagues. At others, he operated within the province for no more than thirty-six hours before returning for debriefing to SOE HQ in Baker Street or to Naval Intelligence at HMS Godolphin. His occasional visits to Baker Street's French Section meant that he was able spend some time, albeit it all too briefly, with Emma – and Catriona.

Their love had grown deeper and even stronger than it had been in their few carefree days together on Tresco. 'In less than two years, Richard, we've experienced more heart-stopping days – both wonderful and cruel – than do most couples who spend a whole lifetime together,' she had said to him on their last brief leave outside London. That each, while still so young, had already lost someone close in the war, added a sharp poignancy to Emma's words. During his horrifying ordeal in the Gestapo cells following his capture in Brittany, it was his love for Emma, more than anything else, that had sustained him and helped him to retain his sanity. As he had stood bound to a wooden post in the ice-cold courtyard at Rennes, facing the firing party and expecting death, his thoughts were only of Emma and the child that he would never see. As well as being his wife, lover and dearest friend, Emma was his emotional sheet anchor.

In between the commitments of his new assignment, Tremayne delivered what Hembury termed 'an outstanding and most telling contribution' to the Admiral's critical strategic conference. The most junior officer at the conference, Tremayne spoke from his heart as well as from his head. The emphasis of his speech was the vital issue of inspirational leadership and of giving people enough belief in themselves to take on assignments they had previously considered impossible.

Hembury was impressed by the degree to which Tremayne had held his audience of senior officers in the palm of his hand. His message – that *real* leaders show humility and, when necessary, act as 'first, among equals' as well as demonstrably setting an example by leading from the front – hit home hard. Hembury was clearly delighted with the audience's enthusiastic reception of his eleventh-hour protégé's straight-from-the-shoulder delivery and the powerful content of his lecture.

'Yours was a most relevant and challenging talk, Richard! You certainly won your conference spurs today – and in front of a very tough, unforgiving audience. I particularly valued your comments about the true test of leadership coming when you have to lead people to success in conditions of extreme adversity. That hit the bullseye with the conference members. You made a most favourable impression on some pretty influential people and lent a significantly authoritative note to this important event. You have my grateful thanks.'

Tremayne was delighted by the Admiral's feedback. Speaking to such a group of people and delivering what was essentially a formal lecture, had been a nerve-wracking experience – especially so *before* the event. He had spent several disturbed nights waking up at unearthly hours to scribble notes on the pad he kept by whatever bed, bunk, or cot he happened to be sleeping in, as fresh thoughts and ideas interrupted his often fitful sleep. On the day, however, he was immediately into his stride, engaging with his audience, as he recalled the advice given to him by John Armstrong, Hembury's Flag Lieutenant: '*Just be yourself, Richard, and remember that if there are NO butterflies in your gut, you're not really with the situation. Talk with the passion you feel for the subject and back up your beliefs with those facts which you know to be true . . .*'

The day following the conference, Tremayne returned to France by Coastal Command Lockheed Hudson. Within a matter of hours, he had been pitched right back into the interregnum chaos and administrative contradiction, which some areas of Brittany had temporarily become.

A major area of evolving conflict – in constant need of reconciliation – was between the necessary expediency of American commanders, almost continuously engaged in battle, and the equally understandable patriotic fervour of the French over reclaimed territory and their deep need to see justice and retribution. Underlying this was a sensitivity and deep-rooted guilt over the degree of collaboration that had inevitably occurred during the occupation. As a result, there had been an unseemly rush to exact revenge in many areas as they became liberated. Brutal summary executions were becoming commonplace. Devoid of pity, or even basic humanity, retribution was carried out against men and women alike. In some cases, punishment was exacted on the flimsiest of evidence.

During what was becoming known as the '*l'épuration*

sauvage', some nine thousand suspected collaborators were executed – many without a proper trial. Tremayne felt, on more than one occasion, that so-called 'justice' was little more than the evening up of old scores, over neighbours' feuds or personal transgressions, where there had been little or no involvement with the occupying forces.

SOE's primary concern was the overriding need to coordinate the activities of the various Resistance groups, in order to provide optimum support to the Allied armies now advancing in several directions through France towards her borders. SOE recognised the need for the French to resolve their political and cultural issues as a matter of some urgency, if the opposing factions in the Resistance were to be able to sustain their collective contribution.

As always, Enever's debriefings of events in Brittany were in Hut 101 at HMS Godolphin which, increasingly, was taking on the appearance – and congenial feel – of a university professor's study. The deceptively benign ambience of the station's Intelligence Centre was unquestionably reinforced by Enever's seemingly easy-going, yet clinically focused style.

Admiral Hembury, a great supporter of the Tresco flotilla and of Enever in particular, was well known in Admiralty circles as 'The Artful Dodger' for his ability to prise equipment – and 'liberate' vital supplies –away from their owners and into the domains of Coastal Special Forces' supplies and stores officers. His persuasive and cogent reasoning, leading to the release – often under resigned protest – of key personnel to Special

Forces, earned him the additional title of 'The Body Snatcher'. Enever, Tremayne and Willoughby-Brown had all been seconded to the Tresco flotilla via the Admiral's exquisitely applied pressure and personal influence.

Enever's office displayed many of the fruits of Hembury's genteel appropriation of others' goods and chattels. These included a beautiful, large Georgian walnut desk, a Victorian captain's chair, several deep leather armchairs, which formerly graced some Admiral's quarters in Queen Anne's Mansions, and a huge, now overflowing, mahogany bookcase. What caught Tremayne's attention this time was Enever's latest acquisition: a well-proportioned English eighteenth-century 'country' table, made of beautifully figured elm. Lying on it was a mysterious looking object of indeterminate shape, covered by a dust sheet.

With his treasured meerschaum pipe clamped unlit between his lips, Enever began. 'Under Major General 'Lightning' Joe Collins, the US VII Corps are advancing like bats out of hell through Brittany and their main thrust continues to be towards the major naval bases – especially Brest, St Nazaire and Lorient. However, if the recent protracted and bloody battle for St Malo is anything to go by, the Yanks could have a monumental task on their hands in liberating these ports for Allies' use. We shall give whatever support we can to assist them, by working closely with the Confrèrie Bonaparte. Since D-Day, this centre of French Resistance continues to grow into a fighting force to be reckoned with.'

He nodded to Lionel, the leader of what was the most

consistently effective Resistance group in Brittany, before continuing. 'French Resistance has already given invaluable help to the Americans and we need to continue to strengthen their hand as much as we can.'

Colonel John Farrell, a Rifle Brigade officer working for SOE, picked up the issue of the long, bloody fight for St Malo. 'When the Yanks finally wrested the port from Jerry, the German commander – an arrogant bastard called von Auloch – appeared for the formal surrender, freshly shaved and immaculate in his best uniform.' Farrell paused with a wry grin. 'The Americans to whom he surrendered were a tough bunch who had fought like hell against stubborn German opposition but, as people who respect courage, they tolerated his flair for showmanship with good humour. The serious aspect of this, gentlemen, is that there are unlikely to be any cheap or easy victories in liberating the main Atlantic seaports. The Jerries are going to defend them to the end.'

Enever took up his story again: 'I am not expecting us to be called upon to support any prolonged assaults to take the Atlantic seaports. Though, no doubt, there is the strong possibility that we will play some sort of Special Forces role in helping to expedite their surrender if the freedom of Brittany, as a whole, is ever in real jeopardy. At the moment, gentlemen, we shall continue to operate from Tresco. We shall, of course, use the secret channels we have already established to and from the Brittany coast, with both our MTBs and our simulated Breton fishing boats – though more about that in a moment, gentlemen. Air cover needed for operations will, as before, be provided either by Squadron Leader Tim Stanley's Hurricanes from St Mary's or by Beaufighters from bases in Devon and Cornwall.' Enever paused while a young Signals Branch Wren brought in tea and – fresh from the galley – some of chef's conversation-stopping 'Nelson slices', glutinous concoctions of fruit, pastry and icing.

Mike Black, an SAS major and, like Farrell, now seconded to SOE, reached for one of the slices, hesitating for a moment with an expression of doubt – bordering on disbelief. Seeing Black's fleeting and very uncharacteristic caution, Tremayne burst out laughing. 'These are uniquely 'Navy', Mike – the Army has nothing like them. You can use them to caulk leaking seams in small boats, load pom-poms with them when you run out of ammunition – and, if desperate, you can *even* eat them! Try one – they're actually very good.'

'Mastering the Navy's more arcane secret weapons is an art – acquired only by long years of experience,' laughed Enever. 'As a Frenchman used to some of the world's finest cuisine, Lionel will confirm that these are, indeed, an *expérience culinaire!*'

'Bien sûr, John – an experience *nevair* to be forgotten!'

Removing his pipe and laying it on his brass ashtray, Enever smiled benignly at the group. 'I'll carry on, gentlemen, while you grapple with our sticky wedges! Our major – and urgent – task is to snatch and bring back to England a senior SS officer who, temporarily, went to ground after the Americans moved so swiftly into eastern Brittany. The latest news is that he has recently resurfaced. Members of Lionel's Confrèrie have tracked him down – after many days of patient searching and surveillance – to a Gestapo Interrogation Centre. This is a large chateau, surrounded by woodland, on the Crozon peninsula, south of and close to Brest. If the fight to recapture Brest becomes the major engagement, which I believe it will, von Greiner – our target – could easily slip away again in the confusion of battle. That, gentlemen, is why we must snatch him before any direct attack on Brest takes place.'

'Who is this man and why, exactly, do we want him?' asked Farrell

'The man we're after is SS-Obersturmbannführer Walter von Greiner. We want him especially for his part in the execution of recaptured escaped British prisoners of war and those taken following commando raids on the French coast. Amongst other things, he is also a senior intelligence specialist, who possesses up-to-date information about German strategies for eliminating Resistance groups within Brittany. Although he has a war criminal's record of terror in France – including Normandy and Brittany, against civilians, Lionel agrees that we can have this guy for his strategic intelligence, but principally to bring him to justice. The information that we do get out of him – and, make no mistake, we *will* get it – about the Resistance, will be shared immediately with the Confrèrie.'

Enever scraped his pipe clean, emptying the contents into his brass ashtray. ' Von Greiner, like too many of his former colleagues from SS Totenkopf, has been responsible for murdering unarmed Allied prisoners since 1940.' His voice and body betrayed the ice-cold emotion he was experiencing. Never before had Tremayne seen Enever fight so hard to control his feelings. 'He will have a proper trial, but I give you my solemn word, gentlemen, that this bastard *will* hang. I have been handed the task by Admiral Hembury of tracing and helping to bring to justice several Gestapo and SS personnel based in Brittany.'

'Hmmm, I suppose,' ventured Black, 'it can at least be said of the SS that they know how to die.'

'So did the Gadarene swine.' Tremayne's swift and cryptic riposte caught some by surprise, though Enever, especially, understood the feelings behind the chilly response.

At this point, Lionel came into the discussion. 'Von Greiner's abduction and subsequent punishment need to de undertaken 'officially' by Allied troops. Any attempts by French Resistance groups to seize and deal with this man – successful or otherwise – will incur unacceptable levels of retribution on innocent French citizens in areas still occupied by the Nazis. It is only two months since the hideous massacre by SS Das Reich of over 640 people at Oradour-sur-Glane. Because of this, we are making sure that the justifiable punishment of war criminals and *collaborateurs* carried out by us, is only in those areas where the Boche have been kicked out.'

Enever looked at Farrell and Black and took a long swig of his tea.

'Thank you, Lionel. So, gentlemen, we need to move quickly on this one. Do I take it that, on behalf of SOE, I have your approval?'

Black was the first to answer. 'I will need to clear my involvement in the operation with Colonel Masefield of French Section, but I doubt if he will have any objections.'

'John?'

Farrell's response was equally positive. 'A telephone call to Baker Street should clear my yardarm.'

'Thank you. It seems that we're in business.'

'So, what's the plan?' asked Farrell.

'Temporarily, gentlemen, we cannot use our fishing boats. Jerry put the kybosh on this, about a week ago, by temporarily forbidding Breton fishing vessels to put to sea. Any fishing boat breaking the curfew, however apparently authentic, would be stopped, searched and impounded and its crew arrested and interrogated.' Enever eased his chair closer to the others, as if to speak more confidentially.

'One option is to parachute in, but the safe drop zones are currently rather too far from our target. Already, several three-man Jedburgh Anglo-French sabotage teams are operating in the area, having parachuted in, and Jerry has become very alert to unwelcome visitors dropping out of the sky.' Catching Black's fleeting look of disappointment, Enever quickly added, 'Mike, I recognise that, to members of the Regiment, the preferred means of insertion into a target zone is often by parachute. Currently, however, we cannot bank on more than about a twenty per cent success rate with a drop and those are unacceptable odds. Another option is to insert by submarine, but she would need to stand too far offshore for the assault party to paddle in. Unable to dive in the inshore shallow waters, she'd be a sitting duck on the surface for Jerry's coastal batteries and E-boats, were she to come in close enough for the paddlers. Our other alternative – and the one Admiral Hembury favours – is to come close inshore in the dark, at the most two cables off, using the captured E-boat that he 'won' for us from RNB

Devonport. The 'snatch team' would then be paddled in dinghies to the shore, to RV with the local Confrèrie unit waiting on the beach.'

'And they,' interrupted Lionel, 'will arrange transport and safe accommodation for you, relatively close to the chateau. It hides its sinister function as an Interrogation Centre under the more innocent cover of a rest and recreation facility for German U-boat crews.'

Enever resumed his story. 'If you agree to this proposal, I will appoint Richard as boat captain, with Lieutenant Willoughby-Brown as his Number One. By the way Richard' – the kindly grey eyes twinkled – 'the E-boat that the Admiral so thoughtfully 'lifted' for us is of similar vintage to the one you stole from Jerry in France so she'll be no stranger to you. She sports the camouflage scheme, insignia and pennant number of the Kriegsmarine's Cherbourg-based flotilla.'

'Seniority, John,' added Enever, nodding to Farrell, 'puts you in command of the operation. Do you all agree that this is our best option?' Enever's question was met with unanimous agreement from the group.

'Thank you, gentlemen, this is how we will do it. Lionel, *mon vieux*, over to you.'

Tremayne could feel his spine tingle as the Frenchman outlined the proposed sequence of the operation. The prospect of action quickened his pulse and the rush of adrenaline began. He could already imagine the low windswept bridge of the E-boat as she surged through the churning sea at over forty knots. For a brief moment, he could feel the exhilaration of the spray from her bow-wave, cascading sparkling white over her deeply flared hull and armoured deck. He yearned to be at sea again, listening to the rumbling growl of the boat's powerful diesels, once more in command of a crew he respected and in whose company he thrived.

His reverie was interrupted as Enever suddenly stepped in and, together with Lionel, lifted off the dust sheet covering the mysterious object. '*Le voila*! This is the Chateau de Trevannec, gentlemen!'

A gasp of admiration from the group greeted the surprise appearance of the exquisitely detailed architect's model of the chateau. 'It was built up from both extensive aerial photographic reconnaissance, courtesy of RAF Intelligence at Medmenham, and photos taken by the Confrèrie,' added Enever. 'Admiral Hembury shamelessly played upon the patriotism of an architect friend of his to get the thing made for us, though he grudgingly admitted to having to part with a case of the finest Claret as payment!'

'Ah, entrances and exits, walls, fences and potential cover – on both approach and evacuation routes – that's just what I need. Marvellous!' enthused Mike Black, as he began the reverse process of seeing the intended snatch through the eyes of the Germans.

'And to help you in your detailed planning, gentlemen, here is a box of pre-war German Elastolin toy soldiers – Jerries and British,' grinned Enever. 'The only problem is the Tommies are all Highlanders in tropical rig and wearing kilts!'

'At least they're carrying rifles and not claymores and bloody bagpipes,' observed Farrell drily. Turning to Black, Farrell asked, 'What think you, Mike? Do we need to set up a diversion, just in case we trigger alarms or set off any booby-traps as we go in?'

'I think that we should *plan* for a small diversionary group, to fool Jerry into thinking that the main thrust of the assault is as far away as possible from the real one. But –' Black stopped for a moment to look again at the windows and doors of the chateau, '– it should be a standby diversion which will be activated only out of urgent necessity.'

'Agreed, Mike. The diversionary group will also need to be flexible and fast enough to act as cover for our exit route.' Farrell suddenly looked at Tremayne, who was listening intently to the unfolding assault plan. 'Richard, I almost forgot, you're now almost as much a Royal Marine Commando as you are a sailor. Do you have any thoughts on entry and exit in this operation?'

'A Marine? A bloody bootneck?! We'd have him as a member of the Regiment any day,' laughed Black. 'Richard's a natural for this sort of work.'

Tremayne grinned. 'Thanks for your vote of confidence, gentlemen.' He took out a folded sheet of paper from his pocket. 'This is a copy of Hitler's Kommandobefehl, ordering the immediate handing over to the Gestapo of all commandos and paratroopers captured from small raiding groups. We now know for certain that those handed over are tortured and subsequently executed – even when wearing regulation British Service uniforms.'

Tremayne paused, to see that he had his colleagues' undivided attention. Enever quickly stepped in. 'Richard also speaks from direct experience. When ashore in Brittany to look for fuel for his MGB, he and his engineer were taken prisoner and brutally tortured. McDonald, the boat's petty officer engineer, was callously executed by firing squad in front of Richard who, in turn, was tied to a stake and forced to endure the terror of a mock execution. He was, against all odds, rescued by a German naval captain from the Gestapo's clutches and removed to a PoW camp – which was contrary to the express orders of the Kommandobefehl.'

Revulsion and undisguised fury greeted Enever's brief, but harrowing, intervention.

Tremayne, nodding in response to his colleague's anger, continued: 'If caught, we will be shot – whatever we are wearing. So, gentlemen, why don't we make the most of the vital element of surprise and go in dressed in German uniforms? I suggest both Kriegsmarine and SS rigs would be ideal, bearing in mind the chateau's dual role. We've got all the paraphernalia that the Jerries love to cover their uniforms in, such as U-boat arm of service insignia, Iron Cross ribbons, wound badges and so on. We also have boat and ships' cap tallies and various badges of rank – all of which are genuine and add to the authenticity of such a disguise.'

Farrell looked up from the model he had been studying, his face alive with enthusiasm.

'Richard, yours is a bloody good idea. It could give us *immediate* tactical advantage, when we are likely to need it most. Moreover, some of us speak enough German to pass ourselves off – initially, at least – as the genuine article. If the rest of you agree, then let's go with it!'

'Count me in! I'm all for it.' Black's affirmative response was instantaneous.

The others were equally positive in their reactions.

'We'll need convincing weapons and I take it, John, that you have access to plenty of MP40s, Lugers, Walthers and the like?' Farrell's sense of pragmatic detail was ever-present in such operational planning.

'Absolutely!' Enever pressed a bell-button on the underside of his desk top and, seconds later, a naval rating, wearing the deceptively innocuous badges of a leading writer, appeared.

'Wade, bring me a goodly selection of our toys please. I want to show off some of our better acquisitions to these gentlemen.'

'Aye aye, sir.'

Minutes later, Wade returned with a small aluminium hand-cart and, at a nod from Enever, began to unload German machine pistols – including a Bergmann MP18, various sidearms and a paratrooper's assault rifle – together with a SS Hauptsturmführer's uniform and several German naval outfits.

'I suggest, gentlemen, we dress according to what we already are. Navy, or –' Tremayne laughed as he saw the pained expression on Black's face. 'Okay, you bloody Pongo, I *know* that there's a letter A between the SS in SAS!'

Farrell, normally urbane and quietly formal, suddenly drew himself up to his full six feet four inches, put on an SS officer's peaked cap and screamed at Black: 'Habt's Acht! Still gestanden, du Scheisser!*'

For a moment there was a shocked silence, then Black spoke – a grin spreading across his likeable, tough features.

'Kin' 'ell, sir! That was *bloody* realistic – I almost shat myself!'

'I did,' quipped Tremayne, amidst roars of laughter from the others.

'That does it John – there's no argument!' Enever reached into the box of props, dragging out a jacket and pair of trousers. 'You definitely *will* wear the senior SS uniform that we have here. That was a frighteningly convincing performance!'

The next two days were spent with the model of the chateau, planning and rehearsing the detail of the snatch. Enever produced full-face and profile photographs of von Greiner

---

'Attention! Stand still, you shit!'

and several of him, in full uniform, in the company of other SS officers, so that members could readily recognise their target.

Promptly at 24.00 hours, at Braiden Rock anchorage, on the night following the operation's rehearsals, Tremayne ordered 'Slip. Bear off forrard. All engines slow ahead'. The low-set, sleek E-boat moved steadily out into New Grimsby harbour, her powerful diesels growling purposefully. Standing next to him on the cramped, armoured bridge, binoculars slung round their necks, were Farrell and David Willoughby-Brown, his first lieutenant. Behind the wheel, eyes on the illuminated gyrocompass, stood Petty Officer Bill Irvine, Tremayne's stalwart, stocky coxswain, who hailed from the back streets of East Belfast. Irvine was a grizzled veteran in his forties, who had fought at Jutland as a boy seaman in the Great War. He was Navy through and through – and Tremayne's rock. Behind the quartet, standing on the signal platform, abaft the bridge and already scanning the area with his night glasses, stood Leading Yeoman of Signals 'Taff' Jenkins. Tough in an understated way and, like Irvine, utterly dependable, Jenkins' mellifluous tones immediately identified him as someone from the valleys of South Wales. Even when badly wounded, in an engagement with E-boats in the Channel, he had remained at his post until Tremayne ordered him to remain below and rest.

Aged twenty-four, Willoughby-Brown, socially out of the top drawer and a language graduate who spoke fluent German as well as excellent French, had become one of Tremayne's closest friends. The two had served together virtually since the formation of the clandestine Tresco flotilla two years previously. Like Tremayne's, Willoughby-Brown's was an RNVR – not regular Navy – commission. Brought up in what was a traditionally 'cavalry' family, WB, as he was widely known, had, by sheer guts and ability, established his credibility as a naval officer. From time to time, much to Tremayne's amusement, his innocent earnestness and transparent honesty did cause Irvine's worldly, experienced eyes to roll heavenwards in utter disbelief. WB and Tremayne enjoyed a friendship based upon the strongest mutual respect and brotherly affection.

Conscious that, closer to the French coast, they would be picked up and then tracked by German radar, Tremayne set a course which would follow the known routes of the Kriegsmarine's own marauding E-boat patrols.

The snatch party, consisting of a well-rehearsed group, included Farrell, Tremayne, Black, Willoughby-Brown, Sergeants Paddy Nugent, SAS and Geoff Kane of the Royal Marines, Corporal 'Blackie' Cotterell and Marine Weaver – both Royal Marine Commandos on secondment to HMS Godolphin.

At first, the aggressive Nugent, Black's right-hand man, who saw all other troops as lesser mortals than those of the SAS, experienced some difficulty in settling in with the three commandos and, for a time, there was considerable friction between them. He quickly made his mark, however, when after being asked by Kane if the SAS had given up eating their young, he retorted – eyeing their green berets: 'Stroll on! Friggin' cabbage 'eads – you couldn't even *produce* your own young!'

Several pints later, in the bar of Tresco's New Inn, they were all swearing eternal friendship, though the derisory comments about each other's units became even more outrageous. Typical of the alcohol-fuelled irreverence were Nugent's question: 'What has an IQ of 144?' and his answer: 'A gross of Marine Commandos!' – countered by Cotterell's riposte: 'The SAS drop out of the sky – just like bird shit!'

Slipping into the tiny chart room with its duplicate gyrocompass, Tremayne quickly checked his bearings and estimated that they were about fifteen miles short of their disembarkation point. They had successfully negotiated the islands and dangerously jagged, rocky islets east of Ushant, so far without inquisitive contact from the enemy. He looked at his watch – it was 03.00 hours – and returned to the bridge.

The slow-running sea was like heaving black treacle, with only the phosphorescence of their bow-wave and wake to break up the otherwise uniform colour. The moonless night was equally black, though more like velvet, and, as yet, there was no discernible distinction between sea and coast.

On course, west of Camaret-sur-Mer, Willoughby-Brown spoke urgently: 'Ahead and to port. What the hell are they, sir?' Tremayne peered through his night glasses, adjusting the focus as he replied. 'Well spotted, Number One! They are – wait, no, they're – got it! They're Jerry Räumboote. I can just make out three of them – heading west, south-west, in line astern. Because there's a trio of them – and only one of us – they are more visible than we are.'

To reduce the E-boat's telltale bow-wave, Tremayne ordered 'All engines, slow ahead, Cox'n'. With the boat already closed-up at action stations, he sent Willoughby-Brown round to all deck gun-positions to order 'Target ahead, five hundred yards off the port bow. Stand by to fire'. After what felt like an eternity, the Räumboote vanished into the still black night as silently as they had appeared; the dying, rippling phosphorescence of their wakes being the only sign of their passing presence.

'Right on time,' thought Tremayne with a grin, as a familiar, adenoidal wail arose from the tiny galley below the wheelhouse –

'There is no snow in Snow 'ill, way down in Summer Lane
But when it's winter time, in the Argentine
It's summer in Summer L–a–n–e!'

'What in hell's name is that?' Farrell was clearly struggling to make sense of the strong West Midlands accent. 'That John, is Able Seaman 'Pablo' Watkins and you are about to be offered a welcome mug of Navy kye – hot drinking chocolate to you – laced with a drop of pusser's rum!'

'God help us! Do I have to endure that caterwauling before I get my – whatever you called it?'

''Fraid so, John, but it will come as a welcome lifesaver when you do get it!'

Watkins appeared, as usual, with the inevitable string of enamel mugs around his neck and carrying a huge aluminium rum fanny in his left hand. Cheerful as ever and doing his best to come to terms with the loss of his closest 'oppo' and 'townie' Brummie Nicholls, he ladled out the Navy's very own steaming nectar with a word for everyone. "Ere yer am, Swain – this'll put 'airs on yer chest. What *would* yo' do without me?'

His eyes never leaving the gyrocompass, the indefatigable Ulsterman grunted a dry response: 'Crack open a bottle of Black Bush to celebrate, so I would.'

Stood to at action stations, gun crews erupted in bursts of laughter as Watkins passed around the deck in the chilly night air.

Some fifteen minutes later, Irvine called out, 'Enemy coast dead ahead, sir, so it is.'

'Thank you Cox'n. Your eyes are as sharp as ever! Take over now please.'

'Aye aye, sir.'

Tremayne turned to Willoughby-Brown who was scanning ahead with his night glasses. 'Time to go, Number One. We need to make ready for landing.'

'Aye aye, sir.'

Though close friends, on duty and in front of others they each maintained the Navy's protocols of rank and role.

As the snatch party assembled on deck in their German uniforms, Farrell called out, 'Everybody, check your weapons. All pistols to be made ready, with silencers. Keep SMGs and grenades handy in your travelling grips.'

Turning to Nugent he said, 'Sar'nt, stand by to flash recognition signal, on command.'

Within minutes they were able to make out the surf rolling in and breaking on the shoreline, like a snaking silver ribbon.

At just over two cables' distance from the shore, Tremayne spoke quietly to the seamen standing to, lining the port side guardrails. 'All hands, lower scrambling nets. Lower and make-fast dinghies. To all gun crews, he called out softly, 'All weapons stand by to fire, range 450.'

'Right, Sar'nt. Three green, one white.' Farrell's terse command immediately followed. Tremayne, his Walther pistol complete with silencer tucked into his belt and his Lanchester SMG in his travelling grip, moved noiselessly up to the forrard scrambling net.

Nugent's multi-lens torch quickly flashed the challenge signal to the shore, where it was just possible to see several indistinct figures gathering at the water's edge.

Agonising seconds passed. Tremayne felt his heart pounding. Tension mounted amongst those on the bridge and boat's deck. Then, at last, came the correct answering signal from the shore.

'Right! Into the dinghies. Quick as you can!' whispered Farrell.

Already allocated as four members to each dinghy, the raiding party quickly climbed aboard. Two ratings to each dinghy slid expertly and silently down the scrambling nets, paddles in hand. As the securing lines were slipped, they immediately pushed off and paddled for the shore. Tension was again evident in the eyes and bodies of their passengers, who sat – weapons now at the ready, travelling grips resting on their knees – hunched up, as if facing a hailstorm.

Conscious of their vulnerability in the flimsy, slow-moving craft, and despite their extensive battle experience, Tremayne became aware of an involuntary bunching-up amongst his fellow passengers – a normal, but often suicidal reaction to imminent physical threat.

On board the E-boat, Irvine ordered Bofors, Oerlikons and MG42s to be trained on the figures emerging out of the dark on shore, to provide covering fire for those approaching the beach from the sea. Moments later, the eight landed and flashed two green signals to Petty Officer Irvine to confirm 'All okay'. The two dinghies pushed off from the shore to return to the E-boat. Once they were secured on board, Irvine slowly turned the E-boat round and set course for St Malo, to return to Allied-held waters, before coming back to pick up the snatch party.

The welcoming party of five heavily armed men and one woman stepped forward as one after an initial, guarded hesitation, prompted by the sight of German uniforms.

Their leader introduced himself as 'Marc' and, in hushed tones, led the group up the rocky beach to an immaculately clean, Kriegsmarine-requisitioned Citroën bus, painted in German naval livery. Stencilled on each side of the bus were black German crosses and it bore official German Navy registration plates. Ominously, the driver wore a German Army steel helmet. At the open door stood a guard dressed in Wehrmacht uniform, carrying an MP40 machine pistol. Was it the snatch party who had run into some sort of trap?

Tremayne's body stiffened, as he eased his silenced pistol from his belt…

Three

The Chateau Keeps A
Strange Cellar

Marc sensed Tremayne's tension and whispered, laughing, 'It's okay, the guard and driver are ours but, like you, they look the part that fate decrees they must play!'

As they moved up closer to the bus and onto the narrow road, Tremayne saw that the Resistance members informally and naturally maintained positions of all-round defence, as if expecting an ambush at any moment. They appeared to be well-disciplined and well-trained, he noted gratefully. All were armed with either Sten guns or German MP40s and all were festooned with grenades and spare magazines.

They scrambled aboard the bus which, after a coughing, muffled rumble, slowly moved off from the RV. Tremayne felt relieved to be underway, clear of the beach and its lack of protective cover. He found Marc's unassuming, quiet confidence professional and reassuring. Dawn was just beginning to break through and, as the sky started to lighten, he was able to see something of the surrounding wooded, rather flat, countryside.

Ten minutes later, they turned off the road and travelled for what he estimated to be close to a mile along a narrow lane, until they arrived at a collection of run-down factory buildings. Clearly, despite its dilapidated appearance, it was still a going concern. From the tarpaulin-covered racks in the store yard, it appeared that the company manufactured a range of ships' chandlery – mostly in bronze, steel and brass – and some of the products looked to be bespoke rather than off-the-shelf. Marc gathered the group around him, while his own people maintained a vigilant watch.

Indicating a large single-storey, L-shaped concrete building, he said, 'These are the factory machine-shops. They are your quarters, gentlemen. I am sorry our hospitality is so limited, but you will be safe here. Under the machine-shop floor is a large underground complex, entered by a trap door that even the employees know nothing of. There are beds, water and the means to cook food but, I'm afraid, very little natural light. The Boche visit the place regularly to check on the movement of their orders as work in progress. Because of their regular calls here, you are safe, since they regard it as 'their' territory and, therefore, secure. The local Gendarmerie also pay the occasional perfunctory visit, drink coffee with the foreman and then disappear.'

Marc paused. 'Any questions, gentlemen?'

'Marc,' asked Black, his brow furrowing, 'you speak faultless English with an American accent. *Are* you French – or are you a Yank?'

Marc smiled broadly. 'I guess I'm both. My father was French and my mother is American, from Virginia, which is where I was brought up. When I was fourteen, they split up and, since I was completely bilingual, my father brought me to Brittany nine years ago. I fell in love with the place and decided to make it my home. I joined the Marine Nationale as a seaman just before the war began. I refused to follow my shipmates to Vichy France so, in their eyes, technically I am a deserter, though I regard my former colleagues as traitors. My father joined the Resistance, but was captured, tortured and finally shot by the Gestapo. I do this because I have a score to settle with the Nazis – I thought the world of my father. He was also my best friend.'

'Thank you Marc, I apologise for the intrusion into your private life.' Black briefly touched Marc's shoulder.

'Not at all, Mike. C'est la vie!' He turned back to the group. 'Let me continue, gentlemen. *Le patron* who is, shall we say, 'commercially cooperative' with the Boche, is not aware of our presence here, so movement in and out must *always* be outside normal working hours – and preferably in the dark. Capstan lathes, pillar drills and other machine-tools will be in operation all day, so any reasonable noise that you make will normally not be heard – but just be careful. When you are at your most relaxed, you are at your most vulnerable – but then, gentlemen, you know all about that!'

Motioning to his group to follow, Marc led the snatch team into the building and opened up a trap door, ingeniously disguised as a built-in foot-scraper to remove any clinging swarf or machine-tool suds from employees' boots as they left the production shop. Well used over many years, it looked the part completely, with no indication whatsoever of its covert purpose.

Settling in the British party, Marc and the Confrèrie members quickly organised a simple but good improvised breakfast – even providing what Willoughby-Brown termed 'a most acceptable *café de pays** '. Within the basement complex was a powerful radio which, as Marc said meaningfully, was 'To be used in emergencies only – and then as briefly as possible. The Boche are very adept at picking up radio transmissions. If ever they were to trace calls from this set – and our hideout – it would be a disaster.' Behind the intense blue eyes, there was a clear, orderly brain, felt Tremayne, as Marc continued: 'If the snatch is successful, transmit, once only 'Jack Daniels' – nothing more. If a failure, or if postponed, send 'Bar closed'. Simply that, gentlemen – other than any necessary revised RV data. In either case, we will be with you within fifteen to

---

**An ordinary, standard coffee*

twenty minutes.'

As light began to filter through the ventilation shafts, Tremayne sensed a growing unease among the Confrèrie members. Marc looked anxiously at his watch. 'We must leave you shortly, before anyone arrives at the factory, but we will be back at 23.00 to transport you to the chateau. That is about half an hour away from here. Remember to carry your travelling grips with you, and behave like last-minute guests who will not tolerate petty hotel officials' piddling bureaucracy.' Marc paused, a wide grin spreading across his finely boned, handsome face.

'Remember, too, gentlemen, you are Nazis, not British, so don't be so damned understanding and 'reasonable'! The British have had years of conditioning as being 'good losers', while the Germans naturally *expect* to win! In any case, the chateau staff are used to people turning up at unearthly hours – and in quantity – by buses from Brest naval base.'

He nodded to the one female member of the group and motioned her to come forward. 'Before we disappear, I want you first to hear Marie-Madeleine's story and details about the chateau's interior layout. She managed to find employment as a cleaner-cum-chambermaid at the place and now knows it like the back of her hand.'

Farrell called to the others: 'Gather round, gentlemen – this is important.'

Through Marc acting as interpreter, Marie-Madeleine described, in clear detail, the location of von Greiner's private suite on the second floor of the chateau, one level above the quarters of the SS and Gestapo members of the interrogation centre. His rooms were accessible via the main staircase – or two lifts – in the lobby, but also by a set of backstairs from the kitchen area, used by the domestic staff. Von Greiner's quarters were identified by a small white metal plate on the door, with SS runes painted on it in black.

The remaining rooms on the second floor were reserved for visiting SS and Gestapo officers and for senior naval personnel. The whole of the third floor was given over to guests, on leave from the Kriegsmarine. The sinister interrogation centre was located in the extensive system of cellars, immediately below the ground floor. Marie-Madeleine estimated that, currently, there were about thirty naval personnel in residence, while around twenty SS and Gestapo members represented the interrogation centre permanent staff, guards and personal aides to von Greiner.

She also pointed out that von Greiner was a creature of habit, who normally retired to bed at about 11.30pm. She further confirmed that there would be two all-night guards on duty outside the main entrance, one at the side entrance and one by the rear door of the chateau, which was for tradesmen and domestic staff. Most of the guards were members of the Allgemeine SS – the specialist troops who ran the Nazi concentration camps – though, occasionally, resident naval ratings were also made to take on guard duties. Located in a corridor, off the lobby, the third door along from the reception desk, was the intentionally anonymous entrance to the interrogation centre. There would also be an all-night concierge and a porter on duty in the lobby, she added.

Glancing anxiously at his watch, Marc said urgently: 'Gentlemen, we really must leave now. We will see you at 23.00.'

Thanking the rapidly departing Marc, Marie-Madeleine and remaining Resistance fighters, Farrell called his team together for an 'O' Group around a large empty packing case, which he had found in the basement. Catching Tremayne's quizzical expression, he said, grinning, 'That, Richard, believe it or not, is the Chateau de Trevannec. I've marked up the external doors with a wax crayon I found here.'

Using a bar of soap to represent their naval bus, Farrell outlined his detailed plan.

'The bus will pull up here. We will disembark as a group, all at once, to confuse the guards about numbers and movements. Sergeant Nugent, Corporal Cotterell and Marine Weaver, you will be dressed as naval junior petty officers and immediately wander off, nonchalantly, silenced pistols to hand, tucked in your pea jackets. You will move to the left of the building, to see where the side entrance guard is located.' Farrell saw that they were giving him their undivided attention.

'You will approach him casually, quietly chatting to one another. If he is SS, you will shoot him and move his body into the bushes. If he's Navy, gag him, tie him up and chuck him in the bushes. Just make a good job of it.'

Nodding to Sergeant Nugent, Farrell then said, 'Move round

to the back of the building and deal with any guards there, leaving Corporal Cotterell acting as guard at the side door, while Marine Weaver 'floats' between the side and rear outside doors.

Farrell then turned to the main group: 'Mike, WB, you and I will stride in through the main door as three arrogant SS officers, looking as if we own the place, and head for the second floor via the main staircase.

Richard, you and Sergeant Kane, dressed as a naval officer accompanied by a petty officer, will follow us in through the front door and make your way to the second floor via the lift. We'll meet up outside von Greiner's suite, approaching it from two different directions.'

At this point, Tremayne came in. 'I think we should also check the backstairs to make sure that, if needed, we have a getaway route there. If Sar'nt Nugent stations himself as guard outside the chateau's rear entrance, we can slip von Greiner out that way, bundle him through the bushes and trees and so into the bus. Marc offered to organise a German Navy ambulance as a back-up option to take away an apparently drunk, or sick, von Greiner and that's an alternative we'll keep on hold for the moment.'

Willoughby-Brown, concerned about the two guards at the main entrance, asked, 'What about those two on the front door, sir?'

'We'll leave them alone, unless they attempt to impede us or raise the alarm – then we'll shoot them.' Farrell's coldly matter-of-fact approach sent a shudder down the backs of some of those present.

Tremayne spoke again: 'As I see it, we keep the operation as low-key as possible, with everything being made to look as normal, or as natural, as we can. We should, by the way, leave at least two of the travel grips behind. They're clearly US officers' issue and, with other suitable doctored evidence inside – I have with me, for example, a London Underground ticket and a dry cleaning receipt – they're one way of telling Jerry that this was not the work of French Resistance.'

'Agreed,' confirmed Farrell. 'I have a recent Lyons Corner House receipt, an incomplete Littlewoods football pools coupon and other odds and sods that we can use to help confirm that this was a British – and not a Maquisard – operation.'

'Richard, let's just go over the details of evacuation by E-boat.' Black reached for the notes he had been taking.

'Right, Mike. The E-boat will set out from north of St Malo at 01.00 hours and will be cruising off Camaret, following the Germans' own coastal patrol routes, by 02.00, awaiting our call. We'll be lying up in our underground bunker, ready to confirm 'Jack Daniels' *or* 'Bar closed' with her coxswain. The RV is a small bay, on the west side of Camaret, at Pen Hat beach. The currents there are dangerous and swimming is not an option, so the Confrèrie have organised two dinghies with paddles for us. The tide should be right for the E-boat to be standing off about a cable's distance from the shore.'

Much of the rest of the day was taken up by going over and over the stages of the snatch and exploring the inevitable 'what if?' questions. Many times during that day, any number of Plan B options were raised, evaluated and either accepted or rejected.

Promptly at 23.00 the bus arrived, complete with Confrèrie members – except for Marie-Madeleine – and, led by Farrell, the snatch party clambered aboard. Four hundred yards short of the chateau, all of the French Resistance members, apart from Marc the driver, climbed out and took up cut-off positions amongst the trees and shrubs on either side of the road.

On the bus, Farrell ordered, 'Check your weapons. Synchronise watches, gentlemen. It is 23.37 exactly.' Looking at each member of the team in turn, he added quietly, 'Make your way, under cover of the trees, back to the bus, parked along the road by the cut-off party, promptly by 00.30. We will wait five minutes maximum. More could be fatal, gentlemen. After that, make your own way back to the factory – before daylight. Good luck everybody!'

Minutes later, the bus drew up outside the main entrance of the chateau, placing itself so that the two guards at the door would be unable to see Nugent, Cotterell and Weaver slip round to deal with the sentry on the side entrance. Tension showed in the faces of those waiting to leave the bus and Tremayne could feel the adrenaline rush coursing through his taut body. Farrell, Black and Willoughby-Brown immediately assumed the confident, arrogant postures of the SS officers they were supposed to be.

Languidly acknowledging the butt salutes of the two SS

sentries, they swaggered up the steps and into the reception area of the chateau. The concierge, obsequiously anxious to please the three SS officers, was dismissively waved aside, as he almost fell over himself in an attempt to relieve the trio of their travelling bags.

Just behind them, in naval uniforms, were Tremayne dressed as a Kapitänleutnant and Sergeant Kane as a Petty Officer Torpedo Specialist. Curiously reflecting his own marksman's skills as a Royal Marines sniper, Kane wore the dark blue lanyard and gunmetal acorn badge of a qualified Kriegsmarine marksman on the right shoulder of his pea jacket. Taking his cue from Farrell, Tremayne likewise airily dismissed the unctuous attentions of the grovelling concierge and led Kane to the first of two lifts, round the corner from the reception desk.

Meanwhile, Paddy Nugent's party strolled round towards the sentry posted outside the side entrance, quietly laughing and punctuating their murmured conversation with several audible 'ja ja's, 'nee's* and the occasional 'doch'. The sentry was an SS Scharführer, steel helmet on his head and an Erma machine pistol slung round his neck. He stepped forward blocking the way, his right arm raised, and screamed a hoarse command at Nugent. The SAS sergeant merely nodded and, with a quiet 'Heil Hitler', carried on walking.

Furious, the sentry yelled again, but this time unslung his machine pistol and, jabbing it into Nugent's face, yelled at him – peremptory flecks of his spittle spraying the Ulsterman's uniform.

---

*nee – colloquial for 'nein'

As he pulled out the silenced Walther P38 from within his pea jacket and fired twice, Nugent muttered, 'Quiet, you noisy bastard.' Shot twice through the heart, the SS man was dead before Cotterell and Weaver stepped forward and grabbed his crumpling body.

'Cheers, lads. Into the shrubbery with him. Make sure he can't be seen. Take his helmet, Blackie, stick it on and sling your MP40 round your neck. He can have his Erma back. Shove some of your mags into your jacket pockets.'

Giving the two Marines a hand, Nugent helped to carry the bulky German into the dense shrubs a few yards away. 'Stay here, Blackie, as sentry. Dennis, remain here too for the moment and look as if you're the sentry's mate, while I check out what's around the corner behind the building. If anyone causes any trouble – shoot them.'

Marching up the stairs in a manner that defied interference, Farrell and the others quickly gained the second floor. At right angles to them, but still out of sight, Tremayne and Kane emerged from the lift at about the same time.

Suddenly, a door in front of Farrell burst open as roars of noisy laughter broke the silence of the corridor. A very drunk naval officer staggered out of the room, plaiting his legs, and collapsed – to raucous cheers – at Farrell's feet.

'So, boys, look at what we have here. The Bohemian Corporal's arse-wipers have come to tell us to be quiet!' The speaker, another leering officer wearing the uniform of Kapitän-zur-See, his Knight's Cross ribbon skewed around his neck and wine stains on his shirt, lurched forward towards Farrell's party, now just joined by Tremayne and Kane.

'You! You drunken, ignorant swine! What is your name?' screamed a chillingly convincing Willoughby-Brown. 'I could have you court-martialled and shot for insulting our Führer.'

The powerfully built naval officer lunged at Willoughby-Brown and made as if to strike him.

'Franzi, come back here and calm down! Don't be a damned fool. You're in enough trouble already, for heaven's sake.' Two pairs of less drunken hands appeared at the door and propelled the belligerent captain, still swearing, and his colleague, who was now grovelling around on the floor, back into the room.

'I apologise, Herr Hauptsturmführer. We were celebrating the sinking of several Allied transports in the Kanal and rather forgot ourselves. I do apologise.' Any bravado this Korvetten-kapitän might have had, had suddenly been replaced by fear of the power that even junior SS officers could wield. His eyes reflected the terror he felt, as he rapidly sobered up in front of the three implacable figures in SS uniforms who were standing in the corridor.

Desperately trying to hide both his relief and his concern about keeping to schedule, Willoughby-Brown snarled, 'This time he is lucky – very lucky – and so are you. You are a disgrace to the Kriegsmarine. Let this be a lesson to you.' Flinging up his right arm, he yelled 'Heil Hitler!' Unsteadily, the Korvetten-kapitän struggled to get his heels together before returning the salute, his face ashen, as he gratefully closed the door.

'Heavens,' whispered Tremayne, his face split into a huge grin as he joined the trio. 'That was in the best traditions of RADA, David. Brilliantly done!'

'I thought we'd blown it for one awful moment,' muttered the normally imperturbable Farrell. 'Thanks, David. You really saved the day.'

Outside, Nugent made his way round to the back of the chateau, cheerfully whistling the marching song *Erika*. As he turned the rear corner of the chateau, where there was far less light than at the main entrance, a tall soldier dressed in SS uniform suddenly stepped out of the deep shadows, his Erma machine pistol at the ready. Swinging it round and pointing it at Nugent's chest, he grunted, 'Du, Matrose. Halt!'

Nugent casually asked 'Zigarette?' and nonchalantly reached into his pea jacket. As the SS soldier froze in horror at the unexpected sight of Nugent's silenced pistol, the Ulsterman shot him twice in the chest. Stepping aside as the German sagged to the ground, dead, Nugent called to Weaver who ran up to assist in removing the body to the nearby bushes. Grabbing the German's steel helmet, Nugent put it on and picked up the Erma from the ground, where it had dropped from the SS man's lifeless hand.

'I'll remain on guard here, at the rear entrance. Just keep contact with Corporal Cotterell and myself – I reckon he and I are about forty yards apart. Make sure that your pistol is handy at all times and keep your eyes open. Let's take a time check

– I make it 23.48.'

Inside the chateau, on the second floor, it was Tremayne who spotted the white plaque and SS runes that indicated the door to von Greiner's suite. Together with Kane, he slipped to the left of the door, while Farrell, Black and Willoughby-Brown took up positions on the right. Farrell whispered, 'Let's hope that ruckus with those drunken naval officers hasn't prompted anyone else to come out into the corridor to see what's been happening.'

Drawing his own silenced pistol, Farrell looked at Willoughby-Brown and nodded, as he gave the door a loud peremptory knock. Touching his first lieutenant on the shoulder, Tremayne whispered, 'Go to it David,' as a querulous, impatient voice from within called out, 'Was? Was ist los?'

Taking a deep breath, Willoughby-Brown called back, 'Herr Obersturmbannführer, my apologies sir! I have an urgent message for you from SS Brigadeführer Knöchlein. I have to await your reply, sir.' Sweat was pouring down Willoughby-Brown's face as he stood back from the door to allow Farrell and Black to move forward to grab von Greiner when he emerged. Tremayne could feel the tension in his body and his mouth had suddenly gone dry, as he shifted his silenced pistol round to the direction of the muttered curse behind the slowly opening door.

'Where is the message and who the hell are you?' The voice was a high-pitched croak. The cropped-headed, overweight body, clad incongruously in purple silk pyjamas, stopped, momentarily puzzled, and then his jaw sagged open in shock as he stared down the barrels of five pistols pointed at his flabby belly.

'What is this? What do you want? Wh-who are you?'

'You talk too much – get back inside, you fat bastard.' Farrell drove the barrel of his silenced Luger hard into von Greiner's bulging gut. The SS officer began to shake uncontrollably as his arrogance rapidly deserted him.

Speaking in fluent German, Willoughby-Brown, his pistol still pointed at von Greiner's belly, said, 'We are taking you to trial for war crimes against Allied prisoners of war. Get dressed, NOW!'

Trembling violently, the SS officer started to protest that he was merely following orders as a soldier. Dressed, he suddenly made a desperate lunge for the door, only to be felled by Tremayne who hit him square on the jaw. He lay writhing and sobbing on the bedroom floor until Black roughly hauled him to his feet.

Farrell checked his watch and said quietly, 'Gentlemen, it is 00.10 hours. Check that there are no papers or other items that we need to take along with us. Search his pockets too.' Turning to Black, he added, 'Get von Greiner's hat and overcoat on him.'

'And David,' Tremayne, nodding, indicated a half-full bottle on the bedside table, 'tip some of that schnapps over the bastard. If he reeks of alcohol as we take him out, it will make his unceremonious departure smell all the more convincing should we meet with anyone. We'll exit via the back door and hightail it through the trees and bushes skirting the drive until we reach the bus.'

His pistol now pushed under von Greiner's chin, Willoughby-Brown hissed: 'If you make any sound, I will shoot you. Do you understand?' White and shaking uncontrollably, von Greiner's terrified eyes were an eloquent enough answer. To reinforce his point, Willoughby-Brown fired a silenced shot, less than an inch from von Greiner's face. Cowering in horror, von Greiner recoiled with a gasp as the chilled schnapps was flung over his face, close on the tail of the bullet, and poured down the front of his uniform under his overcoat.

Tremayne and Kane left first, to make sure the corridors and backstairs were clear. Moments later, Willoughby-Brown led the group out, while immediately behind him was von Greiner, flanked by Farrell and Black, each clutching one of the SS man's arms. Halfway down the stairs leading to the rear exit of the chateau, Tremayne and Kane were suddenly confronted by two SS officers who had emerged from the kitchen, carrying food and two bottles of wine – clearly on the way back up to their quarters on the floor above.

Although Tremayne outranked both, the first – a Hauptsturmführer – arrogantly pushed him out of the way snarling, 'Move your arse, sailor. Make way for *real* men.' The second one grinned wolfishly, adding, 'They've no guts, Wolfi, just pretty blue uniforms to hide behind! Three months on the Eastern Front would teach them respect for the SS.'

Tremayne — conscious that Willoughby-Brown was just about to appear behind him with von Greiner and the others — turned quickly, thrust his right leg between the leading SS officer's shins, and viciously brought his knee up into the man's crotch. With an agonised yell immediately stifled by Tremayne's hand, the SS officer collapsed on the stairs, dropping his supper and the two bottles of wine. As he went down, Tremayne chopped him savagely in the back of the neck with his other hand. The second SS officer's startled shout was cut short, as Sergeant Kane moved in swiftly from behind and thrust his fighting knife under the man's ribcage.

'Let me deal with yours, sir.' There was a chilling menace in Kane's quiet voice, as he swiftly despatched the first SS man.

'Thanks Sar'nt. Let's get rid of this lot, asap, before more of the bastards appear.' Horrified by the sudden ending of two lives in so clinical a manner, Tremayne, shaking, struggled with his emotions as his calm words gave a lie to the numbing shock he felt. At that moment, Willoughby-Brown and the others appeared, as if on cue. Surprise, or horror, registered variously on their faces at the sight of the two dead SS men. Von Greiner went white and, stumbling with fear and disbelief, had to be held up by Farrell and Black.

Tremayne immediately took control of the situation. Addressing Farrell and nodding to the two corpses, he said, 'We'll get these two outside and into the bushes, but Sar'nt Kane and I will need the strong right arms of Mike and yourself, while David keeps watch on this scum.'

'Right, Richard.' As one, Farrell and Black grabbed the limp body of the nearest SS man, while Tremayne and Kane seized the other one.

Laughter came through the open kitchen door and, for a moment, Tremayne froze as one of the senior staff stepped out into the passageway and stopped, mouth open, as he saw the inert figure of the SS officer being dragged along by the two naval men. To ensure a silent kill, Kane had deliberately thrust his knife into the man's kidneys and, fortunately, there was no sign of blood on the front of his uniform. Taking advantage of the sous-chef's shocked surprise, Tremayne — his heart pounding – put his finger over his lips to signify discreet silence and said, in French, 'He is very drunk and very sick. Get back in the kitchen and keep quiet about this – or you will find yourself with the Gestapo in the cellar below. I take it you know what goes on down there?' Tremayne's voice took on a quietly menacing tone. A very hurried, 'Oui monsieur, bien sûr,' saw the rapid disappearance of the terrified French-man. As they passed outside, through the rear door of the chateau, Paddy Nugent moved forward out of the shadows to help Tremayne and Kane remove the SS man. Tremayne paused to check his watch, as Farrell, Black and the other dead SS officer emerged, closely followed by Willoughby-Brown and the hapless von Greiner. It was twenty-seven minutes past midnight, leaving just eight minutes, absolute maximum, until their deadline to return to the bus.

Nugent ran back inside to clear away the bottles of wine

and food dropped on the stairs by the SS officer, as he collapsed when Tremayne kneed him in the groin. The SAS sergeant then rapidly joined the others as they rushed von Greiner and the corpse of the second SS officer deep into the dense bushes skirting the path at the side of the chateau. Black, Kane and Nugent made a thorough job of hiding the bodies – which they expertly covered in intertwined leafy branches, deep in the thicket and several yards away from the building. Led by Farrell and Tremayne, the party made their way through the bushes and well clear of the front entrance of the chateau and the sentries posted there. As a precaution, Black had gagged and blindfolded von Greiner and he and Willoughby-Brown alternately pushed and dragged the terrified and now breathless, shaking prisoner to the bus and the waiting group of Maquisards.

Kane and Nugent brought up the rear of the group, constantly turning to check that they were not being followed. Anxiously, Tremayne looked at his watch again. It was 00.33 and the bus was nowhere in sight. He felt panic rising. He whispered to Farrell, 'John, we've just two minutes before the bus leaves. Let's send Kane ahead to find them and let them know we're close.'

'Agreed.'

The athletic Kane moved at lightning speed in search of the about-to-depart bus. Tremayne and the others were sweating freely as they rounded a bend in the road, in time to see the blurred dark shape of the bus barely outlined against the blackness of the trees behind it. 'Thank God,' gasped Tremayne. Panting, they scrambled aboard, heaving the exhausted von Greiner, fighting for breath, up the steps and into a seat, where he was hemmed in by Sergeant Nugent. Willoughby-Brown, as interpreter, sat behind the SS man, while Tremayne and Farrell sat in front of him. Cotterell, Weaver and Kane, the three Marine Commandos in the party, positioned themselves close to the door, with silenced pistols at the ready should anyone attempt to stop and board the bus. Marc drove, while three of his men – armed with MP40 machine pistols – took up positions at the rear of the bus. All the Confrèrie members were dressed in German uniforms, complete with steel helmets.

Just before 01.00 hours, they arrived back at the empty factory. Still gagged and blindfolded, von Greiner was bundled through the hidden trapdoor and into the main area of the hideout.

In the next room and out of von Greiner's earshot, Tremayne reminded Marc to signal the E-boat out at sea, awaiting the snatch group's call. His well-practised technique maximised signal content, but kept transmission time to a minimum to reduce the monitoring Germans' chances of locating the source of the message. Marc added Tremayne's coded signal to his coxswain to move quickly: *'Tarry not, rash wanton!'*

On board the E-boat and deputising for Sparks, Taff Jenkins' response was instantaneous and even briefer – *'Affirmative'*.

'Jerry radio intercept monitors may guess the meaning of the transmissions, but they won't know when and where,' said Tremayne. 'We will repeat the signal once we're at the RV.' He paused and looked around at the others. 'Hot coffee with a drop of cognac, then, I suggest John, we move.'

'Agreed.' Turning quickly to Marc, Farrell added, 'Right, let's go through the detail of the journey to Camaret and get that sorted.'

Tremayne looked across the room at Kane, Cotterell and Weaver, sitting as a small, tightly knit group in the corner, talking animatedly but quietly together. They were Royals. They were family. That was the way of the Corps – and always would be; like the Navy, yet somehow different. He smiled to himself as he recalled the Royals' own mantra: 'Once a Marine, always a Marine...'

Four

Within A Hair's Breadth

With a large-scale map of the Crozon peninsula spread open before them on the scrubbed top of the old pine kitchen table, Farrell and Marc led the briefing on the group's escape plans. It was Marc who spoke first, urgency obvious in his voice and suddenly tensed shoulders.

'While you were busy snatching von Greiner, Marie-Madeleine took a call from a trusted local Maquisard who reported an exceptionally heavy Feld-Gendarmerie presence around Plougastel-Daoulas on the road to Brest. Apparently, the Boche are after a Confrèrie member, who was arrested but broke free and gave them the slip.' He paused, seeing the questioning look cross Farrell's face.

'Although that's not the road we shall be using to reach Camaret, Marie-Madeleine was told that the man who escaped is believed to be heading for the coast – and presumably a contact with a boat – so the Boche will be covering all roads leading to the sea.'

'Damn, that means we'll be subject to delays and probably searches. Those Feld-Gendarmerie bastards won't be fooled easily – especially by a busload of SS men, accompanied by sailors of all people. By any score, that's a pretty improbable combination of travellers,' fumed Farrell.

Marc smiled. 'Perhaps, but if those sailors were dressed as medical staff and operating theatre personnel, accompanied by SS officers, that would give a very different impression – and one invested with urgency.'

Indicating the still bound and blindfolded von Greiner, Marc added, 'Richard, take this scum's uniform, boots, cap and overcoat and leave the rest of your naval outfit here. His tunic still reeks of schnapps, but sponge it off as well as you can.' Tremayne winced as he looked at the girth of the SS officer's coat and his own slim, athletic waist.

Marc continued: 'We'll strip von Greiner and put him into a hospital surgical gown and heavily sedate him. The others, who were dressed as a petty officer, or seamen, will put on the medical clothes that we have collected. They are some of the most effective disguises we have – believe me! We will use a German military ambulance that Thomas, one of my men, and Marie-Madeleine 'borrowed' from Brest military hospital – right under the noses of the Boche. Thomas's father was German and, though brought up in Brittany, he speaks fluent, accent-free German. As soon as we heard of the escaped Maquisard, we sent those two off, dressed as orderly and nurse, to take an ambulance needed urgently for a senior SS officer, allegedly suffering from acute appendicitis! The French medical staff at the hospital assumed Thomas was German and even organised the ambulance for him. So, if you're stopped on the journey to Camaret and the Feld-Gendarmerie *do* check with the hospital, they should get a convincing story of an urgent case involving a very ill, senior SS officer!'

'Why the hell, Marc, would we be taking an urgent medical case to Brest via Camaret? That doesn't make sense.' Farrell barely concealed his irritation with what he saw as a 'no-go' tactic.

At this point, Tremayne cut in. 'In fact it does, John. From where we are right now, the journey to the military hospital on the west side of Brest, via ambulance then E-boat, would, at a guess, take considerably less than half the time, compared with the route via Plougastel-Daoulas.'

He looked at Marc for confirmation. 'Exactly so. Richard.'

Marc looked at his watch. 'It is now 01.58. The ambulance should be with us in about fifteen minutes then, gentlemen, we must leave quickly, to keep up our story of urgency if the Boche do start checking up on timings with the hospital. I will drive you to the RV. We have a radio on board the ambulance to confirm with your boat that we are in position at Camaret.'

The sound of tyres crunching on gravel announced the arrival of the ambulance. It was 02.15.

Tremayne quickly put on von Greiner's uniform. The greatcoat hid the ill-fitting jacket and trousers which swamped Tremayne's athletic frame. By 02.20 they were on their way in the packed ambulance with Thomas at the wheel and Willoughby-Brown and Black in the front passenger seat. The rest of the snatch party were in the body of the ambulance with von Greiner, weapons loaded and made ready. Farrell and Nugent kept the partition between the driver's cab and the ambulance body open, while Tremayne, Black, Kane and the others surrounded the now comatose von Greiner, ready to simulate adjusting drip-feeds and generally minister to him if stopped and searched.

By 02.40 they were passing through Kersolou, on the outskirts of Camaret, when they were suddenly stopped by Feld-Gendarmerie troops, manning a temporary swing-barrier placed across the road. The first military policeman – a sullen, menacing figure in his grey-green leather overcoat and aluminium gorget who was carrying a MP40 machine pistol – strode up to the driver's obligingly opened window and grunted 'Papers', his free hand already reaching up for them.

Thomas, apparently free from the heart-stopping, sweating tension that Tremayne and the others were experiencing, calmly responded: 'We have a critically ill SS Brigadeführer, whom we are rushing to the military hospital in Brest. We are to rendezvous with an E-boat, on patrol off Camaret, to take the officer by sea to the hospital. We've been told that some damned French terrorist is on the loose near Plougastel-Daoulas and the roads there are not safe.'

'Get out all of you. Stand over there!' The muzzle of the machine pistol was pointing to a low dry-stone wall, close to the other two Feld-Gendarmerie soldiers manning the barrier. 'We will check your story with the hospital.'

At this point, Willoughby-Brown signalled to the others to follow himself and Thomas. Waving his own MP40, Willoughby-Brown screamed furiously at the NCO who had ordered them out.

'You damned blockhead. The Brigadeführer could die while you piss about playing the stupid official! Your name, rank and number, you dolt – NOW!' Willoughby-Brown produced pencil and paper from his tunic pocket and, with a dramatically impatient flourish, began to write. Within seconds, the now querulously protesting Feldwebel* and his colleagues were surrounded by furious, threatening officers and NCOs – all in SS uniforms. As if on cue and rising to the situation superbly, Tremayne was the last to appear – slowly emerging from the double doors at the back of the ambulance with the cultivated, authoritarian bearing of a senior SS officer.

Pushing his way purposefully through the other milling figures, Tremayne went right up to the Feld-Gendarmerie sergeant and, inches from the man's face, hissed: 'Your name!' Snapping his fingers imperiously at Willoughby-Brown, he indicated that

*Sergeant

87

his first lieutenant should write down the name 'Kmetsch'. With his rank, regimental number *and* unit designation similarly recorded, Feldwebel Heinrich Kmetsch's command of the situation disintegrated rapidly and he began to splutter incoherently and apologetically.

With a curt, dismissive wave of his hand, Tremayne pointed towards the barrier and snarled 'OPEN IT!' A peremptory 'Heil Hitler!' ended the encounter, as a now badly shaken military policeman sullenly raised the red, white and black-banded steel pole.

'That was a bit too bloody close for comfort,' said Farrell as they drove on, at speed, towards the coast just west of Camaret. 'I think the next stage would have been silenced pistols.'

'And then the whole of the Crozon peninsula and beyond would have been on full alert, followed by savage reprisals against the locals,' added a pensive Tremayne. 'Thank heavens no one spoke French – or, worse still, Breton – back there. But one thing we damn well failed to do was to leave any traces of 'British' involvement around the place.'

'No we didn't, sir.' It was Kane who spoke up. 'I dropped an empty Gold Flake cigarette packet, just in front of the rear wheels of the ambulance. The Jerries will find it flattened and dirty – but recognizable – when it gets a bit lighter, sir.'

'Thank God for the Royal Marines. Well done, Sergeant! I'll make sure Able Seaman Watkins gives you a double tot when we're back on board!' laughed Tremayne.

'Pushing me luck, sir, a bacon sarney would go down a

treat too!'

'I'll support Sergeant Kane in that, Richard, I could murder one,' grinned Black.

Minutes later, the ambulance stopped on the road, close to the ruins of the strange tower house – once the home of the French poet, Paul Roux – which looked even more mysterious and atmospheric against the pre-dawn sky. Tremayne looked up anxiously. 'We must signal our pick-up. Petty Officer Irvine will be expecting our call. Right Marc, 'Jack Daniels' it is – please transmit!'

Seconds later, the Sparker on the E-boat responded with equal brevity – 'Affirmative'.

Willoughby-Brown whispered, 'Thomas tells me that the dinghies are tucked into the sand dunes just below us. He suggests that we disembark pretty pronto and get chummie here tied to his stretcher and down onto the beach as quietly as possible. Apparently there is a Jerry coastal defence bunker a couple of hundred yards along the road ahead of us. The sentries on duty often take a stroll along the cliff-top road and the beach, to relieve the boredom of watch-keeping, so we must maintain strict silence.'

'There's no sign of that bloody E-boat. Where the hell is it?' muttered Farrell.

'Coxswain will keep her patrolling, as if keeping an eye open for would-be escapees and, as luck would have it, the Maquisard who made a break for it earlier reinforces the need for boats on close inshore patrol.' Following warm farewells to Thomas, who started on his journey to 'lose' the ambulance back at the military hospital, the others moved off the road as silently and quickly as possible.

Sweating with anxiety as much as through physical effort, the party – together with a still sedated von Greiner – made its way down the cliffs and over the dunes. Stifled oaths and obscenities marked the group's, at times, perilous descent down the granite rock face. Feeling for secure hand- and toe-holds, in the dark and carrying weapons, taxed the strongest of nerves and the best of rock-climbing training. Corporal Cotterell and Marine Weaver were both trained in mountain rescue and took charge of lowering von Greiner's stretcher down the steep rock face to the beach below. The others – and especially the Marine Commandos and SAS men – frequently lent a hand, as the stretcher had to be eased and supported over several small overhangs or jagged outcrops of rock.

After what seemed an interminable struggle, the group reached the beach. Leaving Farrell, together with Sergeants Kane and Nugent, to guard the prisoner now tucked into the sand dunes, Tremayne organised the others into two parties – one led by himself, moving left, and the other, with Black in command, going to the right – to search for the dinghies hidden by the local Maquis.

About five minutes later, Tremayne's group found the rubber inflatable boats, complete with paddles. With an urgent whisper, he sent Marine Weaver back to bring von Greiner and the others to the dinghies.

'Sir, look! There's our E-boat, moving south, about three cables offshore.' Corporal Cotterell, pointing out to sea with his machine pistol, whispered hoarsely, his eyes straining to see the MTB in that pre-dawn light when objects can take on the illusory quality of a mirage.

'Well spotted, Corporal. Let's try two green flashes from the torch and hope and pray that she is ours.' Tremayne checked that the green lens was in place and flashed twice. After a moment's heart-stopping delay, the E-boat replied with the same signal. 'Thank God. It's them!' Tremayne and Cotterell made ready the two dinghies and dragged them to the water's edge. In the slowly lightening sky, Tremayne could just make out the others, coming along the beach towards him. The E-boat altered course to port and, running slowly with a barely audible rumble, moved as close as she dare towards the beach. The others had just joined Tremayne's group when a voice, tinged with fear and uncertainty and coming from the direction of the dunes, shouted 'Halt! Wer da?'*

A very young German soldier – clad only in his underpants, open uniform jacket and jackboots – emerged from the dunes, nervously brandishing a pistol.

'Oh shit!' muttered Farrell. 'That's *all* we bloody well need!'

Willoughby-Brown immediately resorted to his arrogant SS officer pose to try and take control of the situation.

'Silence, you idiot! How dare you appear half naked in front a superior officer! Put that pistol down and stand to attention!'

At first it looked as if the German would comply. He

'Halt! Who goes there?'

hesitated, trembling, and then said, his voice quaking with fear, 'You can't fool me. I heard you speaking English. W-who are you?'

'Let me deal with the bastard, sir,' hissed Nugent, easing his fighting knife round from its sheath on the back of his belt.

Tremayne, recognising that a terrified man with a gun is more volatile and dangerous than someone who is relaxed, whispered, 'No! Any sudden movement and the poor sod's likely to start shooting and wake up everyone in the bunker.'

Willoughby-Brown's response was almost simultaneous. 'We are an SS Einsatzkommando* rehearsing the seizure of a British sabotage unit, expected to come ashore here any day now. We will need to speak English to fool them long enough to beach their dinghies, before we can capture them.' Willoughby-Brown meaningfully drew his finger across his throat, leering at the young soldier who, still uncertain and hesitating, looked around at the others as if hoping for confirmation.

Seizing the initiative again, Willoughby-Brown snapped, 'You are supposed to be on duty, *you* should be in the damned bunker. You have deserted your post!' Moving closer to the German, he snarled, 'Put that pistol down, NOW. You are in enough trouble already! You are for the Eastern Front, soldier!'

Bewildered and terrified, the young German lowered the pistol, looking pitifully at the chilling faces and SS uniforms surrounding him. In a blur of sudden movement, Nugent immediately swung round and seized the pistol from the German,

---

* *SS special unit (usually extermination squads)*

ready to thrust his fighting knife into the soldier's throat. Tremayne's urgent command cut through the tension. 'Stop! Let the poor bastard live. We need him to take the story back that it was British commandos he encountered – not French Resistance. We want no reprisals against the local population.'

Kane joined Nugent in pinning the German's arms behind him. Willoughby-Brown, now more himself than an SS officer, smiled at the soldier, who could be no more than nineteen years old, and said, 'You'd better get dressed and send your young lady home before the Maquisards catch you. Far worse than the Ivans on the Eastern Front – *they'd* cut your balls off!'

Once back in uniform, the German was bound and gagged and told that he had been the prisoner of a British commando unit – and was lucky to still be alive. The young French girl, emerging embarrassed and scared from the sand dunes, was given the identical story and told to clear off home once the party was clear of the beach. Grinning, Farrell said, 'I must say, Richard, you're a compassionate bastard, but that *was* the right thing to do. Oh, this bloody war! They seemed such a nice pair of kids whom circumstances have somehow thrown together. I hope they survive all this.'

'Hmmm, John, it seems I'm not the only softie around here. Welcome to the human race!'

Quickly, the party carrying von Greiner slid the rubber dinghies into the surging waves lapping the shore. Against the strong current and incoming tide, they slowly and painfully made their way over to the E-boat, now hove-to some three hundred yards offshore. Tremayne gave a repeat of the recognition signal as they gradually drew closer to the MTB. With arms aching from the effort of paddling in the choppy sea, they were hauled up the scrambling nets thrown over the side of the E-boat and grabbed by strong welcoming hands.

'It's good to see you back, sir, so it is,' were the first words a very grateful and relieved Tremayne heard, as the formidable coxswain dragged him, exhausted, up onto the forrard deck. 'Thank you, 'Swain. Am I damned glad to see *you!*' With everyone back on board and their prisoner stowed below under armed guard, Tremayne immediately moved to the bridge and once more assumed command. 'Right, Cox'n – gently does it round the rocks, then maximum revolutions and take us home!'

'Aye aye, sir.' Petty Officer Irvine's craggy features registered the broadest smile that Tremayne had ever seen cross the resolutely dour Ulsterman's face.

A rather contrived, self-conscious cough caused him to turn round, to find a grinning Able Seaman Watkins standing right behind him. 'Beggin' yer pardon, sir, here's a welcoming mug of kye – laced with pusser's rum, sir!'

'Watkins! Thank you. Whatever would we do without you?' 'Well sir, my missus would have an answer to a question like that, sir!' The relief at being away from the tensions of the snatch operation and the Brittany coast were only too obvious, as bursts of laughter accompanied the irrepressible Watkins and his mugs of rum-reinforced kye around the deck. Once more on the bridge, his binoculars slung round his neck, Tremayne was back in what had become his natural element. On countless occasions he had stood there in fair weather and foul, with his first lieutenant and coxswain beside him. Now, too, as the dawn began to lighten the sky and increase visibility, his thoughts began to drift towards Emma and Catriona. He knew that Emma would be only too aware of the operation and the dangers involved. He also knew that despite her continuing active commitment to Naval Intelligence, she would go through her own private hell of anguish, worrying about him, wondering if – this time – he might not be coming back to her. It was reassuring that John Enever, the Senior Naval Intelligence Officer – and his wife's former boss, would do his utmost to support Emma with his compassion, sensitivity and unique ability to put life into perspective.

With the E-boat running at defence stations, Tremayne's reverie was suddenly shattered by a yell from the watch-keeper in the forrard gun position. 'Aircraft bearing red oh-four-five. Three of 'em sir!' Tremayne immediately pressed the klaxon button for 'action stations' and weapons were traversed and elevated onto the incoming aircraft. 'Stand by all guns! Commence shooting, on my command.'

Sergeant Kane was the first to confirm their identity, yelling, 'They're ours, sir. They're *ours*! Spitfires from Bolt Head, sir.'

Tremayne's response was instantaneous. 'Hold your fire, everybody!' A great, ragged cheer went up from those on deck as the Spitfires flew over, in line astern, each performing a victory roll in honour of the snatch party's coup. 'Y' know, David, that wonderful characteristic Spit's 'Merlin whine' always gets to me. It's a sound like no other!'

'Absolutely,' Willoughby-Brown responded, his eyes following the fast-disappearing trio. 'With those beautiful elliptical wings and elegant fuselage, the Spitfire has to be the most iconic of fighter planes – and oh, such a welcome sight.'

'Rather like our beloved Scillies, David. Just look to port, to the Western Rocks. How enchanting they look in the early morning light. Even with such natural beauty – and in sunlight – they still manage to convey a hint of mystery and silent menace.'

At around 06.30 hours and stood down from action stations, Her Majesty's acquired E-boat ploughed purposefully through the rolling seas between St Mary's and St Agnes. Twenty minutes later, with Samson and Bryher islands off her port beam and with the tide in her favour, the sleek, greyhound-like motor torpedo boat glided through Tresco Flats, past Appletree Point and secured at her anchorage off Braiden Rock. Unable to contain his enthusiasm, a beaming Enever scrambled down the rocky path to greet Tremayne, his crew and the members of the snatch party – still wearing their SS uniforms and hospital attire.

'Welcome home, gentlemen, and my warmest congrat-ulations! Thanks to you, SOE French Section is over the moon. The blower between here and London has been positively steaming, throughout the wee small hours!'

Energetically shaking the many proffered, outstretched

hands, Enever turned back to Tremayne. 'Now, Richard dear boy, gather up your stormtroopers, surgeons and those thug-like medical orderlies — and let's all go and grab breakfast.' Sudden recognition dawned. 'Good grief, Sar'nt Kane, if ever there was a serious miscasting of people and roles — it's you as a male nurse. You look far less sinister in your usual cap comforter and camouflaged Denison smock, festooned with grenades and with a fighting knife stuck between y' teeth!'

Enever grinned as he checked to see that the group was assembled and ready to move.

'Dick and Aileen Oyler are laying on a feast fit for royalty for you — wartime rations accepted — up at the New Inn! Two Royal Marines are already on their way from HMS Godolphin to take care of von Greiner. Woe betide him if he decides to play the 'I'm a brigadier' stunt with them! Come, gentlemen, you must all be starving, we'll talk shop *after* breakfast'...

Five

Operation Dragoon: The Second Channel Of Invasion

S till blindfolded, his face haggard and grey, von Greiner was led, stumbling, into Hut 101 by his two Royal Marine guards. He was quickly pushed into a seat facing Enever, Farrell and Tremayne, with Willoughby-Brown acting as interpreter. At a brief nod from Enever, one of the Marines removed the blindfold. For a moment, the SS officer blinked and struggled to focus his eyes, then shock crossed his face as he recognised his captors from the day before — all now dressed in their own Service uniforms.

Through Willoughby-Brown, and with no preliminaries, Enever opened what was to be the briefest of interrogations. The principal one – in depth – was to be conducted by SOE's French Section in London, whose officers were already on their way to Penzance to collect von Greiner, together with Farrell and also Black and Nugent, currently on attachment from the SAS, and take them to Baker Street.

'You have been brought to England, von Greiner, to stand trial for war crimes against British prisoners of war and against French civilians. Those crimes go back at least to May 27th 1940, to the cold-blooded murder of captured British troops, taken near Dunkirk, when you were a serving officer with SS Totenkopf. Since that day, you have been involved in the torture and summary execution of other British prisoners of war and countless French citizens.' He paused, his eyes looking unblinkingly into those of the SS officer. 'What have you to say to these charges?'

Turning white and trembling uncontrollably like an animal run to earth who knows escape is impossible, von Greiner, incoherent with fear, mumbled,

'Nicht schuldig*.'

Willoughby-Brown translated Enever's curt response: 'That will be for the Military Court to decide.' At this point Farrell cut in, 'You will now be given food and water and then you will be removed from here to where you will be formally arraigned on charges of the war crimes against you. After that, your trial will begin.' Enever nodded to the two guards who

---

*Not guilty

hauled von Greiner to his feet and led him outside, to face the prospect of Royal Navy 'compo' rations. 'Let's hope that giving a prisoner of war a tin of 'Rations: Mixed Bacon and Egg' doesn't constitute unwarranted maltreatment and a breach of the Geneva Convention,' murmured Farrell, with the first smile of the brief, but tense encounter.

In what seemed like an unnatural vacuum after von Greiner was removed, silence hung heavily in the room. It was Enever who was the first to speak, an unexpected tremor in his voice at odds with his normally calm demeanour.

'The SS are the lethal product of Stone Age barbarity, Neanderthal leadership and twentieth century technology. That man's guilt is beyond question, gentlemen, and personally I'd like to have hanged the bastard from the parade ground mast's yardarm. All this must sound so unprofessional and emotional to you.' His voice dropped, as he reached for the handkerchief tucked into his cuff to blow his nose.

'You see, my young cousin was one of over ninety men of the Royal Norfolk's 2nd Battalion, slaughtered by SS Totenkopf four years ago, after they had surrendered at Le Paradis near Dunkirk. Only recently has news of this massacre come to light.'

He struggled to speak and fought back the tears in his eyes as he quietly added, 'The reports of the mass execution, taken from French civilians living close to the scene, are harrowing to say the least. Those lads never stood a chance.' Wrestling with his feelings, Enever managed to compose himself before continuing,

'They were forced to stand against a wall of one of the farm buildings they had been marched up to. Savagely pushed into place and lined up by the SS, they were then systematically machine-gunned to death. Two men survived – or so we believe from the French reports – and were looked after by one local family before they were recaptured, this time by soldiers of the Wehrmacht. We know nothing further of their fate. At the moment, clichés like 'time is a great healer' mean nothing to me. I recognise that the world will move on. It has to – it's the only way. But, for *my* world to move forward again, I have to do all I can to bring these murderers to justice. I say 'justice', but probably what I'm feeling is as base as pure primeval revenge.'

Enever's barely controlled anguish touched Tremayne deeply. So unexpectedly, he too had been suddenly confronted again with his own horrific memories of his Chief Engineer McDonald's callous execution by the Gestapo at Rennes just a few months ago. Never before had he seen Farrell so moved by emotion.

Quickly recovering, Enever turned to Farrell. 'I recognise that SOE have a far greater claim on von Greiner for the calculated murder of so many British agents and countless French citizens who may, or may not, have given them shelter. If we are to distance ourselves from the animal behaviour and code of the SS, then von Greiner must be given a fair trial, under due process of military law.'

His normally patrician features softened by obvious concern at Enever's distress, Farrell briefly touched the naval officer's shoulder. 'I'm so sorry, John. I had no idea that this bastard's actions had touched your family so brutally, but your young cousin *will* be avenged – that I *can* promise you.'

Continuing to look at Enever, Farrell gathered up his papers. 'I must leave now, John, together with those two SAS villains, Mike Black and Paddy Nugent. We're returning to SOE, along with von Greiner, but I do want us to stay in touch.' Turning to Tremayne and warmly shaking his hand, Farrell added, 'Richard, it's been an absolute pleasure serving on ops with you. I hope that, ere long, we will repeat the experience.'

Tremayne saluted the tall Rifle Brigade officer. 'Thank you, sir. The pleasure has been mine. I, too, hope that our paths will cross again.'

Accompanied by Enever and Tremayne, the three soldiers and their prisoner, along with the Royal Marine escort, walked round to New Grimsby Quay – the scene of so many of Tremayne's poignant farewells with Emma – to board the naval motor launch for Penzance. After the cordial quayside goodbyes, where the close bond between Tremayne and the soldiers was so evident, he and Enever slowly made their way back to HMS Godolphin, deep in conversation.

Back in Hut 101, Enever – scraping out his pipe into his brass shell-case ashtray – said, 'It looks as if you and Mike Black will be serving together again well before any of us anticipated.' Tremayne looked up questioningly. 'Oh? *That* sounds intriguing.'

Enever pressed the electric bell on his desk to ring for tea. 'I received a signal early this morning from Colonel Timmins, the American commanding officer in Rennes for whom you and Lionel weeded out those Gestapo interrogators from among the German prisoners he was holding. He's just returned to his old unit, the 1st Special Services Force – known for very good reasons as the 'Devil's Brigade', and has made a special request for your temporary secondment to his team. Clearly you impressed him, as did Mike Black, from the reports given to him by American OSS agents working in Brittany with the local FFI Resistance units. Admiral Hembury has agreed to that, but put a time limit of two months on your attachment to 1st SSF. I need you here at HMS Godolphin for operations being planned against the German-held ports in Brittany.'

'Do you know, at this stage, what's afoot and what our role is likely to be?'

'Much of it, Richard, is still under wraps, but I can tell you this … Ah, Jane, thank you so much – a real lifesaver. Bless you!'

Enever took the two cups of tea, passing one to Tremayne.

'The Yanks have won the battle over British reluctance to open a second front by invading the south of France in force. For obvious reasons, this was originally code-named Operation Anvil – with the implied 'hammer' of the analogy being the Allies' breakout in the north from Normandy. By all accounts, dear old Winnie was strongly opposed to the idea, but was forced to concede and go along with our Allies, which, of course, also included overwhelming pressure from the French. They, understandably, see this as the second necessary channel to the liberation of their country. The operation has now been renamed 'Dragoon' and some believe this change has come about because Churchill was dragooned into accepting a second invasion of France!' Enever smiled knowingly, taking a sip of his tea.

'If the Germans based in the south fight with the same tenacious courage and steely discipline as their counterparts in Normandy, then we might just have bitten off more than we can chew. Casualty rates in the north, for both sides, are frightful and, in addition, over thirty thousand French civilians have already been killed since D-Day. Similar losses in the south could prove to be disastrous.' Enever paused to fill and light his treasured meerschaum pipe.

'However, with few exceptions, we know that Jerry does not have the same numbers of first-class troops stationed in the south. Intelligence reports indicate that many of his forces in Provence and inland from the Côte d'Azur are disaffected Russian nationals of pretty poor calibre.'

Enever looked at Tremayne, a look of concern crossing his amiable face. 'However, Richard, we know that to stiffen the battle capability of these mediocre troops, the Germans have deployed some armoured units of fanatical SS soldiers in the south. They are likely to be moved rapidly to oppose the invasion – but at what stage in its progress, we can only guess.

Based to a degree on this intelligence, Operation Dragoon has been given the green light. Over ninety thousand Allied troops – mostly Yanks and French – will be involved in day one of the invasion, along with more than ten thousand vehicles. British involvement will be mainly by the British 2nd Independent Parachute Brigade with supporting ship-to-shore bombardment by the battleship *HMS Ramilles* – oh, and of course, you and Mike Black, dear boy!'

Enever stopped again to drink his tea. 'Ah, so well named as the cup that cheers.'

'What, primarily, will be our role, John? The Yanks have their own battle-hardened troops who have proved themselves in combat, time and again, since D-Day.'

'Where you and Mike will be involved is as commando-trained specialists – experienced in beach assault and close-quarter battle in the confined space of small islands. That is one reason why Mark Timmins asked for your presence in the 1st Special Service Force's opening role in the planned invasion. They are tough, resourceful troops with an enviable record of success – most recently in winning fiercely contested battles in Italy. They are a mixed group of Americans and Canadians and you'll need to prove yourselves to them, whatever Colonel Timmins has told them about you and Mike. Inevitably, you will face a lot of tribal scepticism about the need for help from a pair of Limeys!'

Enever felt a sense of relief as a he saw the intense interest registering in Tremayne's eyes. 'The other reason, Richard, is that after meeting you and Lionel, he realised that he needed all the help he could get in establishing sound relationships with the French Resistance in the south. Many of the Maquis units there consist of highly independent mountain people who will welcome American firepower, but not what they see as US colonisation of their territory – however temporary that may be.'

=====O=====

Even as Enever was speaking, members of the 1st Special Service Force, along with seven hundred French Commandos de la Marine, were assembling in Propriano Bay in south-west Corsica. Colonel Mark Timmins, reporting to Colonel Edwin A Walker, the officer commanding Operation Sitka – the attack on the three islands guarding the approach to the German naval base at Toulon – was already there. A tall, lean professional soldier from the mountains of New Hampshire, Timmins saw, in Tremayne, qualities similar to his own – independence of thought, decisiveness and highly adaptable self-reliance. From what he had seen of Tremayne, and from discussions with Confrèrie chief Lionel in Rennes, he had learned, beyond doubt, that the Englishman was a courageous, inspirational leader who had the complete confidence of the local French Resistance. That trust, Timmins knew, would be critical once the islands were taken and the invasion force broke out from the beachheads on the mainland. Even before the overwhelming numbers of Allied troops were clear of the coast, the Maquisards would be only too eager to join in and take the fight themselves to the retreating Germans as they fled north to escape the massed breakouts from the beaches.

The Special Service Force's immediate target – the Iles d'Hyères – lay across the channels of the Allies' main seaborne assault, just to the east of Toulon. With batteries of 164mm guns mounted on them, they posed a significant threat to the incoming landing craft heading for the mainland beaches, located anything from three to fifteen miles behind the islands.

The three islands – ranging in surface area from about three miles by one-and-a-half miles to five miles by one-and-a-quarter miles – are Porquerolles, the largest and closest to Toulon; Port-Cros, some seven miles to the east; and, beyond that by less than a mile, the Ile du Levant. Later, when Tremayne saw the map of the proposed invasion channel during the final pre-assault briefing, he was intrigued to see how comparable in size and shape the islands were to some of the larger inhabited isles of the Scillies.

Late the following day – August 13th – Tremayne and Black flew from Wiltshire by RAF Dakota to join Colonel Timmins and the US-Canadian 1st Special Service Force. Arriving under a starlit, clear Mediterranean sky, black as velvet, they were picked up at the landing field and transferred by a US Navy Elco patrol torpedo boat to the American attack transport, *USS Ormond*, at anchor in Propriano Bay. She was a converted former flush-deck, four-stack destroyer, given a new lease of life for Operation Dragoon, along with several other vessels of similar vintage.

They were warmly welcomed aboard by Timmins and one of his aides, Captain Joe O'Connor, a huge, impressive bear of a man. Pointing to O'Connor's ham-like fists, Timmins grinned as he said, 'We always send Joe in first. The Krauts just get the hell out of it whenever he appears. I guess Joe's philosophy is 'Do unto others, before they do it to you'! Joe will lead the assault on the first island and I will join you in the attack on the second.' Tremayne warmed instantly to the affable, shyly smiling giant, who seemed to fill every inch of his uniform with bone and muscle.

Timmins and O'Connor led the way into the wardroom, to introduce Tremayne and Black to the CO, Colonel Walker, and the other officers involved in Operation Sitka. Among them, looking as if he had just stepped off a Hollywood film-set in his immaculate US naval officer's white uniform, was Commander Douglas Fairbanks Junior, the film-star. As engaging and good-looking in the flesh as he was on the screen, Fairbanks greeted Tremayne and Black enthusiastically, as if *they* were the stars. An expert in the arts of naval deception and 'beach jumping' – the technique of laying false trails in beach assault – Fairbanks had recently been appointed to take command of the so-called 'Mosquito Squadron' of powerful, fast patrol torpedo boats. These small, all-wood vessels were known to their crews as 'flaming coffins' on account of the three thousand gallons of high octane petrol they carried on board. Their job was to take the 1st SSF assault teams and their rubber boats in close enough to make the beach landings in the seaborne attack on the three islands guarding the approach to the Riviera invasion beaches.

Large, detailed maps of the southern French coast – from Marseille eastwards to Nice – covered one wall of the briefing room, while another featured an larger-scale map of their objective – the Iles d' Hyères.

Setting the scene for their involvement in Operation Sitka, Colonel Walker opened the pre-operation 'O' Group by confirming the need for Tremayne and Black's specialist knowledge and unique expertise. He took the time to explain the importance of their advisory roles in the assault on the islands and – subsequently – as 1st SSF established itself on the French mainland, around Cap Nègre and beyond.

Moving to the seaborne assault, he began: 'Gentlemen, your first objective is the seizure of Port-Cros, which is the middle one of the three islands you see here.' Walker slid the long wooden pointer across to a small wooded area on the eastern side of the island. 'And there is our primary target – a 164mm gun emplacement – which we will neutralise, along with any Krauts we find there. Once Captain O'Connor's assault teams have secured the island, they will cross the narrow stretch of water by rubber boats to join the other SSF units, led by Colonel Timmins, on the Ile du Levant, and destroy the garrison and any gun emplacements they find there. Within a matter of days, those combined units, together with French Commandos de la Marine and Senegalese infantry, will assault and secure Porquerolles, the largest of the islands. That attack is planned for August 22nd.'

Dealing with questions at this point, Walker described the approach to the seaward side of the islands, which would be by inflatable rubber dinghies launched from the Elco PT boats close to shore. The disembarking troops would immediately begin scaling the island's rocky cliffs – in some places as high as eighty feet. To assist them, the leading assault parties would have Schermuly rockets to fire ropes fitted with steel grapnels, which would provide secure holds for the climbing lines among the rocks on the cliff tops. The only beaches ideal for seaborne landings lay on the landward side of the islands, clearly visible and well within range of the German coastal artillery batteries mounted on the mainland.

Colonel Walker concluded his briefing on a suitably aggressive note: 'Regroup by squads as soon as you reach flat ground, making use of whatever cover you can find. If there are any Krauts around, make damn sure you put down enough lead to gain – and hold – the fire initiative. Move forward quickly and maintain the momentum of your attack, in order to capture the island by nightfall of August 16th at the latest. Ship-to-shore supporting fire will be provided by five US Navy attack transports and, if that doesn't shift the bastards,' he smiled at Tremayne, 'the Royal Navy battle-wagon, *HMS Ramilles* is on call with her fifteen-inch guns. We cannot afford another costly Omaha, gentlemen.'

The following day, Tremayne, Black and the members of the 1st Special Service Force embarked, in glorious sunlight, in the green and grey camouflaged PT boats of Fairbanks' mosquito squadron. Once on board, Tremayne and Black were immediately invited to the small bridge above the wheelhouse by US Navy Lieutenant Jim Dowd. Slim, lithe, muscular and of average height, with strong, clear-cut features, Dowd conveyed an impression of a watchful panther at rest. Tremayne was impressed by the shipshape, business-like appearance of the PT's bridge and easy access to all the boat's essential controls. With enthusiastic authority, Dowd had clearly stamped his youthful presence on his equally young command.

'Say, Commander, would you like to take the wheel an' see how she handles?' was exactly the invitation that Tremayne was hoping for.

'Would I just!' Tremayne's spirits leapt at the prospect. 'Thanks, Jim. By the way, my name's Richard – to hell with formality.' Once in control of her after taking the wheel, Tremayne called down the voice-pipe for maximum revolutions. Responding immediately with a surge of power, the Elco Type 103 PT was quickly up to over forty knots, ploughing through the rolling Mediterranean waves, sparkling white foam cascading over her bow and the for'ard Oldsmobile 37mm gun.

'She's eighty feet long, her beam is twenty feet an' she's fifty-five tons of fightin' fury. She's driven by three Packard V12s, each deliverin' 1500 horsepower.' Dowd grinned with obvious pride. 'At the speed you're goin' right now, I guess she drinks about 160 gallons an hour!'

'Hmmm. I think, Jim, I'd better slow down, or the gallant

Commander Fairbanks will not be best pleased with us. It's bad form to race ahead of the hunt master, but thanks for the opportunity to try her out. She's a real beauty – and sea-kindly. She's responsive and she handles well. Thank you for letting me have my way with her!' Tremayne took in the PT boat's varied and extensive armament. In addition to the for'ard 37mm M9 automatic, she carried a 40mm Bofors aft, while amidships was a twin 20mm power-mounted Oerlikon and several .50 calibre Brownings, as well as four 21-inch torpedo tubes. 'I'd love to have one of these in my flotilla back in the Scillies,' enthused Tremayne, as he reluctantly handed the wheel back to Petty Officer Jake Sikorski, the fresh-faced, smiling coxswain who looked as if he'd come straight from high school. What a contrast he was – mused Tremayne – to the dour, laconic Ulsterman who so reassuringly filled the British MTB's bridge with his powerful, authoritative presence. As the flotilla drew closer to the islands in the softening light of late evening, O'Connor ordered 'check weapons', signalling to the troops on board the other PT boats to do the same.

Tremayne and Black had been tasked with supporting Timmins and the first waves of the SSF troops landing on Port-Cros. Black would lead the way, roping up the rock faces, together with the surprisingly agile Joe O'Connor and the American and Canadian squad commanders. Their job was to get to the top with the squads' automatic weapons as quickly as possible to put down maximum fire, to keep the Germans' heads down, as the rest of the assault force, at their most vulnerable, scrambled up the precipitous rocks. Timmins had deliberately selected the Johnson light machine gun as the squad automatic, instead of the more common BAR – the Browning Automatic Rifle, because it weighed some thirty per cent less, a key factor in roping up the eighty feet or so of near-vertical rock face. To maximise the attacking force's firepower, a high proportion of the troops were issued with Thompson sub-machine guns with twenty-round box magazines. The rest carried either the powerful .30-calibre Garand self-loading rifle, or lightweight automatic M1 carbines. Like British commandos, the SSF troops were equipped with fighting knives and festooned with grenades.

Tremayne was quick to make sure that the American and Canadian troops moved their grenades off their chests to their backs, to avoid dislodging the priming pins, with fatal results, when crawling flat on their bellies. He had picked up that vital and, as it proved to be, timely tip from Marine Commando Sergeant Kane, when he had earlier led the successful raid on the main German radio station in Brittany.

At two cables' distance from the cliff wall, looming menacingly against the now velvet black of a cloudless August night sky, the assault teams' rubber boats and paddles were lowered into the choppy sea. Hand over hand, the troops struggled down the bucking scrambling nets into the bobbing craft, quickly stabilising them for those following. Paddling the four hundred yards or so towards the cliffs – and the search for ledges from which to fire the Schermuly rockets – was tiring work against the offshore tide.

With their rubber boat bumping against the wet, slippery cliff face, Tremayne and Black eased their way along until they found a ledge wide enough to place and fire the rope launcher. The squads in the following boats took their lead from Tremayne, seeking whatever footholds they could find. Quickly, the first Schermuly grapnels were stabilised and fired, shooting the climbing ropes to the cliff tops where the grapnels lodged among the scattered rocks and crevices.

Ensuring that the grapnels had taken hold, the leading squads began swarming up the climbing ropes. In places, where the rocks were lower or less steep, the SSF troops nimbly scaled the cliffs without ropes, carefully picking out finger- and toe-holds as they climbed in the pitch dark. With not the best of heads for heights, Tremayne opted to climb by rope, close behind the SAS officer, who gave a masterclass demonstration of rock-climbing techniques.

Even in the chill of night, Tremayne's shirt was soaked with sweat as, gripping the climbing rope, he recalled his urbane first lieutenant's apt description of abseiling during commando training as 'a bowel-liquefying descent into oblivion'. As he struggled up, he also remembered the words of the Royal Marine instructor at Achnacarry Castle: '*Don't look down, sir. Keep your eyes on the rock face and look and feel where you're going to put your hands and feet.*' Behind him, he could hear grunts and muttered curses in accents from places ranging from Alberta to Alabama, as the mixed group of Canucks and Yanks clambered up after him.

At the top of the precipitous climb, Mike Black signalled silence as the troops regrouped under their squad leaders, seizing whatever cover they could find. As Tremayne scrambled up to him, Black signalled to the squad leaders with a red-lens torch to join him and Joe O'Connor.

Their first major objective – the 164mm German artillery gun – was situated about half a mile ahead and to their left. Before they reached that, they knew that they had at least one manned enemy machine-gun pillbox emplacement to neutralise. Intelligence sources had also confirmed the existence of several old stone forts on the island, which housed the German garrison, believed to be upwards of 250 troops. Further into the island was a cave, which could pose a problem to lightly armed troops should the Germans decide to use it as a fortified safe haven.

Black handed over the command of the operation to O'Connor as he and Tremayne resumed their advisory roles. In a short cliff-top 'O' Group, crouched among the sea gorse, O'Connor quickly reminded his NCOs of their task and its objectives,. Meanwhile, on board the *USS Ormond*, Colonels Walker and Timmins were finalising details of the 1ˢᵗ SSF's subsequent role in the main assault on the French coast, once they had taken the islands threatening the invasion channel.

O'Connor stood up and checked his Thompson gun, making sure the safety catch was on and the magazine was securely pushed home. 'Okay, let's go…'

Six

Channel Of Invasion
Cleared And Open

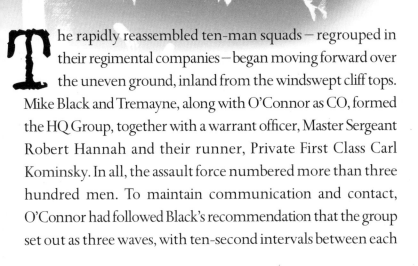

The rapidly reassembled ten-man squads – regrouped in their regimental companies – began moving forward over the uneven ground, inland from the windswept cliff tops. Mike Black and Tremayne, along with O'Connor as CO, formed the HQ Group, together with a warrant officer, Master Sergeant Robert Hannah and their runner, Private First Class Carl Kominsky. In all, the assault force numbered more than three hundred men. To maintain communication and contact, O'Connor had followed Black's recommendation that the group set out as three waves, with ten-second intervals between each extended line of men. One officer, together with a senior NCO, was placed at the centre of each line, with an NCO on each extreme flank. Other NCOs remained with their squads. Tremayne picked Sergeant First Class Caleb Jackson – a lean, laconic and thoughtful Alabaman, and New Yorker Sergeant John Kovacs who, together with his squad, would act as point, scouting some fifty yards ahead of the first wave of infantry.

As had become their tradition on night operations, the men of the Devil's Brigade blacked-up their faces and hands with GI boot polish. Tremayne's somewhat hesitant and rather reluctant attempts at camouflage with the strong-smelling goo amused Mike Black: 'Your genteel upbringing shows up even more than your stark white ears, Richard!' Despite the tension of anticipation and the frustration of coordinating an attack in the darkness of a moonless night, everyone seemed in high spirits as, fanning out from their start position, they began their advance to contact, to neutralise the first German machine-gun post some five hundred yards ahead and an estimated seventy yards off to their left. Tremayne felt very much at home with the 'can-do-will-do' approach to battle of the North Americans.

Scouring the map of Port-Cros, Tremayne had earlier spotted a narrow dirt road among the several that criss-crossed the small island. This particular one passed within a few yards of the pillbox, on its west-facing side. Most likely little more than an ancient cart track, and represented on the map by dotted lines – broken in places, he had recommended this to

O'Connor as what was probably the best route to their objective. The broken dotted lines suggested overgrown vegetation or uneven terrain to Tremayne and, therefore, the possibility of cover. Approximately two hundred yards beyond and to the east of the machine-gun post lay the 164mm coastal battery artillery emplacement. In the darkness, it was well nigh impossible to gauge accurately what distance remained. Tremayne, leading the point section, instinctively checked both the safety catch and 'pig-sticker' bayonet of his Lanchester – the Royal Navy's own unique sub-machine gun. Its fifty-round magazine and provision for a bayonet gave it distinct survival advantages over many other similar weapons. It remained Tremayne's chosen gun for close-quarter work. He felt his gut churning with a mixture of anticipation and fear. He was sweating freely and the adrenaline raced through his body as they drew closer to where the pillbox must be. 'Stay alert and bloody well concentrate,' he muttered to himself.

Tremayne froze and whispered an urgent 'Down – hit the deck!' as a sudden burst of laughter, just ahead, announced the presence of the German machine-gun crew.

'No more 'n thirty yards ahead an' jest a mite to the left, sir.'

'Johnny Rebs' of the 4th Alabama attacking Union soldiers at the First Battle of Manassas must have sounded just like that, mused Tremayne, as he snaked his way on his elbows closer to Caleb Jackson, his Lanchester cradled in his arms. As he did so, he whispered to Sergeant Kovacs to join them.

'Thank you, Sarn't. Well spotted. Take command here. I'm going ahead with two of Sergeant Kovacs' men to suss out the ground.' Addressing both NCOs, Tremayne whispered, 'I want two satchel charges made ready and bring up a couple of the squad LMGs with plenty of spare mags for when we return.'

Turning to Kovacs, he whispered, 'Right Sarn't, I want two of your men with me as scouts, while I take a look-see to find out the lie of the land. Depending on what we find, we'll assault with either a left or right flanking attack with at least the first wave of troops. We'll either return together, or I'll send a runner back with orders.'

Tremayne quickly checked his ammunition pouches to make sure that the spare magazines for his Lanchester were ready for instant use.

'Questions?'

Kovacs was the first to respond – the clipped Bronx accent in marked contrast to Jackson's Southern drawl. 'McBride and Polanski will be your scouts, sir.'

'Thanks Sarn't. Get them up here, please.'

To Jackson, he whispered, 'Send a runner back to Captain O'Connor to keep him in the picture and let him know what I'm doing, Sarn't, as soon as I move off. Have two squads ready to assault – one with two LMGs, the other ready to attack from the flanks on Captain O'Connor's command. Tremayne smiled, his teeth showing white in the dark, 'We want *our* Little Round Top to be a success, Sarn't!'

The Civil War analogy struck an immediate chord with Jackson, who grinned back, 'Yessir, we sure do – this time around!'

Seconds later, Tremayne was joined by McBride and Polanski, who had already been briefed by Sergeant Kovacs. McBride – a powerfully built Canadian – carried a Thompson, and Polanski – a slim, athletic-looking man –brought with him an M1 .30 calibre carbine.

'Stick close and keep your eyes open. Safety catches on – let's go.'

After slowly and silently crawling forward for about ten yards, Tremayne found what appeared to be low hedge, broken in places, little more than three feet to his right. Signalling the others to remain where they were, he slid along the thorny bushes to the next gap and discovered a small dirt track on the other side of the hedge. Another burst of laughter – this time louder – fixed the position of the German machine-gun post no more than twenty yards somewhere along the track. With his eyes now well adjusted to the dark, Tremayne could just make out the squat, menacing outline of a bunker and what he estimated to be three – possibly four – Germans lounging outside, talking and smoking. He crawled back to McBride and Polanski, his finger to his lips indicating silence, and whispered, 'The bunker's close and I want to find out where its firing apertures are. Do you both have grenades?' Both nodded a silent 'yes'. Tremayne checked that his own two grenades were secure, before he spoke scarcely above a whisper, 'We're going to keep this side of the hedge and move up until we're opposite the bunker and can see what it's like. Depending on what we find, I want you, Polanski, to crawl back to tell Sergeant Jackson what we're about to do and then rejoin me asap, complete with a couple of satchel charges.'

Silently, the three moved forward again, hugging the rough ground. Five minutes later, they arrived almost opposite the concrete bunker, at a narrow gap in the hedge. About fifteen feet away were two German soldiers, leaning against the bunker and chatting with what appeared to be another two men, now back inside, and manning a machine gun, judging by the direction of conversation, surmised Tremayne. One firing aperture was almost directly opposite his group and there were another three, set symmetrically, one each side of the square bunker.

As the Germans began to speak – and laugh – more loudly, Tremayne whispered, 'Let's move on twenty yards, slip over the cart track, work our way back to the bunker and stick the satchel charges, plus my grenades, through the aperture on the far side.' Nodding to McBride, he said, 'You and I will finish off anyone still alive after the explosions, while you,' he turned to Polanski, 'get back at the double to Sergeant Jackson and report. Understood?' Both nodded in the affirmative. 'Okay, let's – oh shit! This bastard's coming for a piss.' The one German, still roaring with laughter, made his way over to the hedge, inches from where Tremayne lay and, undoing his flies, began to urinate – missing the Englishman's head by a hair's breadth.

His laughter suddenly froze as he looked down and saw,

in the dark, the three still figures below him. 'Ach, Mensch. Gott in Himmel! Was...?'* His terrified shriek was cut short, dying as an agonised groan as McBride's fighting knife drove into his heart.

Tremayne heard the distinctive sound of an MG42's action being worked, before a measured burst of fire sprayed bullets inches above their heads. 'You two – roll to the left and get round the bunker with the charges. Move!' As another controlled burst shredded the hedge, Tremayne rolled rapidly to the right and into a shallow ditch he'd passed only minutes before. A sudden sharp cry told him one of his men had been hit. With scarcely time to take aim, Tremayne returned fire, raking the area of the aperture with his Lanchester. Instantly, he rolled further to his right, just as the Germans began desperately 'hose-piping' the area he had vacated. Leaping the hedge but keeping low, he raced up to the bunker wall, pressing himself against it. Pulling the pins out of both grenades simultaneously he hurled them, one after the other, through the side aperture close to his shoulder and flung himself to the ground.

Panic-stricken shouts inside confirmed that the Germans realised what had happened. Screaming in terror, they scrabbled, too late, for the door at the rear of the bunker. The grenades detonated simultaneously. Tremayne was just getting up to finish the job and check on his own men, when an almighty explosion flung him to the ground and the massive reinforced concrete bunker shook to its foundation. Hearing a sustained

---

Oh, man. God in heaven! What...?

burst of automatic fire, he raced round the bunker to find a grim-faced McBride cradling his MI in his arms. 'That's just about evened the score for Frank. They shot him. Polanski's dead, sir, so I used a satchel charge on the bastards after your grenade exploded and emptied a magazine into what's left of 'em, sir.'

For an instant, Tremayne shuddered at the thought of the obscene results of the explosions in such confined quarters. McBride's brief, matter-of-fact report brought him right back to the moment. 'Thank you. I'm so sorry about Polanski. He was a good soldier. I wish to hell I'd had the time to get to know him as a man.'

'He was a great guy, sir. He was my buddy. I have his dog tag. Let me write to his mother, sir – I know the family well. When we went on leave from Fort William Henry Harrison in Montana, I stayed with Frank and his folks in Wyoming.' The big Canadian fell silent, embarrassed, yet drained of emotion and conscious that perhaps, in British eyes, he had spoken too much and shown more of his feelings than the British do.

Tremayne briefly touched McBride's shoulder. 'I have also known the pain and sense of complete emptiness that follows the loss of a good friend. Each time it happens, it doesn't seem to get any easier.' He recalled, all too sadly, the brutal break-up of the seemingly indestructible Pablo Watkins-Brummie Nicholls partnership on the D-Day landings. 'Perhaps, in a way, that's a good thing. To lose that would be like quitting the human race.' Tremayne looked at McBride who was regarding him seriously, his eyes beginning to fill with tears.

Raw grief was beginning to take over from the temporary self-anaesthetising effects of adrenaline-charged action.

'We'll take care of him for you. I'll speak with Captain O'Connor as soon as we return. Take your time to grieve for Frank — you'll need it. But right now, the best honour you can do him is to be the soldier you — and he — know you are.' Tremayne smiled. 'Come on. Let's get back to Sergeant Jackson before that Johnny Reb starts to re-fight Gettysburg in our absence!'

The first sign of a return smile crossed the big, awkward Canadian's tough yet sensitive face. 'Thank you for that, sir, I sure appreciate it.'

Within minutes, they were back with Jackson and Kovacs who had been joined by the HQ Group and the rest of the invasion force, now temporarily lying up, deployed, in positions of all-round defence.

Tremayne reported quickly, but in sufficient detail, to O'Connor and Black, the sequence of events in the destruction of the bunker. He was concerned that, for post-action reports, O'Connor took on board the parts played by both McBride and Polanski in the brief, but bloody firefight.

Black was the first to speak. 'Joe, the whole garrison — wherever they are — will be now on the alert after the noise of that engagement. I suggest we push on with all speed to take the artillery emplacement. Use the three squads of the first wave, with the second and third waves in reserve. Send out scouts, as before, in the advance to contact.'

'Sure makes sense to me. We'll scout ahead at squad strength, but with the Krauts awake and waiting, we'll deploy three-man recce teams on both flanks.' The big Irish-American looked with concern at Tremayne. 'You okay to take the point again?'

'Of course Joe.' Tremayne's reassuring and confident grin confirmed his readiness. 'That's what they pay me the big money for!' Turning to Sergeant Jackson, he said, 'Sarn't, pick your squad, we're point. That 164mm gun is our objective.'

'It'll be Kovacs' squad, sir. I reckon we owe that to Polanski, sir.'

'Good luck, Richard. We'll be right behind you.' Tremayne's smile lit up his face. 'Thanks, Mike.' The solid, unspoken bond between the naval officer and the SAS major, born of their shared experience of operations together, was as strong and natural as instinct itself.

Turning to Jackson, Tremayne ordered, 'Sarn't. Take the right flank, please, with Sarn't Kovacs on the left. I'll have McBride next in line, on my right.

Extended line – advance to contact!'

'Yessir! Jes' like we done when we whupped them Blue Bellies* at Shiloh!'

Jackson's broad grin confirmed that he had fully cottoned on to Tremayne's sense of humour and awareness of American history.

The squad moved silently but quickly forward, eyes straining to see through the darkness of the clear, dry summer night. O'Connor let Tremayne's point section cover fifty yards,

---

*A derisory Confederate term for Union soldiers

before he ordered the remaining squads of the first wave, together with the second line, to advance in support. The third wave he held in reserve, under the command of Canadian Lieutenant Ian McKenzie, formerly of the Seaforth Highlanders of Canada before he joined the 1st SSF. Although he had left his native Ullapool during the Great Depression thirteen years ago, at the age of nine, McKenzie had never lost his soft, lilting West Highland accent. Hearing McKenzie's voice on board the *USS Ormond*, Tremayne had sought him out and spoken at length with him. Immediately, a friendship had developed between the two men, based on a shared love of the Scottish Highlands and an interest in the Gaelic language.

Now some three hundred yards ahead of McKenzie's position, Tremayne's scout squad was close to its target. The red lens of Tremayne's signal torch flashed once each way, right then left. Within seconds, Jackson and Kovacs were at his side. With eyes now fully accustomed to the darkness, they could make out the long barrel of the coastal defence gun raised, Tremayne estimated, to an angle of thirty degrees and pointing menacingly across the intended line of the planned seaborne assault on Toulon. Complete silence reigned, apart from Jackson's whispered comment to Tremayne: 'It 'ud be jes like one of them turkey shoots against them landing craft, sir.'

'We'll move in for a closer look, Sarn't, but I don't like this complete silence, there's something unnatural about it.' The first pre-dawn streaks of grey were just beginning to lighten the sky. Tremayne paused to recheck the magazine and bayonet of his Lanchester. Turning to Kovacs, he whispered, 'Sarn't, take two men and —' The flat crack of a Mauser, the sickening thud as a bullet hit human bone and a sudden shocked moan all seemed to happen almost simultaneously.

'Sniper sir! I just caught his muzzle flash. He's in the gun emplacement—somewhere over towards the left corner I reckon.' Grateful for the slow-speaking Alabaman's sharp eyesight, Tremayne muttered, 'Well spotted, Sarn't. We'll get that bastard before he does any more damage.' Moments later, Private First Class Krause slid alongside on his belly. 'It's Private Dolan, sir, shot clean through the forehead as he raised himself up to stretch for a look-see.'

'Thank you, Krause.' He hoped he didn't sound callous. 'I'm sorry about Dolan. That sniper must have very good eyesight to pick out individuals in this light. Did *you* see his muzzle flash too?'

'I guess not, sir, though I reckon, from the angle of shot, it was ahead and most likely where Sergeant Jackson said — just over to the left, sir.'

Addressing Jackson, Tremayne whispered, 'I want your two best marksmen in this section to pin the bastard down with sniping shots. They're going to have to be patient and bloody accurate — and make damn sure they don't shoot any of us. I want them to move forward, into cover, one on each flank. Tell them I'll signal them — three red flashes, repeated — to let them know that we're ready in position and therefore to raise their fire above us, but to maintain the pretence of continuous sniping. I want you to send a runner back to Captain O'Connor, to let him know why we're held up and what we're doing to deal with the problem.'

'Yessir.'

Turning to Kovacs, he continued, 'You and I, Sarn't, with the rest of the squad, are going to nail this sniper. While our two guys keep his head down, the rest of us will crawl up to the emplacement and lace it with grenades before we rush in. We'll take a couple of satchel charges to blow up the gun and temporarily disorientate the bastard – if we haven't blown him up too.'

With Tremayne leading, the squad advanced on the gun emplacement, crawling rapidly and taking advantage of the uneven ground for cover. Beresford and Gavrilovich, the two marksmen, maintained the impression of carefully aimed shots to keep the German sniper's head down, but without knowing precisely where he was hiding.

At less than twenty feet from the gun emplacement's stone and sand-bagged wall, Tremayne turned and gave three red flashes from his signalling torch – repeated – to the marksmen behind and yelled 'Grenades!' Seven arms went up and seven grenades landed in the compound, exploding together. Kovacs and one of the troopers hurled in the satchel charges, which went off with a deafening roar; flame and smoke rising around the gun, its barrel now pointing skywards at a crazy angle.

Vaulting over the low wall, Tremayne led in the squad.

'In lads, quick as you like!' Within seconds, they found the crushed dead body of the sniper who had sought refuge from the marksmen behind the gun. Kovacs, savagely muttering 'sonofabitch', instinctively put a burst of four rounds into the sniper's head, blowing away the back of his skull. The satchel charges had flung the heavy weapon off its mounting and it had landed on the sheltering sniper, killing him instantly. Nearby and curiously untouched, lay his Mauser rifle, its Zeiss telescopic sights still in perfect condition. Tremayne sent the runner, who had just returned, back to let O'Connor know – 'Mission accomplished'.

Minutes later, the rest of the invasion force was taking up positions of all-round defence at the destroyed gun emplacement, with O'Connor, Black and McKenzie enthusiastically congratulating Tremayne and the assault squad on their achievement. By 05.00, in the chill light of dawn, it was now possible to see something of the island and its rolling terrain – so like areas of St Martin's, mused Tremayne, as, with some nostalgia, he was reminded of the Isles of Scilly. By 06.30, after another 164mm gun had been located – this time, a prominently sited, cleverly constructed replica designed to lure Allied bombers away from the genuine article – the western half of the island was securely in the hands of the invaders.

Following a hasty breakfast of GI 'compo' rations heated – rather than cooked – on hexamine stoves with coffee tasting of the petrol cans in which it was 'mashed', O'Connor ordered the advance to continue.

Advancing cautiously across open country, towards Fort Arbussier and the island's port, the invasion force was fired on by a body of German troops who were first driven back before counter-attacking spiritedly and inflicting casualties on the SSF. The German infantry, well equipped and backed up by intensive, sustained machine-gun fire from a network of cleverly sited, deadly MG42s, continued the fight with the utmost determination and courage. Over two hundred strong, they posed a major obstacle – and threat – to the SSF, using mortars as well as their automatic weapons to great effect.

Calling up both an airstrike from rocket-firing Hawker Typhoons and supporting naval bombardment from the four-inch guns of a British destroyer, O'Connor forced the Germans to retreat, which they did so in good order, into three stone-built Napoleonic forts – Arbussier, L'Eminence and Lestissac –and a large cave system.

Repeated assaults on the forts and cave went on through-out the day, with the 1st SSF losing casualties against the well-defended strongholds and being unable to dislodge the German defenders. The Germans had ringed the forts and entrance to the caves with more well-sited MG posts, which made frontal assaults far too costly for the Americans and Canadians. The four-inch guns of the British destroyer had proved to be completely useless against the solidly constructed old forts and merely bounced off. Similarly, the six-inch weapons of the American cruiser, the *USS Augusta* proved to be equally ineffectual.

In one attack against the Germans, the assault led by O'Connor, with Black and Tremayne in support, was pinned down in a cemetery and took heavy casualties, losing many good officers, NCOs and enlisted men. Tremayne, Black and O'Connor were all wounded, fortunately not seriously, when a German mortar bomb exploded near them. Tremayne and Black suffered only minor injuries from small mortar bomb fragments and remained on the battlefield with field dressings on their arms and shoulders. O'Connor, however, received more severe shrapnel wounds which required surgery and he was evacuated by PT boat and returned to the ship's surgeon on the *USS Ormond*. With O'Connor's withdrawal from the battle, Mike Black assumed overall command of the operation.

German resistance remained fierce and tenacious and the engagement became a succession of attacks and counter-attacks, with no signs of surrender from the garrison. Black radioed for greater fire support from the Navy to dislodge the Germans from the stone fortresses and cave. With nothing heavier than bazookas, the invasion force simply did not possess the firepower necessary to destroy the German fortifications.

Black's request for assistance to Colonel Walker resulted in US Navy Admiral Forrestal's surprise – and very welcome – arrival on the island to read the situation at first hand. He immediately called for the support of *HMS Ramilles'* fifteen-inch guns. The great British battleship steamed majestically into range and two salvoes of her mighty weapons, two days after the seaborne attack had begun, quickly brought about the Germans' surrender. A soldier appeared at the entrance to the cave carrying a white flag and, at 22.00 hours, the German garrison surrendered.

Colonels Walker and Timmins attacked the Ile du Levant with thirteen hundred troops and, once more after several bloody engagements, the determined Germans eventually surrendered in the face of superior naval firepower. August 22nd saw the delayed seaborne assault on Porquerolles take place, this time with Tremayne and Black again taking part in what were essentially advisory roles to Colonel Timmins. With them were several hundred French Commandos de la Marine and a large detachment of Senegalese infantry, whose very presence created considerable unease amongst the Germans.

Intense fighting took place spasmodically across the island until the garrison – outfought and outgunned – finally capitulated, surrendering to the French and Americans rather than the Senegalese.

That night, Colonel Timmins sent his cryptic signal of the SSF Brigade's victory in the Iles d'Hyères, to the Allied General Headquarters: 'Channel of invasion cleared and open!'

Seven

A Political Goulash

With the Allied invasion of the south of France in full swing, Tremayne and Black's continuing support to Colonel Timmins, following the capture of the Iles d'Hyères, took the form of legal and civil administrative guidance. As the full force of Operation Dragoon began to hit home, the important bases of Toulon and Marseille fell to the Allies at the end of August after bitter fighting.

With French troops back on French soil, supported by thousands of active local Resistance fighters, revenge against suspected collaborators became a major, widespread issue. Innocent people were tortured and executed on trumped-up charges of 'collaboration' in the hysteria of guilt and shame, which tainted the genuine desire to see justice done. All too often, 'justice' became the alibi for revenge and retribution.

At the same time, French forces under General de Gaulle were entering Paris. When the German garrison in the city surrendered – in defiance of Hitler's order to fight on and 'burn Paris' – witch hunts for collaborators began there almost immediately. As concurrently, in the south, the innocent were punished along with the guilty, it seemed to Timmins and Tremayne that much of liberated France was hell bent on expunging guilt, as much as ensuring the due process of law over collaboration.

In the role of co-liberators with the French, the Americans were in a difficult, politically fraught position, where the utmost diplomacy and great sensitivity were required of them. The growing influence, in some regions, of the Communist Maquisards, opposed to the Gaullist FFI, created not only political divisions, but also resulted in uncoordinated resistance and sabotage against the Germans. Too many Resistance operations lacked the necessary cohesion and control, because of the political diversity and conflicting aims of the different Maquis groups.

Timmins had called an urgent operational meeting with Tremayne and Black who were now joined by the Canadian Highlander lieutenant, Ian McKenzie.

Timmins took the lead: 'Here in Vichy France, gentlemen, we have the added problem of genuinely confused and divided loyalties. When Field Marshal Pétain was appointed leader of the compromised Vichy regime, his overt stance of loyalty to France understandably appealed to the largely conservative elements of the middle-class population in the south. To many, he was still the hero of Verdun who had fought so gallantly during the First World War.

'Ian, like you Richard, studied law at university and I know he will add to our efforts to assist the local authorities to sort out and make sense of some of the challenges thrown up by our substantial presence in the liberation.'

Turning to the softly spoken Highlander, Tremayne held out his hand, smiling, with the traditional Gaelic greeting of welcome: 'Ceud mile fàilte!'*

An even broader smile lit up the tall Highlander's amiable face as, initially surprised then obviously delighted, he enthusiastically shook Tremayne's hand: 'Gu'n robh maith agad!'**

Timmins continued: 'In order to make the most of a bad situation – and in the face of force majeure, especially so within the southern, Vichy-controlled area – the French authorities have collaborated with the Germans. While such cooperation has sat relatively comfortably with the more conservatively nationalist elements of the population, the Communists, Jews and other sections of society have become major sources of active resistance against the Nazis.'

Timmins paused as a young uniformed orderly appeared with coffee, indicating an aged fruitwood table at his side.

'Thanks, Murphy – set 'em down here. It seems, for instance,

'A hundred thousand welcomes!'
** 'Thank you!'

that the anti-Jewish legislation in Vichy was implemented and vigorously pursued by the French authorities – not just the Nazis. Furthermore, gentlemen, the Vichy authorities have created a French paramilitary police force – the Milice – a brutal bunch of thugs who have actively collaborated with the Germans to crush Resistance groups in the south. They have willingly cooperated in the capture, torture and execution of Maquisards – particularly the Communist factions – and have even fought in set-piece battles against the partisans, alongside German troops.'

'To put it mildly,' interjected Tremayne, 'it seems as if Vichy France has developed as something of a 'political goulash', with an improbable mixture of ill-assorted ingredients.'

'Too damned right and, in such insecurity and instability, self-preservation has become the common, shared imperative for all and sundry. As in all wars, the victors are the only ones who are able to exact revenge and punishment – and, boy, are they doing that right now.' Timmins took a sip of his coffee.

'We cannot eliminate injustice and unfairness – that's just not on the cards. We don't have the time – or the necessary resources – if such a task were even possible. We can only intercede on a limited and local scale, but if we are only able to ensure justice in one case, that will be a one hundred per cent improvement on complete failure. What we can't afford to do, gentlemen, in an area such as this – where there are so many Communists, Gaullists and other Resistance factions – is to turn an attempt at justice into a political crisis.'

Timmins paused, looking at each of the three officers in turn. 'Is all this making any sense, or is it just so much 'noise' and no 'signal'?'

Black was the first to reply. 'It's making complete sense, sir, and the message I'm getting, loud and clear, is that we *don't* give up – but we do need to tread carefully, to minimise the local resentment towards 'foreign' liberators, which we've already encountered. Luckily, in Operation Dragoon, there is, from the outset, a far higher proportion of French troops involved than in Operation Overlord. At the moment, sir, we're as much the adjunct as the main body of liberating troops. We need to be seen as assisting in the liberation of France *for the French people*, not as a foreign, occupying force merely replacing the Germans.'

'Right, Mike. The key question remains, though. Which are the truly representative bodies of the French people in *this* area: the very substantial PCF – the French Communist Party – or the conservative middle classes, who saw Marshal Pétain as both the saviour and representative of the essential spirit of France?'

Timmins drained his coffee cup.

'Though I agree we *are* walking on egg shells, we might take the view – 'Fifty million Frenchmen, fifty million shades of political colour' – and just get on with the job,' added Tremayne, as Black and McKenzie nodded in agreement.

'Okay, gentlemen, action it is. So, into the minefield – or into the goulash, as you prefer!'

Timmins unrolled a large-scale map of the mountainous area immediately north of Hyères and Toulon. Taking a bayonet off his desk to serve as a pointer, he indicated the town of Solliès-Pont. 'Here, gentlemen,' he said, tapping the spot with the tip of his bayonet for emphasis, 'is where a group of ten Miliciens have been cornered in a café by a large group of Communist Resistance members who are out for blood – and nothing less. US Army Intelligence want those guys for questioning about Allied prisoners of war known to have been held in the area – and who, if still alive, will be moved north as the Germans and their friends in the Milice flee north.' Pausing to light a Camel from an ornate, beautifully engraved cigarette case, Timmins exhaled luxuriously before continuing. 'I've briefed Ian on the route and put a jeep at your disposal. Carry sidearms with you but leave any carbines or automatic weapons in the vehicle. Ideally, I'd like all ten Miliciens for questioning. The information they hold is crucial to us, since some of the PoWs held in captivity by the Milice and their Kraut buddies are US and British Special Forces guys. Most of them, I guess, may have been executed by now but I need to know about them and their fate – and anyone else who has been captured on pre-invasion operations in the south. Find out what you can and bring me back one of these guys for questioning.'

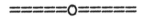

Ten minutes later, as they walked to the MT compound to collect their jeep, they passed a row of houses and Tremayne smiled at the unmistakable sounds coming from a radio of the Glenn Miller orchestra playing *Chattanooga Choo Choo.* 'Hmmm,' he mused, '*liberation à la sauce américaine!*' Mike Black, joining in with off-key vocal accompaniment, was only allowed to get as far as '...track twenty-nine and you can give me a shine' when a grinning Tremayne cut in with, 'Thank you, Major Black. Don't call us – we'll call you!' Laughing, the trio clambered into the jeep, stowed their weapons and, with McKenzie at the wheel, they set out to negotiate the release of the Miliciens cornered by the Maquisards in the nearby town café.

After an uneventful journey of some forty minutes, they drove into the town to discover, to their horror, a noisy crowd of spectators and five corpses, flung into a heap at the foot of a hastily erected temporary gallows. Standing on benches beneath the gallows, with hangman's nooses already round their necks, were the remaining five Miliciens. All were deathly pale and all bore extensive bruising to their faces. One was sobbing uncontrollably while a further three were visibly shaking. The fifth one stood to attention, looking over the heads of the Communist Maquisards and assembled jeering crowd, his face a mask of contempt.

McKenzie stopped as near as possible to the gallows with a screech of brakes, while Tremayne and Black leapt out and pushed through the crowd up to the Maquisards, who were on the point of kicking over the benches the prisoners were standing on.

'Stop! Arretez vous! Arretez!' yelled Tremayne frantically. 'We need to interrogate your prisoners. Stop the execution!'

A large, bear-like Maquisard, who appeared to be in charge, nodded to his men – now behind the two British officers – who then savagely punched Tremayne and Black in the back and pinned their arms to their sides. McKenzie looked on helplessly as members of the Maquis surrounded his jeep like a solid phalanx, preventing him from coming to the aid of his colleagues and knocking him back into his seat when he tried to get up. Having already secreted the ignition keys in his pocket, he tried to ward off further blows to his head and body until he raised his bloodied hands in surrender, shouting, 'Je suis pas Anglais. Je suis Ecossais!'*

At this point, the crowd of Maquisards stopped beating him but remained closed up round the jeep. Tremayne attempted to remonstrate with the Maquis leader who swore at him and punched him in the mouth. Swinging his leg, Tremayne managed to kick the Frenchman in the crotch, who doubled up – grimacing with pain. Immediately, other Maquisards pitched into Tremayne and Black, knocking them both to the ground. Recovering, the bear-like creature gestured to his colleagues who hauled the bruised and battered British officers to their feet. Punching Tremayne in the solar plexus, the man hissed, his foul breath reeking of alcohol, 'Now English you will watch them die.' Badly winded, Tremayne struggled to regain his breath, but was unable to speak, except to gasp, 'We need to question them, we –'

---

*'*I'm not English. I'm Scottish!'*

'Shut your mouth, English, and watch!'

At a signal from 'the bear', the benches were suddenly kicked away. Choking and jerking violently, the five Miliciens died as the crowd whooped and cheered. Some of the celebrating spectators yelled curses and jeered cruelly as the obscene twitching ceased. Tremayne, so brutally reminded of his engineer's callous murder by the SS and his own horrific mock execution, felt again the despair and anguish he had known on that terrible early morning in Brittany, only months ago.

After the bodies were released from the nooses and flung on the floor to join their dead comrades, many of the crowd pressed closer to spit on them before drifting away, completely ignoring the three officers. The Communist Maquisards began loading the ten corpses onto an ancient Renault lorry, as 'the bear' strode back to Tremayne and Black growling, 'Go home, English, and keep your noses out of our affairs.' He pushed Tremayne in the back towards the jeep and, as he did so, Black caught Tremayne's quickly muttered message: 'Let the bastard come as far as the vehicle.'

Approaching the jeep, Tremayne sensed that the large Maquisard was about to deliver some foul-mouthed final farewell. Without warning, he turned on the unsuspecting Frenchman, feinting a blow with his left hand towards the dead, tawny eyes.

Then, as the Maquisard lifted his arms to protect himself, Tremayne stepped back and uppercut him with all his strength, the man's jaw breaking with an audible crack. The Maquisard crashed to the ground in a heap, out cold. 'That makes us quits, you arsehole.' Tremayne grinned at Black through bloodied swollen lips. 'Ah, here they come! Put a burst over their heads, Mike.'

With McKenzie already gunning the engine, Black and Tremayne grabbed their automatic weapons from the jeep and fired several short bursts over the furious Maquisards, advancing at the double to rescue their leader who was stretched out at Tremayne's feet.

The temporarily halted mob soon recovered and, rallying to the yell 'À l'attaque!' began to charge again towards the now rapidly moving jeep.

'Time to go, Richard. It would be bad form to outstay our welcome.' Smiling grimly, Black ostentatiously took deliberate aim with his Thompson gun, causing the yelling mob to draw back once again. McKenzie accelerated to maximum revs, raced out of the town centre and onto the road back to base.

'Mission failed and, what's more, I have probably done irreparable damage to relationships between the Communists and the invasion forces in this area,' said Tremayne ruefully.

'For certain, we didn't secure the release of those captured Miliciens for interrogation, but frankly that was 'mission impossible'. As for those Commies, what were we supposed to do — kiss the bastards?'

Tremayne took some comfort from Black's sense of realism and from the still bloodied, but imperturbable Highlander who, grinning, said, 'It was only when I told them I was a Scot — trading on the Auld Alliance — that they stopped hammering hell out of me!'

'By the way, young Tremayne,' added Black. 'That uppercut you delivered is what's called a real 'cog-heaver' where I come from. It was devastating! Are you sure you don't want to transfer to the Regiment!?'

'I'm flattered Mike, but I've had a love affair with navy blue for too long! Thanks, anyway. In any case, my film-star good looks couldn't take too many batterings like that!'

'God help us, Ian – would y' just listen to the man!' laughed Black, checking the magazine on his sub-machine gun.

Minutes later and still feeling sore, as well as angry and disappointed after their encounter with the Maquis, they pulled into the MT compound and quickly made their way to the CO's office.

Expecting an almighty rocket from Colonel Timmins on return to SSF HQ, the three were relieved to hear him state that theirs had, indeed, been an impossible mission. 'I already had one of my SSF guys in the crowd on reconnaissance. He's from north-east Maine and French is his first language. He's a fluent speaker and can disguise his North American accent and pass – for a time at least – as a Frenchman. He saw what went on and slipped away from the crowd, just before you, in an old gas-driven Citroën that we've doctored for him to get maximum speed out of it. He reported, likewise, that he couldn't even get near enough to those poor bastards to speak to them.'

'Once a crowd is worked up, howling for blood, sir, few are likely to influence them – except a voluble, angry leader hell bent on vengeance. I believe, too, that because of the Gestapo-like brutal record of the Milice – especially in this area – we were on to a loser, but we *had* to make an attempt to get them out,' replied Tremayne.

'Looking at your faces, it seems as if you guys had one hell of a hard time with those Commie bastards and I do thank you for your efforts.'

'All part of the service, sir,' grinned Black, 'but all three of us are frustrated to hell that we didn't succeed in bringing out just one of those Miliciens for interrogation.'

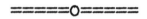

Following the failed mission to secure the release to Allied custody of any of the Miliciens, Tremayne spent further time attempting to negotiate with the local power figures established, and emerging, within the region – with varying degrees of success. One operation involved ensuring the safe release to Colonel Timmins of several German naval personnel, taken prisoner close to the coast by an FFI unit. Showing the signs of rough physical treatment in captivity, the very relieved Germans were only too ready to talk to Timmins and his interrogators when they reached SSF HQ. As Black had wryly commented, 'That success goes some way towards restoring our shattered egos!'

Though enjoying the company of Timmins, Black and

McKenzie in helping to restore some sort of civic normality within the areas newly liberated by 1ˢᵗ SSF, Tremayne was relieved to receive the welcome signal – two weeks later – from Commander Enever, ordering his return to Tresco.

The enchanting Isles of Scilly with their familiar emerald seas and glorious beaches, his colleagues and shipmates of the Tresco flotilla and – above all – Emma with, now, the added bonus of Catriona, all pulled at his heart. 'Much as I'm tempted by so privileged an invitation, *these* are what make me want to remain Navy and not transfer to the SAS,' he mused, as he stowed his kit into his grip prior to the journey back to HMS Godolphin.

Eight

Bryher – The Island Of Hills

Tremayne bade farewell to Timmins, Black and McKenzie with mixed emotions. In testing conditions – both on the field of battle and in working with the civic authorities and the different Resistance factions – a strong bond had developed between them. He had found Colonel Timmins' positive, yet understated leadership style ideal to work under. Timmins always spelled out the 'what' and 'why' of an operation and its objectives with the utmost clarity, yet he trusted others to work out their own 'how best to's – as long as they delivered. He raised others' self-confidence by frequently demonstrating his confidence in them. What is more, Tremayne liked the tall, lean New Hampshire American and his quiet, authoritative approach. Their relationship had grown strong on a basis of mutual affection, respect and trust.

In Ian McKenzie, Tremayne had found something of a soulmate. Their shared interest in the Gaelic language and culture and love of the wild remoteness of Highland mountain scenery, led naturally to a close friendship – bordering on kinship – between the two of them. For considerably longer, he had valued his relationship as comrades in arms with Mike Black. He and Black had fought on several different fronts, facing danger and knowing fear together. He had also learned much from the SAS major about survival techniques that had undoubtedly saved his life on more than one occasion. In action, he and Black made a great team, but he knew that he was returning to an even greater one at HMS Godolphin.

Interrupting his reverie with a succession of bone-shaking jolts and bumps, the drab-olive US Air Force DC3 touched down at RAF Netheravon airfield in Wiltshire. On disembarking, Tremayne was immediately transferred to a waiting RAF Westland Lysander, to take him to St Mary's for the next leg of his journey to Tresco. Still dressed in British army khaki battledress, but bearing naval insignia, he clutched at his commando woollen cap comforter against the gale-like propeller draught of the Lysander's powerful Bristol Mercury engine. He quickly scrambled up into the cockpit, to an outstretched hand and a cheery 'Welcome aboard, sir. I'm Flight

Lieutenant Jim Avery'.

In Avery's lively, engaging company, the flight to the Scillies passed quickly. The Lysander pilot had had considerable experience in both inserting and retrieving agents — mostly SOE personnel — to and from Brittany and he and Tremayne were soon on common ground. Avery's operations regularly took him into the depths of Brittany, to remote — often hastily improvised — airfields. On two recent occasions, one the result of betrayal and the other due to sheer bad luck, he had been forced to make his escape under German fire. 'Rather a bit hairy, sir,' had been his rueful, self-effacing summing up, much to Tremayne's amusement. 'Some of the bravest passengers I take are Vera Atkins' young ladies, as they are known, sir. The casualty rates amongst those enormously courageous SOE ladies are horrendous. What the hell the bloody Gestapo do to them before they execute them, heaven only knows, sir.'

The sudden reminder of his own time as a prisoner of the Gestapo sent a shudder of revulsion through Tremayne, as the unforgettable terror and sense of utter isolation of that captivity momentarily overwhelmed him.

The Lysander's large, extensively glazed cockpit provided excellent viewing and Tremayne felt his spirits soar again as the Isles of Scilly appeared on the horizon virtually dead ahead. Initially they looked like a collection of indeterminate brown smudges on the shimmering sea and then, gradually, they began to take on their more familiar recognizable forms, to the point where Tremayne could readily identify individual islands.

Nearest was the Hanjague, known to Scillonians as 'th' Onjig' – rising out of the sea like some primeval monolithic monument. Following immediately behind, he saw the welcome sight of the red and white striped Daymark at the eastern end of St Martin's island. A dramatic visual daylight marker of the islands' presence, it had been serving mariners as an orientation point for close on three centuries. Ahead and to port was the larger mass of St Mary's and, between that and St Martin's, was the picturesque scattering of the Eastern Isles. Ahead and beyond those lay the island of Tresco, its distinctive, lush southern half standing out in dramatic contrast to its barren, rocky northern area.

In the bright sunlight of a late August midday, Tremayne now had a clear view of the islands, each with its many cherished memories for himself and Emma, chronicling through their emotions and senses the growth of their burgeoning relationship. Tresco was where they first spent time walking together, when each had felt pangs of guilt for seemingly betraying their love for a recently dead partner. The Eastern Isles saw them begin to put their grieving into the context of needing to move on, but without forgetting their former loved ones. It was Tresco, again, where each finally acknowledged that they had truly fallen in love and that it was, indeed, time for a new beginning.

Flying low over the beautiful shallow coastal sea, Tremayne was again reminded of its emerald and turquoise transparency, with the patches of dark seaweed fronds reaching up towards the surface like the gnarled, grasping fingers of green Man-of-the-Woods. All at once, the south of France — and the obscenities of war — seemed an eternity away. He was home.

Landing at St Mary's airport he saw, parked close to the runway, a khaki-painted Hillman Minx with RAF roundels on its doors. Saluting Tremayne as he scrambled down the Lysander's footholds, the ever cheerful Avery smiled and said, 'There's your transport, sir, down to Hugh Town harbour, where one of your harbour motor launches will be waiting. Good luck, sir!'

With an exchange of waved 'cheerios', Tremayne walked briskly over to the Hillman, returning the salute of the LAC driver who stood to attention, holding the door open for him.

'Afternoon, sir! Leading Aircraftsman 'Iggins, sir. I'll 'ave you down at the 'arbour in just a jiffy, sir.' True to his word, the reassuringly maitre d'-like Higgins deposited Tremayne on Hugh Town Quay some ten minutes later and with considerable precision, right next to the steps leading down to the boats bobbing in the water below.

The waiting HML, moored alongside the Hugh Town Quay, was manned — to Tremayne's joy — by Petty Officer Irvine and no less than Leading Seaman 'Pablo' Watkins. The latter, saluting, took Tremayne's grip with a poker-faced — 'Good to see yo' back sir.' Swain thought as 'ow yo' might 'ave decided to stay, what with all that ooh-la-la-froggie food and stuff, sir.'

Irrepressible as ever, thought Tremayne, as he returned the seaman's salute and shook his hand. 'You should know by now, Watkins, that I couldn't possibly stay away. Neither Petty Officer Irvine nor I can resist your culinary masterpieces.'

'Well, I don't know about that, sir, but I think yo' both like me cooking!'

To Tremayne's amusement, he caught a glimpse of the most fleeting of smiles –masquerading as a facial twitch – as it crossed Irvine's dour Ulster countenance. 'Hmmm,' mused Tremayne, contentedly. 'I am indeed home again!'

Commander Enever, as ebullient and enthusiastic as ever, was waiting to meet Tremayne on the quay at New Grimsby harbour. Tremayne raced agilely up the steep stone quayside steps, saluted, and shook Enever's outstretched hand warmly. 'So good to have you back on board, dear boy. Let's talk as we walk – both of us have so much to say to bring one another up to speed.'

In the time that he had been away, Tremayne learned from Enever that the Germans were clinging with fanatical resistance to the major Atlantic seaports in Brittany. Though their capital ships had long ceased to be a menace on the high seas, the Kriegsmarine still maintained a deadly presence in the English Channel, with its U-boats and E-boat flotillas, from those same bases on the extreme west coast of France.

The Allies – especially the US High Command – had decided that, judging by the recent bloody battle for St Malo, taking the ports would turn out to be a prolonged and costly operation. It seemed that, strategically, it made far more sense to go flat out, moving eastwards, together with the British, French and

Canadians, for the Reich itself. Hence, apart from Brest, the other Atlantic seaports were allowed to remain as small German-held enclaves, surrounded by Allied forces, with the FFI and other Resistance groups committed to making life hell on earth for the besieged garrisons.

While he had been involved in Operation Dragoon and the battles for the Iles d'Hyères, the Tresco flotilla had remained active in the insertion and recovery of agents in Brittany, as well as in Channel sweeps against predatory E-boats. Hermann Fischer had gained a DSO as the result of what Enever termed 'his fearsome Vortrekker courage', and the flotilla had lost one of its Fairmiles in a particularly bruising encounter with the German Navy's MTBs. In that incident, Lieutenant Mick Taylor, the Fairmile's skipper, had been badly wounded, but was recovering well in the RN hospital at Devonport. He, too, had been recommended for a DSO for his part in the action. Lieutenant Quilghini and Sub-Lieutenant Simmonds had each been mentioned in despatches.

'Oh, Richard, one intriguing scrap of news is that Admiral Canaris, head of the Abwehr and Hitler's 'spymaster', has been removed from office and arrested. This, I gather, is something to do with the recent attempt on the Bohemian Corporal's life at the Wolf's Lair in East Prussia on July 20th. As yet, though, we know nothing of his fate. It does suggest, however, that German naval and military Intelligence Services are not currently in the best of health — which is to our distinct advantage! It seems, from unofficial sources, that the wretched fellow was trying to hunt with the hounds and run with the fox – both at the same time.'

As they approached the gates of HMS Godolphin, Enever lightly touched Tremayne's arm. 'We'll have a quick spot of lunch in the wardroom and then, dear boy, into the bathtub and on with your best bib and tucker. There will be an ML ready at New Grimsby Quay at 15.00 hours to take you to Penzance. Emma and Catriona will be arriving on the evening train and you are starting a much overdue week's leave with effect from 17.00 today!'

Caught by surprise, Tremayne was over the moon and his lunch with Enever passed as a most happy, light-hearted occasion – with most of his thoughts on anything but naval matters.

Hours later, a delighted Tremayne, immaculate in his best uniform, was already waiting on platform four when the express train from Paddington pulled into Penzance station, just eight minutes late. Resplendent in its dark green GWR livery, belching thick white smoke and with hissing steam escaping from its highly polished valve gear, the gleaming Hall class locomotive *Hagley Hall* ground to a noisy, steel-screeching halt. 'Like a fiery, mechanical dragon returning triumphantly to its lair,' mused Tremayne, as he anxiously scoured the long line of chocolate and cream carriages, searching for Emma.

As the carriage doors were eagerly flung open and passengers began to spill out onto the platform, he looked for her dark chestnut hair and her lithe, trim figure. His pulse quickened as more carriage doors burst open – yet still she didn't appear. Had Catriona suddenly been taken ill? Had Emma been caught up in last minute work with SIS and missed the train? Surely not one of those bloody doodlebugs? Memories of that terrible blitz on Plymouth, which had cruelly killed his first wife Diana, suddenly flashed across his mind. For a moment, he went cold and an involuntary shudder ran through his body. It had been Emma who had saved his sanity after that horrific tragedy, restored purpose and perspective to his life and given him love — the like of which he had never known before.

Then he saw her waving happily, her face radiant. In her left hand she carried a canvas, leather-bound holdall and there was Catriona — swathed in a cradle-like sling over Emma's right shoulder and held close to her breast. Relieved beyond words, Tremayne pushed forward through the milling crowd to grab the holdall as Emma summoned one of the hovering porters to take her suitcase from the carriage compartment. For a moment, they simply stood locked in one another's arms while passengers smiled knowingly — and some, no doubt, enviously — as they struggled past on their way to the uniformed ticket collector. That moment, when time itself had no relevance, was theirs.

'Dearest Emma, how wonderful it is to see you — and you Catriona!' He paused, incredulous at the changes in his daughter's size and appearance since he had last seen her. 'Looking at that determined little face, darling, I reckon that our daughter would make a great Leading Wren Stoker Mechanic!'

'Hmmm, yes,' Emma's eyes sparkled with amusement, 'she *does* look rather like *you*, Richard. I can't wait to see if she grows up with your sailor's rolling gait!'

'I've organised a taxi, let's catch up with the porter and pile into the cab. There's a motor launch at the harbour, courtesy of dear John Enever, waiting to take us across to Tresco.'

Settled in the cab, Tremayne continued, 'Dick and Aileen Oyler are expecting us at the New Inn and Dick has managed to find a small hired fishing boat for us, complete with outboard motor.'

'So,' said Emma with Tremayne's arm around her, 'Bryher, at long last, is on the cards for a visit?'

'Absolutely, and until our three-badge Wren Stoker is old enough, we'll travel by engine power, rather than by sails, while we're in the islands.'

Emma took Tremayne's hand, smiling happily, 'I just can't wait to see you building sand-castles and paddling in the shallows!'

'Playing the role of Dad, let loose on the beach with bucket and spade, will be a rare privilege – and a sight to behold I promise you,' laughed Tremayne.

The harbour motor launch, manned by two seamen from HMS Godolphin, pulled away smoothly from Penzance harbour, setting her sleek, but sturdy hull into the Atlantic rollers. Emma sensed that Tremayne was eager to step up onto the small bridge above the wheelhouse and, in his words, 'get the feel of the boat and her capabilities'.

'Up aloft, Lieutenant Commander, I know that you're dying

to be on the bridge. Go, Richard, Catriona and I will be fine here in the wheelhouse.' Emma grinned, 'If your daughter does become bored, I'll introduce her to those twin Lewis guns, aft, and let her empty a magazine or two!'

Tremayne laughed. 'Just make sure she doesn't shoot up the bridge or the jackstaff. I won't be long – and thank you. You read me like a book – but then, you always have!'

Tremayne scrambled up the companionway to the small bridge, returning the salutes of the two seamen.

'Carry on, I'm just missing being on a bridge – it's months since I had the feel of a boat's wheel in my hands.'

'Here, sir, please take it!' The elder of the two – a killick seaman – handed the wheel over with a broad grin. Tremayne immediately called for maximum revs, maintaining the boat bow-on to the rolling whitecaps. Because of Emma and Catriona, he attempted no manoeuvres, but simply revelled in the role of boat captain once again like an enthusiastic cadet. After five minutes, he handed the wheel back – thanking the leading seaman.

Emma smiled as he returned to the wheelhouse. 'Happy?'

'Yes – thank you for being so understanding. It was so good to be in command of a boat again, albeit for such a short time.'

Emma found his naturally boyish grin to be one of his many endearing characteristics. In her company, away from the brutality and cruel excesses of war and what he had once described to her as 'the unremitting commitment to barbarity', she saw how he gradually relaxed and began to look less careworn.

Under her self-contained 'front' she, too, regularly went through agonies of fear and anxiety, forever wondering if he would return from whatever operation he happened to be on at that time. There were many occasions when she was grateful for her continuing, albeit now part-time, role with SIS and the degree to which it occupied her time and thoughts. It temporarily took her mind off Richard and the numbing sense of dread that so often overcame her when he was away. While her SIS colleagues' messages of 'Keep your chin up, girl, and press on – he'll come through', might sound trite, Emma knew that underneath the seemingly hackneyed phrases, there was a genuine concern and affection for her. She also knew that their messages offered the only reality open to her. There were no options.

Tremayne unintentionally broke her reverie. 'I've been playing at commandos for too long. I need to be a sailor once more.' He paused, looking at her, intently. 'But far more than that, I need time to be a *real* husband and father.'

Deep in conversation – now more light-hearted and frequently punctuated by laughter, they were both surprised at how quickly they seemed to reach Tresco and New Grimsby harbour.

Dick Oyler was there at the quayside with his tractor and cart, ready to take them up to the New Inn. Their welcome from Aileen was as warm and as 'Irish' as ever with the promise of roast beef for supper, thanks to Dick's persuasive bartering power with a local farmer. They were given an equally enthusiastic homecoming by an ecstatic Bertie, Tremayne's black labrador, whom the Oylers regularly took into care on his many absences at sea or on operations in France.

'You'll be coming out with us, Bertie, it's been far too long since we walked together over these islands!' laughed Tremayne, stroking his dog's ears and ruffling the thick curling fur around his neck.

Back in what they always considered to be 'their' room, and with Catriona fed and back in her crib — built specially for her by the Bryher boatmen, they tumbled into one another's arms. Emma finally said, 'I'm famished, let's go and sample Aileen's wonderful cooking. But,' she added, looking at Tremayne mischievously, 'let's not take *too* long over eating as we have other priorities to catch up on too!'

Supper turned out to be a delightful surprise reunion with David Willoughby–Brown and his fiancée, Lucy Caswell. Sensitive and uncannily perceptive, Aileen Oyler had sensed, quite rightly, that a foursome would be right for the occasion and had taken the initiative to make it happen — much to everyone's delight. At around ten thirty, Willoughby-Brown and Lucy bade the Tremaynes goodnight and wandered off, hand in hand, along the road down to the beach. Standing outside the door of the inn for a final farewell, Tremayne looked up at the clear night sky. 'As if to order, the moon is shining. How *do* you do it, Emma — and where did you park your broomstick this time?'

'Now, that would be telling. Just stop blethering, sailor, and awa' up the stairs wi' ye!' The laughing blue eyes and the teasing, exaggerated Glaswegian accent said it all…

They awoke to a fine morning with the early sun casting its bright light through their open window. For both there was the unbelievable sense of wonder that they were together again. Checking that all was quiet in the 'engine room', with their little Wren Stoker Mechanic still fast asleep, they made love once more, giving themselves to one another with less urgency than they had the previous night.

As they finished breakfast, Henry Hall and his dance orchestra were playing the quick-step tango, *At the Balalaika,* on the inn's radio. 'Come on, Richard, on your feet!' laughed Emma, dragging Tremayne out of his chair. Having been told by dancing partners on more than one occasion that he had two left feet, Tremayne took hold of Emma rather self-consciously and cautiously attempted the tricky steps. More quickly than he had expected, he was into the rhythm of the catchy tune and whirling round the dining room floor – albeit with less panache and confidence than most ballroom dervishes, much to Emma's amusement. More by sheer good luck than any skill on his part, he just managed to steer clear of Aileen who had come in with a pot of fresh coffee, but ended up on the floor in a heap with Emma.

'If you can cause such chaos with just two of us, Richard, I dread to think what you might do to an eightsome reel!' said Emma, laughing, as she struggled to her feet.

After breakfast they made their way past the row of quaint old cottages – with their carefully tended, colourful gardens

— down to New Grimsby Quay and the small, weathered, red and white fishing boat. Broad in the beam and about twenty feet long, she was sturdily constructed with all the build integrity of a Bryher-made boat. A small white cuddy, designed to protect her passengers from rain and spray, created sheltered family space for all three. Intended to be gaff-rigged, her Breton-red sails were temporarily stowed forrard in a built-in locker. Her Mercury outboard coughed twice, noisily throbbing into life after Tremayne's third energetic pull, and she drew away smartly, heading across the water for Church Quay on Bryher.

Moored and landed, and heading inland for Watch Hill, Tremayne carried a borrowed Royal Marine Commando Bergen rucksack containing Aileen's picnic lunch, while Emma took her place beside him with a happily burbling Catriona slung across her breast.

Pink striped trumpets of sea bindweed, misty blue sea holly, and straggly clumps of snow- white sea rocket growing along the low sandy dunes of the seashore soon gave way to a profusion of wild roses, fuchsia and mesembryanthemums in the hedgerows. In the adjoining fields, Emma's attention was caught by densely grouped sapphire blue agapanthus and purple and cream acanthus.

'Those acanthus, or 'bear's breeches', look like giant, primeval lupins. What a dramatic show of colour they make! I'm just so glad that, at long last, we've made it to Bryher — it's a beautiful island. Like all of them, Richard, this one has its own unique character and atmosphere. I love it!'

Tremayne smiled at Emma's childlike enthusiasm and fascination for the flora, fauna and captivating scenery of the islands, which had endeared her to him from the very outset of their relationship. He knew, too, that it was the enchanting ambience of the islands which had played a subtle and indefinable – yet key – part in the growth of that relationship.

Pausing regularly to take in the stunning views of Tresco and Hangman's Island to the east and the twin humps of Samson to the south, they steadily climbed Watch Hill up to the ruins of the old lookout. Dating from the time of the Civil War, it was now little more than an oval enclosure, protected by an ancient wall about three feet high.

'Let's stop here, Emma, and have some of Aileen's coffee before we move onto Shipman Head Down.'

Standing up to look westwards, over the island of Gweal and beyond, to the wild, jagged Norrard Rocks pounded by Atlantic rollers, Tremayne found some of the horrific memories of the Chateau de Trevannec, the seizure of von Greiner and the taking of the Iles d' Hyères beginning to slip into perspective. These and many other experiences, like the cruel deaths of McDonald and Nicholls however, would never be completely erased from his memory nor, he acknowledged, should they be.

For Tremayne there remained a recurring, fundamental dilemma: how to fight a war and win battles while retaining the essence of common human decency. In his darkest moments of introspection, this was the issue that always returned to haunt him. But precious time with Emma, the tranquil beauty of the Scillies and his new role of father each helped to take away the rawness of the horror and pain. Together, they represented a restorative therapy that no other source could hope to provide.

'A penny for them – though I believe I can guess.' Emma's was a timely interruption. Her face registered intense concern, giving a lie to her apparently light-hearted request.

Tremayne smiled. 'Sorry! Forgive my rudeness and preoccupation. Just lately, I'm in danger of becoming awful company. I was just thinking how many times you have helped me cope with the grimmest aspects of this bloody war and my part in it. Dear God, Emma, I shall be glad when it's behind us.' Tremayne paused and took Emma's hand. 'Don't let me spoil this beautiful day by wallowing in self-pity. I just want you to know, Emma, how very much I love you and need you.'

Fighting back the tears which were beginning to well up, Emma said quietly, 'It's not self-pity, for heaven's sake, Richard. If you can't talk to me like this, I shouldn't be your wife and that would be something I just can't even begin to contemplate.' For a moment, they stood silently with their arms locked around one another and then Tremayne quietly said, 'Thank you for that, dearest Emma. I count myself the luckiest man alive.'

As they prepared to move on again, he realised how little consideration had been given to exploring the pressures currently confronting Emma. His preoccupation with the horror of his own recent experiences was, he recognised, in danger of dominating his thinking. Emma's characteristic unselfishness in concentrating on his concerns, meant they had only talked briefly about her continuing part-time role, working for SIS as a naval liaison officer. Her cousin and close friend Morag had moved in with her to help look after Catriona. As Emma had so light-heartedly put it, 'I'm rather like a highly paid cleaning lady, working afternoons only!' Feigning a very passable Cockney accent she had simply said, 'Yer know, I does it to oblige, dearie!' Despite her making light of it, Tremayne knew only too well the importance of her work and how highly she was regarded – both within SIS and in SOE circles.

Hell Bay did not disappoint as a primitively dramatic spectacle of the pure power and restless force of nature in action. From the quaintly named Badplace Hill, they looked down to see the rollers roaring in and crashing onto the rocky shore below, sending up spumes of sparkling white foam onto the cliffs above the bay.

As well as the many sea birds swooping and diving over the Atlantic breakers, Emma spotted a kestrel hovering over the ramparts of an ancient fortification by Boat Carn, searching for prey on the headland. On Bryher, as on many other islands, the elusive puffins were nowhere to be seen, much to Emma's obvious disappointment. The principal alternative to the various gulls and smaller terns, were the black and white oystercatchers probing the rocks below for limpets, with their long orange beaks. Tremayne attempted several reasonably passable imitations of the colourful wader's distinctive 'peeeep' call, much to Emma's amusement — especially when the oystercatchers suddenly veered off as a group to the south. 'Must be something I said,' laughed Tremayne.

After exploring some of the many ancient cairns they, too, moved south off Shipman Head Down, skirting Great Popplestone and climbing Gweal Hill for views of the southernmost of the Norrard Rocks. They then made their way to the long sandy sweep of Great Porth Bay where, by the large granite outcrop of Great Carn, they settled down for Aileen's picnic lunch. Its surging power broken by Moon Rock, Merrick Island and many other rocky islets nearby, the sea rolled in serenely, its waves lapping gently at the shoreline of golden sand and scattered rocks. Changing into swimming trunks, Tremayne waded out into the shallow, freezing water before plunging in for a quick swim. Using his powerful crawl stroke against the chilling impact of the deceptively cold sea, he swam strongly, revelling in the exhilaration of pitting muscle against nature. He remained in the crystal clear emerald waters for a further ten minutes, before walking back up the deserted beach to fling himself down beside Emma under the warming sun. Catriona lay close by, fast asleep on the folded blanket after her midday feed, protected by the shade of Great Carn.

The all-too-rare happiness of being in each other's company after so long apart — and in such different worlds — delayed their need to explore as they lay alternately talking, laughing and dozing in the early afternoon sun. After two blissfully relaxing and soul-restoring hours they packed up and moved on, walking around Heathy Hill down to the charming Stony Porth beach, then round to Rushy Bay at the foot of Samson Hill. From there, they had uninterrupted views of Samson island, the southern end of Tresco and St Mary's.

'Samson intrigues me,' said Emma, gazing at the twin humps of the uninhabited island no more than a few hundred yards across the sea from Bryher. 'I'm sure it's all in the imagination and therefore quite unjustified, but there is a curious air of mystery about that island. Aileen did hint that it was haunted and I'd love to visit it — especially as we have the boat for the whole week.'

'Right, you're on!' laughed Tremayne. 'Let's do that tomorrow if this glorious weather continues to hold, but right now, I have other needs. I — '

Emma cut in smiling, 'Really, Richard, you're usually far more subtle and gentlemanly, but I suppose,' she added with a sigh of mock resignation, 'a poor girl has to do her husband's bidding — I do seem to remember saying something, during a state of intoxication, about love, honour and OBEY!'

Tremayne laughed. 'Quite right too! But I was merely going to suggest nothing more exciting than a cup of tea at some tea rooms which Dick Oyler told me we would find along the road back to Church Quay! In the likely absence of a Pablo Watkins brew, I'd willingly settle for some of Joe Lyons' best.'

'Oh, Richard, for one heart-stopping moment, you raised my hopes,' laughed Emma, 'but yes — I really would like some tea, though I still hope that the moon will be shining again tonight!'

Laughing and talking they walked up Samson Hill, passing several ancient Bronze Age graves. Pausing at the top to look out over the awesome jagged Western Rocks and St Agnes and Annet beyond Samson, Tremayne said, 'It is indeed the 'island of hills'. We must have been up and down at least half a dozen since we started this morning.'

Twenty minutes later they arrived at the small tea rooms, tired but happy. A welcome pot of tea soon arrived, together with the unexpected treat of homemade scones, jam — and locally produced clotted cream.

Their day on Bryher ended with the walk to Church Quay, past All Saints Church, and finally back to the small fishing boat. Over a very relaxed dinner in the New Inn back on Tresco, a smiling Tremayne said, 'What a perfect day that's been, it couldn't have been better.'

'It *has* been wonderful — and thank you for that,' Emma looked at him, 'but it's not over yet darling and, unless I'm mistaken, that very obliging moon will be shining again tonight!'

The rest of their week's leave together flew by all too quickly. They were days of laughter, discovery of new places and joy in each other's company — and in their new roles of parents. As Tremayne commented, they were days for stockpiling memories for the rest of their lives. The day after their boat trip to the island, Dick Oyler reported that the unusually low tide meant that they could walk across New Grimsby Sound to Bryher. Aileen happily volunteered to look after Catriona while Tremayne and Emma made the return trip – allowing enough time to complete the walk and take time out for a picnic, sitting together on the quay at Bryher.

Their third and fourth days were spent revisiting their favourite haunts on Tresco, recalling so many poignant memories of the previous two years. With the fishing boat still at their disposal – and the continuing fine weather – they later took in St Mary's, St Agnes and St Martin's and the Eastern Isles. They left the final day to visit Samson and experience its unique – yet benign and peaceful – silence, before returning once more to Bryher. Roaming over its many hills, they deliberately took their time to take in the magnificent panoramic views. It had been an unforgettable leave. Each knew that they were even more deeply in love than in the heady days of their time serving in the Tresco flotilla.

Their parting this time, after so many happy days together, was almost unbearable. Tremayne felt helpless, desperately wishing that he could turn the clock back a week as he stood on New Grimsby Quay, waving goodbye to Emma. It moved him deeply to see her lose her fight with the tears, which added a haunting sadness to her beautiful face. All too quickly, the motor launch carrying her back to Penzance disappeared from sight, northwards through New Grimsby Sound. As he turned to walk towards HMS Godolphin, an inexplicable sense of foreboding almost engulfed him. It wasn't fear about his survival, but an unaccountable premonition of indefinable dread involving Emma…

Nine

Perhaps A Friend For Life

T remayne quickly slipped back into his role of flotilla commander — even sooner than he had hoped for. Allied supplies and troop reinforcements — principally US and Free French — to support Operation Dragoon were continually being transported south, by both sea and air. Despite the Germans clinging ferociously to the Brittany ports, the Allies had gained complete mastery of the air over the Channel and Western Approaches. What remained as threats to the Allied surface vessels, en route to and from southern France, were the aggressive E-boat flotillas and considerable number of marauding U-boats, looking for easy pickings in the waters to the north and south of Ushant.

While Naval Intelligence rightly saw the days of such predators as numbered, realists acknowledged that their lethal potential would continue to be a problem for several months ahead. Therefore, Allied shipping continued to be vulnerable – particularly troop ships and transports – especially to night attacks under cover of darkness.

Tremayne was ordered to take his flotilla – two Vosper MTBs, captained by himself and Lieutenant Pierre Quilghini, the Camper and Nicholson MGB under the command of Lieutenant Hermann Fischer and the Fairmile 'C', skippered by newly promoted Lieutenant Maurice Simmonds – to carry out patrols off Ushant and await further orders. Enever would radio those orders to him in code. Like Tremayne, all boat captains held RNVR commissions and already had more combat experience – on land and at sea – than many regular serving officers based in home waters.

The four Tresco flotilla boats had been up-gunned to combat the renewed E-boat menace in the Channel. Every boat was now equipped with power-mounted six-pounder quick-firers, fed by Molins auto-loaders, as their principal bow gun. Secondary armament included 40mm high-angle Bofors and/or twin 20mm Oerlikons. Added to these, according to boat captains' individual preferences, were either .50 or .30-calibre, belt-fed Brownings or drum-fed Vickers 'K' .303 machine guns.

Currently carrying depth charges as a matter of course – in readiness for attacks on submerged U-boats – and using the recently fitted latest sonar detection equipment, all four boats now had far greater capability to locate and sink submarines operating below the sea's surface. The Vosper MTBs each carried just two torpedo tubes – the other pair having been removed to save weight. For ease of identification following losses and new additions in the flotilla, the four boats had recently been renumbered: Tremayne's Vosper as 1510, Quilghini's as 1511, and Fischer and Simmonds' boats as 1512 and 1513 respectively.

At precisely 18.00 hours, on a clear evening at the end of August, Tremayne ordered 'Slip. All engines slow ahead'. With a throaty roar of powerful petrol motors, the flotilla surged forward from the anchorage at Braiden Rock, heading south, direction Ushant. Once in deeper water, with Samson island soon astern off their starboard beam, Tremayne signalled: *'Diamond formation. Speed twenty-two knots'*. The flickering Aldis lights rapidly conveyed Tremayne's order, and the other boat captains' acknowledgements, as the boats slid effortlessly into formation – Tremayne leading, Simmonds directly astern, Fischer taking the starboard station and Quilghini to port. Tremayne's speed of twenty-two knots was set specifically to accommodate the slower Fairmile and Camper and Nicholson – both of which struggled to top twenty-seven knots. By contrast, the Vospers could make forty knots – as Willoughby-Brown uncharitably said – with a good following wind and half the crew manning paddles. Even this was bettered by the forty-three knots of the German E-boats' Daimler-Benz diesels.

Clear of St Mary's by fifteen miles, Tremayne signalled:

'*Test weapons*'. The reassuring ten-second sustained cacophony which followed told the boat captains and their crews that all was well, as spent brass cartridge cases of various calibres tumbled, clattering, into collecting bags or spilled noisily across spray-swept decks. Tremayne smiled to himself as he glanced to his left at Willoughby-Brown who was scanning the now greying horizon through his binoculars, his fine-boned patrician features a picture of composed concentration. To his immediate right, eyes switching between his gyrocompass and the rolling sea ahead, stood Petty Office Irvine, redoubtable both as a coxswain and as a man. On so many occasions, Tremayne had described the awesomely competent and dependable Ulsterman as his 'Rock of Gibraltar'. Standing behind the coxswain with little enough room on the Vosper's cramped bridge, also searching the grey waves through a set of Bausch and Lomb Admiralty Pattern binoculars, was Leading Yeoman of Signals 'Taff' Jenkins. Describing himself as an exile from the Valleys on loan to the Navy, Jenkins' sense of duty was legendary. Severely wounded in a recent engagement, he had had to be ordered from his post, protesting defiantly, as he was helped down the companionway to rest below deck, barely capable of walking. Now fully recovered, his quiet presence and lilting Welsh voice filled something of the painful void left by Leading Seaman 'Brummie' Nicholls who, for so many cross-channel operations, had occupied the corner next to Irvine. Nicholls's place in the crew had been taken by Leading Seaman 'Scouse' O'Reilly, a man with a razor-sharp wit and, like Pablo Watkins, always with a ready answer — whatever the occasion.

Tremayne felt a sense of completeness. All three of those on the bridge had been with him for long enough to become a 'band of brothers'. His engine room artificer — a newcomer — was Angus Buchanan, known simply as Chief, whose elder brother had also served for a time under Tremayne in the Tresco flotilla.

A mournful wail suddenly arising from the boat's tiny galley confirmed that Leading Seaman 'Pablo' Watkins was about to come round with mugs of kye for all those of the duty watch. Willoughby-Brown's elegant right eyebrow assumed its customary exaggerated curve of mock horror, as the strangulated aria floated up from below —

'When my Navy days are over And I 'ave gone beyond recall, I'll buy a great big fish and chip shop And pee the profits down the wall'

'A certain urban vitality about it, wouldn't you agree, sir?' commented a straight-faced Willoughby-Brown. 'But I doubt that it will make Glyndebourne.'

Tremayne choked back his laughter, grimacing at his first lieutenant — he often sensed a restrained puritan disapproval from his East Belfast coxswain whenever Willoughby-Brown's urbane humour erupted on the bridge.

Stifling a snorting giggle, he managed a barely controlled, 'I'm sure you're right, Number One.'

Moments later, Watkins's deadpan face and a rum fanny

full of welcome, freshly made hot kye appeared on the bridge.

'Evening, sir. Not too late, I 'ope, sir?'

Tremayne fleetingly caught Watkins's surreptitious wink, intended for Taff Jenkins, who studiously ignored it with exaggerated concentration on some indeterminate spot on the horizon.

'Never, Watkins. The delay has merely given us more time to anticipate its arrival.'

Beaten to the repartee punch for once, Watkins looked up questioningly at Tremayne then, slowly, a big grin spread across his amiable face. 'Blimey, sir, I'd never 'ave thought of an answer like that, sir.'

Further banter was cut short by an urgent shout from Leading Seaman McIlhenny, the gun-layer on the forrard six-pounder.

'Periscope, sir! Ahead and off the port bow – three hundred yards, sir!'

All binoculars swung round, rapidly being refocused, as the first lieutenant yelled, 'Got it, sir. There!'

Following Willoughby-Brown's pointing finger, Tremayne shouted, 'Well spotted, McIlhenny. Thank you.' And then more quietly, 'Well done, Number One.'

Nodding to Irvine, he said, 'Port ten, Cox'n. All engines – full ahead.'

Yelling through the loudhailer to the forrard six-pounder and port Browning gun crews, Tremayne called, 'Periscope, three hundred yards – OPEN FIRE!'

Turning to Taff Jenkins, he ordered, 'Yeoman, make to

all boats: '*Am engaging submarine — three hundred yards ahead. Form line astern on me. Stand by*.' To Willoughby-Brown, he snapped, 'Number One, standby aft with Able Seaman Sharpe to release depth charges.'

The bursts of six-pounder shells and .50 calibre Browning bullets churned up the sea around the periscope, turning it into a boiling cauldron. Cheers went up from both gun crews as the shots quickly found their mark and the slender tube was blown to pieces. Already crash-diving, the submarine created eddies of swirling waves as she slipped further below the surface. Approaching the spot where the U-boat had just vanished, Tremayne called to Willoughby-Brown, 'Release depth charges!'

Seconds after the first pair rolled over the stern chutes, the twin rumbling explosions sent columns of white water shooting up into the air. Lack of debris, or oil, confirmed two misses.

'Yeoman, make to all boats: '*Attack with depth charges in line ahead. Good hunting!*'.'

With Lieutenant Quilghini's Vosper leading, sparkling water cascading over her sharply raked bow, the three boats swung round, following Tremayne's course, dropping successive pairs of depth charges as they came. Just as before, explosions were followed by columns of white water, but nothing else. Then, as Simmonds's boat — the last in line — passed over the area of the U-boat's rapid departure, an explosion louder than the rest, accompanied by dark grey water and a telltale shower

The Channel To Freedom

of debris, confirmed a hit. As cheers rang out from the deck of Simmonds's Fairmile, a large quantity of leaking oil began to spread, like an obscene black stain, over the surface of the surrounding sea.

Tremayne called to Jenkins, 'Yeo, make to all boats: '*Slow ahead. Stand by for surfacing sub'*.'

With the boats' engines running almost silently, the crews on deck could hear the distinctive wheezing rumble of the U-boat's tanks blowing as she began her ascent from the depths below. Slowly, her long sleek nose poked its way through the breaking waves and, as she emerged, righting herself, Tremayne could clearly see her shattered periscope and the extensive wreckage and gaping hole, just aft of her conning tower, where Simmonds's depth charge had severely damaged her hull.

'Hmmm. Type VIIC, the regular old workhorse of the U-boat arm, sir, mounting an 88mm gun forrard,' announced Willoughby-Brown, studying the U-boat through his binoculars.

With his Vosper turned beam-on to her, Tremayne ordered all guns to fire at her many weapons. In a matter of seconds, her bow deck gun and the formidable anti-aircraft armament abaft her conning tower were destroyed in short, deafening bursts of fire at point blank range. The U-boat crew opened the conning tower hatches, cautiously emerging, shocked, to see their guns blown to mangled, useless wreckage and four heavily armed motor boats standing off, only yards away, with their weapons trained on them. Among the first to clamber out was the U-boat commander, a Kapitänleutnant, a Knight's Cross at his throat, his distinctive white-topped cap confirming his role as the submarine's skipper.

The hopelessness of his situation was only too obvious. He could no longer defend himself on the surface and his boat was incapable of operating submerged. Barely able to continue travelling, even at minimum revolutions on the surface, there was little he could do. He solemnly saluted Tremayne and shrugged with a rueful gesture of helplessness. Willoughby-Brown, speaking fluent German, called him to muster his complete crew on deck and get ready to be boarded.

A combined boarding party of eight ratings and a petty officer were quickly mustered from Tremayne's boat and Simmonds's Fairmile. Armed to the teeth and under the command of Willoughby-Brown, they pushed off in two rubber dinghies to board the stationary U-boat. All four boats of Tremayne's flotilla made an obvious point of keeping their weapons trained on the German submarine.

Slowly and sullenly, the German crew members assembled on deck as the boarding party scrambled aboard the U-boat and clambered down inside her conning tower. Seconds later, the sudden sound of muffled shots from within the submarine carried across to the British boats. Agitated, the German captain and several crew members began to rush to the conning tower gallery and companionway, ready to scramble back inside the U-boat. Tremayne ordered a burst from his Brownings over the heads of the German crew – who were now milling about on the deck, confused and apprehensive – and shouted through his loudhailer that those attempting to climb back inside should re-form in line on deck and remain there. Another sustained burst from the twin Brownings focused the minds of those still hesitating, who continued to collect in groups of threes and fours, shouting excitedly. Quickly, they re-mustered, silently in line, as the U-boat captain took command, calling them to attention then standing them at ease. Rarely did his eyes leave Tremayne's face.

Minutes later, Willoughby-Brown and the boarding party emerged, carrying the U-boat's confidential books and signal codes. He told the German commander that a petty officer, who had remained below contrary to orders, had attempted to conceal the books and had fired shots, wounding a member of the boarding party. He had been shot dead by return fire.

With the German crew still lined up under Tremayne's guns, Willoughby-Brown's boarding party returned to their respective boats. The wounded rating was carried back to Simmonds's MGB to await pick-up by Coastal Command Catalina, which would transfer him to the Royal Naval Hospital in Plymouth. It was only too obvious that the U-boat's crew of over fifty men could not be carried securely by the four British boats for any distance, especially as Tremayne expected to be committed to a new operation that evening. The last thing he wanted was the encumbrance of prisoners of war, almost equalling the number of crew members on each of his boats, with the attendant need to suspend operations and return to base.

Tremayne's telegraphist had picked up the stricken U-boat's Mayday call and its acknowledgement, confirming that an R-boat flotilla of air-sea reconnaissance and minesweeper motor launches was on its way to pick up the crew. They would be arriving from Brest within the hour. He knew that his flotilla outgunned and could easily sink the R-boats as and when they attempted to rescue the crew of the stricken U-boat but, with his need to be free of prisoners, such an attack would be self-defeating. Though they were the enemy, Tremayne was not prepared to abandon what might be left of the badly damaged U-boat's crew to the dangerous, unpredictable waters of the Bay of Biscay. Nor was he prepared to allow the U-boat to remain afloat and possibly taken under tow to a German port in Brittany.

Through Willoughby-Brown, Tremayne told the U-boat captain that he knew rescue was imminent. He ordered him to abandon ship and take to personal flotation equipment and the submarine's life rafts, telling him he was about to sink their vessel by gunfire. Tremayne allowed the Germans to recover the body of their dead petty officer, which they brought up on deck wrapped in a Kriegsmarine ensign.

With the German crew standing off, half a cable's length away from their U-boat and huddled together in life jackets and on their life rafts, Tremayne ordered, 'All boats – open fire!' He was grateful that, mercifully, the submarine's end came quickly as, riddled with shellfire, she slowly and majestically slid into the grey depths to her watery grave.

Tremayne and Willoughby-Brown joined the German officers in saluting her passing, while her crew, struggling to sit at attention on the bobbing life rafts, gave her a rousing 'Hoch! hoch! hoch!' Through his first lieutenant, Tremayne told the German captain that they had just picked up four small blips on their radar, moving at speed in their direction. Rescue was at hand. As the four British boats started their engines, Tremayne was deeply moved to hear the sound of singing, carried across the water, of the poignant traditional German lament sung for the dead petty officer: 'Ich hatt' einen Kamaraden, Einen bessern find'st du nicht…'*

Setting a course, south-west, away from the four R-boats identified on their radar, Tremayne radioed Enever, in code, to let him know of the encounter with the U-boat. To Jenkins, he called, 'Yeoman, make to all boats: '*Resume diamond formation. Speed twenty-two knots*'.'

Within minutes, Tremayne received a signal by radio from Enever, which congratulated him on the destruction of the U-boat and gave him the expected orders, confirming the mission of his patrol off Ushant.

He was to take his flotilla to a point some eighteen miles west by south of his present position, to locate and destroy a German 'milch cow' submarine and what Naval Intelligence 'Y' Service radio intercept operators had confirmed as two U-boats, due to rendezvous with her and deliver fuel and ammunition supplies. The vessel was known to be regularly

---

'I had a comrade. A better one you won't find…'

lurking in the area and refuelling U-boats for operations in the Bay of Biscay.

Tremayne immediately signalled his three boat captains: *'We will locate and sink suspected 'milch cow' U-boat and her two customers. Follow the leader'*. He radioed RAF Coastal Command to let them know his new RV, so that they could pick up the wounded rating from Simmonds's Fairmile.

Briefing Willoughby-Brown on the operation he said, 'There were believed to be ten of these so-called Type XIV 'milch cow' U-boats – some of them supplying up to twenty-five submarines with fuel, ammunition and other supplies at sea. We know from Naval Intelligence that all ten have been sunk – the last one shortly after D-Day. Latest information is that a similar vessel is successfully operating near here. We can only assume that it's an improvised conversion – possibly of a Mk IX fighting U-boat – fitted out to supply a 'wolf pack', recently cobbled together and tasked with sinking vital invasion fleet supply ships. It's been spotted twice from the air during the last few days – once in the early dawn and the other time on aircraft radar during the middle of the night, at around 02.00 hours. Unfortunately, on both occasions, the aircraft had neither bombs nor depth charges and insufficient ammunition to sink the vessel – or its customers.'

Via Leading Yeoman Jenkins's busily flickering Aldis signal lamp, Tremayne sent a much-abbreviated version of the same message to each boat captain, calling for a briefing on board HMMTB 1510 in one hour, on reaching the intended

RV. The sea was running with only a moderate swell, but visibility was already decreasing as the late evening light began to fade. Later, Tremayne knew there would be some light from a waning harvest moon and the sky had remained cloudless all day, with hope of a fine, clear night.

With boats hove-to and closed up at action stations at the RV, boat captains repaired to Tremayne's MTB, leaving their first lieutenants in charge of their vessels. As Quilghini, the last to come aboard, struggled up the scrambling nets onto Tremayne's deck, the low rumble of aircraft engines – approaching from the north – carried over the gently churning sea. Through his loudhailer, his voice clear in the calm early night air, Tremayne called all boat crews to stand by to fire on command. He quickly turned to Jenkins, 'Yeo, send up one green and two white flares' – the challenge and recognition signal agreed with Coastal Command.

Seconds later, the distinctive roar of Pratt and Whitney Twin Wasp engines, accompanied by responding green and white flares, confirmed the arrival of the expected RAF Coastal Command Catalina flying boat. In the fading light, her white undersides showed up starkly against the darkening sky. After circling the four boats, she landed alongside and the wounded rating was quickly transferred on a stretcher via the flying boat's dinghy.

Her pilot confirmed with Tremayne that he was one of those pilots who had seen a 'milch cow' submarine transferring supplies to a pair of Mk VII U-boats in the area some three nights ago. Their combined heavy anti-aircraft fire had dissuaded him from hanging around – especially as he had virtually nothing left with which to attack them. 'Three 37mm and probably as many as ten or twelve 20mm ack-ack guns could make a bit of a mess of a big, slow-flying kite like this old girl. At the most, I had about one hundred rounds of .303 calibre left, which just about scratched their paintwork when my starboard dorsal gunner laced 'em with it.'

He began checking his switches and instruments in preparation for take-off as he added, 'There's no doubt that one of 'em *was* a supply U-boat and that she was provisioning the other two – but with what, we couldn't really see.' With a cheery grin, he gave a thumbs-up sign and yelled 'Good luck!' – just before the big flying-boat's engines coughed briefly, then roared into life as she slowly began to move forward in readiness for take-off.

Tremayne and his boat captains recognised that catching what was the principal German U-boat supply vessel in the Bay of Biscay could turn out to be a very protracted affair, requiring a good deal of patience. Without doubt, the several U-boats continuing to pose a major threat in the seas around Ushant and into the Channel were heavily dependent for supplies from either the besieged Kriegsmarine bases of Brittany, Lorient and St Nazaire – which were subject to regular Allied air attacks – or from a mobile source at sea.

The latter, despite the vulnerability of having to re-victual on the sea's surface, gave far greater flexibility, while the vastness of the ocean's expanse provided endless RV options. What the Germans had still not realised, however, was that their Enigma code had been cracked and so details of RVs, transmitted by radio, could be quickly identified. Being able to react fast enough and reach those rendezvous in time was a problem for the Allies, especially with operations Overlord and Dragoon stretching resources to their limit.

Gathered in the MTB's tiny wardroom, Tremayne reported to the boat captains that Commander Enever had relayed by wireless the latest intelligence picked up by Naval 'Y' Service radio intercept operators, which was that a supply submarine and two 'customers' were due to rendezvous that night at 01.00 hours in the area where they were currently stood-to. The approximate location had also been confirmed by the Catalina pilot.

'There are no certainties in this game,' said Tremayne, 'only strong possibilities, gentlemen.' He looked around the cramped room. 'And, at best, this is what we have here.'

Discussion broke off as Leading Seaman O'Reilly knocked on the door and came in carrying a tray with four glasses of beer. 'Good evening, sir. I found some bottles in the galley and thought you might like a glass of ale, sir.' He paused briefly to gauge Tremayne's reaction before continuing, 'Leading Seaman Watkins 'as cooked a pile of snorkers for supper, sir. Shall I bring some in, sir?'

'You'll be in trouble if you don't,' grinned Tremayne. 'And thank you, O'Reilly!'

Tremayne's plan of action to destroy the supply submarine was simple: 'I propose that the flotilla will systematically sweep the area within what would be a succession of five by one-mile 'boxes', starting from our present position with the five miles running north to south. We will then continue to sweep, moving south and north but always shifting one box eastwards until we've covered an area five miles wide. Then we will repeat, moving back westwards, revisiting the area previously swept. In all we will have searched an area of twenty-five square miles of sea twice over.'

The group broke off their briefing as O'Reilly reappeared – complete with sausages, fried eggs and chunks of bread fried to a light golden-brown.

'Gastronomic bliss,' enthused Fischer, adding to Tremayne's thanks, while Quilghini, French as ever, smiled and said – with more than a little feeling, 'Though it may not be *suppair* at Les Deux Magots, it is most welcome and robustly delicious – and so very 'Rosbif' as we might say, no?'

'We might indeed, Pierre,' laughed Simmonds as he speared one of the rapidly disappearing chunks of fried bread with his fork, 'though I suspect Sartre and Hemingway – and other habitués of that wonderful café – would approve of this too, y' know!'

Tremayne took up his briefing again. 'Taking the standard 'A-B-C-D' quartered partitioning of the box, Maurice and I will take the leading port and starboard sweeps, 'A' and 'B' respectively, positioned a thousand yards apart, while Hermann and Pierre will take 'C' and 'D', five hundred yards apart and five hundred yards behind us. The range of our new sonar submarine detection equipment will easily cover a five by one-mile imaginary 'box', sweeping in such a pattern.'

Tremayne stopped briefly to eat some of his supper, before resuming once more. 'The sweeps will commence at 24.00 hours. We will maintain radio silence and signal by Aldis lamps. We will be able to keep limited visual contact by moonlight, using night glasses, for most of the time. Our speed will be a consistent fifteen knots, which should cut down engine noise to a reasonable level. Submerged, Jerry will be making only about six knots, so we should be able to pick up any sonar signals at that speed and with our pattern of sweep. On the surface, his U-boats will be capable of around twelve knots.'

'How long do you intend to sweep?' asked Fischer. 'For as long as it takes?'

'We'll maintain this method for three hours. Then, if necessary, we'll review the situation and, depending on the light and condition of the sea, we may vary our search pattern. RAF Bolt Head is on standby to come to our assistance with a couple of Beaufighters if we need them. As you all well know, gentlemen, luck plays a major part in locating submerged submarines – it's essentially a matter of being in the right place, at the right time. Despite the consistency of intelligence reports, we're searching for pretty small needles in one hell of a vast haystack.'

After further questions and discussion lasting some twenty minutes, the boat captains returned to their motor boats and, at 24.00 hours, the flotilla moved off to begin a sweep of the area, taking up the search formation agreed with Tremayne.

Slowly and monotonously, two hours passed with neither sight nor sound of a U-boat. Tremayne and his first lieutenant anxiously scanned the sea through their night glasses, looking for the telltale phosphorescent trail of a raised periscope. Below them, in the wheelhouse, sat Leading Seaman Watkins, his eyes fixed on the sonar image recorder screen before him. With fingers hovering over the transducer training hand wheel, he waited patiently for the first sonic signals warning of a U-boat's presence...

=====O=====

Some ten miles to the north and moving slowly south, at periscope depth, to his refuelling RV with two U-boats, was Kapitänleutnant Otto Böhm, Commander of Milchkuh U-boat U471. Recently sunk in Toulon harbour by American bombers, she had been recovered, refloated and rapidly restored to life in her new role as a supply submarine – just days before Allied troops captured the port in Operation Dragoon. Her deck gun had been removed, as had her torpedo tubes, and her anti-aircraft armament now consisted of two Flakvierling quadruple mounts, giving her formidable firepower from eight 20mm cannon. Thanks to a far-sighted senior Kriegsmarine captain, U471 had been rescued from her early grave and U-boats, operating in and around the English Channel, now had the vital services of much-needed replenishment fuel, ammunition and supplies from a new Milchkuh.

In prudently occasional UT* radio contact with his two potential customers, Böhm knew that they too were on a converging course for the pre-dawn tryst and morale-boosting delivery of crews' personal mail, as well as diesel oil and cannon shells of different calibres. One customer he knew well enough already – a Mk IXC U-boat commanded by one of his closest friends, Kapitänleutnant Wolfgang Kohler. The other was an unknown quantity for him – one of the new Mk XXIII, small but deadly coastal submarines capable of penetrating the Tommies' estuaries to reach shipping thought to be invulnerable by the British.

Her commander was Oberleutnant zur Zee Günter Heinzeller – equally unknown to Böhm.

Close to Böhm in the U-boat's control room stood Leutnant zur See Kurt Hansen, his trusted and capable first officer. Both officers, along with the rest of the crew, wore the drab grey-green denim battledress rather than naval uniform as it was better suited to moving quickly and easily in the cramped conditions of a U-boat's interior. Böhm and Hansen both wore their epaulets of rank and decorations. At his neck, the U-boat commander displayed his Knight's Cross, awarded for courage in action against Allied anti-submarine escorts in the Atlantic and, on the left breast of his battledress blouse, were pinned the Iron Cross First Class and U-boat war badge.

Unterwasser Telefonie – underwater telephone

Hansen wore the Iron Cross Second Class on his blouse, along with the U-boat war badge. Having served for a time with a Marine Infantry Division in the hell of the Eastern Front, he wore a tank destruction badge on the right sleeve of his battledress blouse. He had earned this badge for singlehandedly destroying a Soviet T-34 tank with a hand-held Panzerfaust rocket launcher. Short, tough and strongly built with unruly fair hair kept in place by his naval officer's peaked cap, Hansen was held in awe by officers and ratings alike.

He and Böhm were executive officers, whose authoritative professionalism was softened by their very human and engaging leadership styles. Both, in their different ways, commanded the complete loyalty of the crew. Böhm – in contrast to his first officer – was slim, tall and elegant with carefully groomed dark hair. Like Hansen, his courage was legendary – and well beyond the confines of his U-boat. On two occasions, much to his anger, photographs of him had appeared in *Signal* – the Nazi military propaganda magazine – following daring, successful attacks on Allied shipping.

At thirty-one, Böhm was older than many of his crew. He had been commissioned in the former Reichsmarine before Hitler came to power. With his thoughtful demeanour and caring manner, he was known to his crew as 'Onkel Otto' – a fact which hadn't escaped him and which amused him no end. His wife Helga and young daughter Ursula – 'Uschi' as he called her – lived at his home in Duhnen, near Cuxhaven on the German North Sea coast. Hansen had married Helga's younger sister, Inge, when he and Böhm were both serving at the Cuxhaven Kriegsmarine minesweeper base prior to the outbreak of war.

Both officers had been bitterly disappointed over the failure of the Wehrmacht's July 20th bomb plot, at the Wolf's Lair in Rastenburg, to remove Hitler from power. Along with so many in the Kriegsmarine, the Bohemian Corporal was variously despised and detested among the officers and ratings on board U471. After the attempt on Hitler's life, Böhm had put himself at considerable risk by refusing, point-blank, to have a Nazi motto painted on the newly refloated U-boat. Instead – and much to his crew's approval – he had a local signwriter in St Nazaire paint 'Immer voran!'* on his boat's conning tower, under the U471 pennant number, accompanied by the helmeted head of a mythical Valkyrie warrior.

By some miracle, the dangerous irony of the boat's new artwork and the name given to von Stauffenberg's failed operation – Valkyrie – escaped the authorities' notice during the murderous, vengeful aftermath of the attempted assassination.

Checking the U-boat's course and speed, Böhm turned to the rating manning the training mechanism, rotating the boat's hydrophones and searching for any sonic signals triggered by the moving presence of surface craft.

'So, Schultz, no sign of the Tommies?'

'No, Herr Kaleu**. So far – all is quiet.'

'Keep searching, Schultz. I don't want any surprises.'

---

* *'Ever onward!'*
***German naval/military verbal abbreviation for Kapitänleutnant*

Looking at his watch, he nodded to Hansen.

'Up periscope! Let's see what the world looks like again. We should have enough moonlight.'

Böhm slowly rotated the periscope, carefully searching the sea around. The moon was shining silver on the rolling waves – a picture of peaceful and yet dramatic beauty.

'Here, Kutti, take a look,' he grinned, 'your eyes are younger than mine!'

As Böhm handed over control of the periscope, Helga's gentle face, soft dark hair and smiling grey-green eyes filled his thoughts suddenly and unexpectedly. For a moment, he felt almost overcome with homesickness and a need to be with her in their house overlooking the island of Neuwerk and the mysterious, frequently mist-shrouded Wattenmeer.

'Oh this damned war – how much longer?' Böhm suddenly felt tired and drained of energy.

He called to a rating watching the Papenberg depth meter: 'Maltzahn, organise some coffee, please. It's going to be a long night and we need to stay awake.'

Hansen confirmed all was clear and handed back the scope to Böhm. 'Thanks Kutti, take her up – we'll give the boys a chance to enjoy their coffee in the night air on the Wintergarten*.'

Turning to Gentzen, his second officer of the watch he said, 'Get me our customers on the UT, Willi, if you will. I'll talk with Kaleu Kohler first, then Oberleutnant Heinzeller.

---

*U-boat crew's nickname for the boat's anti-aircraft platform aft of the conning tower

I now make it just over twenty minutes to the RV.'

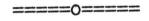

On board HMMTB 1510, Tremayne was on the bridge with Willoughby-Brown, searching the horizon with his night glasses, when he was interrupted by an urgent call from Leading Seaman O'Reilly. 'Three blips, five thousand yards almost dead ahead, sir, moving slowly towards us on the surface. 'Bout a thousand yards between each of 'em but closing fast on the centre one, sir.' At that moment, the four British boats were continuing their sweep and moving from south to north.

'Thanks O'Reilly. Keep tabs on 'em and let me know immediately anything changes.'

'Aye aye, sir.'

Calling to Jenkins, who had taken over manning the ASDIC, he shouted, 'Yeo, make to all boats: *'Three radar blips five thousand yards ahead. Close up. Form line astern — twenty-seven knots'.*'

'Right Number One, sound action stations!'

Searching the sea ahead with his night glasses for any signs of enemy vessels, Tremayne continued to address his first lieutenant: 'I wish to hell that we had four Vospers, we'd be well within range before those U-boats submerged. Any minute now, the bastards will spot us and crash-dive. We'll continue on this course, in line astern and closed up tight, to minimise our radar profile, but as we come to within a thousand yards of them, we'll attack in line abreast for maximum shell and depth-charge saturation – and to disperse their fire.'

Meanwhile, taking in the fresh air of the clear late summer night, drinking coffee or smoking on the conning tower and anti-aircraft platform, were many of the U46 crew members. Engineer Warrant Officer Schumacher's fine tenor voice was leading the singing of *Erica**, an old marching song, with everyone enthusiastically roaring the oft-repeated line 'Ein, zwo, drei, Erica!'

'So, the boys are in good heart, Kutti. It's a relief to hear them singing like this.'

'You've welded them into a fine crew, Otto. They'd follow you to hell and back. Simple things like a sing-song under the night sky are a wonderful boost for morale. I think that –. Aha, so our friends are about to join us!'

Böhm looked round to see two U-boats approaching from astern in the dark, one to port and the other to starboard. As they drew closer, he saw his shipmate of many years, Kapitänleutnant Wolfgang Kohler, salute and then wave his white-topped U-boat commander's cap – and he heard those on Kohler's boat joining in the singing at full volume as they drew alongside to starboard, cheering and waving.

'So, Wolfi, great to see you! How are things?' yelled Böhm

The plant, heather – and also a German girl's name

through his loudhailer, above the boisterous choral efforts.

'In fine form, thanks. Off for a week's leave in a fortnight – haven't seen Katya in months! How about you, Otto?'

'Likewise, fine thank you! Ah, here comes my other guest – the little Elektroboot. Bear with us a moment, Wolfi.'

Silently, the small electric-powered U-boat slid slowly along U461's port beam. Leutnant zur See Heinzeller had members of his crew lined up at attention on the 'Wintergarten' platform while he, standing at attention on the conning tower, had raised his right arm in a Nazi salute.

'Just look at that arsehole, Kutti,' muttered Böhm, as he returned the greeting with a formal naval salute.

'I'll bet he's got a damned swastika tattooed on his left tit!' grinned Hansen.

'We'll get rid of that bastard as quickly as possible. Secure the lines for transferring ammunition and fuel with him, Kutti, and then organise the same for Kaleu Wolfi, if you will.'

Transfer of fuel and supplies to both U-boats was underway, supervised by all three first officers and supporting teams led by petty officers, when Gentzen came rushing up the companionway onto the conning tower platform, his face anxious. 'Herr Kaleu. We've just picked up a blip on our radar screen, heading straight for us at high speed. Range about three thousand metres'.

Böhm pressed the klaxon button to sound the alarm for action stations, shouting to the other U-boat commanders through his loudhailer to uncouple fuel hoses and release lines at their end and clear away for action.

Yelling to Hansen, he called, 'Number One, stow gear, close torpedo storage hatches and get everyone back inside. Pronto!'

Shouting to the Flakvierling gun crews he yelled, 'Off the platform *immediately*. Get below!'

Quickly, Böhm waved to Kohler. 'Viedersehen Wolfi, we'll see you in – ' His words were suddenly cut short as, with an awesome whoosh, several shells straddled the water, exploding immediately astern of the three U-boats. Calling to his first officer, Böhm shouted, 'Quick, Kutti, stand by to dive. The damned Tommies have found our range with their first salvo.'

In line abreast, their six-pounders firing on automatic as they came on at speed, the four British boats were closing rapidly on the three submarines. With the utmost speed, the German commanders were attempting to clear their decks of crew members and transfer gear and supplies, but shells were now beginning to strike home with deadly effect, fatally puncturing hulls and upper works alike. At a closing distance of two thousand yards, seventy per cent of the armour-piercing and high-explosive six-pounder shells were hitting home, quickly making it impossible for the U-boats to dive safely and limiting their chances of escape. Through his night glasses, Tremayne looked on in awe as pieces began to fly off the U-boats under the unrelenting and increasingly accurate bombardment. One U-boat, smaller than the others and to the right of what he assumed to be the supply submarine, was already on fire. As they closed to a distance of a thousand yards, he could see flames raging around the conning tower of the vessel, which Willoughby-Brown identified as one of the latest Type XXIII electric-powered coastal submarines.

The submarine to the left of the 'milch cow' was firing back from her forrard 105mm and, within seconds, put a shell through the hull of Quilghini's Vosper, followed almost immediately by another one through her bridge. Tremayne could see the 'milch cow' struggling to swing her stern round to her starboard to bring her two quadruple Flakvierlings to bear on her tormentors while she, in turn, was taking damage from them.

Advancing to little more than a cable's length away from the U-boats, the British continued to pour in a devastating fire. The small Mk XXIII submarine, which was completely engulfed in flames, suddenly blew up with an almighty explosion. A sheet of bright orange flame shot skywards, followed by a pall of dense smoke. Within seconds she rolled over to port and sank. To the left of the 'milch cow', the U-boat – whose gun crew had fought with such courage and determination – was now defenceless, her forrard 105mm a grotesquely twisted wreckage of mangled metal and dead bodies. Her hull and conning tower were riddled with holes where the six-pounder shells had done their best to tear her heart out. Tremayne could see that she was already beginning to settle in the water, her bow lower than her stern.

The 'milch cow' – skippered and crewed with determination

and bravery like the other U-boats – was, against all odds, gallantly continuing to return fire from her multiple AA guns, now engaging the British boats, point-blank, over open sights.

Through his loudhailer, Tremayne yelled above the din to his forrard gun crew to concentrate on the U-boat's Flakvierlings. These lethal weapons were pumping out hundreds of rounds per minute of flat trajectory shells and, at a range of two hundred yards, were taking their toll on the British motor boats. Within seconds, they too finally fell silent as a concentration of high explosive shot blew them to pieces, exploding their magazines.

Tremayne signalled: *'Cease firing. Stand by to pick up survivors'*. An eerie silence descended over the carnage and wreckage and a pathetically small number of U-boat crewmen were struggling in the water in their inflatable life jackets and flotation suits. Some were clinging to any of the flotsam that they could lay hands on, which was beginning to surface and float around as the only reminder of the boat that had sunk minutes before. More men appeared from the upper works and decks of the two severely damaged submarines, dropping into the sea and swimming towards the British boats which moved slowly to meet them.

On board U461, choking in dense smoke and clambering over wreckage and mangled equipment, Böhm, his right arm broken, struggled to find any of his crew members who were still alive and help them over the side. He had already discovered Hansen, badly wounded in the leg, and managed to lift him down into the water with the help of Schulz and Schmidt, one of the specialist torpedo ratings. Genzen, his young second OOW* who was only recently out of Flensburg Officer Cadet School, lay dead, as did Maltzahn – he of the ever-ready smile – whose coffee never seemed to taste of the inevitable acorns of the ersatz issue brew.

Along with his surviving warrant officer engineer, Schumacher, he opened the U-boat's sea-cocks and, very slowly, she began to settle.

'Time to go, Schumi. It's time to leave her. Out you go.' Böhm dragged himself onto the U-boat's deck and, with tears in his eyes and standing briefly at attention, he saluted the crimson ensign, his broken right arm limp by his side. Looking at the riddled conning tower with its proud emblem, he murmured, in farewell, 'U461 – immer voran!' Then, silently, he slid into the water, dropping the boat's weighted confidential books into the sea – just in case the Tommies were able to board and search her before she sank.

With scrambling nets flung over the sides of their hulls and decks lined with ratings reaching out with boat hooks – or throwing ropes and life belts to the swimmers – the British boats circled slowly, searching for survivors. Tremayne and Willoughby-Brown stood together on the Vosper's foredeck, looking on horrified as swimmers – chilled to the bone in the cold, black oil-covered sea – began to call out for help. Watkins, O'Reilly, Sharpe and others reached out to grab the wrists of survivors as they struggled to climb up the scrambling nets,

---

*Officer of the Watch

their hands too cold to pull themselves up and onto the deck.

Tremayne noticed one swimmer, who was struggling in the water, reaching up to grab the scrambling net then falling back because of what looked like a broken arm. Leaning out as far as he could, he reached down to grab the German's good arm, but yet again the man fell back into the water, exhausted. Flinging off his sea boots, his uniform coat and his cap, Tremayne dived into the water, gasping with the cold as he surfaced. Quickly he swam round to the German and heaved him far enough out of the water for O'Reilly to grab his shoulders and drag him onto the Vosper's deck.

'Alright, sunshine, I've got yer. 'Old on now and you'll be as right as ninepence, kid!'

Shivering with cold, Tremayne called out, 'Thanks O'Reilly. Careful with his right arm, I think it's broken. Get some morphine into him asap.'

'Aye aye, sir. Willco! We'll soon 'ave 'im all sorted and in pisspotical order, sir.' Despite the cold, Tremayne grinned as he wondered just what the injured German must be making of O'Reilly's thick Scouse accent and choice phrases. The next thing he knew, Willoughby-Brown and Watkins were quickly hauling *him* out of the water and wrapping him in a dry blanket.

The German — similarly wrapped — struggled to sit up, grimacing in pain.

He saluted Tremayne with his left hand and, speaking good English, said,

'Kapitänleutnant Otto Böhm. U-boat Commandant. I am

grateful to you for saving me. I could not swim for much longer. Tell me, please, is my first officer, Oberleutnant zur See Hansen, alive? He was wounded in the leg.'

'Lieutenant Commander Richard Tremayne. Welcome aboard. One minute please, while I check…'

An affirmative nod from Willoughby-Brown answered Tremayne's question.

'Yes, Oberleutnant Hansen is on board this boat. He is injured, but he's alive, and has been given morphine. My first lieutenant is dressing his wound. I will let you know the names of other survivors on my boat shortly. We will check all wounded – and signal ahead for transport to a naval hospital. We will give you hot drinks as soon as we can.'

Calling out to Jenkins, Tremayne shouted, 'Yeoman, make to all boats: *'Report casualties and damage. Follow the leader, diamond formation, twenty-five knots. We're going home'.'*

Nodding again to Willoughby-Brown, he said, 'Take over, Number One, while I dry out. Please get Watkins to organise some of his torpedo propellant for crew and PoWs.'

'Aye aye, sir.'

Within minutes, Tremayne was back on the bridge to receive his boat captains' reports from Jenkins.

'Signal from 1511, sir: *'First lieutenant killed. One PO and three junior rates wounded. Forrard gun severely damaged.'* From 1512, sir: *'Two ratings dead. PO wounded. Extensive damage to upper works and hull.'* 1513 signalled: *'Self wounded. One rating and one PO dead. One rating wounded. Damage to wheelhouse and hull.'* That's it, sir.'

'Thank you, Yeo. That's more than ebloodynough. Add one PO and two junior rates wounded from us, plus the shambles of what was once the foredeck. Make to 1512: *'Details of your injuries please'.*'

Within a matter of seconds, Fischer's yeoman of signals' lamp flickered in reply: *'Both legs wounded. Shrapnel. Otherwise in braw fettle!'*

'Yeoman, please send: *'We'll fettle a pint out of you yet. Good luck!'.*'

Tremayne, together with his first lieutenant, slipped below to see his own wounded crew members, leaving Petty Officer Irvine in charge on the bridge.

Tremayne's crew casualties, along with four injured and seven unwounded Germans, were stretched out on mattresses in the cramped crew's quarters. Sharpe and Able Seaman Wade were keeping guard, Lanchesters cradled in their arms. Spending time with each of his wounded, Tremayne assured them that their injuries would be tended to in hospital, as quickly as possible. Addressing the German prisoners, Willoughby-Brown gave them a similar message.

At Tremayne's request, Willoughby-Brown spent time getting to know Böhm and Hansen, to find out whatever he was able to glean about the extent of German 'milch cow' activities in the Channel and Bay of Biscay. As Willoughby-Brown later reported, both German officers remained completely professional, giving nothing away about German naval and military issues. Both, however, opened up to a considerable degree on personal and general topics. Both, too, disassociated themselves from Hitler and the Nazi Party. Böhm was clearly delighted to learn from Willoughby-Brown that his close friend Kaleu Kohler, though badly wounded, was alive and being cared for on one of the accompanying motor boats.

Tremayne radioed Enever to report the destruction of the 'milch cow' and the other two U-boats. When he told the SNIO of the numbers of casualties and PoWs, Enever ordered him to make for Penzance where he would be met by an armed guard and representatives from both HMS Drake in Plymouth and from Helford Naval Special Forces flotilla. Severely wounded British and German casualties would be transferred to a local hospital, accompanied by naval medical orderlies and guards, while prisoners – including those lightly wounded – would be taken directly to the sick bay of a PoW camp in Cornwall.

Willoughby-Brown reported that Böhm had asked him if he knew the Isles of Scilly. 'For a moment he had me worried and I thought that he must be on to us. When I told him that I was aware of them, but didn't really know them, he seemed disappointed and obviously wanted to tell me something about them.'

'You have me worried too, David. Tell me more.'

'He expressed unbounded gratitude for the kindly treatment his grandfather received from the Scillonians as one of the few passengers rescued from the Hamburg-Amerika Line steam packet, *SS Schiller*, when she sank off the Retarrier Ledges in 1875.

'Apparently, his grandfather was a fourteen-year-old at

the time and was rescued from the ship by escaping in one of the two serviceable lifeboats to make it to shore in the wild, pounding seas on that terrible night. Tragically, both great-grandparents perished in the disaster which, I gather, was the *Titanic* of that time. Grandfather is still alive and frequently talks to Böhm about the experience. The grounding of the ship – and his grandfather's rescue – all happened at night in the pitch dark, which made it even more of a horrifying and unforgettable experience. Böhm's intention is to visit the Retarrier Ledges as soon as he can after the war, to be-able to tell his grandfather that he too has been there and seen for himself the terrifying rocks that wrecked the *Schiller* and destroyed his family.

'So, he told me that there were only thirty-seven survivors out of more than 370 passengers and crew.'

'Hmmm,' murmured Tremayne, 'he seems a pretty good guy to me. He fought like hell, he cares for his crew and he's a professional who understands the tragedy of war and yet appears to bear us no grudges. Retarrier Ledges are but a short deviation off our course. We'll take him there, en route to Penzance. Set a course for Retarrier, David. A cable's distance off, we'll have him up on the bridge and he will be able to see them by the light of dawn. The sea's running reasonably and the sky already looks clear.'

'Thank you, Richard. All this sounds unusual to say the least, but Böhm is a thoroughly decent fellow and I just have a feeling that you'll gain a friend for life. By the way, like you he read law at university – at Göttingen actually – and plans to take silk as and when.'

Almost imperceptibly, 1510 altered course ten degrees to port, Tremayne having signalled Quilghini to lead the others to Penzance, maintaining twenty-five knots. '*On small goodwill errand – will rejoin you at Penzance, if not before. Good luck.*'

Tremayne ordered: 'All engines, full ahead.' Responding with a muffled roar, the Vosper surged forward, cutting through the waves, water cascading over her bow.

Turning to Willoughby-Brown, who had now rejoined him on the bridge from the chart room, Tremayne said, somewhat self-consciously, 'Diverting to the Retarrier Ledges may seem an odd thing to do, David, but it's a small step towards reconciliation – the direction we have to move in sooner rather than later. It's a shift in mindset that I've been aware of for some time. Somehow, I just know that it's the right thing to do with Otto Böhm.'

'I'm sure it is. He and those of his crew with whom I've spoken, seem to value basic human decency just as much as we do. I feel that, were we to have been prisoners of theirs, we would have been treated with the same degree of consideration and care. Clearly he too wants to see an end to this bloody war. Undoubtedly, he is feeling intense grief at the loss of so many of his crew.'

Later, as dawn broke and the still clear sky began to lighten, Willoughby-Brown, searching the horizon through his binoculars, called softly, 'There they are – there are the Scillies!'

'Well spotted, Number One. It's good to be back in home waters.'

'Cox'n, ten degrees to port. We'll take her well clear, south of Pednathise Head and Gilstone Ledges, then bear north-west for Retarrier Ledges. With the rising sun behind us, they'll stand out sharp and clear. Kapitänleutnant Böhm should have a fine view of those rocks this morning.'

'Aye aye, sir.'

Less than twenty minutes later, with the promise of a Watkins culinary miracle as an early breakfast for prisoners and crew alike, Tremayne ordered 'All engines, slow ahead' as the MTB approached the Retarrier Ledges. Dramatic and awesome – and silently sinister in the pale golden light of a fine sunny dawn, the tearing, jagged rocks bore testimony to the Ledges' destructive history.

Tremayne spoke to Willoughby-Brown, standing next to him on the bridge and obviously fascinated by the sight of the dreaded Retarrier rocks, a mere cable's distance away.

Bring Kapitänleutnant Böhm onto the deck please, David, and let's see his reaction when confronted by the stuff of his nightmares! I hope he will be impressed.'

Minutes later, Böhm appeared on the bridge, escorted by Willoughby-Brown, rubbing the sleep from his eyes and looking quizzically at Tremayne as the MTB closed to within a cable's length of the Retarrier Ledges.

Tremayne smiled and nodded to his first lieutenant who began speaking in impeccable German.

'There, Otto, look over there – just two hundred metres off our port beam – that is the monster that your grandfather came up against in the *SS Schiller* sixty-nine years ago – and which has haunted him ever since!'

Böhm gasped and, for a moment, stood stock still, white-faced, as he gripped the side of the bridge as if to brace himself against some cataclysmic or seismic happening.

'I just can't believe that, at last, I am here – after all the family stories, the returning memories, the terror from the past.' He paused, as if struggling to find the right words for Willoughby-Brown to translate. 'It – it's as if, after all these many years, I have come to confront a ghost. But in so doing, I have also come closer to the presence of my ancestors who have featured so much in the stories of my own childhood and beyond.' Böhm paused again, gazing intently at the evil-looking rocks, imagining their awesome destructive power as, battered by waves, the huge vessel – almost a hundred metres long and weighing nearly 350 tonnes – was smashed against them. For a moment, sadness engulfed him as he thought of the 335 souls lost when the *Schiller* broke up and sank. He also thought of the many members of his own crew who, only hours before, had died when his U-boat had been virtually destroyed by British gunfire. Turning to Tremayne, his face still pale with shock, he said, 'How can I ever thank you enough for your compassion and caring. You understand just how important this is to me. I still find it impossible to believe that I am right at the very place where my forebears and so many of my people died – it's as if a part of me lies here too.' He stopped for a moment, his voice even quieter, 'As it does back there, off Ushant.'

Tremayne briefly touched his arm and, through Willoughby -Brown, said, 'That never gets any easier and I'm pleased that it doesn't. I would hate to reach a stage where I accept the death of my crew members as routine. I am glad, however, that perhaps we have helped you to put some ghosts to rest.'

The three stood chatting for a short while, before allowing Böhm to be alone with his thoughts for a few more minutes.

With a very grateful Kaleu once more below, Tremayne ordered, 'Set course for Penzance. All engines full ahead!'

At a steady forty knots, the Vosper bore west by north-west round St Mary's island, heading for Land's End. As the mainland coast came into view, O'Reilly, manning the boat's radar, yelled, 'Think I've got 'em, sir. Three blips in arrowhead formation 'bout nine thousand yards, sir.' Gradually, Tremayne's boat overhauled the slower moving trio and, four miles short of Mousehole, resumed the lead into Mount's Bay and Penzance harbour.

Several RN three-tonners and ambulances were lined up along the quay and on the road leading to the docks. The British and German wounded were the first to disembark. As Böhm was escorted to a waiting ambulance, he turned to salute Tremayne and shake his hand, passing him a note with his address in Duhnen.

'Please, Richard, write to me when this nonsense is behind us. I will not forget you or David and the kindness you have shown me and my crew.'

Tremayne, touched by the German officer's gesture, smiled and gave a final wave as Böhm was helped into one of the ambulances. He and Willoughby-Brown then turned to seek out Fischer and the other wounded members of his flotilla. He soon found the South African, who had been badly injured by shell splinters below both his knees.

Though pale and drawn, he grinned at Tremayne, irrepressible as ever. 'I won't be in hospital long enough for you to visit me with bloody grapes – just set up the bottles for when I return! Oh – I almost forgot – and give Commander Enever a cuddle from me!'

Exhausted and drained, yet curiously elated – a paradox which he did not have the energy to make sense of at that moment – Tremayne set course for home, taking his battered flotilla back to Tresco...

Ten

Blockade Busters

D uring the weeks following the successful destruction of what was believed to be the Kriegsmarine's last supply U-boat, the Tresco flotilla's motor boats underwent extensive repairs. The two Vospers each required replacement six-pounders, Quilghini's boat needed major reconstruction of its bridge, while the wheelhouse of Fischer's big Camper and Nicholson had to be virtually rebuilt, reinforced with tougher armour plate. All boats had sustained serious gunfire damage to their hulls and deck fittings, involving considerable time in dry dock. The repair shops at Tresco had never before worked so hard and to such tight timescales, pressed to have all four boats back in action as a matter of extreme urgency. Because of the relatively high numbers of casualties incurred by so small a flotilla, HMS Godolphin was awaiting a new first lieutenant for Quilghini's boat, as well as several petty officers and junior rates. Such replacements were not to be found easily because of the nature of Special Forces' operations and the strict – yet often unorthodox – selection criteria. Neither Enever nor Tremayne were prepared to drop standards just to fill vacancies quickly, although each acknowledged the pressing need to be fully operational as soon as possible.

Tremayne and his crew transferred to the captured E-boat and were joined by units from the Helford River flotilla in maintaining anti-U-boat and E-boat sweeps around the Bay of Biscay and the entrance to the English Channel. En route one day to RN barracks at Devonport for a major inter-Service briefing – in collaboration with C-byrån, Swedish Military Intelligence – Tremayne was able to call at Penzance to see Fischer. Exuberant as ever, despite his wounds, the happy-go-lucky South African was clearly enjoying the attention of so many attractive nurses. Seemingly the perpetual bachelor, Fischer – who had, in fact, had a brief but unhappy marriage in South Africa – appeared to be having a succession of field days, much to Tremayne's amusement. Despite the caring and genuinely needed succour, Fischer admitted that he was missing active service and needed to be 'back with the lads' as quickly as recovery allowed. However, Fischer's timescales for recuperation and idea of 'fit for purpose' were somewhat more optimistic than those of the medical officers responsible for his return to active service.

The Allies were continuing to advance slowly across France on several fronts. Although the Americans had decided to leave the Brittany ports in German hands so as to concentrate on the advance eastwards, the US VIII Corps captured Brest on September 18th after a long, bitter and bloody fight. As General Patton had remarked: 'Once the American army has put its hand to the plough, it should not let go.'

More than 35,000 troops defended Festung Brest*, including General Ramcke's 2nd Fallschirmjäger Division of paratroopers – once described by Hitler as 'tougher in battle than the Waffen SS'. Essentially a soldier's general and a Knight's Cross holder, he was affectionately referred to by his paratroopers as Vatti Ramcke – 'Papa' Ramcke. Opposing them were three US infantry divisions, strengthened by several Ranger battalions and supported by a large group of well-armed FFI Resistance fighters.

Updating Tremayne on the costly, protracted battle in which the Americans suffered ten thousand casualties, Enever said that the siege had taken the form of a 'corporal's war' with much of the fighting taking place at quad level, painstakingly whittling away German resistance street by street and building by building. Ramcke had laid waste to the dock and harbour installations, rendering them completely useless to the Allies as a port or naval base. When the Germans finally capitulated, Ramcke had the gall to ask the US officer taking them prisoner, whom he outranked, whether he had the

---

*Fortress Brest

credentials to accept the garrison's formal surrender. Pointing to his tough, heavily armed soldiers, the American brigadier general quietly replied: '*These* are *my* credentials.'

Enever mentioned the ever-present threat from E-boat flotillas and isolated U-boats, which would continue to operate out of the Atlantic ports still held by the Germans in Brittany.

'I suspect that until we have achieved victory in Europe, Lorient and St Nazaire will remain as safe havens for both sets of predators. Allied Supreme Commander, General Eisenhower, seems to be committed to a strategy of containment, rather than one of destruction, of the garrisons defending these ports. However, I also believe that Admiral Hembury will ask us to do something further to reduce the threats to Allied shipping in the Bay of Biscay and Channel – possibly in conjunction with SOE agents and the FFI.

'Knowing the Admiral, I don't think that he will be overly bothered about obtaining Ike's permission to go ahead with any initiatives that he decides are necessary.'

Enever paused. 'There is, Richard, a major, urgent operation for which our gallant Admiral has specifically requested your help but, before I go into that, let me organise some coffee. I could murder one right now and imagine that you could too!' Enever rang the bell button on his desk to summon a Leading Wren from Secretariat Section.

'First, dear boy, some background information to set the scene for the operation.' Enever patted his pockets, searching for his pipe. 'As you know, the Swedes have been walking a pretty tricky tightrope between the Germans and ourselves and they have continued to trade with both of us. Essentially, the Swedish Government has adopted a simple, pragmatic approach to the diplomatic negotiations involved in conducting business with both belligerents. Understandably, self-preservation lies at the basis of their trading stances – hence noticeable shifts in their willingness to trade more with one than the other as the fortunes of war have shifted.'

'Ah, thank you so much, Lucinda. Oh – and my goodness – warm Nelson slices too! Unashamed luxury – tuck in dear boy!' Enever paused to offer Tremayne one of the Navy's 'lifesavers'. 'Seize a wedge before they go cold.'

Tremayne smiled to himself at Enever's uninhibited delight and enthusiasm for the simplest of pleasures. It was, he reflected, the SNIO's natural joy of life itself that made him such an engaging boss, colleague and companion.

'The Swedes have clearly read the signs accurately and know that it's only a matter of time now before Germany capitulates. For at least a year now, at our insistence, they have reduced their exports of iron ore, machine tools and ball-bearings to the Germans, despite their proximity to the Reich and German-occupied Norway and Denmark. Their Intelligence Service – the C-byrån – has been collaborating with British SIS, feeding vital information through, and they have also been supplying us with desperately needed ball-bearings for our war effort. And this is the point, Richard, where you come in.' Enever took a sip of coffee.

'Using Camper and Nicholson MGBs, operating out of the east coast Coastal Forces bases, the Navy – and, more often than not, the merchant navy – have been blockade running to Sweden to bring back vital ball-bearings for our armament industries. Sir George Binney, an old Etonian and graduate of Oxford – and a most enterprising RNR officer, has been the instigator and driving force behind this very vital operation, code-named 'Bridport'.

Unfortunately, due to frequent dense fog in the North Sea and an unprecedented number of broken crankshafts – and hence engine failure – recently, the operations have been less than a complete success. British MGBs have been given rather more than a facelift to make them look like merchant navy launches. They've even flown the 'red duster' instead of the white ensign so as not to embarrass the Swedes when calling at the port of Lysekil to collect the goods. To reinforce the mercantile illusion, merchant navy officers and Hull trawlermen have courageously acted as the crews for these hybrid vessels.' Enever stopped again to finish his coffee.

'You're probably wondering where all this is leading, Richard?'

'I think I can guess,' Tremayne smiled. 'You want me to take my lot over to Sweden to collect a large, urgently needed consignment of ball-bearings, as back-up to Operation Bridport?'

'Hole in one, dear boy! You will also be carrying a large supply of small arms and ammunition, which the Swedes have agreed to take on to contacts in the Danish Resistance.

Apparently, the Swedish Government has already begun to explore plans to attack the Germans in Zealand, in support of the Danes, by crossing from Skåne in force. As you will appreciate, this is still top secret and not for discussion outside this room but, right now, the idea is being given considerable thought in Swedish Intelligence circles.'

'Hmmm. Sounds quite a proposition. Now I see some immediate point to the recent conference on relationships with neutral Sweden and its Intelligence Services. Is *my* boat to be 'doctored' to look like a merchant navy vessel?'

'No, certainly not. Before the war, we sold some earlier Vospers to the Swedish Navy. These craft bear a strong enough family resemblance to our current boats, though they are smaller and less well armed. Their own later MTBs – especially those built at the Kockums yard at Malmö – also happen to look similar to British Vospers, particularly those of ours which only carry two torpedo tubes. Because of such similarities we'll use your boat, with some necessary cosmetic changes including an all-over coat of lighter grey paint and a large white, shadowed-dark grey 'T' pennant number on her bow.

'Naval Intelligence has found a couple of Swedish ensigns for us. As soon as you pass through the Skagerrak Strait off the northern tip of the Jutland peninsula – near Skagen and north of the entrance to the Kattegat – hoist the Swedish colours. You will of course be operating under cover of darkness which will aid and abet your disguise. We'll drape tarpaulins over your new six-pounder which, by the way, will be fitted tomorrow.'

'Because of the sensitive political nature of such an operation in neutral waters I imagine, John, the cry is 'keep a very low profile' and that, should we have to defend ourselves, we do so with minimum force?'

'Exactly. Much of the operation has been set up with Colonel Nygren of Swedish Intelligence and the plan is this...' Enever noisily scraped out his pipe and then clamped it, empty and unlit, between his teeth, before unrolling a large-scale wall map of the Skagerrak, Kattegat and surrounding coasts of Denmark, Norway and Sweden.

'You will proceed to the harbour of Lysekil, north of Göteborg, via an archipelago of low, rocky islands and islets.' Enever indicated the chain of low-lying isles, known as the 'granite belt', with a wooden pointer. 'The operation will take place in three days' time when there should be enough of a harvest moon to assist you in navigating the islands and finding your way to the RV. Admiralty charts of the area around the archipelago and entrance to Lysekil harbour are available for you,' Enever indicated rolls of paper on his desk with his pipe, 'and you'll need to take time to study these.

'Colonel Nygren has organised things so that you will secure alongside a Swedish Baltic trader, the SS *Trollhättan,* moored immediately against the main harbour jetty. Her skipper, Captain Erik Larsson, is a former Swedish naval officer who is no lover of the Nazis. Nygren planned the transfer of kit to your boat in this way, because you will be secured on the blind side of anyone on the jetty and completely covered from most eyes by the *Trollhättan*'s bulk. His view – and mine too – is that the fewer people who know what's going on the better.

One problem we have been warned about is that of Larsson's Second Officer, Berggren, who is anti-British and who is known to have contacts among the German Abwehr. They, as you can well imagine, operate around Göteborg and along the coast, from as far south as Malmö and north up to the Norwegian border. The Germans' none too subtle hints of the potential use of military force to ensure Swedish collaboration, have created something of a 'fifth column' in the country. Consequently, there are enough willing amateur spies and people anxious to save their own skins should Hitler move against Sweden.'

Enever rang for more coffee.

'One other complication is that you will be acting as return ferry to a junior member of the British Legation staff in Stockholm: a certain captain, The Honourable Peregrine Thornby-Smythe.'

'The Honourable *who*?! Where the hell did he acquire a moniker like *Peregrine?* Oh my aching arse, John! Can't he just be flown out with the diplomatic baggage?'

''Fraid not, dear boy. There's the risk that he and the information he's garnered may be shot down. The Luftwaffe is still very much in evidence in the skies above the areas of the North Sea close to Scandinavia. He's gathered a great deal of vital intelligence about German troop dispositions in both Denmark and Norway and about their anti-invasion coastal defences. With the liberation of those two countries now in sight, it is essential that SIS have this information as soon as maybe.' Enever looked at Tremayne, an expression of apologetic resignation on his amiable face.

'By all accounts, he's been a bit of an idiot and is persona non grata with the Swedes because of a succession of scandalous affairs with Swedish society ladies and half the Legation female staff. When he does turn up at SIS HQ, he's due for a right roasting from Brigadier North, his controller. Apparently, there have been times when his many amorous liaisons have come perilously close to compromising his role as a spy. On one occasion, the clown started a most torrid affair with what he assumed to be a Swedish lady who turned out to be the mistress of the German military attaché's ADC in Stockholm. Her Swedish – and English – were completely fluent, though she, like her paramour, was German through and through. We have yet to establish the extent of the pillow talk and any possible lapses of security. Otherwise, the silly fellow has been a most skilful espionage agent.'

'While perhaps a double-barrelled name of Wright-Pratt might be more appropriate for him, I have to admit to developing a sneaking regard for this fellow – and perhaps a degree of envy too,' laughed Tremayne. 'The Honourable Peregrine sounds sufficiently *dishonourable* to be very human. I look forward to meeting him and I'll bring him back for you, John. I'm sure that young Willoughby-Brown is going to find him fascinating company! Under that deceptively guileless front of his, WB has a razor-sharp brain. He has, too, a seemingly innocuous way of wheedling information out of people – usually without them realising it.'

Enever's briefing took a further fifteen minutes. Then Tremayne put his boat crew in the picture, having first persuaded Captain MacPherson, HMS Godolphin's ill-tempered and arrogant commanding officer, to release Royal Marine Sergeant Kane to accompany them on the operation.

'I need Sergeant Kane's experience and skill as a fighting man – especially if, for any reason, we are forced to give battle on land, sir. Aboard ship, he makes an admirable deckhand and he can handle all of the MGB's main weapons.'

If only on the basis of – 'why be merely difficult when, with only a little more effort, you can be a real pain in the arse? – MacPherson was automatically predisposed to refuse the request. However, the steel in Tremayne's eyes – and his body language – told MacPherson that he would have one almighty fight on his hands were he to refuse. He knew too that such a refusal would, ultimately, bring Admiral Hembury's scalpel-like wrath down upon his head. MacPherson had no alternative but to concede, which he did with customary bad grace.

The next three days were spent on the Vosper's painstaking refurbishment, culminating in the attractive light-grey livery of the Royal Swedish Navy MTBs. With her paint freshly dry, Tremayne barely had time to take her out with her crew and run in her newly overhauled engines before Operation Viking was underway. Operations boxes, containing the crew members' personal weapons, were fitted onto her decks in exactly the same manner as those set up for use on the fishing boats for undercover expeditions to Brittany. Five extra operations boxes were similarly secured on deck containing Sten guns, Bren guns, grenades and ammunition for onward passage to Danish Resistance fighters. Below decks, the structure had been adapted and storage space was created to hold the anticipated forty-ton consignment of the urgently needed ball-bearings from the SKF* Göteborg plant.

During those same three days, Tremayne, Willoughby-Brown and Sergeant Kane had been boning up their conversational Swedish from three phrasebooks, which Enever had managed to produce for them – seemingly out of a hat. Willoughby-Brown – a natural and gifted linguist – quickly emerged as the most adept and fluent of the three.

'Right, David, if we get into any trouble we'll send you in first,' laughed Tremayne. 'You sound the most convincing of all of us.'

Tremayne's Vosper – MTB T42 of the Kungliga Flottan** as she had temporarily become – slipped her moorings at Braiden Rock at 07.30 hours and set course for the Royal Navy's Coastal Forces base at Harwich, her refuelling stop.

Berthed overnight, revictualled and with her fuel tanks full, she left Harwich at 06.00 the following morning, still flying the white ensign, her course set north-east for the Skagerrak. From there, off the northernmost tip of Jutland, she would make her way to her midnight tryst with the Baltic freighter SS *Trollhättan* in the port of Lysekil. On call to provide air cover

---

*Svenska Kullagerfabriken (Swedish ball-bearing factory)
**Swedish Royal Navy

for T42 were a squadron of Beaufighters from RAF Duxford, which could give protection – out and on the return journey – as far as the west coast of Denmark.

Tremayne knew that he and his crew would be at the mercy of Focke-Wulf Condor reconnaissance aircraft on patrol over the North Sea, who would report his presence to both Luftwaffe fighter-bombers and torpedo-carrying Arado seaplanes from their Norwegian base at Stavanger. In the North Sea, he was also wide open to attack, at flotilla strength, from E-boats from Ostend, Ijmuiden, Den Helder and, once they were close to the German Bight, from Wilhelmshaven. With T42 stood-to at defence stations and the temporary tarpaulins removed from the forrard six-pounder, Tremayne, Willoughby -Brown and Leading Yeoman of Signals Jenkins maintained a constant search of the horizon through their binoculars.

Almost due north of Emden and north of the Frisian Islands, the sharp-eyed Willoughby-Brown detected first the smoke and then the indistinct outlines of what was probably a German destroyer squadron moving west at high speed.

'We're probably too small to be seen, but a pound to a penny they will have picked us up on their radar and may have called in the 'greyhounds' to come sniffing,' said Tremayne, who called for maximum revolutions. 'We'll maintain increased speed for twenty minutes to clear the area, then reduce to thirty knots again.'

Forty miles west of the coast of Schleswig-Holstein, to the north of Cuxhaven, with the sea running strongly and the sky a uniform dull grey, Jenkins suddenly began adjusting the focus of his binoculars and yelled, 'Off the port beam sir, low in the sky, aircraft approaching.'

'Thank you Jenkins. Number One – sound action stations.' Then Tremayne shouted, 'All guns – aircraft bearing red two-five-oh. Stand by to fire, *stand by!*'

With the white ensign conspicuous, Tremayne wondered for the briefest of moments what the Germans would make of the very un-British livery. Would they open fire as a matter of course, despite the mixed international messages T42 was giving off?

Rapidly, in response, the six-pounder, Bofors and Oerlikon gun crews traversed weapons, continually adjusting elevation, as the aircraft drew ever closer. Sharpe and O'Reilly, each manning the new twin .30 calibre Brownings to port and starboard, abaft the bridge, likewise swung their machine guns round, ready to engage as the aircraft came into range. For a second, Tremayne's thoughts flashed back to Enever's briefing and his reference to the merchant navy officers and seamen who did this same perilous run with no weapons on board and with unreliable engines that had frequently broken down. 'How the *hell* did they cope?' muttered Tremayne to himself.

His thoughts were abruptly cut short by an urgent shout. It was his Leading Yeoman of Signals. 'Two of 'em, sir. Ju 88s – nasty buggers, sir. Altitude 'bout two 'undred feet.'

When excited, Jenkins's voice sounded even more strongly

of the Valleys. For a fleeting moment and curiously detached from the sudden impending threat, Tremayne reflected, 'Hmmm, always on top of the situation, Jenkins would make an ideal outside half,' and then smiled at the utter incongruity of the thought.

Through his loudhailer, Tremayne yelled over the approaching roar of the Ju 88s' engines,

'Range five hundred and closing – all guns FIRE AS YOU BEAR!'

Turning to Irvine, he ordered, 'Cox'n, port engine, full ahead! Starboard engine, full astern!'

That sudden, swinging manoeuvre saved them. At the same moment, at a range of around three hundred yards, both fighter-bombers opened fire with their 20mm cannon. The shells whistled closely overhead, churning up the sea in a succession of splashes off their stern. As the two Ju 88s closed, their twin Junkers Jumo engines screaming at maximum revs, all of T42's gunners maintained a murderous fire until the barrels of their guns were too hot to touch. The aircraft roared so low overhead, that Tremayne could clearly see his gun crews' cannon shells and bullets striking home and pieces flying off wings and fuselages. Pure adrenaline was coursing through his body. 'Follow them round, lads. Don't lose the bastards. Shoot just ahead of them – let 'em fly into your cone of fire,' he yelled. 'Keep bloody well firing!'

As the fighter-bombers drew away, to prepare to make a return attacking run, so the angle of elevation dropped and the bow six-pounder joined in, firing on automatic, its shells exploding around the disappearing aircraft. All at once, the heavily overcast grey sky was brightly lit up with a flash of yellow-orange flame as the forrard Hotchkiss gun's heavy shells hit home and one of the Junkers, bursting into a ball of fire, plunged into the sea.

'Stand by for the return trip,' shouted Tremayne. 'Gunners – mark your target well and fire as you bear.' Catching the imperturbable coxswain's eye, he added, 'Swain, stand by to zigzag, all engines full speed ahead.'

'Aye aye, sir, though I think the other one's not coming for any more, sir, so he isn't.'

Tremayne looked up to see the rapidly disappearing Ju 88 sweep round in a wide arc, then straighten up on a course heading in the direction of Stavanger.

'You're right, by heavens, Cox'n. It's not often that Jerry gives up that easily. It may be that he was already low on ammunition and my guess is that neither aircraft was 'bombed-up' for the attack.'

At around 22.00 hours, north of the Danish coastal town of Skagen, and now in the velvet darkness of a clear late September evening, Tremayne hoisted the blue and yellow naval ensign in keeping with their ruse de guerre as a Swedish MTB on patrol. In the wheelhouse, Tremayne checked his charts and called up to Irvine, 'Bear off, a couple of points to starboard, Cox'n. Keep her steady at thirty knots, please.'

'Aye aye, sir. The sea's getting rougher, sir, so it is.'

Tremayne had already felt the sea beginning to churn as he pored over the charts. 'Thank you, Cox'n. We're now entering Ålbæk Bay where the waters of the Skagerrak and the Kattegat meet, so the sea will liven up for a while.'

Back on the bridge, he spoke to Willoughby-Brown. 'Better put the tarpaulin back on the six-pounder, Number One. If any non-participating Swedes do rumble us, I don't want us to look too belligerent.'

With the crew maintaining defence stations, eyes were sweeping the now barely discernible horizon through night glasses. It was Willoughby-Brown who was first to make out the waves breaking as white streaming foam over the first of the outlying islands of the archipelago.

'Almost dead ahead, sir, the start of the 'granite belt'.'

'Thank you, Number One. Have Sharpe and O'Reilly on the foredeck as extra lookouts.'

Ten minutes later, he ordered Irvine to reduce speed to twenty knots as they moved into what, for them, were the unknown waters of the archipelago itself. Under a clear night sky and with the deep gold of an autumnal moon reflected on the sea surrounding the emerging islands, Tremayne found the scene almost magical and, in some ways, reminiscent of the Scillies. Here, one difference was the generally lower, more rounded silhouettes of the Swedish islands, compared with their fearsome, jagged counterparts to the west of Cornwall – especially those of the Western and Northern Rocks.

As they threaded their way slowly through the archipelago,

the lights of Lysekil suddenly appeared ahead and off the port bow.

'How very different from Britain and much of the rest of Europe,' said Tremayne, 'and how good it is to see a town lit up at night once again.'

'It seems unbelievable now,' responded Willoughby-Brown, slowly adjusting the focus of his night glasses, 'just how much we all took for granted so few years ago.'

'Sir, we've got company, coming up fast astern, sir.' It was the calm voice of Sergeant Geoff Kane, the Royal Marine manning the stern twin 20mm Oerlikons.

'Well spotted, Sar'nt.' Tremayne and Willoughby-Brown swung round, their binoculars centring on a phosphorescent bow-wave, now little more than a cable's length behind them. Tremayne ordered 'Action stations' and 'Clear away the tarpaulin off the Hotckkiss six-pounder', yelling to all gun crews to stand by to open fire. Shouting to O'Reilly and Sharpe, who had moved from bow lookout to man the six-pounder, Tremayne said, 'If we are stopped for any reason, keep your ears open for my orders. I may have to speak rather than shout.' He repeated the order to Kane and to the ratings manning the midships Bofors.

To Irvine he said, 'Maintain twenty knots, Cox'n. But give me maximum speed when I call for it.'

'Aye aye, sir.'

Turning to Willoughby-Brown, he said quietly, 'Can you make out who, or what, she is, Number One? All I can see is

– Damn! The bastards have switched their bloody searchlight on.'

The sudden blinding light was immediately followed by an accurately placed burst of automatic fire, which straddled the water immediately ahead of them.

'We're in Swedish national waters so we'll stop, Number One, but issue automatic weapons to all crew members – just in case.'

To Irvine he called, 'Stop all engines, Cox'n.'

As the following boat – an MTB – drew alongside, Tremayne was horrified to see that it was a German E-boat. He called quietly to the gun crews to train their weapons on the vessel, adding, 'Stand by to blow the bastards out of the water, lads.'

Willoughby-Brown shouted though the loudhailer in fluent German: 'You are guests in Swedish territorial waters. What in hell's name are you doing, firing at us? Explain yourselves immediately.'

A moment's hesitation, and then the German commander shouted back: 'You are not Swedish, I think. Who are you?'

'The bastard may be playing for time. Tell him that we *are* Swedish,' muttered Tremayne.

'Of course we are Swedish. What the hell do you think we are? We are flying our naval ensign, can't you see? You have fired on a neutral vessel. Why?'

'Your boat looks British – one of the newest Vospers, no less. The Swedish Navy has no such vessels.'

Tremayne muttered a swift reply to his first lieutenant as the increasingly tense stand-off continued.

'Then your intelligence is out of date, my friend. If you are going to spy on us, at least do it competently. Now move out of Swedish waters. You are not welcome here.'

'So, the cowardly Swedes, who are afraid to fight and grow fat making a profit out of us and the enemy, try to order the Kriegsmarine about. Maybe we should teach you a lesson!'

To pre-empt any further threats from the E-boat commander, who was revelling in escalating the situation with what he assumed to be easy meat, Tremayne quietly ordered the six-pounder gun crew to aim their gun directly at the E-boat's bridge and put a burst just feet above the heads of the commander and those standing with him.

Five rapid flat thumps saw the heavy shells pass within a terrifying three feet of the Germans' heads and the disappearance of their radar antenna, radio mast and jackstaff.

The atmosphere was electric. Seconds seemed like an eternity. A tense, menacing silence added to the threat of mutual obliteration. No one spoke. Would the Germans return fire and risk the bloody carnage of a point-blank suicidal exchange of fire, in which they were outgunned and at a distance of just ten metres? Tremayne could feel the sweat pouring down his back, soaking his shirt.

Then, as quickly as it had escalated, the tension began to evaporate as the German commander, clearly shaken and his bluff called by Tremayne's overwhelming response, screamed,

'You stupid, clod-hopping Swedish blockheads.' His impotence now only too obvious, he yelled, 'You will live to regret this insult to the Kriegsmarine,' and ordered, 'all engines slow astern.' As the E-boat reversed away, its now very deflated commander threw up his right arm in a defiant Nazi salute, more in an attempt to recover a humiliating loss of face than as any mark of maritime courtesy.

'Keep all weapons trained on the bastards. Keep them backing off,' called Tremayne, his voice raised just enough for his gun crews to hear.

Willoughby-Brown, in contrast, shouted in Swedish through his loudhailer at a level that could be clearly heard on the E-boat above the rumble of its Daimler Benz diesels. 'All engines, full ahead' – his command echoed immediately, but quietly, in English by Tremayne.

Speaking into his voice tube on the bridge, Tremayne called down to the tiny galley. 'Watkins, some rum-drenched kye all round would be most welcome.'

'Aye aye, sir. I bet it would, sir. Back there, sir, I nearly gave birth to a set of wooden jugs!'

'Bloody well done, Number One,' said Tremayne, touching Willoughby-Brown's shoulder. 'As the gallant Duke said of Waterloo – a close-run thing!'

'Indeed it was, sir.' Willoughby-Brown's calm composure undoubtedly masked a whole range of emotions and reactions, mused Tremayne, and he felt the need to offer his first lieutenant an explanation.

'I took what I admit was extremely high-risk action and my reason, apart from short-circuiting that idiot's attempts to bring things to a head, was that I recognised his pennant number as one belonging to the Baltic-based 3rd S-Boot Training Flotilla. I reckoned that, while the arrogant bastard was anxious to impress his trainee crew, he would back down – with only inexperienced officers and ratings on board – if we frightened him enough.'

'Excuse me, sir, but 'ere's a drop of what Mr Willoughby-Brown calls me torpedo propellant, sir.' Leading Seaman Watkins had, for once unnoticed, clambered up beside Tremayne.

'Thank you so much, Watkins. Another of your most welcome lifesavers. But tell me, why no serenade from the galley? This is, I think, the first time I can ever remember you appearing on the bridge with a rum-fanny full of kye and no song to precede your arrival.'

'Well, sir, begging yer pardon, I was bloody scared – and you've no doubt heard of stress incontinence, sir. Well, I was –'

'Do spare us the details, Watkins!' said Tremayne, as he and Willoughby-Brown burst out laughing. 'But thanks for the kye.'

With the entrance to Lysekil harbour less than two miles away, Tremayne ordered Jenkins to stand by for the challenge signal flashed from the shore on their approach to the seaport. Colonel Nygren had confirmed that they would be challenged by two red lights followed immediately by one green one and that they must reply in reverse order. Several minutes later, the challenge and successful response were made and MTB T42 gently glided into Lysekil harbour, her engines turning over slowly, until she secured alongside the SS *Trollhättan*.

'Maintain duty watch at defence stations,' Swain. The first lieutenant and I will be back as quickly as we can. Please have the shipment of arms and ammunition for the Danish Resistance brought up on deck and supervise their loading at this end when the *Trollhättan*'s deckhands appear. Their mate in charge will most likely speak some English.'

Tremayne and Willoughby-Brown were welcomed at the head of the temporary gangway, connected to the MTB's deck, by Captain Erik Larsson and taken to a reception area on board the *Trollhättan*, where they were introduced to Colonel Nygren and several of Larsson's officers. Over seemingly endless glasses of schnapps, conversation rapidly became lively and the British officers were soon made to feel at home. Larsson, short by Swedish standards, retained the smartness and crispness of manner of a former naval officer. His fair hair was cut *en brosse* and his alert light blue eyes took in the turnout and demeanour of his guests as a matter of course. Clearly, from the degree to which he so readily engaged with them, he approved of what he saw. In such convivial company, where Nygren also related easily to the two Britons, discussing shared interests in remarkably fluent English, Tremayne immediately picked up the ill-disguised hostility of Berggren, Larsson's second officer. He had no doubt that the Nazi-approving Swede would be on the radio to his contacts in German Intelligence, detailing the exchange and destination of the cargos both leaving and joining MTB T42 – vital ball-bearing shipments to Britain and weapons to the Danish Resistance.

After about twenty minutes, a tall, slim and strikingly handsome man joined the group. He wore the impeccable dress uniform of a captain of a British regiment of Hussars, his trousers superbly tailored in fashionable 'cavalry' style. His expensive, immaculately polished boots must be by Lobbs, or Duckers of Oxford, thought Tremayne as, fascinated, he watched the elegant officer's somewhat theatrical approach.

'Aha,' said Larsson, a beaming smile crossing his otherwise serious countenance, 'this, gentlemen, is our naughty boy from the British Legation. Come and have a drink, Perry!'

So, mused Tremayne, *this* was the notorious rake he was due to escort home – and to a scorching reprimand by the SIS. Brigadier North, his controller, had described the Honourable Peregrine Thornby-Smythe to Enever as: 'Intellectually brilliant, but psychologically flawed, he is charming to a fault, but with an almost non-existent sense of responsibility. He possesses the libido and sexual proclivities of a buck rabbit.'

In his customary way, Enever had added his own colourful description for Tremayne's benefit: 'As some Frenchman or other once said, 'Any hussar who lives beyond the age of thirty must be a blackguard' – and Thornby-Smythe can't be too far off that fateful milestone!'

Tremayne was greatly amused to see how easily his first

lieutenant and the honourable lothario sparred with one another in light-hearted and completely inconsequential cocktail-party conversation where sparkling, ever-ready wit fired the mutual cues and prompts. The Swedes looked on, seemingly bemused by the rapid-fire exchanges punctuated by regular outbursts of laughter. Only too aware of Willoughby-Brown's sharp intelligence and penetrating insights, Tremayne knew that, under the apparent froth of superficial conversation, his first lieutenant would be cleverly probing for answers and information from their temporary charge.

Larsson, on the pretext of showing him some wall-mounted photographs of sister ships of the SS *Trollhättan*, steered Tremayne out of Berggren's earshot.

'Richard, there's no doubt that my Nazi second officer has already alerted the Abwehr to the purpose of your trip to Lysekil. It doesn't take a genius to work out that any homeward-bound member of a military attaché's staff travelling by high-speed boat, rather than by aeroplane, is most likely loaded with intelligence information. The Germans know only too well the vital importance of ball-bearings to a nation's war effort – we sell them vast quantities too, especially since your bombers have begun bombing their own manufacturing plants at Schweinfurt and elsewhere.'

Larsson looked earnestly at Tremayne. 'Your MTB will leave at dawn, when loading is complete, in the company of the Swedish Navy destroyer *Mjölner*, which will escort you as far as the area north of Skagen. Make sure that you continue to fly the Swedish naval ensign while you are accompanied. We are also providing you with temporary air cover. A SAAB 18 reconnaissance bomber will be overhead – apparently working in conjunction with you – as T42 and the *Mjölner* seemingly sail together on a Kungliga Flottan 'routine patrol'. You will be safe up to that point but, from there on, I believe that – thanks to Berggren – you are likely to be hunted relentlessly by aircraft as well as by surface units of the Kriegsmarine.'

'Erik, we are deeply indebted to you and I am grateful for the help that you are providing for us. I appreciate, too, that there is enormous potential embarrassment for you and for the Swedish Government in this operation if –'

Larsson put up his hand, stopping Tremayne in mid-sentence. 'Let me worry about that, Richard. As you would say, we know which side our bread is buttered on. We see the tide has turned irrevocably and, in a few months – perhaps a year at the most, Germany will be defeated and we will all need to start rebuilding Europe, if not the world.'

He grinned at Tremayne. 'I cannot undo what Berggren has already passed onto his Nazi friends, but I'll damn well tie him up with so much watchkeeping and sea-going duties during the next few days, while we're shifting timber between Finland and here. I'll make sure that he doesn't go ashore again for the best part of a week. And when he does, I'll see that Per Lindstrom, my first officer whom you've just met, accompanies him for what will be an inescapable drunken run ashore. That will keep him out of action for another twenty-four hours! In the interests of Swedish Secret Military Intelligence, Colonel Nygren is very curious to know just what Berggren has been up to on his many 'unofficial' meetings with the Abwehr at the German Embassy. Nygren does not want him to have even the slightest suspicion that he is under observation. So, no attempt is to be made – yet – to clip Berggren's flapping wings. Our Military Intelligence have an agent – a female secretary – on the staff at the German Embassy who is monitoring Berggren's activities and Nygren wishes that to continue, unhindered, for a while longer.'

Larsson held out his hand to shake Tremayne's. 'I must leave you now, Richard. It won't do to appear too conspiratorial. Per Lindstrom will look after arrangements for your departure at 05.00. I wish you Godspeed and safe sailing tomorrow. I hope we meet again in more settled times!'

Right on time the next morning, T42 slipped her moorings at Lysekil and, escorted by the destroyer *Mjölner*, headed out to sea, setting a course north by north-west. Some ten miles clear of land, the two vessels – travelling in line abreast with *Mjölner* to starboard between T42 and the coast – were joined by the SAAB 18 of the Swedish Naval Air Service.

Hugging the Swedish coast, to minimise German radar contact from monitoring stations in Denmark and Norway, Tremayne's MTB parted company from her destroyer and reconnaissance bomber escorts some forty miles north of Skagen. Signalling – by Aldis lamp – grateful farewells to the Swedes, he set course for Harwich, his crew stood-to at defence stations.

They had successfully unloaded the weapons intended for the Danish Resistance and taken on board the forty-ton consignment of precious ball-bearings, together with the equally important Honourable Peregrine Thornby-Smythe and his vital intelligence for SIS.

The delicate shade of green that his already genteelly pallid features had turned on entering the turbulent seas of Ålbaek Bay, suggested that his previous experience of boats must have been confined to a punt on the Isis or a rowing boat on the Serpentine. Claiming that death would be a merciful release, and much to the crew's ill-disguised amusement, he had retreated below, and stayed there, clutching a large galvanised bucket.

"Eaving 'e was, sir, when I left 'im,' said Watkins with a grin as he ladled out kye to those on the bridge and weapons positions. 'Trying to 'elp, sir, I did offer 'im an 'ot pork sausage sandwich, but some'ow I don't think 'e was in the mood, sir.'

'I'm *sure* he wasn't, Watkins!' laughed Tremayne, as the vision of the Honourable Thornby-Smythe, head over a bucket, heaving uncontrollably and surrounded by countless crates of ball-bearings, flashed across his mind. Turning to his first lieutenant, he said, 'Better try him with a dose of scopolamine – we have some in the medical kit. It may help to make life seem less ghastly for him.'

'Aye aye, sir. Apparently, the Jerries also use it as a so-called 'truth drug' in interrogation. Perhaps, after a couple of spoonfuls, the Honourable Peregrine might open up about some of his affairs – that could be quite entertaining, sir!'

'There are times, Number One, when I do worry about you!' Both dissolved into silent laughter as Willoughby-Brown slipped below to try and ease their passenger's suffering.

Tremayne checked both his charts and the gyrocompass, as they would shortly be entering the waters of the Skagerrak, with Denmark to port and Norway to starboard. The Kungliga Flottan ensign still flew, flapping frenetically in the strengthening breeze. In such fraught times and so far from its base, in waters which frequently became the scene of air and sea battles, a Swedish MTB might invite more questions than its presence might answer. But, as Tremayne had reasoned, such a cover, however flimsy, might just provide precious minutes in which to gain the fire initiative, or even turn a situation to his advantage and completely fool the enemy, which the white ensign never would. At sea beyond southern Jutland, the Swedish flag would be an improbable sight, unless en route to a German North Sea naval port, which could so easily be checked and disproved on the spot by ship-to-shore radio.

In planning his return strategy with Enever, Tremayne had, as was his natural tendency, decided to keep his options open. Depending on circumstances, one stratagem – inspired by Thornby-Smythe's presence – was to travel in the guise of a vessel taking a Swedish naval attaché to Wilhelmshaven, using the excuse that air travel in the area was unsafe because of both the RAF and the Luftwaffe. His second cover story was that they were carrying desperately needed ball-bearings for the German war effort – also to be landed at Wilhelmshaven – for onward transportation by rail to the Ruhr, in a vessel which the British would possibly not apprehend. Once he had passed Wilhelmshaven, however, he knew he would have a real problem.

Larsson had thoughtfully stowed on board enough Swedish naval sea-going working rig for at least half of Tremayne's crew to wear, in case they were stopped at sea by patrolling German surface craft. Those on deck had already changed into Swedish naval clothing above the waist, with everyone – officers included – wearing nondescript Kungliga Flottan forage caps.

The redoubtable and fervently patriotic Irvine had protested most strongly about donning what he saw as rig courtesy of pantomime hire.

'My elder brother, who fell at Zeebrugge in the First World War, would be turning in his grave if he could see me like this, sir, so he would.'

The sea and sky had seemed uncommonly empty to Tremayne, as he, Willoughby-Brown and Jenkins maintained a constant scanning of the horizon with their binoculars. They had not even seen the merest telltale trace of smoke in the far distance. As planned with Enever, he had alerted the RAF of his impending return and they had confirmed that three Beaufighters were already on their way to provide air cover. Because of the weight of their cargo, the Vosper was struggling to make twenty-eight knots. In the increasingly heavy sea she was rolling heavily, making the passage home soaking wet for those on deck as waves crashed over her bow, sending chilling cascades of spray over the forward gun position and the open bridge.

For a brief moment, Tremayne wondered about Thornby-Smythe and how much he must be suffering in the rough conditions. Apart from ensuring that he was warm and dry and that the contents of his bucket were regularly thrown overboard, which was already being done, there was little else that he could do for him.

When T42 was some eighty miles due west of Flensburg, Able Seaman Sharpe, who was monitoring the boat's radar screen, shouted from below, 'Bridge! Five small blips heading this way, at speed, on the port beam. Range seven miles.'

'Thank you, Sharpe – well done.' Turning to Willoughby-Brown, Tremayne said, 'Sound action stations, Number One. Make sure all – '

'Sir! Three aircraft on the screen, coming in astern of us from the north, sir. 'Bout five miles away, sir.' This time, there was no mistaking the urgency in Sharpe's otherwise calm voice.

'Thank you again, Sharpe. Jenkins – radio RAF Duxford, giving our position and details of blips of both aircraft and surface vessels. We're going to need those Beaufighters pdq.'

The klaxon for action stations had already sounded and all weapons were now manned, the gun crews quickly checking ammunition and ensuring that traversing and elevating mechanisms were all in perfect working order.

Within seconds, Jenkins shouted up to the bridge, 'RAF have acknowledged, sir. Beaufighters will be with us in about twenty minutes, sir.'

'Hmmm, the first fifteen minutes are going to be exciting, Number One, until help arrives.'

Tremayne called across to Irvine, 'Stand by to zigzag at maximum revs and be prepared to get every last knot of speed out of her, Cox'n.'

To the gun crews, he shouted through his loudhailer, 'Keep your eyes open for aircraft coming in astern of us and stand by to fire, on my command.'

Minutes later, Sergeant Kane — acting as gun captain of the twin stern Oerlikons and desperately trying to shade his eyes — shouted, 'They've changed direction, sir, and shifted their angle of attack! They're coming in from the east, sir, on our stern port quarter, with the sun behind them.'

'Cunning bastards,' muttered Tremayne.

'Hard a-port, Cox'n, then zigzag, full speed ahead.'

To gun crews, he yelled, 'All guns STAND BY TO FIRE! They're coming in at us out of the sun. A double tot for the first man to confirm their identity!'

It was Kane, with the sharp, calculating eyes of a sniper, who secured the prize.

'Me 110s — three of 'em, sir.'

'Well done, Sar'nt. You'll be the one to splice the mainbrace! The Swedish flag and paint job may just fool 'em, Number One.' Tremayne looked across at Willoughby-Brown, following the aircraft with his binoculars and then called through his loudhailer: 'ALL GUNS, STAND BY. Everyone else wave at the bastards. They'll see us easily in the —'

The sudden eruption of cannon and machine-gun fire from the three Messerschmidts was deafening and the shelter over the after companionway disappeared as so much shredded timber and steel.

'ALL GUNS – FIRE AS YOU BEAR!'

At a height of what Tremayne estimated to be two hundred feet, the three aircraft were over and away in a trice, with everything from .30 calibre rounds to six-pounder shells competing to straddle and destroy them. Slowly and gracefully they turned to port and then came racing back, engines roaring, for a second attack – this time, bow-on.

Reacting to the manoeuvre, Tremayne yelled 'Down everybody, DOWN!' as 20mm cannon shells and 7.62mm bullets struck home along the top of the bridge and thudded into the roof of the wheelhouse. Tragically, Taff Jenkins failed to move quickly enough and was killed instantly by a burst of machine-gun rounds in the head. Distraught, Tremayne rushed across the bridge to his chief yeoman of signals crumpled against the steel bulkhead, but he was too late. The mellifluous Valleys voice had been stilled forever. Never would he don the proud red jersey of Wales, but if St Peter ever formed a XV, up Topsides, he would certainly pick Jenkins as his outside half.

The desperate need for urgent action took over from shock and Tremayne raced round the wheelhouse to the operations box, hell bent on vengeance. Crashing open the lid, he snatched up a Bren gun, checked its magazine and action, cocked it and took aim at the leading Me 110 as the trio returned for a third strafing run.

'Gun crews! Mark your targets well. FIRE AS YOU BEAR!'

Tremayne let the first oncoming Messerschmidt fill his sights. Deliberately, he squeezed the trigger and kept his finger on it, emptying the magazine and swinging the Bren just ahead of the fighter-bomber's nose as it roared over, less than two hundred feet above the MTB. Flying into a lead and steel curtain of the combined fire of the Bofors, the Hotchkiss six-pounder, twin Oerlikons, the Brownings and Tremayne's Bren gun, two aircraft began to disintegrate in mid-air. Seconds later, one blew up while the other plunged into the sea – oily, black smoke pouring from its starboard engine.

From the outset of the attack, Irvine had been furiously zigzagging the Vosper and, though more damage had been inflicted on the MTB, there were no further casualties. Of concern to Tremayne was that her Carley floats and rubber dinghy had been ripped to shreds by cannon fire, denying her crew the means of survival in the sea if she were sunk in action.

He knew, too, that in addition to further punishment from the remaining Me 110, within minutes he would have to face the combined attack of five E-boats. In the heat of the engagement, Willoughby-Brown had radioed RAF Duxford again to speed up the arrival of the desperately needed Beaufighters. Without their support, T42 would be sunk without trace and her precious cargoes of ball-bearings and vital intelligence would be sent to the bottom of the North Sea.

The surviving Messerschmidt banked steeply and then turned purposefully into an attacking run, firing immediately as its pilot lined it up on his target – the MTB. The combined noise of so much weaponry, firing fully on automatic, was deafening and disorientating. Despite his courageous determination to press home the attack, the German pilot was clearly disconcerted by the concentrated volume of hot metal coming his way and hitting his aircraft. This time, his shooting was off the mark and the majority of his cannon shells and bullets flew overhead, splashing into the sea astern of the MTB. Able Seaman Davis, the rating serving the after twin Oerlikons with Sergeant Kane, was badly wounded in the attack and one of the stern depth-charge chutes, luckily empty, was reduced to a shambles of torn and twisted metal. Willoughby-Brown dashed to the Oerlikon position, along with Leading Seaman Watkins, to tend to Davis's wound, give him a shot of morphine and take him below deck.

A sudden yell went up from Sergeant Kane, 'We've got 'im, sir,' and he immediately resumed firing, pumping 20mm shells into the Me 110 as flames and thick black smoke suddenly erupted from the front of its slender fuselage. Seconds later, there was an explosion as the plane's remaining ammunition blew up and it plunged into the sea, sinking before T42 could save its pilot and rear gunner.

The shock of Jenkins's death and fighting off the persistent attacks of the Messerschmidts had temporarily taken Tremayne's attention away from the five rapidly approaching blips on the radar screen. Calling down to O'Reilly who had resumed his scan, Tremayne shouted, 'Those five blips – where the hell are they?'

'Closing fast, sir. 'Bout three thousand yards, sir. Maintaining course directly for us, sir. Oh, wait, something else is on the screen, sir. A surface vessel is approaching from the north at almost ninety degrees to the five blips and what look to be another five aircraft, paralleling this vessel, sir.'

'Thank you, O'Reilly. Keep me posted on any changes.'

Nodding to Willoughby-Brown, Tremayne said, Looks as if it's going to become rather busy – who the hell I wonder, Number One, are this little lot? There's no sight of our three Beaufighters from Duxford. At our reduced speed, we don't stand the devil in a church's chance of taking avoiding action. Check the state of ammunition with guncrews, please. They must be bloody low, especially the Oerlikons and Brownings.'

As the first lieutenant returned to the bridge to report on the state of ammunition, McIllhenny, gun captain of the forrard six-pounder, shouted, 'Aircraft approaching, two o'clock, and destroyer or frigate coming this way, sir, dead ahead. To starboard, five E-boats approaching at speed, sir!'

'Thank you, McIllhenny. Well done.'

Willoughby-Brown, silent while McIllhenny reported on the rapid approach of so much partially unidentified traffic, spoke: 'Brownings and Oerlikons each have only a hundred or so rounds left. The six-pounder is down to less than fifty shells and the Bofors has three more clips of six rounds each, sir. And,' added the first lieutenant – his face a continuing mask of studied concern, 'I believe we've also run out of Nelson slices, sir.'

Tremayne burst out laughing. 'Tell me Number One, does that impossible sense of humour of yours ever desert you?'

'Only when the wardroom bar runs out of gin, sir.'

Picking up his loudhailer, Tremayne called, 'All guns, stand by to fire!' then added, 'And make *every* shot count, lads, there's sweet 'fox' 'able' ammo left.'

Tremayne and Willoughby-Brown scanned the horizon ahead and to starboard, trying to identify the vessels and aircraft closing in on them – the five E-boats now menacingly close.

Tremayne picked up his loudhailer just as Willoughby-Brown – familiar with the workings of the Aldis signalling lamp and proficient in Morse code – assumed the role of temporary acting yeoman of signals on the bridge, replacing Taff Jenkins.

Tremayne called to the gun crews: 'Target, bearing green oh-four-five. Five E-boats. ALL GUNS – COMMENCE FIRING, AS YOU BEAR.'

Almost as if on cue, what was now recognisable as a Grimsby-class anti-submarine frigate, opened fire on the rapidly closing E-boats. Swinging sharply to starboard to bring her single 4.7-inch rear turret to bear, she straddled the German MTBs with her first salvo of accurate ranging shots. Moments later, her second salvo from her two single turrets began striking home, this time exploding on the E-boats. Tremayne could see T42's six-pounder and Bofors simultaneously hitting the German MTBs, which suddenly broke formation into a clever, scattered Stichtaktik.*

Tremayne yelled through his loudhailer, 'All guns, mark your targets well, you're low on ammunition!'

Willoughby-Brown, pointing to the five twin-engined aircraft which were now on the scene – appearing out of the low cloud base, yelled, 'Beaufighters – and five of 'em, sir!'

''In the nick of time, Number One. The RAF is in good form, thank heavens.'

Sweeping in low over the rapidly dispersing E-boats, the Beaufighters opened their attack with rockets and cannon fire. A violent explosion and billowing plume of black smoke signalled the immediate end of one of the E-boats while another, under the hail of deadly rockets, stopped dead in the water and slowly rolled over before disappearing into the bleak depths of the North Sea.

As T42 drew closer to the zigzagging frigate, manoeuvring to avoid a torpedo attack from one of the E-boats, Tremayne's heart leapt as he briefly saw her pennant number – U47. She was his old ship – *HMS Fleetwood* – off her normal Atlantic station and just out of Harwich following a minor refit. Forgetting all protocols of rank, he grabbed Willoughby-Brown's arm. 'Just look at her, David, she was *my* ship – called 'the happiest

*A manoeuvre that allows a group of E-boats to attack a target simultaneously from several directions

ship in the Royal Navy' — and she's bloody well here!'

His unrestrained whoop of genuine joy and wildly waving cap brought a wry — and very rare — grin to his coxswain's normally serious countenance and an even rarer unsolicited comment: 'She's a fine wee ship and handled well, so she is, sir.'

Praise indeed, thought Tremayne, as he quickly returned to directing fire onto the remaining E-boats. Within seconds, another one brewed up under the Beaufighters' aerial rocket onslaught and the combined impact of *Fleetwood*'s 4.7-inch quick-firing guns and T42's main armament.

The devastating, concentrated fire of one of the E-boat's lethal 20mm anti-aircraft four-barrelled Flakvierlings brought down one of the Beaufighters in a massive explosion. Crashing into the sea in a near vertical dive, Tremayne could see that there would sadly be no survivors. Badly damaged, with black smoke issuing from her port engine, another Beaufighter veered off to the north-west in the direction of its base in East Anglia.

Likewise, the two remaining E-boats broke off the engagement and made an attempt to escape, heading at high speed in the direction of the German coast. The *Fleetwood*'s maximum speed of sixteen knots was no match for the forty-two knots of the Germans and her captain contented himself with firing a succession of parting salvoes until the E-boats, one trailing smoke, disappeared out of range of the frigate's punishing guns.

Tremayne waved his cap in acknowledgement as the three Beaufighters tore off in pursuit of the Germans. Turning to Willoughby-Brown, he said, 'Number One, make to *HMS Fleetwood*: '*Many thanks,* Onward*, *your timing was impeccable. It's a joy to see my old ship again!'*

Moments later, Willoughby-Brown translated *Fleetwood*'s reply, 'She's acknowledged, sir: '*Glad to be of help. Rejoin us on board whenever conditions permit. You will be most welcome!'*

Tremayne smiled. 'Seeing her again was like being in the company of a dear old friend. It's quite ridiculous how sentimental sailors become about their ships but *HMS Fleetwood* was, indeed, a very happy ship and I'm proud to have served in her, David.'

Turning to Petty Officer Irvine, Tremayne said, 'Cox'n, take us to Harwich, if you will. Keep her speed to twenty-seven knots and then, when we've deposited our honourable gentleman into the none too welcoming arms of his controller and unloaded the shipment of ball-bearings, you may take us home as fast as you like.

'I know you hate the charade of pretending to be a Swedish coxswain, so, while I take the wheel, you go below and change back into Royal Navy rig.'

'Aye aye, sir – and thank you sir!'

As Irvine disappeared to dress once more in the RN rig of the day, Tremayne grinned at Willoughby-Brown and, affecting a passable Ulster accent, snapped, 'I'm an Ulsterman, so I am – not a bloody troll!'

---

*'Onward' – HMS Fleetwood's ship's motto

At ease with the boat's wheel in his hand, Tremayne said, 'When we arrive back in Tresco, I'll also be bloody glad to shed the alien rig, paintwork and pennant number and officially become part of the good old Andrew once again.'

Tremayne and Willoughby-Brown bade farewell to their still rather pale green passenger at Harwich, wishing him well.

'I'm going to need all the luck in the world to untangle myself from this little lot, I'm afraid, but thank you for your courtesy and hospitality. You've been most considerate hosts. I just hope that the intelligence I've brought back for my lords and masters will help to mitigate the list of charges they will undoubtedly throw at me. Do please come and visit me, gentlemen, when I'm behind bars!' With a struggle, the unhappy erstwhile lounge lizard managed a rueful smile as he lurched, rather than strode, to meet his destiny.

Less than twenty-four hours later, exhausted but exhilarated, Tremayne and his crew moored safely once more at Braiden Rock and went ashore for detailed debriefing and whatever Naval Intelligence next had in store for them...

Eleven

A Shock For Tremayne

A cool breeze blowing off the white-capped sea chilled the mid-morning air, despite the bright September sun. The white ensign fluttered proudly from the tall, painted steel mast. At the head of HMS Godolphin's small, packed parade ground, the awesomely insulated figure of Captain MacPherson dominated the scene. He called the assembled ship's company to attention and, with his sword, saluted Admiral Hembury. Returning the salute, the Admiral stepped forward to address the immaculately turned-out ranks of navy blue and white. Almost imperceptibly, he nodded to MacPherson, who responded with the commands – 'Parade – stand at ease. Stand easy!'

Just hours before, Hembury had arrived from the mainland to publically congratulate the flotilla members – most notably Enever, Tremayne and what he termed 'you happy few' on their successes in supporting Operation Dragoon, their actions in the Bay of Biscay and the Channel and, most recently, in Swedish waters. With his ability to switch from the serious or grave, to the light-hearted and back again, Admiral Hembury smilingly referred to the combined crew of the Tresco flotilla as 'Tremayne's Premier Cru'. As Enever later stated, 'At that point, some of the sailors did look rather blank – or was it blanc?!'

Generous in his praise and appreciation, the Admiral was also quick to express his deep sorrow over the deaths and injuries sustained by the Tresco flotilla. He acknowledged the pain such casualties caused within a small, tightly knit Service community like HMS Godolphin where, necessarily, there was strong mutual support and close camaraderie amongst members of the ship's company, but especially among boat crews. In such circles, where living on adrenaline was the norm, the depth of bonding and unspoken – yet intense – sense of community was palpable.

The loss of comrades was felt deeply, despite the ever-present and seemingly unfeeling sentiment of 'push on regardless'. Tremayne knew from people of his father's generation, who had fought in the First World War, that it would be in his later years – with the added poignancy of passing time – that he would perhaps experience the greatest sense of loss for his shipmates.

With impeccable timing, right on the closing of the Admiral's parade-ground address, Squadron Leader Stanley led nine Hurricanes of the St Mary's Flight 1449, in arrowhead formation, in a low-level fly-past over the assembled ship's company. Just beyond St Helen's island, they reformed in line ahead and, one after the other, performed victory rolls as they flew back to their base on St Mary's.

With quite uncharacteristic bonhomie – but probably a desperate need for approval – Captain MacPherson ordered 'Parade, off caps!' and 'Three cheers for Admiral Hembury'. As Hembury was very much a sailor's admiral and held in great affection by the ship's company, the rousing, uninhibited cheering echoed around HMS Godolphin's parade ground. Obviously moved by the enthusiastic reception, Hembury thanked officers and ratings alike, before MacPherson called the parade to attention. As he ordered – 'Parade, right turn. To the marquee, quick march!' – the Royal Marines band, which Hembury had brought over from Plymouth, struck up *Heart of Oak* and the ship's company stepped off, smart as paint, as if they were on the barracks square at Pompey, Chatham, or Guz.

With his customary – and so appropriate – level of pure theatre and a fine sense of occasion, Admiral Hembury had organised a memorable lunch under a huge marquee for the ship's company. The atmosphere he had created following the parade-ground address was more that of a celebratory gala than a formal Service function and the ship's company revelled in the relaxed, informal – yet still thoroughly naval – spirit of the day. The band played a mix of light patriotic airs and popular tunes of the day. 'Jolly Jack', not known for inhibition or shyness on such occasions, boisterously sang along with some of the band's numbers — and with particular gusto whenever the sailors had produced their own bawdy lyrics to the tunes.

A smiling Admiral Hembury took Enever to one side. 'Y' know, John, the Tresco flotilla has performed miracles under you and young Tremayne and I am so pleased to see the lads – and lasses,' he added with twinkling eyes, 'relaxing and enjoying themselves. They richly deserve that, as indeed you all do.' Hembury took Enever's arm and steered him further out of earshot of the noisy tables.

'Needs must, I have to talk shop with you, John. As you well know, there is a certain understandable logic in Ike's decision to leave the Atlantic Brittany seaports besieged, but still firmly in German hands. Between them, SOE and SIS are doing a good job of insulating the Jerries, inland of the ports, through the efforts of the Resistance, the Jedburgh sabotage teams and both the British and French SAS units. In fact, Major Black and Sergeant Nugent, whom you know well, are both on covert operations there as we speak. However, the Germans still have more or less the full use of the port and harbour facilities for their damned U-boats and E-boats. Resistance attacks on the installations themselves need to be initiated and coordinated from the inside, as it were, to achieve maximum destructive impact against the Germans' near-impregnable U-boat pens. These are monstrous, virtually bomb-proof structures in reinforced concrete and RAF raids so far have been less than successful.'

Hembury took two glasses off a tray being carried round by a young Wren and passed one to Enever. Taking a clearly relished sip, he continued, 'Bomber Command does, of course, possess the hugely destructive Tallboy bombs, but because of the collateral damage they can cause on exploding, the RAF is reluctant to use them with so many housing estates and apartment blocks so close to the docks of Lorient and St Nazaire. Many of these, I know, have already been destroyed – and on an appalling scale. The number of further civilian casualties likely to occur is completely unacceptable, so further raids are out – especially from the altitudes at which our bomber crews need to go in. In the earlier raids on Lorient, thousands of French civilians have been killed by Allied bombers.'

Admiral Hembury glanced briefly at Enever, as if preparing to deliver bad news.

'So, what realistic options do we have that will result in minimal casualties to French civilians – and, hopefully, to ourselves – in our attempts to curb Dönitz's destructive U-boat operations? Current thinking in Intelligence circles is that we need to get agents into the U-boat pens who can plant explosives on the submarines, with timer fuses, and then slip away before the charges go off. Far easier said than done in what are heavily guarded docks. We'd only have one bite of the cherry, so it has to be a meticulously planned and coordinated, one-off operation. It is one with the inherent risk of potentially appalling casualties amongst the saboteurs, unless thoroughly orchestrated and managed.'

Admiral Hembury paused to take a particularly large, reinforcing swig of champagne.

'This, John, is where I should like your views and comments. Former Second Officer Tremayne is, as you know – although now a mother – a civilian intelligence specialist, operating within SIS as a naval liaison officer. Of late, her work has increasingly taken her into the shadowy, disputed boundary territory between SIS and SOE. Her job title is primarily a *nom d'espion* for what is a considerably wider espionage and intelligence brief. Like her husband, Emma Tremayne is doing sterling work. Inevitably, her liaison role has taken her more recently into the realms of SOE's French Section and the activities of the redoubtable Vera Atkins.'

Hembury stopped to check that Tremayne was well out of hearing range of their conversation. Looking intently at Enever, he continued, 'So, now for the crunch issue, John. Vera Atkins's colleagues are pushing Emma's SIS controller to release her temporarily to SOE to act in a similar role in Brittany, to coordinate the activities of the Resistance and Allied sabotage teams. She would, of course, be operating under cover, behind German lines, inside the Lorient 'pocket' and then, likewise, at St Nazaire. She may sometimes even commute between the two. A woman – given the right operating cover – is likely to have just that little bit more freedom to move around unchallenged than a fit-looking young man.

'There is no question that, because of her high intelligence, fluency in French, her extensive understanding of the workings and politics of anti-Nazi sabotage operations in Brittany and – above all – her rock-steady temperament, she is the best there is for this vital role. In the intensive preparation she has already been given at the Jedburgh teams' training school at Milton Hall, near Peterborough, Emma came out top of the class in virtually every subject – except unarmed combat where she emerged with a very creditable third place in a group of ten trainees. Her pistol shooting, apparently, was rated as 'outstanding'.'

Admiral Hembury looked searchingly at Enever's serious face before he asked, 'How do *you* think young Tremayne will take this? Before you answer, the dilemma I have, John, is that Emma is so perfectly typecast for the job, while Richard Tremayne is the ideal flotilla leader – I know of none better – and I cannot afford to have him disaffected by this sudden turn of events. He has a vital continuing role to play himself in the coming months.'

Enever took what, at that defining moment, was a much needed drink of his champagne. He drew a deep breath as his attention was suddenly caught by a burst of merry, carefree laughter from Tremayne and Willoughby-Brown and those seated closest to them.

Clearing his throat before responding, he said, 'Lord help us, sir, what an absolute hell of a dilemma.'

Enever stopped briefly, his face showing the anxiety of deep personal concern.

'I now understand, sir, why Emma's cousin and close friend,

Morag, was so subtly 'engineered' by Intelligence into the role of her babysitter and housekeeper. But whatever has been Emma's reaction to all this, sir?'

'Marvellously positive – and so typical of the girl – just as we've all come to expect of her. With barely a pause, she looked me straight in the eyes and said 'If it will help to shorten the war in any way, sir, I'll do it. Just please make sure that Catriona and Richard are looked after if anything happens to me'.'

'It is one bloody awful turn-up for the book but, like God, SIS and SOE work in mysterious ways their wonders to perform. I'm afraid we have to move forward – and quickly – on this one. SIS and SOE must have our answer by 17.00 hours this afternoon. By 23.00 hours, Emma should be on her way to Lorient by RAF Lysander.'

'I take your point on urgency, sir. One issue to bear in mind, however, is that Richard is not fully aware of the intense level of involvement of Emma's role – nor the degree to which her reputation and standing have risen within senior Intelligence circles at both SIS and SOE. Might I suggest, sir, that we let him finish lunch and then the three of us sit down together and talk him through what has transpired between SOE and SIS – I believe that news such as this would be better coming from both of us.'

'Agreed, John. Grab him at 14.00 hours and we'll disappear to your office together. In the meantime, let's think about how we should best broach the issue with young Tremayne.'

The meeting in Hut 101, which Tremayne had assumed was to be either a pre-operational briefing or an update on Allied naval strategies, had initially left him numbed. For a while, he could not believe what he was hearing. Mentally and emotionally, he was quite unprepared for the shock news. He had, as Enever had suggested to Hembury, no real inkling of the key importance and contribution of Emma's role to Military Intelligence, beyond the general impression of clandestine activity that she had been allowed to give him.

His feelings ranged from complete shock, to a sense of betrayal by the Intelligence Services, and then to despair as, in his mind's eye, he visualised Emma in a similar situation to his own, when he had been held as a prisoner, brutally beaten and interrogated by the Gestapo.

He shuddered, sickened, as he remembered the haunting words of Jim Avery, the Lysander pilot who had flown him home to St Mary's from RAF Netheravon after his return from Operation Dragoon: *'Some of the bravest passengers I take are Vera Atkins's young ladies. . . I take in more than I bring back out. . . What the hell the bloody Gestapo do to them before they execute them, heaven only knows, sir.'*

An icy chill ran through his body as he recalled the inexplicable feelings of foreboding he had experienced as he and Emma said goodbye when their leave ended just two weeks ago. Had that unaccountable sense of dread been a premonition of what was unfolding, out of his control, around Emma and him right now? The joy and delight of their all-too-brief time together had served to remind them of their hopes and plans for the now foreseeable future, when the war would come to an end and life could start in full for them. And now this.

Tremayne felt yet again the leaden despair he had known when he had faced the firing squad at Rennes less than nine months ago and when McDonald, his chief engineer, had been so callously murdered. For one crazy, hideous moment, he saw Emma's body hanging from an execution post, just as he had seen Mac's sagging corpse, before the SS officer in command of the firing squad had walked up and put a final pistol shot into his chief's head.

Aware that the Admiral and Commander Enever were looking at him intently – concern registering on both their faces – he knew he had to take an immediate grip of his churning emotions, get his head together and begin thinking straight.

Turning to Admiral Hembury, his voice taut but controlled, he said, 'If Emma has said yes, sir, there *is* no option and I must make it as easy as I possibly can for her to undertake this assignment. Whatever my feelings are on this matter, sir, I will not falter in carrying out my own duties as flotilla commander. I will draw on whatever extra strength I might need from the officers and men with whom I serve. My primary duty is to them, sir. I cannot – and will not – fail them.'

Later that night, a Westland Lysander stood on the runway at RAF Tarrant Rushton in Dorset, its engine already running at high revs, as the young woman – carrying a cheap leather holdall of French manufacture and wearing obviously French clothes – walked steadily towards it. Her heart was pounding and her stomach felt in turmoil as she drew close to the aircraft's open door. Clutching the chic French beret she wore over her dark, chestnut brown hair against the rush of air from the Lysander's propeller, she climbed the passenger steps to the cabin.

'Hello, I'm Jim Avery, your pilot. I take it you're Emma Tremayne. Welcome aboard!' The hand was outstretched in friendly greeting and Emma gladly shook it. At that moment, it represented the comforting security of the normality she so desperately needed to steady her shaking body and to calm her nerves. Never before had she known such physical fear.

The grin was warm and cheerful, without being unnaturally so. 'There's a flask of hot coffee with more than a smidgen of rum in it and a packet of cook's 'mystery' sandwiches for you, if you'd like a bite to eat on the journey. Whatever is in them, only cook knows, but they're usually pretty good!'

Avery's attempts to allay her fears were not wasted on Emma and she was grateful for his easy, unobtrusive conversation.

'Tell me,' he said, once they were airborne and climbing steadily to their planned altitude of ten thousand feet, 'are you related to a Lieutenant Commander Tremayne who commands the Tresco-based Special Forces coastal flotilla? Yours, if I may say, is a pretty uncommon name and you and he are the only Tremaynes I've ever met.'

Already inclined to slip into giving her well-rehearsed cover name – Giselle Trenet – Emma paused for the briefest of moments before replying, 'Yes, he is my husband. I believe you flew him from RAF Netheravon to St Mary's.'

Glad of Avery's reassuring company, Emma struggled to keep her mind in gear for her forthcoming meeting with the members of Jedburgh team at her destination, just outside the besieged port of Lorient and in an area recently secured by the French Resistance. She checked the contents of her handbag for the umpteenth time – especially the details of her impeccably forged identity card, confirming her to be Madame Giselle Trenet (widow), twenty-five years of age and a Clerk (Technical) employed on the large civilian staff at the naval base in Lorient. She found her Benzedrine tablets to help her remain awake and shuddered as her hand touched the rubber-coated cyanide suicide pill – necessary if captured and unable to face the prospect of torture under interrogation. For a moment, hideous unreality engulfed her.

At three minutes to midnight, the Lysander touched down at the makeshift airstrip close to the port. Avery shook Emma's hand and smiled, transferring some of his relaxed confidence to her. 'Good to have the pleasure of your company, Emma. I hope I'm the lucky one to take you back home. Do please give my regards to your husband – he's one helluva guy!'

The reception party waiting on the runway consisted of three members of the Jedburgh team and a young woman from the local French Resistance.

'Hello, Emma, it's good to meet you.' The voice was warm and welcoming and suggested Anglo-Irish origins. 'I'm Tim, the team leader, and my fellow 'Jeds' are François, a captain in the Free French Army and Bill, a lieutenant from a US Ranger battalion. Simone is from Lorient and is our invaluable courier. You and she will be working together quite a lot. By the way, we never use our surnames with one another and, from now on, please get used to being 'Giselle' and temporarily forget Emma Tremayne. Within a couple of days, it'll feel quite natural, I promise you!'

Taking Emma's holdall, Tim led the way to a heavily armed jeep festooned, SAS-style, with a Browning .50 calibre heavy machine gun of awesome firepower firing forward and twin .303 drum-fed Vickers 'K' machine guns pointing ominously aft.

'I'm afraid it will be a bit cramped and a pretty bouncy ride, but at least it's better than walking,' apologised Tim with an amiable grin. 'We'll take you to our secure base in liberated France for a welcoming glass of very drinkable plonk, and then you can get a good night's sleep before we put you in the picture tomorrow morning.'

Already, Emma could feel herself beginning to feel at home with the team and more at ease with herself. Her principal concern now was how Richard must be feeling about what, for him, would have been such a sudden and completely unforeseen turn of events.

Over the promised glass of a quite respectable *vin ordinaire*, Emma was able to get to know her new colleagues. Tim, of medium yet muscular build with dark curling hair, was a major in the 5th Royal Inniskilling Dragoon Guards – 'The Skins'.

His family had gone over to Ireland with Cromwell and had long been part of the old, so-called Protestant Ascendancy – 'for too bloody long' as he had put it. 'Ireland is for the Irish – not we 'blow-ins' – but how I do love that fair country with all its wonderful idiosyncrasies.'

The engaging soft lilt in his voice effectively masked his dedicated, professional approach to soldiering – especially to the role and work of Special Forces. 'Our regimental motto,' he added, largely for Emma's benefit, 'is *'Vestiga nulla retrorsum'* – we don't retreat.' An experienced soldier and saboteur, he was also completely fluent in German – a language which lent itself well to his naturally authoritative demeanour.

François, small, compact and wiry, had served as a senior NCO in the Chasseurs Alpins – the French specialist mountain troops nicknamed Les Diables Bleus, before he escaped from Vichy France to England to join De Gaulle's Free French Army. There he had taken a commission and had been rapidly promoted to captain. His regiment – the 99th – traced its proud lineage back to the Régiment de Royal Deux-Ponts, which led the successful attack on the British and Hessian redoubts in the Franco-American victory at Yorktown in 1781.

He was, like Tim, an explosives expert and fully trained underwater swimmer – among many other skills. François was also a versatile practical man, seemingly able to turn his hands to almost anything involving technical or commonsense ingenuity. He acted as the Jedburgh team's unofficial motor mechanic, treating their jeep with loving care and a pride of possession as if it were his very own.

Bill, the US Ranger officer, was tall, lean and athletically built with slow, deliberate speech and a deceptively relaxed and easy-going manner. His fair hair had been allowed to grow out from its crew cut to give him a less obviously 'American' appearance. Loose-limbed and supple, Bill was a natural for scaling apparently impossible rock faces, tall buildings and man-made structures that other, lesser mortals would leave strictly alone. Like the other two, he was a crack shot with most infantry weapons and, like François, an awesome adversary with a fighting knife in his hand. The only one of the team who was not a first-rate linguist, he had, as he put it, learned to 'grunt' his way through conversations with foreigners – 'including you British' he said to Emma, his face deadpan apart from a teasing glint in his eyes.

Later, sharing a small room with twin bunk beds with Simone, Emma got to know much more about the French girl. Slim, like Emma, and of similar small bone structure, she had fashionably cut short fair hair and, as Emma noted, most intelligent brown eyes. They were of a similar age with many shared interests. Simone's husband had served in the French airforce at the outset of the war. He had been shot down around the time of Dunkirk and she had heard no more of him. She still did not know whether he had been killed or taken prisoner and shipped off to Germany as slave labour.

'I have never given up hope,' she said, barely above a whisper through her tears, 'that one day, he *will* come home to me.'

To bring Emma quickly up to speed, they spoke nothing but French together with Simone using every opportunity to call Emma 'Giselle'.

'So, Giselle, I notice how you pronounce, for example, the word 'aujourd'hui' as 'arjardhui' which marks you out straight away to the French as someone likely to come from rural Picardie or Artois. Your cover story, I know, is that you were born and lived the early part of your life in the Vaud region of Switzerland, which would account for other slight differences in your accent. I suggest that we add some years spent in Picardie to your history where, we'll say, your father was involved in the silk-weaving business somewhere near St Quentin – for example, Vadencourt. That would lend a subtle ring of authenticity to your varied pedigree! By the way, your Swiss passport could be your saviour if captured. Don't lose it!'

Simone laughed – a merry, bubbling sound like a rushing Highland mountain burn, thought Emma wistfully, joining in the laughter.

The next day, life as a secret service agent began in earnest for Emma.

'We need you to develop, as quickly as you can, a feel for both the territory in which we operate and your role in it,' said Tim at his early morning 'O' Group briefing.

'Our friends in the Resistance, with the help of Simone, will get you from here, through the Germans' defensive lines, to one of our safe houses in what's left of the residential area of Keroman, the harbour district where most of the German U-boat pens are located. There you will establish your base where there is, of course, already a short-wave radio. Your task, Giselle, will be to meet with, get to know and coordinate the espionage and sabotage activities of the FFI Resistance members – with us and a dissident Communist Resistance faction. The Commies are anxious to have a go at Jerry and, unless we involve them pdq, there's every chance that they'll go it alone and, possibly, go off at half cock. They don't lack guts and they can be damned cunning saboteurs, but they do lack the patience to plan what we see as having to be a thoroughly prepared operation. We can, of course, ignore them and simply go ahead with just the FFI but, for many reasons, I would rather collaborate with them and have their support.'

'Is it possible that we could use them to conduct a major diversionary attack, while the other groups combine to place the explosives on the targets?' ventured Emma.

'Hmmm, while politically that could be fraught, it does have possibilities. I'd like to keep that one in reserve and think about how we could convince the Communists that such a role was central to the operation. Thank you for that, Giselle.'

Tim acknowledged with a nod two newcomers who had just entered the room.

'You will be given detailed maps and a list of Resistance members, with instructions on how to contact them – all using the codes you were taught to use at Milton Hall. It is vital that you do not take any of this information around with you –

except in your head. There are no hiding places in the safe houses you will occupy that can be guaranteed one hundred per cent so all written material must be kept here in Allied territory.'

Tim stopped and looked closely at Emma.

'Clear so far, Giselle?'

'Yes, thank you. So far so good.'

'Do you have any questions? Are there any points of clarification?'

'At this stage, no thank you. I really want to get a feel for the situation at first hand as quickly as I can.'

'Fine, Giselle. Now let me introduce you to our two new arrivals. They know your husband extremely well and will be working on our patch – but on a very different operation from ours. If anyone can lead you into trouble, these two villains will! The plug-ugly one is Major Mike Black of the SAS and the good-looking one is the recently promoted Sergeant Major Paddy Nugent – also from that dubious band of Hereford cut-throats.'

As the two SAS soldiers shook her hand, bombarding her with questions about Tremayne and asking her to pass on their warmest regards to him, she began to feel more confident, in their enthusiastic company, about what lay ahead. Their relationship with her husband and his oft-expressed affection and respect for them, gave Emma a more personal and tangible reassurance. Here was a direct link to Richard and, therefore, from him back to her.

Tim motioned Simone over. 'The bikes have been stashed in the jeep. Bill will run you and Giselle down to just above Pont-Scorff.' He glanced at Emma. 'That, Giselle, is where the German-held territory begins, immediately to the north of Lorient. Simone will show you one of the less dangerous ways through their lines and down into what's left of the residential area and to one of the safe houses we have there. This is one of the routes that you will take when you go in on your own. Resistance members will be around, though you won't see them.'

Emma felt her heart pumping as an overwhelming sense of terror and a desperate need to flee gripped her. For a moment she froze. As if in a dream, she heard herself saying, 'Fine, Tim. Thank you. I'll take my lead from Simone and follow what she does.' Yet there seemed to be neither connection nor congruence between the terror she felt at that moment and the words she uttered. It was unreal, as if she was in some sort of trance, looking down on herself from above. She knew that she must, as a matter of urgency, break out of the numbing detachment that threatened to immobilise her and start functioning again.

As unobtrusively as she could, she took several deep breaths and climbed into the jeep behind Bill and next to Simone. Seeing Emma's sudden death-white pallor, Simone smiled and took her hand. 'It will get better, Emma. The first time is always like this. Just stay close to me and you'll see just how easy it really is. Now, I must start calling you 'Giselle' again.'

When the jeep stopped, in the shelter of some derelict, bombed houses that marked the start of no-man's-land, the girls unloaded their bicycles. With Simone leading, they pushed their bikes alongside a tall hedge that skirted a large field.

'This area is patrolled by the Maquisards to deny the Boche its use and we really won't meet any Germans until we pass through that village over there, which is about a kilometre away.' Simone pointed to what was little more than a hamlet of mainly damaged houses and a church. 'They are very wary of the Maquisards who take no prisoners here since the Ouradour-sur-Glane massacre by the SS. They don't just capture them and execute them – they normally torture them first, *then* kill them.' She looked knowingly and quite unapologetically at Emma.

'We'll see them manning checkpoints and defensive positions as we begin to move into the outskirts of Lorient, which is really where the Boche's cantonment begins. Make sure that your wedding ring is on the correct finger as I showed you last night and have your identity papers handy. Remember, your airman husband was killed over Dunkirk. Until you get used to meeting Germans, leave the talking to me, Giselle. But, if you are questioned, remember your cover story that we agreed last night. Don't forget,' added Simone with a comforting smile on her face, 'you are Scottish – and a Fraser at that. Forrit the tartan!'

Emma, caught unawares by hearing General Sir Colin Campbell's passionate exhortation to his High Command, burst out laughing. 'That's a marvellous boost to my confidence, Simone. Wherever did you learn that?'

'Oh, in some history book somewhere when I was reading about the British at war in the Crimea and India.'

They began to pedal as they emerged from the field and moved towards the village. Passing through that and apparently chatting and laughing light-heartedly, they began to see the first of the ring of German fortifications. Seeing the enemy at close quarters is always something to concentrate the mind – and for Emma it was just that. The ugly coal-scuttle helmets, the menacing field-grey uniforms and silent, arrogant scrutiny sent a cold shudder through her body.

'Keep laughing and chatting, Giselle,' said Simone, a smile still playing around her generous mouth.

'Relax your body. Nod to them, if you will, but don't wave except to return the gesture – and even then, do it discreetly and casually. Act as if you have been used to the bastards – as I have – for the last five years. They're probably mentally undressing us right now. Just take them for granted, Giselle – like horse droppings on the road!'

Emma giggled at the analogy. '*That* has put them into perspective, Simone!' Her breathing was steadying again and she knew that her brain was back in gear and functioning once more. She smiled to herself as she recalled the other part of Sir Colin Campbell's famous demand of his superior: 'Let ma ain lads at them!'

Entering Keroman and the district bordering the dock area, they were stopped at their first roadblock and checkpoint – two guards and a black, white and red counter-balanced steel swing pole straddling the road.

'Just follow me, Giselle. Watch what I do and listen carefully to what I say. But be casual and polite,' whispered Simone. They dismounted from their cycles, identification papers at the ready. The guards were youthful Kriegsmarine sailors and, according to their cap ribbons, from a U-boat flotilla – not Feld-Gendarmerie* or SS.

'So, what have we *here*, Franzi? Two *beautiful* young ladies looking for two lonely sailors like us! Aha, ladies, your luck's in!'

Their French was passable, but their harsh pronunciation murdered that beautiful language.

'Your papers, please, ladies.' Emma felt the sailors' eyes were far more on Simone and her than on their ID papers. The younger one, Franzi, gauchely attempted a quick, fumbled kiss from Simone who looked him straight in the eye, responding in German, 'Nein, nein! Matrosen nicht! Andere Städchen, andere Mädchen!'**

Both seamen burst out laughing and gave a mock salute before they raised the hooped barrier, painted in the German national colours, and cheerfully waved them through, still roaring with laughter and making ribald comments.

'My first test,' said Emma, as she and Simone cycled clear of the checkpoint, 'and curiously, I felt okay – just a bit apprehensive. The Feld-Gendarmerie, though, would be a

---

*German Military Police who frequently manned roadblocks and checkpoints

**'No, no! No sailors! Other towns, other girls!' – a phrase used to suggest philandering, especially amongst sailors in seaports

very different matter. Those two were both nice lads and such typical sailors.'

'They were the damned Boche, Giselle, and that says it all,' grimaced Simone without a trace of a smile on her serene face, her delicate Renoir complexion now flushed with anger.

Minutes later, cycling slowly through the maze of streets and countless houses destroyed in air raids, they reached an area where there were several buildings – damaged but still standing and inhabited. These were mostly small business properties such as ships chandlers, engineering repair workshops and producers of small ferrous and non-ferrous castings and the like – all associated with the servicing and repair of boats, ships and small dockyard equipment.

Simone whispered, 'Stop here and look casual and relaxed.'

Emma followed Simone as she nonchalantly dismounted and wheeled her bike through a covered entry between two of the terraced brick buildings to an ancient wooden door, covered in peeling, dark green paint, which served as the main entrance to a third adjoining building.

Producing a rusting steel key, Simone opened the deliberately unlubricated old lock, which responded with a series of tortured, metallic squeaks, and pushed her bike inside, signalling Emma to follow.

There was a pervasive dank, musty smell suggesting dry rot and, due to the small windows, the place was dark – until Simone pulled together the obligatory blackout curtains, even though it was early morning, and switched on the lights. The kindest thing that Emma could say about the room was that it was clean and comfortably furnished. A small forge and built-in workshop, reminiscent of the old Black Country nail-making factories, occupied an area at the back of the building. A selection of metalwork hand tools lay on the worn top of an ancient engineering work bench. Bags of furnace coke were piled into one corner, while built onto the wall behind the still warm forge was a large, solid elm set of well-worn shelves, backed with planking of the same timber and standing about seven feet high. Scattered on the shelves were more small hand tools, used tins of paint, an oil can and sets of protective gloves, along with forge tongs and a pair of brass-trimmed bellows of indeterminate age.

'We keep the forge operating, Giselle, to show the Boche that this is a working business in constant use. Occasionally, Kriegsmarine engineers and French technicians working at the naval base call here for small repair jobs.'

'Is there another way out if a nosey German patrol decides to come searching for any of us – or are we like rats in a barrel?' asked Emma.

'To German eyes, and to those of any French employees of the Boche, there is absolutely *no* other exit!' Simone's emphatic response puzzled Emma.

'But, Giselle, look again at that old set of shelves. Permanently built onto the wall? Mais non, rien du tout! See the three large, rusty iron hooks screwed to the side panel of the shelves with forge fire irons hanging from them?'

'Yes, of course!'

Despite her curiosity, Emma wondered just where all the mystery and drama were leading.

'Now, Giselle, grab the middle hook and twist it towards you – use some strength!'

Using both hands, Emma twisted the hook as ordered and then gasped as the complete shelf unit, including the planked elm backing, swung open to reveal a flight of old, well-used stone steps leading down into a long passageway beneath the building.

'Good grief, Simone, wherever does it lead?'

'Switch the lights on and you'll see. It's an old smugglers' escape route for shifting contraband goods and escaping from Revenue Officers, which dates from early in the last century. It was wired up for electricity about five years ago when war looked inevitable and it also has a water supply laid on, as you are about to see.'

Emma clambered down the steep, worn steps and discovered an area off to the right – about twelve feet by eighteen feet – with a sink and cold-water tap, a small table, four chairs and two single mattresses on the floor, placed to one side. A compact short-wave radio stood on a wide shelf, secured to the wall by steel brackets. Beyond a tiny enclosed lavatory at the end of the open space, the brick-lined passage continued, tunnel-like, for at least a further fifty feet. Set in the end wall of the passage was a small wooden door. Turning the wrought iron door handle, Emma suddenly found herself in the yard and entry of a derelict house, damaged in one of the many Allied air raids on Lorient. A good deal of rubble and badly burned architectural timber still lay around, adding to the abandoned feel of the place.

'That was a bit of luck that the bombs hit this house and not the one you use,' said Emma.

'Exactly! Now look carefully at the set of elm plant-pot shelves, which, though about thirty centimetres lower, mirror the tool shelves that you opened in the old forge. Ingenious, isn't it? To open this one – if you come into the safe house via the back way – you just grab this support bracket under the middle shelf, twist it and pull hard. And voila! It is connected to the wrought iron door handle inside. As Tim said, not one hundred per cent secure but, so far, it has served us well.'

'Who knows about this passageway, Simone?'

'Obviously all the Jeds and the two SAS guys, escaped PoWs and Allied aircrew shot down and picked up by us when they were on the run. Oh – and two of the FFI members who have used it on operations – Maurice and Pascal.'

'But none of the Communists you want me to liaise with and bring into the fold are aware of this secret passage?'

'No, certainly not.'

'Then I suggest we keep it that way, Simone. Meetings that I will need to set up will have to be in the main house and forge, but the passageway and escape routes must remain a secret. The fewer who know about them the better.'

'Agreed. There is a telephone in the main building for making contact, Giselle, but I would strongly advise that you use the short-wave radio as little as possible and then only in very short transmissions. The Boche use radio-detector vans frequently and the Resistance — and SOE — have lost several good people located and picked up this way. Individual soldiers, from detection teams of the Abwehr, also walk around the area with portable receivers and aerials concealed under their uniforms and an earpiece hidden by their helmets. They've even used female Milice officers, disguised as mothers pushing prams around the area, with receivers hidden under the blankets and pillows. Telephone calls are also regularly monitored and they too can be traced to the source. In lots of these old terraced properties there are shared, central fuse boxes. While the operator is still transmitting, the Germans remove the fuses one by one. Then, voila, if the transmission stops, they know in which of the connected houses the operator is located. So, Giselle, to counter that, the Resistance — including us — have started to use car batteries for our wireless sets, which we recharge ourselves!'

'Even so, I take the point about using the radio and telephone as little as possible — and then only in short transmissions, using the 'covers' that I have been given, especially as I shall be using the same location more than once.'

Simone lightly touched Emma's arm, 'Giselle, we are going to cycle back now. I want you to lead and be the first to be stopped and questioned by the guards manning the checkpoints. Today, we do it together. Tomorrow, you will travel on your own, but I will join you here later. You will also be met here by a Resistance member, probably Maurice, who will light the forge and make a few small forgings as part of your cover. You will be acting as secretary to what passes as a two-man business. I will give you two telephone numbers, which you must commit to memory. One is that of the Communist Resistance leader – code-named 'Philippe'; the other is that of the Jedburgh team's HQ where you will sleep again tonight.

Stopped by a different pair of guards, this time unsmiling members of the Wehrmacht, Emma carried off the encounter well, without raising any suspicions and exuding an appropriate air of resignation that such irksome intrusions on her life were inevitable and unavoidable.

Back at the 'Jed' base, she was congratulated and debriefed by Tim. 'You've passed your critical first-day test with flying colours, Giselle. Well done – we are all delighted!'

That night, Emma lay wide awake, desperately trying to sleep, her thoughts wrestling with the terrifying prospect of tomorrow – and how she longed to be back safely with Richard and Catriona. How impossibly far away England – and especially Tresco – seemed, with its inviting, emerald waters and haven-like tranquillity. That was not just another country – it was another world…

Twelve

Mayhem In Parallel

he German submarine pens at St Nazaire and Lorient have withstood countless Allied air raids and remain impregnable. The damage inflicted in the costly, but successful raid by British commandos on St Nazaire docks in Operation Chariot has been repaired and the U-boat pens are back in use once more,' explained Enever at his pre-operational boat captains' briefing. 'Our intelligence is pretty well bang up to date, gentlemen.'

Enever let down the large rolled-up map of Brittany on the wall behind his desk and looked around at the serious attentive faces.

'As you all well know, the intention is that containment, rather than destruction, is to be the fate of these ports. They are far too strongly defended to be taken in set-piece siege operations without prohibitive cost – in men, equipment and time. Since the pens sheltering numerous U-boats and E-boats remain indestructible from the air – and a seaborne assault would be suicidal – we are going to rely on other means to destroy at least some of the boats lurking in them. At the moment, I'm not able to say much about that, but I will put you in the picture just as soon as I can.'

Enever deliberately avoided Tremayne's sharpened interest in his reference to 'other means', but suspected that his flotilla commander was already putting two and two together and seeing Emma's hand – and head – involved in the 'alternative' strategies.

He continued: 'The Royal Navy are in force in the Bay of Biscay to try to corral as many of the U-boats and E-boats as possible and both the Fleet Air Arm and RAF Coastal Command are also playing a major part in their containment – and destruction. Nevertheless, some are still getting through into waters used by us to ferry fresh troops and supplies to the battle zones in France and they continue to sink our ships with considerable loss of life.'

He paused for a moment to smile reassuringly at Tremayne before continuing, 'As the war in France moves inexorably towards the frontiers of the Reich and the Germans are thrown increasingly onto the defensive, our attacking role will diminish – except as a response to specific and what will be largely isolated threats. What we will be increasingly called upon to do, gentlemen, is to bring back our agents from France – and elsewhere in Europe. They will remain a major priority for us until *all* of them are safely home.'

Enever paused to ring the push-button bell on his desk for coffee. Tremayne, he noticed, was already beginning to look somewhat less tense and drawn.

'Now to our other immediate priority. We have been tasked with facilitating the escape to the West of key German scientists and other important figures – especially experts in submarine and rocket technology – before they fall into Soviet hands. I say 'escape', gentlemen, but, initially, our role will most certainly be that of 'body snatchers'. In such a role, we most certainly have Admiral Hembury's approval and blessing!'

Enever looked up to gauge the reaction to his comments, noting one or two raised eyebrows and puzzled looks.

'That may sound intensely disloyal to our Russian allies but there is already considerable disquiet within Intelligence circles over what will shortly become our post-war relationship with the Soviet Union. Pressure is also coming from US Intelligence sources for the British to be more guarded on the immediate post-war appropriation of key German scientists and technological resources. Of particular concern to us – and the Yanks – are the latest impressive German advances in U-boat 'Schnorkel' technology. This crucial area of research, with its long-term implications for developing the new generation of submarines, is a prize we do *not* want to go to the Russians. On that point, Admiral Hembury is quite uncompromising. Soviet submarine technology is already well advanced and, post-war, could begin to steam ahead of ours. We also know that they intend to expand their submarine fleet dramatically, with the aim of operating underwater, in force, throughout the Mediterranean. Once established there, another route to the Atlantic and our waters is theirs.' Enever stopped as the young Communications Branch Wren came in with coffee.

'Bless you, Jane. Dehydration and, in some cases,' he said looking around him, 'last gasps for want of liquid, were perilously close!'

Indicating to the boat captains to 'seize a brew', Enever took up his story again.

'Largely, I suspect, as a result of Dönitz's devastating U-boat strategies, large, powerful, long-range submarines will become the capital ships of the future as the increasing vulnerability of battleships renders them obsolete. As recently as July of this year, Soviet Special Forces frogmen discovered a supply of T-5 Zaunkönig acoustic torpedoes aboard a sunken German U-boat, the U-250. While there are, admittedly, some indications that they *will* share the scientific secrets of these weapons with us, we know that they are anxious to develop their own submarine technology from captured German sources. We, gentlemen, must do the same, with the assistance – willing or otherwise – of Jerry's best U-boat scientists.'

Enever looked around the room, gratified by the absorbed

attention of his audience. Once more, he saw raised eyebrows and surprised looks exchanged by some of those present.

'Two leading U-boat specialist scientists are located near the Keroman submarine base at Lorient, trapped there in the besieged German pocket, albeit currently well out of reach of the Soviets. From the latest Resistance intelligence, it appears that their quarters and experimental workshops and laboratories are close to the Villa Kerillon – the so-called Chateau des Sardines – the building formerly occupied by Admiral Dönitz at Kernevel, by Larmor-Plage. Naturally, these are heavily guarded and they cannot be snatched from there.

Latest intelligence from our SAS team, operating with their French counterparts in and around Lorient, is that plans are believed to have been made to fly these two scientists back to Germany by means of a Kriegsmarine Naval Air Service flying boat. What we don't yet know is from where *exactly* in Lorient – and when. Since no airfields are available to the Germans within their enclave, they can only exit by air from the sea's surface. Most likely, therefore, the flying boat will be that good old standby of the German Air Sea Rescue Service – a Dornier 24.'

Enever briefly checked the time on his wristwatch.

'We have learned, however, that their transfer is likely to take place within the next few days. If we lose them from under our noses in Brittany, the devil knows where the hell they'll end up. But I'll lay odds that the Soviets will go flat out to capture them using Special Forces snatch squads, once they move further east to German naval bases at Kiel, Cuxhaven or Flensburg.'

'Do you already have a preferred method of snatch and extraction?' asked Tremayne, 'and do we have photos and details of the two guys we intend to grab?'

'For this operation, I also intend to use the latest captured E-boat, which Admiral Hembury has borrowed, on our behalf, from the Coastal Forces flotilla at Lowestoft. British MTBs would simply be blown out of the water on sight by the overwhelming German coastal and harbour defences. I may also involve, as back up and as a possible decoy, one of our disguised fishing boats, probably the *Monique*, but I'm still thinking it through,' said Enever.

'In answer to your second question, Richard, here are copies of photos of our two would-be victims – Professor Joachim Piening and Doktor Ingenieur Rolf Schepke. The two scientists – and as much of their research data as we can grab – are our objective and the operation will take place under cover of darkness. The details still have to be worked out, but Flight Lieutenant Dick Pritchard from the St Mary's squadron will join us as the much needed pilot. He's had previous Coastal Command experience on Catalina flying boats and has a working knowledge of the Dornier 24. The SAS snatch squad will consist of Mike Black and Paddy Nugent and probably a captain of the French Special Air Service. Your role, Richard, will be to act as guard boat and to lend firepower – and whatever other support may be needed by the body snatchers to facilitate their seizure of the two scientists and to make their escape from wherever within the vast Lorient harbour area – but more of that later.'

Tremayne and the others looked with considerable interest at the pictures of the two German scientists, taking in details of their appearance, turnout and bearing. Professor Piening was tall and slim with receding, unkempt, long white hair. His equally white goatee beard, piercing, intelligent pale eyes, preoccupied expression and pronounced stoop, marked him out as the archetypal aged academic. Tremayne guessed that he was probably in his early sixties.

Dr Ing Schepke was a burly, grim-faced individual with a florid complexion, tightly clamped lips and thick, straight black hair. Considerably younger than the professor, he was clean-shaven and possessed some of the hardest, most unforgiving eyes that Tremayne had ever seen. Enever had told him that the two complemented one another in terms of the marriage of scientific theory and the practical testing and proving of hypotheses. Piening's capacity to conceptualise, crystallise and model ideas was matched by Schepke's ability to turn abstract theory into workable know-how and – ultimately – into 'do-how' and some of the tangible advances that marked U-boat technology as among the best in the world.

Clearly, together, they formed a formidable and enviable resource that British Intelligence was most anxious to seize before the Russians did. The scientific synergy possessed by Piening and Schepke for developing ever more threatening technological advances in submarine warfare, was viewed by the more desperate elements of the Oberkommando der Marine as on a par with the creation of Hitler's latest 'vengeance weapons' – the V1 and V2.

Unknown to Tremayne – deliberately so – the snatch, though a critical operation in its own right, was also intended to serve as a major diversion to the sabotage operations concurrently being engineered by Emma, the Jedburgh team and local French Resistance. Partly aimed at deflecting German counter-espionage resources away from following up the planned covert attacks on the U-boats at Keroman, SIS and SOE were collaboratively orchestrating their activities to throw the penned-in German garrison of Lorient into confusion and panic as they were hit simultaneously on two very different fronts.

To confound the defenders even more, Enever had organised an aerial bombing and rocket attack on their outer-dock naval installations around Port-Louis and Larmor-Plage. These lay at the entrance to the estuary leading to the nearby U-boat pens at Keroman, and the attack was timed to coincide with both the seizure of the two scientists and the detonation of the limpet charges placed on the submarines. Ideal for a tactical strike, the aircraft – making what was to be a diversionary, low-level, hit-and-run raid – were de Havilland Mosquitoes. Capable of almost four hundred miles per hour and armed with 20mm cannon, rockets, or high-explosive bombs, they were scheduled to swoop in in two separate waves, creating maximum mayhem, noise and panic, and then fly out again as quickly as they had appeared on the scene. Timing of their appearance and accuracy in the placing of their bombs and rockets were of critical importance to the safety of both the saboteurs and snatch squads at work below them. Five night-fighter Mosquitos, the Mk XIX variant, temporarily attached to RAF Bolt Head, were to accompany the attacking aircraft to act as protection for the bombers and rocket-carrying planes.

SOE had signalled Tim – Emma's controller and leader of the Jedburgh team – in code, by radio, to stand by to synchronise their destructive sabotage in the U-boat pens with the other planned operations – within days rather than weeks.

=====O=====

As a consequence of the joint SOE-SIS planned escalation of operations in and around Lorient, Emma had been forced to move much more quickly than expected in gaining the confidence of the local Communist Maquisards. Visiting her 'office' at Keroman irregularly but in ones and twos, posing as would-be buyers and salesmen to allay suspicion, they had progressively – but quickly – come to trust her open, no-nonsense and transparently honest approach. As, apparently, a Swiss national from the Vaud region, she had unashamedly traded on her adopted rural origins and peasant family background, which had helped to dispel any associations with the despised 'bourgeoisie' for the Communists. Her innate sensitivity and perceptiveness helped her to engage readily with the left-wing Resistance members on their terms and in ways which naturally echoed their culture and backgrounds, rather than her own. Sooner than expected, she had also managed to build a reassuringly positive working relationship with Philippe, the key figure in the Communist Resistance group, based upon mutual respect and personal regard.

Though, initially, he had argued and disagreed over issues of ideology, Emma had skilfully focused their meetings on sabotage tactics and the operation at hand and deliberately avoided becoming enmeshed in arguments over doctrinaire politics. The very authenticity of her commitment to the team's task objectives and her undoubted trustworthiness – allied to her tactical competence – had won over the fiery Communist leader who had given her the nickname 'Comrade Guguss', a reference to the straight-talking, satirical journal from the Vaud region of Switzerland.

Maurice, a local FFI man and member of her support team, who convincingly carried off the cover role of forge master, was frequently to be seen shaping hot metal components at the blacksmith's hearth. He came across naturally as a man of the people, relating as a fellow worker to the visiting Communist Resistance members, reinforcing the 'comradely' political tone of their collaboration with the Jedburgh team.

Emma's toughest challenge had been to persuade the Communists – especially Philippe – to accept the supporting role of neutralising the guards around the U-boat pens and inner harbour, to allow the saboteurs to place limpet mines, unhindered, on the submarines' hulls. She had eventually succeeded after a good deal of persuading, cajoling and hard-nosed horse trading, whereby their part in the sabotage would be given high-profile prominence in the press reports that would follow the action. Published acclaim would appear both in liberated France and within the German enclave, despite Emma's cautionary note about giving away too much confidential information and the risk of reprisals within occupied Lorient and further south in St Nazaire.

Pascal, the other FFI Frenchman attached to the Jedburgh team, rarely appeared due to often unexplained 'other commitments'. Whenever he did, Emma felt a disturbing sense of unease in his presence, especially when Maurice or the other team members were not around. Though she instinctively recognised that there was something of the sexual predator in the man and that he made her flesh creep, there was, she sensed, also a more sinister, thinly veiled air of menace about Pascal. His behaviour strongly suggested that he didn't see himself as part of a dedicated team and, for much of the time, he acted as a loner who deliberately pursued his own private agenda.

Little seemed to be known about his background, other than that he had served for a time in the hated Milice in Vichy France, but had deserted and joined the ranks of the FFI. Tim had picked him up during an operation in the mountains of Haute Savoie, when a Jedburgh team had fought alongside the SAS and their French counterparts and defeated a combined

Gebirgsjäger and Milice unit. FFI stragglers, including Pascal, had appeared on the scene towards the end of the engagement, joined in the battle and then, when the action was over, left with the Allied troops. Something about Pascal just did not add up. The more Emma thought about it, the more she began to realise that her feelings of intense disquiet stemmed from her growing belief that the man was inherently evil. Not wishing to make a fool of herself by appearing too primly 'British' or prissy in Simone's eyes, she had not mentioned the matter to the French girl. What her sixth sense told her, however, was that if real harm were to befall her, Pascal would somehow be involved. She also had a gut feeling that, as a matter of urgency, she needed to broach the issue – initially at least – with Simone rather than Tim.

At HMS Godolphin, Enever was engaged in regular telephone contact with Admiral Hembury and both SOE and SIS, pulling together the linked sequential steps of the snatch and coordination of that complex operation with the sabotage of the U-boats and the diversionary Mosquito air raid. Daily, he telephoned or radioed Mike Black in Brittany for the latest intelligence on the planned departure to Germany of the two scientists, and particularly for up-to-date details of the arrival of the Dornier flying boat to take them out of Lorient. Through

Tim, the leader of the Jedburgh team, he managed to establish a radio link which allowed an overjoyed and much relieved Tremayne to speak with Emma on one of her frequent returns to the Jeds' HQ in the liberated zone outside Lorient. He was aware of the unsettling effect – as well as the reassurance – that such contact could generate, but he was anxious to allay Tremayne's concerns about Emma's dangerous role whenever she crossed into the German occupied enclave on her meetings with the local Resistance.

Tremayne knew that his radio conversations with Emma would be monitored by German wireless-intercept operators, so they talked about her cover role as 'NAAFI canteen manageress' and his as 'victualling officer' responsible for supplying Allied canteens in Brittany. For the purposes of their overheard conversations, Catriona had become his 'secretary and assistant'. To allow for any slips of spontaneous affection, or concern for safety, they deliberately gave their dialogues the flavour of a hot, clandestine affair which, Tremayne could tell, greatly amused Emma. She, for her part, consciously exaggerated her Scots accent, from softly spoken West Highlands lilt to broad Glaswegian dialect, so that wireless-intercept operators monitoring her short transmissions from Lorient docks would not recognise any modulations or tonal similarities in the two voices. Not for the first time in their relationship had they been grateful for Emma's ability as a mimic. Deliberately, she had not raised the issue of her fear of Pascal with Richard.

Some twenty-four hours later, Enever received the signal he was expecting from Mike Black. In code, the message read: *'Rare species of bird will migrate 01.15 hours, two days' time. Point of departure — love's beach. Don't be late, sweetheart. Three green ones will do.'*

Enever decoded the signal, grinning at the words 'love's beach' — and Black's ingenious phonetic licence.

Tremayne joined him in Hut 101 shortly afterwards.

'So, Richard, the snatch is to be from Larmor-Plage. Recognition signal will be three green flashes from you to him. The date will be October 10th.'

Enever began searching for his pipe among the papers on his desk and found it with an audible grunt of pleasure and relief.

'Using our new E-boat, you will RV at sea with Mike, Paddy and Guy — the French SAS captain — off Pointe du Talut, two miles west of Larmor-Plage, at exactly midnight. They will be in a small fishing boat approximately one mile off shore. Remember the signals. Our fishing boat *Monique*, skippered by Pierre Quilghini — who is now recovered from his wounds, will also be there to act as escort to the SAS team's little fishing boat. Just ignore her unless there's a major hitch. You will then proceed with the E-boat, as if on Kriegsmarine local coastal patrol, to Larmor-Plage to locate the Dornier. David Willoughby-Brown, with his fluent German, will hail the Dornier aircrew and explain that you have vital intelligence from OKM in St Nazaire, which *must* go with the two scientists to Germany. Get WB, Mike, Guy and Paddy onto the sponson of the Dornier as quickly and as quietly as possible. Each will carry a silenced pistol. Your task, Richard, is to secure that aircraft and its two passengers and ensure it gets on its way to England asap. Mike's latest intelligence is that the two scientists will be brought to the flying boat by a Kriegsmarine harbour launch at around 01.00 hours for their 01.15 departure. I suggest that you explain your unexpected presence to them using the vital intelligence stratagem, but use your fertile imagination and initiative as circumstances dictate. You will also need to transfer Dick Pritchard, the RAF pilot, from your boat to the Dornier.'

'Will we need any recognition signals for the Mosquitoes when they launch their attack?'

'I think not. They have been told of your presence and role, but three green signal flashes to them would be dangerous. The risk of using those is that, if they are seen from shore, collusion will be suspected and you are likely to be fired upon by the massive coastal defence artillery. At such point-blank range, you run the very obvious danger of being blown out of the water.'

The following day, Tremayne checked the fuelling, provisioning and arming of the Lowestoft E-boat, rocking gently on her mooring warps at Braiden Rock anchorage. Like others that he had commanded, she was of the S100 series – a sleek, purposeful looking craft, capable of a consistent forty-two knots and up to forty-six knots in short bursts of rapid acceleration. Her original 20mm bow gun had been replaced by a heavier

37mm weapon, while amidships she carried twin 20mm high-angle Hispano-Suiza cannon. Towards her stern, but mounted forrard of her mine and depth-charge chutes, was a 40mm Swedish Bofors quick-firer. She also carried two torpedo tubes and a variety of 7.92mm MG42s. Her pennant number, wheelhouse flotilla insignia and mottled blue-grey-brown camouflage identified her as a vessel from a St Nazaire-based S-Bootflotille. Flying proudly, yet somewhat incongruously, from her jackstaff was the Royal Navy's white ensign.

Twenty-four hours later on a chilly autumn evening, shrouded in a thick, damp sea mist, she quietly slipped her moorings, moving slowly through the shallows of Tresco Flats, her powerful diesels turning over with a low, effortless rumble. Once in The Road, with St Mary's on her port beam, Tremayne ordered 'All engines, full speed ahead'. They were on course for Lorient…

Thanks to Emma's personal influence and skilful persistence, the Jedburgh team had finally secured the collaborative support – albeit with some reluctance – of the Communist Resistance faction. They had eventually agreed to take care of the German sentries, guarding one major unit of U-boat pens, while Tim and François – wearing shallow-water divers' dry suits and swim-fins with closed-circuit breathing apparatus

— swam into the pens and placed their explosive charges. Bill, the US Ranger officer, would act as liaison man with Philippe's Communists to ensure optimum synchronisation of their elimination of the guards with the progress around the U-boat pens of the two frogmen. Latest intelligence, orchestrated by Emma, confirmed that there would be six U-boats in the pens targeted for the operation that were likely to remain there for at least a week.

In the time since she had arrived in Brittany, Emma had made close to a dozen daily visits to her 'office' in the dockyard area. With her customary sensitivity and awareness, she had developed both the skills — and more importantly, the mindset — to enable her to deal with the German guards at the roadblocks covering the approaches to the harbour. At her most comfortable with the naval sentries, she engaged in limited banter with them, though deliberately never beyond the point of casual clichéd conversation and the exchange of friendly greetings. With Wehrmacht troops — and especially when confronted by the more questioning members of the Feldgendarmerie — she adopted a polite, matter-of-fact approach, but never one which was so 'professional' or slick as to betray her SOE training.

On the day the sabotage operation was due to take place, she found herself both more alert and less relaxed than usual. Her heart was pounding as she approached the black, white and red-banded swing pole of the barrier. This time, the guards were Feldgendarmerie soldiers, the aluminium gorgets suspended around their necks proclaiming their identity. With them was an officer from the dreaded Milice. Though French, the Milice had an unenviable record of betrayal, torture and murder of their own countrymen, in collaboration with the German forces of occupation. The Milicien looked up as she drew near and said ominously, his hand raised to indicate that she should stop immediately, 'I've been told about you, madame. I want to talk to you.'

Panic gripped Emma. She braked nervously, more sharply than usual, and almost stumbled as she came to a sudden halt. Dismounting from her bicycle at the roadblock, her hand trembled uncontrollably as she fumbled in the handbag slung around her neck for her identity papers. She gripped the handlebars of her bike tightly with her other hand to steady herself. After two weeks of constant use, with daily correction by Simone, her already fluent French had matured dramatically. At a signal from one of the German military policemen, the Milicien stepped forward.

'You've been reported to us as a newcomer here. Who are you? What is your business here, so close to the docks? Where have you come from? Why?'

Deliberately designed to faze her and throw her off guard, the barrage of questions, fired off like a machine gun, triggered her intensive training at Milton Hall as she fought to control her rising terror. Handing over her pass and still steadying her body by hanging on tightly to her bicycle, she replied with a calmness in her voice that surprised her.

'I am Giselle Trenet, aged twenty-five. I am a wid—'

'I can see that. I can read, damn you, woman. We want to know exactly who you *really* are.' His smile was ice cold. 'Perhaps you should come with me to the Gendarmerie for a little talk.'

Desperately struggling to fight the paralysing fear that threatened to overwhelm her, she managed to say — without her voice breaking and giving away her disintegrating control — 'Certainly. As you wish, monsieur. Perhaps you would also like to see the office where I work, it is only about two hundred metres from here.'

Emma's apparently calm and factual response caught the Milicien by surprise. Whatever he may have suspected of 'Madame Trenet' — or hoped his questioning and her terror of the brutal reputation of the Milice might have uncovered — slowly began to evaporate as he looked searchingly into the steady, unblinking blue eyes.

Changing his tack, but pursuing his goal of disconcerting her, he asked, 'You are a widow, I see. How did your husband die?'

Momentarily caught unawares, she suddenly recalled Simone's apparent widowhood, drawing upon her story.

'He was a pilot in the Armée de l'Air and was shot down near Dunkirk, along with several other airmen.'

A look of triumph crossed the Milicien's ferret-like features as he framed a question aimed at exploding her composure.

'What aircraft was he flying when he was shot down?'

Fortuitously, Simone had volunteered what, at the time,

had seemed to Emma like unnecessary detail. She would be eternally grateful for that apparently superfluous piece of intelligence.

'Morane-Saulnier 406. Why do you ask, monsieur?'

'I ask the questions here. You answer them. Understood?'

'Of course, monsieur.'

'Now, on your way. We'll call at your office another day for a further little chat.'

The cold eyes bored into her as if scanning every recess and cranny of her mind.

Trying not to show the unbounded relief that she felt, Emma deliberately climbed back onto her bicycle unhurriedly and firmly pushed down on the pedals, heading for the street where her office was. Badly shaken by the encounter, she struggled to get her head together again as she moved off.

The sudden harsh shout cut through her faltering attempts to regain a sense of normality.

'Madame, Halt! Come back here!'

Utter despair gripped her. She shook with terror as she dismounted and turned to walk towards the Milicien and military policemen who stood silently staring at her, machine pistols cradled menacingly across their folded arms.

'You will need this if you don't want to find yourself arrested as a member of the Resistance. A careless mistake like that could cost you dearly!'

A sneering smile distorted the bloodless slit that passed as his mouth, as the Milicien held out her identity card which, in her confusion and terror, she had forgotten to take back from him.

'Thank you, monsieur. That *was* stupid of me.' What Emma hoped would sound a confidently apologetic response came over as mumbled and barely audible as she took back her pass, mounted her bicycle once more and rode away, perspiring with fear…

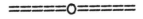

Lifting their Cockle Mk2 two-man canoe out of the ancient Renault van that was parked along the lower, open reaches of the Blavet estuary, Tim and François – already wearing their dry suits and shallow-water breathing apparatus – slid the rigid canvas boat into the cold black waters. They had slipped across the German perimeter defences in the dark, on foot, carrying their swim-fins in their hands. Once across the defence line, in thickly wooded country, they had rendezvoused with two Communist Maquisards who had driven through the back lanes in the van, organised by Emma working closely with Philippe's group. The van also contained their Bergen rucksacks, loaded with explosive limpet mines – sufficient for four charges per submarine. Each charge weighed four pounds, giving both swimmers around fifty pounds to carry. Apart from their commando fighting knives, both carried silenced Browning pistols in waterproof wrappings.

After synchronising their watches with the two Maquisards, Tim and François stashed their heavy Bergens into the canoe's stowage spaces, scrambled into their seats, unshipped their double-bladed paddles and pushed off. Until the time came to cross the estuary, when they would be at their most vulnerable, they hugged the shoreline south of the Pen-Mané headland, paddling silently in unison. Bill — the third Jedburgh team member, together with Philippe and the rest of the group, would be waiting for them across the estuary, close to the target, ready to signal them in once the German guards were being dealt with.

At Keroman, hidden in a dockside fuel dump, were Philippe and eight of his men, dressed in the uniforms of the Milice. Posing as additional sentries, seconded to assist the German naval personnel already standing guard over the two pens holding the six U-boats, they would appear on the cue of two flashes of a red light from Bill, lying up close to the shore and awaiting the swimmer-canoeists. Splitting into three groups, they would eliminate the guards and take over as sentries. As well as their Milice MAS36 machine pistols they each carried a British commando Fairbairn-Sykes fighting knife — by anyone's reckoning a lethally efficient weapon at close quarters. By 23.45 hours, the cloudy sky and drizzling rain of an already black moonless night were thankfully keeping visibility down to a reasonable minimum for the raiding parties. The swimmer-canoeists' major fear was that, despite the intense darkness, a particularly alert guard using binoculars might just pick up their presence during the paddle across to Keroman.

Luckily for them, it was Bill, searching the surface of the water in front of him, who eventually spotted the barely visible phosphorescent bow-wave of the solitary canoe at 23.53. Immediately, he signalled Philippe and his group to begin their hideous slaughter of the sentries. He then repeated the same signal to Tim and François to paddle ashore – their progress marked by more telltale phosphorescence, glistening dull silver, as their double-bladed paddles dug into the calm, black water of the estuary.

Guided by Bill, they paddled the last fifty yards or so, close to the entrance of the first U-boat pen, where they stowed their canoe on a small stony beach. Removing the explosive charges from their Bergens, they set the timers for detonation at 01.15 hours and carefully transferred them into converted canoe buoyancy bags. These rubberised, waterproof containers were connected by a cord line to their divers' weight belts – now devoid of lead weights – so that as the two swimmer-canoeists took to the water, the attached bags swung below and behind them. Donning their facemasks and connecting their oxygen supply, they slid into the icy, uninviting water. Silently, they slipped beneath the gently lapping waves and swam round into the huge, reinforced-concrete U-boat pen, just as the first sentries fell to the knives of the Maquisards, who began to replace them as guards. The butchery had begun.

Entering the first U-boat pen, the two swimmers found three boats moored alongside one another with just about enough room for a frogman to manoeuvre between them. Previous intelligence, via Emma, had already confirmed that it would be impossible to squeeze even a boat with a beam as narrow as the twenty-eight-and-a-half inch breadth of a Cockle Mk2 between the submarines' hulls. The U-boats were all Type VIIs, carrying up to fourteen torpedoes, stowed well forrard of the conning tower. Emma had also informed the Jedburgh team that the boats were fully armed and ready to go to sea. The two swimmer-canoeists laboriously placed one limpet charge against each side of every U-boat, about six feet below the surface of the water and right on the outer casing of the hull where the torpedo store was situated. A further two charges were also magnetically clamped one each side of the boats, aft, outside their engine compartments.

The hollow clang of metal being attached to metal by the limpet mines' strong magnets gave the two in the water some anxious moments and, briefly surfacing, they looked to see if any U-boat crew members were emerging on deck to investigate the noise. After a wait of several anxious minutes, none appeared.

Swimming round to the second pen, they discovered, as Emma had reported, a large ocean-going Type IXB U-boat, equipped with up to twenty-two torpedoes. Moored alongside her were two more Type VII boats. Dragging their now considerably lightened buoyancy bags of charges behind them, they had just completed clamping limpet charges to the large boat's hull, when the forrard hatch opened and three ratings, led by a petty officer, scrambled out and up onto the deck. Just below the surface of the water, Tim and François were horrified to see the sudden appearance of several powerful torchlights being directed down along the sides of the U-boat's hull, shining down onto the surface of the black, oily sea above their heads.

They could be discovered at any moment. Urgently tapping François's shoulder, Tim indicated that they needed to move immediately round to the cover of the U-boat moored alongside and wait. Any violent action at this stage could trigger a general alarm – something they needed to avoid with around forty-five minutes still to go before the charges were due to blow. Swimming slowly to minimise surface disturbance of the water and confident that their oxygen would create no betraying bubbles to mark their passage, they silently slipped away.

For what seemed an eternity, the two divers watched anxiously from their cover as the German sailors, leaning precariously over the sides of their boat, slowly and carefully swung their torches back and forth over the length of her hull. Tim looked at his watch. Those forty-five minutes preceding the explosions would reduce drastically, limiting their opportunities to complete their task, if the Germans remained on deck for much longer. A further ten, very tense, minutes passed when suddenly they heard a surprised shout – 'Ach, Scheiss!'

One of the Germans had dropped his torch into the gently swelling water, its rapidly fading light mocking him as it sank out of sight. A burst of laughter followed the curse and, after unmercifully ribbing the unfortunate seaman, the party clambered back down the U-boat's companionway, closing the hatch after them. Eventually, with only twenty minutes to go before their charges were due to detonate, the two frogmen completed their task and swam quickly back to their canoe, to paddle away and gain protection from the blasts of their charges and the exploding torpedoes. Both were only too aware from their training with the Royal Marines of the obscene effects on human tissue of underwater explosions.

They paddled flat out for the temporary security of a small, low-lying island, situated roughly halfway between Keroman and the Pen Mané headland, located opposite one another in the Blavet estuary. Tim checked his watch, his paddle resting for a moment on the canoe's wooden cockpit coaming. The air raid by the Mosquitoes was also now only fifteen minutes away. The aircraft would be heading straight for the nearby naval installations and HQ buildings and their attack would provide the cover that Tim and François needed to paddle on to their planned return destination just beyond Pen Mané. There, concealed in the coastal woodland, was the waiting Communist Maquisard driver and ancient Renault getaway van – organised, after much persuasive negotiation, by Emma.

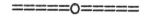

Following her harrowing encounter with the Milice officer and Feldgendarmerie military policemen, Emma returned to her office, to Maurice and to the final pre-ops meeting she had instigated and set up with Philippe and his team. At her insistence, they went over the critical sequence and details of the operation several times, until she was satisfied that the more maverick elements of the group would stick to the agreed plan – unless unforeseen circumstances genuinely forced them to do otherwise and use their initiative for the survival of the group. They knew, from SOE transmissions, of the diversionary air raid which, like the Jedburgh swimmer-canoeists, they too would use as a cover for their getaway and escape back to their various boltholes – not all of which were in the liberated zone.

Before the meeting finally broke up, they celebrated the forthcoming operation with a marvellous gourmet supper of *langoustines rôties sur une tarte fine d'oignon blanc* – prepared by one of the team who was a restaurateur in east Lorient. Philippe, with a knowing grin, provided four bottles of a very worthy *vin de pays d'Oc* as an accompaniment. Held up at the local checkpoint, luckily by young sailors, he had readily declared the wine – saying it was to celebrate the wiping out by the Milice and Wehrmacht of a group of Communist Maquisard bastards in neighbouring St Nazaire. Having bountifully handed the sailors a fifth bottle to share in the celebration of that fictitious triumph, he left them, somewhat bemused, vowing 'eternal brotherhood' and 'death to all Communists!' and went cycling on his way, whistling happily.

Pascal joined the group in time for the end of supper, having just returned, he claimed, from a local FFI telephone wire cutting operation, close to the German defensive perimeter to the west of the enclave.

Philippe checked his watch and announced that it was time to go. Pascal, who had not been told what was planned – as he was FFI and because the Maquisards were only too aware of his former Milice background, asked where they were going and what was happening.

'We're off back to our homes, mon ami. Today was the wrong one for any activity,' lied Philippe with a meaningful glance at Emma, who caught it and nodded almost imperceptibly in response.

Maurice left with the others, leaving Emma alone with Pascal. Draining the dregs of one of the *vin d'Oc* bottles into his glass, he leered at Emma.

'Well, Giselle – if that *is* your name, how cosy this is. Just the two of us, eh?'

He pulled a vicious-looking Service stiletto from under his jumper and began ostentatiously peeling an apple. All the time he looked at Emma, his face an obscene, twisted mask and said, his voice full of controlled menace, 'I think you and I should have a nice, quiet little talk, eh? And you can tell me who you really are. My friend in the Milice is very interested to know all about you. He told me he spoke to you at the checkpoint today…'

At 23.45 hours, Tremayne was cruising slowly eastwards,

two miles off Pointe du Talut near Lorient, his E-boat's three
Daimler-Benz diesels turning over at quarter revolutions with
their low distinctive rumble. Beside him, on the cramped bridge,
stood David Willoughby-Brown, Petty Officer Bill Irvine and
Leading Yeoman of Signals 'Yorky' Rayner who had joined the
crew as Taff Jenkins's replacement. Apart from the coxswain,
whose eyes rarely left the sea ahead or the gyrocompass directly
in front of him, all the others were using binoculars to scan
the invisible horizon and the sea around them for any sign
of *Monique* and the small fishing boat carrying the SAS snatch
squad. Below, catching up on his sleep in the mess deck, was
Dick Pritchard, who was to pilot the Dornier and its precious
cargo home to England.

Tremayne, knowing that Emma was somewhere close by
on the occupied mainland of southern Brittany, fought to retain
his concentration on the mission. Many times during the night
crossing from Tresco, his thoughts had inevitably turned to her.
As always, one of Leading Seaman 'Pablo' Watkins' adenoidal
musical renditions – followed by the inevitable mug of rum-
laced kye as only Watkins could make it – lifted his spirits.

'Yo 'm lookin' a bit peaky, sir, beggin' yer pardon, so I thought
as 'ow this might 'elp, sir,' he said, a look of genuine concern
on his amiable features.

'Thank you, Watkins – much appreciated! You know, you'd
make a better psychologist than Freud, Jung and Adler put
together!'

'Blimey, sir, *they* sound like a firm of bookies from up Alum

Rock!'

Tremayne thought it wiser not to risk asking what, or where, Alum Rock was.

With all weapons manned, the E-boat was closed up at defence stations. Visibility was particularly poor that night, although the sea was almost like a millpond. Yorky Rayner's disciplined concentration and sharp eyes were the first to see *Monique* and then the much smaller fishing boat that she was carefully shadowing, a cable's length ahead of her.

'Well done, Rayner. Well spotted.' Tremayne nodded and smiled at the serious, rather shy Yorkshireman.

'Make the signal to the smaller boat— three green flashes — and wait for their acknowledgement.'

'Aye aye, sir.'

The reply from the SAS team was almost instantaneous.

Tremayne nodded to Petty Officer Irvine, 'Take us alongside, Cox'n.'

Calling to the rating acting as gun-layer for the bow 37mm cannon, Tremayne shouted,

'O'Reilly, stand by to assist our guests. Lower scrambling nets. Secure their fishing boat and lash her astern. We're going to need her for the Dornier aircrew we take prisoner.'

Moments later, Black, Nugent and Captain Guy Duval were on board the E-boat, shaking hands with Tremayne and Willoughby-Brown.

Black smiled at Tremayne as he said, 'I've seen her Richard and she's in fine form. She's doing a great job over here. Nobody else I know could have won over those hard-bitten Communists like Emma has. Tim Galway, her controller, is full of admiration for her.'

'Thanks, Mike! That's good news indeed, but I promise you, I'll be so bloody glad when she's back home again.'

Tremayne nodded to Willoughby-Brown. 'David, join us please in the wardroom and let's go through the final details of the snatch, now that these villains have arrived.'

At 00.35, the E-boat moved off to Larmor-Plage, maintaining quarter revolutions, with the Île de Groix fine on her starboard beam. Tremayne was very conscious of the amount of artillery that, in an instant, could be triggered by radar signals from any one of several coastal batteries along the seaward edge of the German enclave on the mainland. He anxiously scanned the coast, some two miles off to port. Though Black was able to give him the current German challenge and response signals, Tremayne knew that their coastal defences randomly used secondary or back-up signals, which changed on a daily basis and of which Black had no up-to-date knowledge.

The darkness remained almost impenetrable and the visual boundary between sea and land was little more than an indistinct monotone blur. Then, suddenly, it was Leading Yeoman 'Yorky' Rayner's twenty-twenty night vision that again identified their quarry – the Dornier 24, moored off Larmor-Plage. The briefest sudden gleam of light from either the cockpit or, possibly, an opening passenger door, had caught his eye and, as he refocused his binoculars, he saw the vague outline of the flying boat.

Tremayne ordered 'Action stations! Port twenty, Cox'n. Full speed ahead!' and, in Irvine's steady hands, the E-boat swung her deeply flared bow and surged towards the Brittany coast and the estuary, flanked by Larmor-Plage and Port-Louis.

'We'll look as if we're on urgent legitimate business if we approach at maximum revs, gentlemen.'

Tremayne addressed the three SAS officers and his first lieutenant, now all crowded onto the bridge. Willoughby-Brown picked up the loudhailer to announce to the Dornier's crew that SS officers would be coming aboard the flying boat with vital intelligence to accompany the two scientists back to Germany. Carrying their silenced pistols, Black, Nugent and Duval would take the aircrew prisoner and secure the scientists in their seats, while Dick Pritchard would take over as pilot.

With impeccable timing, the first wave of Mosquitoes roared over Larmor-Plage and Port-Louis. Rocket and bomb explosions turned the quiet black night into a lethal fireworks display, just over half a mile to the north. Seconds later, more muffled but bigger explosions came from the Keroman U-boat pens as the limpet mines and on-board torpedoes detonated. The Mosquitoes turned for a follow-up strafing run, firing rockets into the submarine pens and dropping bombs on Keroman to confuse the Germans and delay their discovery of the real cause of the U-boats' destruction. Within minutes, the second wave of De Havilland fighter-bombers would be unloading their rockets and bombs onto the naval complex to add to the chaos, carnage and destruction.

Meanwhile, paddling furiously for the comparative safety of the shore – and the ancient Renault van waiting beyond Pen Mané, were Tim and François, cheering wildly as the world began to explode behind them.

With spray cascading over her bow, the E-boat rapidly decreased speed and engine noise to draw alongside the Dornier, conveying an impressive sense of urgency. A hatch and a door opened in the flying boat's hull and her captain shouted across to the figures he could now make out, crowding the E-boat's bridge and foredeck.

'You're in one hell of a hurry. What's wrong? What the devil is going on ashore? I thought that the damned RAF had decided to give up on Lorient. Don't hold me up now – we must move before we're bombed out of the water!'

Willoughby-Brown, wearing a Kriegsmarine officer's peaked cap, yelled back through his loudhailer, 'You're damned right. The RAF *are* back. We won't keep you – we don't want to be bombed either! I have SS and Kriegsmarine Abwehr officers on board with vital intelligence, to accompany Professor Piening and Dr Schepke back to the Fatherland. They must convey this urgent confidential material personally to the two scientists. Are they on board yet?'

'Yes – they're just settling in.'

At a whispered word of command from Tremayne, Able Seaman Young threw a line to the German airman who secured it round the flying boat's wing strut as Irvine slowly manoeuvred the E-boat close alongside. With pistols at the ready, the three SAS men sprang onto the plane's low, broad sponson, acting as a float on the sea's surface. Quickly recovering from the shock appearance of the enemy, the flying boat captain attempted to draw his own automatic from its holster, only to be laid clean out by Nugent's fist. Tremayne ordered his port machine gunner to traverse his twin Brownings menacingly at the Dornier's bow and dorsal machine-gun turrets while Sharpe, manning the midships Oerlikons, swung them round, threatening the aircraft's tail-gun position.

Black and Nugent, shouting and waving their pistols meaningfully, stormed aboard the Dornier. Duval remained standing on the sponson, directing the five emerging aircrew prisoners – their hands clasped firmly on their heads – to the removable gangway, which was secured to the E-boat's hull. They were met there by Tremayne, Willoughby-Brown and O'Reilly – all armed – and then directed aft. Under Pablo Watkins' appropriately baleful eyes and threatened by the business-like Lanchester he so obviously relished waving under their anxious noses, they were searched by Leading Telegraphist Rayner.

'What the bloody hell d' y' call this, Sunshine?' demanded Yorky Rayner as he extracted a Luftwaffe ceremonial dagger from beneath the flying boat bow-gunner's leather aircrew jacket. 'That'll look good on the wall over me mantelpiece. You don't find too many of these up in Middlesborough!'

After being searched, they were directed by ratings down a scrambling net and into the small Breton fishing boat lashed immediately astern. Though only a little over half a mile from the nearest point on the coast, but now with a strong swell running, Tremayne had ordered two full naval-issue water bottles to be put into the little boat's stowage locker. Her sails had been made ready to be unreefed and raised.

Addressing the five prisoners, still shocked by the sudden and dramatic turn of events, Willoughby-Brown said, 'We have little enough room on the Schnellboot, so we are turning you loose in this fishing boat to sail back to Larmor-Plage, which is about one kilometre away in that direction, gentlemen.' He pointed towards the still indistinct coast.

'We could, of course, make you swim or we *could* shoot you.' A look of terror crossed some of the startled faces staring up at him. 'But then, that wouldn't be 'weak, amateurish and British' now, would it?'

Clearly enjoying the airmen's discomfort and confusion, Willoughby-Brown closed with an engaging smile and threw the sailing boat's painter to one of the Luftwaffe men standing in the vessel's bow.

'On your way, gentlemen – and good luck! Thanks for the Dornier!'

On board the flying boat, Piening froze – his face a mask of shock as the SAS men burst into what served as the makeshift passenger area of the Dornier. He made a desperate, futile attempt to hide an expensive hide attaché case, just before

Nugent grabbed it from him. Passing the heavy case, which was bulging with documents, back to Duval, who had now moved into the pilot's cockpit with Pritchard, Nugent turned his attention to Schepke. Seemingly from nowhere, he had suddenly produced a Walther P38 and was pointing it at Black, who stood off, lowering his own automatic.

'You won't shoot me, gentlemen.' The voice was a contemptuous sneer. 'You want the professor and me alive. Now, both of you, stand together where I can see you. Return Professor Piening's papers at once, or I will shoot you.' He raised his pistol, pointing it directly at Black's head.

'It seems as if you've won, Dr Schepke. Well, at least we tried.' Black carefully placed his Browning automatic on the cabin floor.

Calling to Duval in the aircraft's cockpit and maintaining his disarming, conciliatory tone, Black said quietly, 'Guy, Dr Schepke has a pistol to my head, please bring the professor's briefcase back.'

Duval, trained and conditioned in the same stable, responded in an equally non-threatening manner.

'Okay, Mike. Hell, what a damned shame! Here, take it. Be careful, it's very heavy.'

'Cheers, Guy. You're right it *is* heavy. Whoops-a-daisy!'

Distracted, Schepke's attention switched to the attaché case falling to the floor, losing concentration on Black for one crucial second as the SAS man deliberately dropped the bag.

In an instant, Nugent leapt forward like a panther, seizing

Schepke's momentarily relaxed wrist. Grabbing the stubby barrel of the Walther with his other hand, he viciously wrenched Schepke's arm upwards, clear of everyone. Caught unawares, the German gasped in agony, releasing the weapon before he could squeeze the trigger. Nugent flung the Walther back to Duval and punched Schepke hard in the solar plexus. As the bear-like scientist started to collapse, badly winded, Nugent immediately hit him again with a savage hook to the jaw. The big man went down with a pitiful groan, struggling for breath as he lay doubled up on the floor. Professor Piening cowered in his seat, looking on in horror.

'Thanks Paddy – and Guy!' Black grinned ruefully at his colleagues. 'Must tell 'em back at Hereford – the training *does* work!'

Turning to Schepke, the quietness of his voice emphasising the intended menace, he said, 'I admire courage, but try that again, Dr Schepke, and I will really hurt you.'

Speaking to Nugent, he ordered, 'Tie 'em both up, Paddy – hands and feet.'

He then sent Duval to man the forrard turret's machine gun, while Nugent, after trussing up the prisoners, went aft to take over the powerful dorsal 20mm cannon.

'We'll have to leave the rear 7.92mm unmanned, while I look after the gruesome twosome and keep them out of Dick Pritchard's way. Calling to the RAF pilot, Black asked, 'Have you cracked it Dick? Are we ready to go?'

'Ready, willing and able, Mike. Mooring lines are slipped!'

Seconds later, the three BMW Bramo nine-cylinder, one thousand-horsepower engines spluttered, their props turning slowly, then roared into life.

'Thank heavens for German engineering,' laughed Black.

Opening the cabin door he yelled to Tremayne, 'We're off, Richard! Thanks for your help. Be seeing you – and Emma – back in Blighty *very* soon. Take care, old son!'

Tremayne waved back, wishing the SAS officer, 'Good luck and a safe journey!'

As he ordered, 'Take us home, Cox'n. All engines – full speed ahead!' he was cruelly reminded that he was deserting Emma and leaving her behind somewhere so frustratingly close by – and in a perilous, sinister world. The thought was unbearable but, despite the anguish he felt, he was grateful for Mike Black's reassuring words. Emma *would* be back soon. She *had* to be. Tremayne knew he had to believe that and cling on to the hope that, in a matter of days now, they would be together again.

He took some comfort from the fact that yet another snatch operation been successfully carried out, right under the Germans' noses. On the first occasion, just a few months ago, he had played a key role in seizing and bringing to justice a leading SS war criminal. This time, two crucially important scientists – and a great deal of vital technological intelligence, of incalculable value to future British naval strategy – had been seized and he had also played a major part in this operation.

Closed up at defence stations, the Kriegsmarine flag lowered and stowed and the white ensign hoisted once more, the Tresco flotilla E-boat headed for the Isles of Scilly.

Several hours later, the E-boat nosed its way into New Grimsby harbour on Tresco and the Braiden Rock anchorage.

An uncharacteristically subdued Enever waited for Tremayne and his crew at the top of the steep, rocky path leading up from the familiar, improvised jetty.

'Welcome back, dear boy, once again you've raised the reputation of the Tresco flotilla to new heights. The whole joint operation has been an unqualified triumph. I simply can't thank you enough for making possible the seizure of those two scientists and their invaluable knowledge and expertise.'

He paused and placed his hand on Tremayne's shoulder, his eyes full of concern. 'Richard, I'm so sorry. I have to tell you that Emma appears to have gone off our radar. She should have turned up more than eleven hours ago, back at the Jedburgh HQ in the liberated zone, but, so far, there has been no sign of her. We will do all in our power to find her.'

Thirteen

Tremayne's Nightmare

Emma fought to control the paralysing fear rising in her. Almost choked by it, she was scarcely able to breathe. Her heart was pounding like some frenetic internal hammer, completely beyond her control. Her mouth was dry and, for one helpless moment, she was unable to speak, to answer the sinister presence sitting so close to her, sadistically enjoying her obvious terror.

She cursed her decision not to carry a sidearm. Yet she knew that to be found with one would mean instant arrest, followed by brutal interrogation, torture and probably the most hideous form of execution. Though caught off-guard and near petrified by the sudden and horrifying turn of events, Emma knew that in order to survive and to keep both her mind and body intact, she must not allow Pascal's attempts to impose his will on her to succeed.

Slowly, as she struggled to regain control of herself, flashes of random recall of her training at Milton Hall and her instructor's stark words came back to her: '*Use feminine guile, ma'am. Move in close, feint to his crotch with your weaker hand and IMMEDIATELY jam two fingers in his eyes with your stronger hand. As his hands instinctively go to his face, knee or kick him, as hard as you can, in his testicles. If you have anything heavy to hand – a small rock, poker, bottle – anything, hit him on the head with it VERY hard. Then hit the bastard again, ma'am. Remove any weapons he has – and RUN!*'

The Marine Commando instructor's dispassionate way of describing how to cripple her fellow human beings had horrified Emma at the time. Right now, his calm, matter-of-fact coaching began to act like an emotional sheet anchor, steadying her disintegrating nerves. Slowly, she was starting to get her head together again as calculating reason began to take over from blind panic.

'So, herdsman's daughter from the Vaud's alpine pastures – if that's where you *do* come from – are you going to answer my questions? As my colleague Lucien from the Milice asked you this morning – *who* are you and *why* are you here?'

He edged even closer, his rancid breath making her shrink from him and want to vomit.

'Ah, so you're afraid of me, eh, pretty woman?'

'No – your breath stinks like a sewer.'

The sudden hard slap to her face shocked her for a moment, but she was now mentally in gear. Though the vicious blow stung, she was already in survival mode and thinking more clearly. She knew she *must* focus her thoughts on how to put this evil creature out of action and escape – using the training she had been given for such a situation. As a matter of urgency, she must find – or create – an opportunity to incapacitate Pascal and break his physical and psychological hold over her. Her very freedom and life depended upon that. She MUST get away, back to the safety of the Jedburgh base.

She also thought of Richard and Catriona – *they* were her reason to survive. Survival and escape were paramount. But how? She had demonstrated competence – and, just as important, confidence – during 'mat time' in unarmed-combat training. More of her instructor's words came back: '*If your life depends upon it, ma'am, you CAN'T afford to be nice. Remember! It's him or you, so cripple the bastard!*'

'Let's do this the easy way – the nice, *friendly* way, Giselle – I don't want to hurt you.' His soulless eyes frequently returned to the silk blouse stretched over her breasts, making her feel unclean. She felt contempt and a loathing for the man. Any attempt to rape her and she knew, at that moment, that she could kill him.

Her breathing was now steady and she felt a detached calm that she knew would give her the necessary 'steel' to do Pascal real harm in order to get away from him.

'What *is* this all about Pascal? What the hell is going on? You *know* who I am.'

'Oh, but that's just it, I don't – at least not all there is to know about you and who your controller is. Neither does my Milicien friend, who has been observing you coming and going for nearly two weeks now. You *are* a Resistance member. He suspected that was the case and now I know it for sure.'

Pascal looked at his watch.

'He'll be joining us in less than half an hour but, in the meantime, you and I can get to know each other a lot better.' Perspiration began to form around his top lip and, once again, her sensitive nostrils were assailed by his foul breath and, now, by his revolting body odour, brought on by his growing excitement. 'Oh, yes, Giselle, *very much* better.'

He moved across to the shelving unit and opened it, indicating the hidden stairway, before crossing the few feet back to the chair next to her.

Emma felt both revulsion and fear as Pascal's sickening intentions became all too apparent.

'We're going to complete the jigsaw puzzle about you and this viper's nest and you, pretty woman, are the one who is going to tell me and my friend all about this little set up.' Emma shuddered as his claw-like hand caressed her thigh.

His hooded eyes moved back to her breasts, a sickening leer crossing his face.

'My friend suggested we make this as enjoyable as possible and, when he arrives, we'll have a nice, exciting threesome together – you'll like that, now, won't you Giselle? I wonder if that will be a new experience for you, eh?'

Pascal reached out, groping Emma's thigh once more, grinning lasciviously as she recoiled, revolted.

He leered at her again – his twisted mouth alternately registering triumph and lust.

'We work by suspicion, gut feel – and by listening to rumours. When we can pin a rumour to a person or group we soon extract the truth from them. We have even impressed the Gestapo with our interrogation techniques.'

He stopped to check his watch again – 'Come on, Lucien, damn you. Hurry up!' – and stared meaningfully at Emma.

'So, Giselle, time for just you and me to have a little fun now, eh?'

Emma stood up and Pascal rose, mirroring her movement. The stench of him was overpowering.

'*Use feminine guile, ma'am. Move in close!*' Again, her instructor's vital words rang in her ears and Emma knew that it was now or never. Soon there would be two of them to deal with.

She slipped her left hand provocatively towards his crotch, trying to form her mouth into a seductive smile. As Pascal moved closer, in excited anticipation, she jammed two fingers of her right hand savagely into his eyes – once, twice in rapid succession. As he screamed in agony, she stood back and kicked him with all her strength in his crotch.

He shrieked, doubling up. 'You bitch, you bitch!' he gasped, clawing desperately at the excruciating, crippling pain in his genitals.

In desperation, she reached for one of the empty wine bottles left on the table. Quickly wrapping a tea towel around its neck to protect her hand, she brought it down with full force on his unprotected head. He moaned – an unearthly, unnerving sound – and collapsed on the floor near to the open secret stairway.

'*Hit the bastard again.*' Her commando instructor was still with her – in spirit at least. She hit Pascal a second time, smashing the bottle in pieces over his head. He lay silent, his skull a bloody mess. Shocked and horrified by what she had done, she stood back, shaking violently.

Fighting to restore control of her emotions, she forced herself back to the moment, focusing on the words: '*Remove any weapons. . . and RUN!*' Emma recoiled as she patted Pascal's jacket and felt his still body, before she discovered the hard bulk of a pistol. Reaching inside, she pulled out a Walther P38, 9mm German military sidearm and checked both the magazine and the action, as she had been trained to do at Milton Hall. In Pascal's left side pocket she found a full spare clip of eight rounds of ammunition. She felt in his other inside coat pocket and removed the wallet that contained his identity papers. Emma also took the bank notes that she found, knowing that money might mean the difference between freedom and capture, if help were needed while on the run before she reached the Allies' lines to the north of Lorient.

Still shaking from her ordeal, Emma alternately dragged

and pushed Pascal's inert body to the top of the stairs of the secret passageway. Luckily, though tall, he was of slight build but, even so, she found that the effort needed to move him to the top of the stairs and roll him down had left her trembling and exhausted. She swung the shelves back into place

and glanced at her watch. It was 11.20pm – less than two hours to go before the submarines were due to be blown up and the planned diversionary air raid would take place. It was now long after curfew and far too dangerous to move by bicycle through the streets of Keroman and the heavily guarded dock area.

Stupidly, she thought, she had neglected to check Pascal's pulse. If he were not dead, would he attempt to come back at her through the door she had just closed or would he escape through the back exit in the alleyway and raise the alarm? She considered the possibility of returning to the blood-covered mess lying in the cellar and putting a bullet through his head, but Emma knew that cold-blooded killing was beyond her. She could kill to defend herself in the terror of the moment were her own life at risk, but this was something way outside her moral boundaries.

She slipped the Walther into the pocket of her fashionably long coat, which she put on against the cold she was now feeling – due to shock as much as the autumnal temperature.

'Hot tea, lassie, with plenty of sugar!' she told herself, as common sense – as well as her survival training – kicked in. Minutes later, with a mug of steaming hot tea in her hand, she sat drained of energy on the chair she had occupied when Pascal had made his obscene advances. She shuddered as the recollection of the evening threatened to engulf her.

Sudden violent banging on the front door and a voice screaming 'Milice! Open up! OPEN THE DOOR!' brought her back to the present.

'Coming!' she shouted as confidently as she could, checking that the pistol was deep in her pocket and out of sight. She opened the door to the Milice officer who had questioned her at the checkpoint that morning.

'Good evening, monsieur. Please come in. How can I help you?'

For a moment, the Milicien was caught completely off guard by Emma's apparent matter-of-fact composure. He stared at her and said, 'Where the devil's Pascal? He told me he would be here too.'

'He called in about two hours ago. Then, I would think probably around an hour later, he left us – that is me, the forge operator and some customers – saying he had to meet someone, but I don't remember him mentioning whom. He did say that he might not be back. I'm only still here because I have to clear up after the customers finished supper. We'd put on a display to advertise and display some new forged products for ships' chandlers, you see.'

Emma felt her heart racing, waiting for the Milicien's next question and wondering how long he would stay before he finally gave up waiting.

The cold, suspicious eyes stared right through Emma.

'I find this very curious, Madame Trenet. Pascal and I had a firm appointment here for 11.30pm and Pascal is not the sort of man to fail to keep such a meeting without telephoning me first.'

Suddenly, the Milicien's eyes spotted the remains of the shattered bottle and patches of blood on the floor, just beyond where Emma stood.

'Mon Dieu, what the hell is that?'

Emma caught her breath. 'Oh, that. One of our customers drank rather too much and decided to treat us to a one-man cabaret. He tried dancing the can-can while juggling some of the wine bottles and fell over, smashing one of the bottles and cutting his hand badly.'

'Which doctor or hospital has he gone to?'

'Neither, monsieur. One of the other customers, who seemed to know a lot about first aid, helped me to clean and dress the cut. Soon after that, the party broke up and people went home before the ten o'clock curfew.'

The Milice officer looked again at Emma. 'I don't believe you. I think you are lying. You are coming to Milice headquarters with me. We'll get the truth out of you there, you little bitch.' He smiled – a chilling experience. 'And Pascal and I will have our fill of pleasure with you too.'

Emma casually put her hand in her pocket around the pistol's ridged butt.

He began to open the flap of his pistol holster as two 9mm

bullets from Emma's Walther hit him in the chest. For an instant he stared at her, his face a mask of utter disbelief, and then he crashed to the ground with a sharp gasp. Emma quickly removed his revolver – an old French Modèle 1892. She attempted to move him to the entrance to the secret passage but he was too heavy. His irregular breathing seemed to become more laboured and progressively fainter. For a moment, she looked down at him and burst into the flood of tears that she had been holding back since she had reduced Pascal's head to a bloodied mess less than half an hour before.

'Dear God, what have I done? What in heaven's name have I got myself into?' For some minutes, she sobbed uncontrollably, holding her head in her hands. The tears were followed by a complete draining of her feelings. All that she held dear suddenly seemed so impossibly far away and beyond her reach. It would be all too easy to give in to the trance-like inertia and overwhelming sense of numbness, where there were no more demands upon her.

It may have been her Highland spirit, underpinning the motto of her tough Fraser of Lovat upbringing – 'Je suis prest'*, or the thought of Richard with his strong sense of purpose and direction that forced her back into conscious decision and action. 'For heaven's sake, get moving lassie,' she muttered to herself.

She switched off the light and, very slowly, she carefully pulled aside the edge of one of the front window curtains just the merest fraction to survey the land outside. The street was

---

*Taken from the French, 'I am ready'

deserted. There were few hiding places in front of the house due to the number of bombed-out buildings, the rubble of some of them having been cleared away. In the darkness, she walked across to the other window and looked out. Once again, the street from that angle appeared empty.

Emma checked her watch — 00.05. The destruction of the U-boats and arrival of the Mosquitoes was an hour and ten minutes away.

Milice HQ — and most likely the Gestapo — would be aware of Pascal's role in infiltrating the Resistance house and of Lucien's follow-up visit. There was, therefore, the risk of German troops — or a squad of Miliciens — arriving before long to see why the two had not returned to base, complete with a female saboteur as their prisoner. Reopening the door to the secret passageway, Emma was relieved to see that Pascal was lying still, his breathing harsh and rough. With her pistol pointing at him, she cautiously eased her way past his inert body and carefully checked all the rooms for any incriminating papers or other signs of the Resistance members' presence. There were none. Tim's strict instructions had been carried out to the letter. She reclosed the doorway to the passageway and cellar.

She slipped outside into the short entry where she had parked her bicycle. It had gone — stolen or hidden, no doubt, by either Pascal or Lucien. She had considered riding a bicycle to be too dangerous after curfew. Being stopped at such an hour would mean immediate arrest and the inevitable consequences. On the one hand, a bike would have given her far more speed for getting away – especially in the dark and under cover of the forthcoming air raid – should she run into a street patrol. Walking and running, however, she could conceal herself more readily, but escape might not be so easy.

Looking up and down the street, Emma saw that all looked clear. Remaining in the shadows, she swapped the magazine in the Walther, now holding six bullets, for the fresh eight-round one in her pocket. She checked the action, made sure the safety catch was on and slid the pistol back inside her coat. She was grateful that Simone had reminded her to wear dark clothes, just in case she might be forced to travel late at night to return to the liberated zone.

The autumn night was cold, with a chill breeze blowing in off the sea. Emma tugged her beret down closer and wrapped her scarf more tightly around her neck. She carried her identity papers in the handbag slung across her chest. She moved off unhurriedly, keeping close to whatever walls remained, bending low to minimise her silhouette. Her rubber-soled shoes made no noise on the pavement. The only sounds cutting through the otherwise silent night were those of machinery associated with the repair, or constant movement of ships and boats in the vast natural harbour. The occasional curse rang out – in French as well as in German – as some unfortunate sailor or Breton dockyard matey on the night shift hammered his thumb or dropped some important piece of equipment whilst working on the U-boats around Keroman.

As she passed one group of dockyard buildings, shrouded

in darkness, a dog suddenly began to bark. Emma hurried on silently as a door was flung open and someone in uniform stood framed there, until the electric light behind him was quickly extinguished. A harsh German voice swore at the dog, which had been tethered outside. Luckily for Emma, the German, whoever he was, did not release the animal but cursed once again and went back inside the building. Just as she turned the corner of the road, where a new succession of bombed, terraced buildings began, she heard the measured tread of a foot patrol marching in her direction. In the darkness, she estimated they must be about a hundred yards away at the most. From what she could see, there appeared to be about six or seven of them. To go back around the corner, looking for cover behind her, would probably start the dog barking again. She felt panic rising as she desperately tried to find somewhere to hide without having to move forward towards the oncoming patrol.

Emma continued to hug walls and the stacked piles of rubble along the shattered road. Close to the remains of the destroyed house, she could just make out a section of neatly piled bricks and lumps of concrete with a narrow gap before the next orderly stack of debris. She wriggled her way through it, keeping her movements to a minimum, and pressed herself as close as she could to the remains of a wall that formed the inside of the irregularly shaped cavity. The stench was appalling. She had discovered, by chance, what was obviously one of the local, unofficial urinals. She felt around the stones, located a narrow recess to one side and tucked herself into it, concealed from the street.

The marching feet were right outside the gap between the remains of the houses when, to her horror, she heard the order 'Abteilung, halt!'* Seconds later, one of the German soldiers came in to relieve himself, farting noisily. He grunted with obvious satisfaction as he rebuttoned his flies, broke wind once more and strode out onto the road, back to his waiting colleagues.

They had obviously decided to take a prolonged break and were now leaning against the shattered remains of the house front wall, smoking and chatting. They stayed there for an agonising fifteen minutes, which seemed like an eternity to Emma. She heard a sudden movement and in came another soldier to use the unofficial loo.

Singing boisterously and off key, he vigorously splashed the wall close to her, his accompanying song being the popular Lale Andersen hit *Drei rote Rosen gab sie mir*'**. Rejoining his comrades at the roadside, his emergence from the improvised pissoir was greeted with hoots of raucous laughter. 'If that's *all* she gave you, Uwe, you're alright!'

The command 'Abteilung, vorwärts marsch!'*** came as a great relief to Emma and she slipped out of the stinking cavity into the fresh night air. Despite the earlier horror at the forge and the continuing danger of her flight back to the Jedburgh HQ, her sense of humour remained undiminished. She

---

* '*Squad, halt!*'
** '*Three red roses she gave to me*'
*** '*Squad, forward march!*'

smiled wryly to herself, as she mused, 'Richard, darling, you are just *not* going to believe it when I tell you what I have been through tonight. I reckon my King and country owe me!'

She estimated that she still had roughly a mile to travel to reach the indeterminate and dangerous enclave boundary area where the Resistance dominated the ground. Though a comparatively short distance away, most of her journey was through a heavily guarded, built-up district, teeming day and night with German naval and military personnel and with occasional members of the sinister Milice.

If stopped by any of these, Emma knew she would be in immediate and serious trouble. She had even considered posing as a streetwalker if stopped, but she remembered that – despite official warnings – they all operated within a confined area, swarming with potential clients, which could further limit her chances of making a run for it.

A very slowly and stealthily navigated five hundred yards further on, Emma came past the entrance to another narrow gap between neatly collected heaps of rubble. She stopped, retraced a couple of steps and crept in noiselessly between the carefully gathered piles of wreckage, her hand on the butt of the Walther in her coat pocket. The gap was empty and, fortunately, there was no stench of stale urine, which suggested no regular visitors.

There, too, Emma found several small hiding places tucked away, created by the stacking of irregular-sized lumps of stone, chunks of concrete and bricks – many of them fused together by the fires started by incendiary bombs. Emma looked at her watch and decided to make this her temporary base until the limpet mines and torpedoes were detonated by the Jedburgh frogmen and the rockets and bombs of the simultaneous air raid enabled her to move, in the ensuing mayhem. She estimated she now had about forty minutes to wait.

How she would love something as simple as a hot cup of tea – or a wee dram of her father's favourite Glen Rothes single malt! For a moment, she allowed herself the luxury of visualising the wild, primitive scenery of Sutherland and Wester Ross – and her Highland home. She was so glad that Richard shared her passion for the Highlands. She had teased him when he had attempted to speak Gaelic, finding himself in a terrible mess as he mangled the unfamiliar phonetic combinations of consonants and vowels that characterises the Celtic tongue. 'Give me French any day – it's such a beautiful language!' he had laughed.

'Oh, dearest Richard, where are *you* right now?' she murmured, as loneliness engulfed her in her bleak, cheerless hideout. She did her utmost to keep herself warm, jumping up and down and rubbing her limbs and body, but the cold penetrated her clothing, adding to her misery, as she waited for the fireworks to start.

At exactly 01.15, the limpet mines and torpedoes began to explode in the U-boat pens and she heard the welcome whining roar of Rolls Royce Merlin engines as the first wave of Mosquitoes raced in, firing their rockets and dropping high-explosive bombs around Port-Louis and Keroman.

'Time to go Emma,' she said to herself. Checking her pistol once again, she moved out into the night, now lit up with the bright orange-yellow flames of successive explosions. At such close quarters the din was deafening – and continuous. Above her, the detonating AA shells from the German 88s and 20mm Flakvierlings tore the black sky apart with repeated vivid flashes, seeking out the British fighter-bombers. A multitude of searchlights ineffectually probed the sky, searching for the marauders.

Lethal shrapnel fell onto the streets and buildings below from the countless airbursts, making movement in the open an even greater hazard. Emma ran through the streets, retracing her daily route by bicycle. Someone shouted something at her in German but she ignored the man and ran on, bracing herself for the shot intended to stop her flight. No shot came.

A group of sailors rushed past her, running in the opposite direction without giving her a second glance, clearly bent on some urgent task in the U-boat pens. Fine shards of hot shrapnel – most likely from the 20mm four-barrelled AA cannon shells – began to fall all around her and she dodged into a large arched doorway to shelter from what had been some perilously near misses.

'Mam'selle, tuck in here. You'll be safer with us.'

The voice was very authoritative and very German, although the French – apart from the mutilated pronunciation – was good. In that same instant, more shrapnel from the

Germans' massive anti-aircraft barrage fell clattering into the street in front of them.

Emma turned to thank the speaker and then froze in horror as she realised that he and his companion were senior NCOs in the military police. Both wore the distinctive aluminium gorgets around their necks and orange piping on their shoulder straps.

Recovering quickly, she said, 'Thank you, Mein Herr. I had to work late at my company tonight, to complete the paperwork for urgent orders for the Kriegsmarine. I need to be back there early in the morning and decided to risk the curfew to get home and snatch a few hours' sleep.'

'Ah, now which company would that be, Mam'selle and for what orders are you completing paperwork for our navy?'

Off the top of her head, she gave the name of one of the forge's competitors and identified the products as small components for E-boat power-operated gun mountings. Like her earlier response to the Milicien at the checkpoint when, in a moment of inspiration, she had plucked the name Morane-Saulnier out of her memory bank, she gratefully recalled Richard's enthusiastic references to power mountings with his boat's weapons. Though now very afraid, she felt that her response had a ring of authenticity about it.

The more senior of the Feldgendarmerie NCOs looked searchingly at her and replied,

'So-o. That sounds as if it might be important work, but

we'll check to make sure. When the raid finishes, you had better come with us and we will give you transport home – *if* your story is true, Mam'selle,' he added, continuing to scrutinise her face for any betrayal of her composure.

Emma felt sick at his offer, which would mean the end of her attempt to escape, but, despite her increasing fear, she managed a convincing, 'That is most kind. That really would be helpful, Mein Herr. I'm very tired now – it's been a long day and somebody has stolen my bicycle. A lift home would be wonderful – thank you.'

At that moment, his walkie-talkie crackled into life.

'Was? Ach, Scheiss! Zu Befehl!'* I must go, but my colleague will take you to our headquarters.'

He spoke rapidly to the other NCO and departed hurriedly, running in the direction of the U-boat pens. As he left, the second NCO turned to watched him go. Like his departing colleague, he was wearing his soft Service forage cap rather than his steel helmet. Drawing her pistol out of her pocket and holding it by the barrel, Emma smashed it down as hard as she could on the military policeman's head. As he collapsed with a grunt, she hit him again with all her strength. A surge of pure adrenaline gave concentration and a necessary edge to her thinking. She ran into the street and kicked a few of the still-hot shards of shrapnel close to the prone figure of the military policeman. With her foot, she pushed the largest of the jagged steel fragments into the pool of blood oozing from the wound in his head.

---

* *'What? Oh shit! As ordered!'*

'Let's hope whoever finds him thinks he's been hit by German shrapnel,' she murmured to herself and, checking that there was no one close by, she continued running along the street. The Mosquitoes' bombs began falling behind her with almost simultaneous explosions. They may not be doing much serious damage, she thought, but they were keeping people's heads down and under cover.

As if on cue, more Mosquitoes, paralleling her line of escape, roared in – pounding dockyard installations and German Admiralty buildings at Keroman and Port-Louis with rockets and cannon fire.

Then, with just half a mile to go, she saw her way blocked by a heavily manned German mobile AA battery of three lorry-mounted, four-barrelled Flakvierlings firing what seemed to be inexhaustible volumes of 20mm shells at the rapidly moving Moquitoes. At this end of the town, there were few buildings left standing and the only cover she could see was that afforded by countless loosely stacked piles of rubble on both sides of the road. The area looked completely desolate and uninviting.

Emma moved into the first of the bombsites and began working her way forward towards the AA battery. The ceaseless staccato banging of the anti-aircraft guns was deafening and the acrid stench of cordite pervaded the night air. More Mosquitoes came tearing in, flying, she guessed, at an altitude of little more than two hundred feet. At that height, the scream of so many Merlin engines – each of 1480 horsepower – was awesome. The very air seemed to vibrate. Emma found herself instinctively crouching low and ducking as she made her way through the debris of so many demolished buildings. Frequently, she stumbled and tripped over scattered bricks, lumps of concrete, jagged roof timbers and twisted steel joists. In this part of the town, closer to the German defensive perimeter, the tidying up of the bombsites had been far less thorough, due to the frequent deadly attentions of Maquis snipers and the deliberately irregular arrival of indiscriminately aimed mortar bombs.

It took her a further hour of stealthy scrambling – and alternate waiting and crawling to dodge the foot patrols – to reach the start of the woods and fields that marked no-man's-land and, beyond that, safety. Normally quiet, but with an underlying sense of menace and fear as Germans and Resistance troops probed and skirmished to reaffirm their respective territorial boundaries, the area was – at the best of times – a dangerous place to be.

That night, the perimeter area was full of Wehrmacht troops and Navy marine fusiliers, deployed to counter anticipated attacks by Allied ground forces under cover of the air raid.

Emma decided it was too risky to move forward any further. She eventually found a small clump of trees close to a low hedge, which offered reasonable shelter from the wind and any rain that might fall. Though movement by day would be risky, the number of Germans patrolling the perimeter made further progress towards Allied-held ground too dangerous.

She looked at her watch – it was 02.47. She snuggled down into the thick undergrowth, wrapping her clothes tightly around her and covering herself with small branches and foliage – prepared for a long, cold wait...

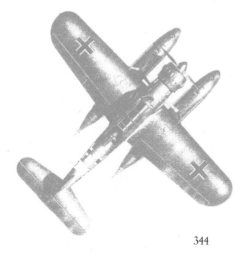

Fourteen

Heart Of Oak

Tremayne found it nigh on impossible to concentrate. He could not get Emma out of his mind. Where was she? Was she alright? Was she still alive? The thought that she might be in some Gestapo cell was beginning to eat into his very being. Yet both his training and his common sense told him that his salvation lay in close involvement in his work. In order to function, he knew he had to push such crippling thoughts out of his mind. People depended upon him. They looked to him to be an effective, committed flotilla leader and boat captain. He had assured Enever that he would let neither him down, nor his boat crews. To Tremayne, the keeping of a promise was sacrosanct.

Behind the scenes, Enever was in constant radio contact

with the Jedburgh team outside Lorient. Because of the frequency of transmissions between HMS Godolphin and Major Tim Galway, every communication was in code. Enever knew that any sudden rise in wireless traffic would alert German radio intercept monitors and result in an immediate major effort to break the code to find out what was afoot. If the code were cracked – and that could be a matter of hours, depending upon the resources deployed – a massive hunt to capture Emma would follow right away.

What he hoped, but was unsure of, was that the Abwehr had not yet broken the code that RN Intelligence was currently using. As late as 12.00 hours, there was still no news of Emma on the day following the successful operations at Larmor-Plage, Port-Louis and the Keroman U-boat pens. The destruction of six U-boats and the spiriting away of two top scientists would quickly be associated with the increased frequency of radio transmissions and attempts by British Intelligence to recover one of their own. That Emma was in the greatest of danger was not in doubt. Enever recognised that all too well. The fact that she had formerly been one of his protégées in Naval Intelligence served to increase his efforts to bring her out of the occupied enclave as a matter of extreme urgency.

By 12.35 hours, Enever learned to his horror from 'Y' Service-monitored German radio transmissions that the discovery of two critically injured Milice officers and a badly wounded Feld-Gendarmerie Oberwachtmeister had been linked to Emma. That connection added comparable urgency to the Germans' determination to capture one 'Giselle Trenet'. She now headed the local Gestapo 'wanted' list as a 'highly dangerous French female saboteur' who must be caught at all costs and of whom they had eyewitness descriptions. Despite the gravity of the situation, Enever was forced to smile – a mark of both his admiration and wonder.

'Heavens above, girl! What *have* you been up to? It sounds as if you've been leaving bodies all over Lorient!' he spoke out loud, seated alone at his desk.

Tim Galway assured Enever that he was rapidly organising both the FFI and Philippe's Communist Maquisards to monitor and secure escape routes for Emma through the German perimeter defences and into the liberated zone.

'Right now, Emma's 'channel to freedom' is receiving the same attention as that for France itself, as far as we're concerned,' said Tim, by telephone, to Enever. 'Effecting her escape is our top priority. We will do all we can to get Emma home, but at the moment the border area is swarming with the Boche. They're bloody edgy and shooting at anything that moves.'

Enever passed on the news to Tremayne, in a sensitively vetted form, emphasising the hopeful and positive aspects of the information that Tim Galway had given him.

'The intelligence that we've had this morning, Richard, from the Jedburgh team leader is that Emma put two Miliciens and a Feld-Gendarmerie Regimental Sergeant Major out of action – all of whom are going to feel very sore for a very long time. 'Y' Service operators are closely monitoring all German wireless transmissions in the area, which is largely where Tim Galway's up-to-date detailed information is coming from. What Tim tells me, too, is that Emma did an incredible job of winning the Communists over. Apparently, they have never before collaborated so wholeheartedly – and in a back-up role at that – in any other operation involving the FFI and a Jedburgh team. He's absolutely over the moon about what she has achieved in so short a time.'

Enever paused to look at Tremayne, his face registering concern as he sensed the anguish in the other man.

'One piece of good news in all this, Richard, is that SOE have aborted any action against St Nazaire, which was to have been the Jedburgh team's other main sphere of operations.'

'Thank you, John. As you must know, I'm immensely proud of Emma for what she's been doing and I –'

'As we all are – I can assure you, Richard.'

'I'm intrigued to know just what five feet four inches and nine and a half stone of young womanhood did to put three men out of action. This is an Emma I just don't know!'

Enever was relieved to see Tremayne's boyish grin return.

'Well, if you really must know, dear boy, she shot one, floored another with a wine bottle and bashed the military policeman over the head with the butt of the pistol she'd taken from a Milcien – or so the monitored German report tells us.'

'My godfathers! I can see I'll be spending the rest of our married life surrounded by bodyguards and terrified to be left alone with her!'

Once again, Enever was gratified to see Tremayne's sense of humour coming through his obvious deep concern about Emma. He knew, too, that the faster Tremayne was involved in a testing operation, together with the members of his crew, the better he would cope.

To that end, Enever had fortuitously received urgent intelligence from SOE, via Admiral Hembury, about an imminent German military mission and delivery of small arms to the Irish Republic for the IRA. As part of the Nazi strategy of using so-called 'vengeance weapons', along with the V1 and V2, the Abwehr had been directed to develop their existing contracts with the IRA to mount a campaign of organised terror on the British mainland. This was to be far more intensive and much more professionally coordinated, in order to achieve levels of destruction and disruption infinitely greater than the limited, though dangerous campaign of 1938/1939.

The IRA was only partially stood down and feelings were running high within Republican circles in the south over the issue of detainees held in Northern Ireland. German Intelligence, operating out of their Embassy in Dublin, had picked up on the strength of feeling and made plans to capitalise upon the emotion of patriotic fervour, as well as the deep sense of social injustice. Reading the situation well, German Intelligence had found a good deal of enthusiasm and support for a major campaign of terror on the mainland of Britain amongst past and present IRA members and associated political groups. Though the bombing campaign would be across the whole of Britain, the concentration would be principally upon England – the perceived archenemy of the IRA – and focused on cities and major towns.

Vital communications centres and essential public utilities such as water, gas and electricity would be among the prime targets, along with places where large numbers of the population were likely to be gathered including cinemas, theatres and football stadia.

Seizing the chance for some opportunistic horse trading, the Army Council of the IRA linked any organised commitment of their volunteers to a major bombing campaign, to a guaranteed supply of arms to the IRA to replace their rusting First World War British Army Lee Enfield rifles and 1920s 'Chicago Piano' Thompson sub-machine guns.

Because of the history of inexcusable British insensitivity and the brutal atrocities of the Black and Tans – especially the Auxiliaries – twenty or more years ago, still strong in the memories of people in and around the area, Cork was chosen to be the centre of operations. Commanders and Flying Column leaders of the old local IRA Brigades – such as Tom Barry –were still regarded as the great heroes of the fight for Irish freedom and had acquired cult status. Local eloquent martyrs to the cause of liberty – such as Terence MacSwiney and Tomás MacCurtáin – also lived on in the hearts and political consciousness of people in Ireland, but especially in County Cork. The Germans, in early discussions with senior IRA members, were also told that the government in Dublin would not wish to be linked either directly, or by implication in any way, with the indiscriminate slaughter of innocent civilians – especially women and children – on the mainland. On the complementary arguments of its recent bloody history and sheer realpolitik, it was therefore decided that Cork should become the centre of the German military mission's influence.

'How do the Germans plan to reach Cork and how many of them are in the military mission?' asked Tremayne.

'A mole planted in the Abwehr by SOE, who alerted us to the operation, confirmed that about a dozen Wehrmacht and Abwehr specialist advisors, together with explosives, five hundred Mauser rifles and two hundred MP40 sub-machine guns will be transported by U-boat – a large, ocean-going Type IXB. The submarine will anchor in Youghal Bay at 05.00 hours the day after tomorrow, just over twelve miles offshore and outside the territorial waters limit near to Cork City and its port of Cobh. There, she will RV with a large Irish crabber – the *Róisín Dubh* – the Black Rose to you, Richard – and transfer both the firearms and the members of the military mission. The crabber will then sail into Cobh – which is just about the largest natural safe harbour in Europe, if not the world – and land her cargo directly to the waiting IRA. Revenue and customs officers are not expected to be very much in evidence at that time of day – by order of the local IRA Brigade.'

Enever broke off his briefing as a Wren, from Signals Intelligence branch, brought in a snack lunch for him and Tremayne.

'Your task Richard, as flotilla commander, is to be there in time to intercept and seize the cargo and the German members of the military mission. Do not, on any account, engage the IRA in battle unless fired upon first. Of far more significance, do not get into a fight with the Irish Naval Service if it appears on the scene from its base on Haulbowline Island. They have six ex-RN Vosper MTBs and, like the U-boat, could blow you out of the water since you will be taking our fishing boats *Monique* and *Muguette*. In any case, Ireland is a neutral country and our role is not to push them into Jerry's welcoming arms. The ideal solution for us is that you capture these people outside Irish territorial waters and signal that you have them captive, giving your position over the radio for all the world to monitor. That may not stand up in an international court of law, but at least it's a start in demonstrating that we tried to preserve Ireland's neutrality. With your greater speed and the combined engine power of two hefty fishing boats, each much bigger than the *Róisin Dubh,* you should have little problem in shouldering her into international waters.'

'Sounds like two brutish front-row forwards bundling a diminutive scrum half into touch!' laughed Tremayne.

Enever's briefing continued for another hour, during which he and Tremayne talked through the detailed sequence and tactics of the stopping and boarding of the *Róisin Dubh* and seizure of her guests and cargo.

The biggest surprise was that *Monique* and *Muguette* would pose as Breton fishing vessels from liberated Brittany, trawling the rich waters off south-west Ireland. Both boats would be needed to accommodate the captured members of the German military mission. The plan was for the retrieved weapons to be dumped in the Irish Sea. Tremayne and Willoughby-Brown, together with Daniel Lejeune – a new Free French naval rating seconded from SOE – would be the French speakers on board the *Monique*. On *Muguette*, a much-recovered Lieutenant Quilghini, together with Able Seamen Philippe Harberer and André Duhamel, would affirm the 'Frenchness' of that boat. On board *Monique*, Tremayne would have Petty Officer Irvine, Petty Officer 'Derby' Allen as his engineer, Leading Rates Pablo Watkins and Yorky Rayner, together with Able Seamen Young and O'Hanlon. A newcomer to HMS Godolphin, O'Hanlon originally hailed from County Tipperary and was a fluent Irish Gaelic speaker. Always useful in what Enever termed 'vulgar brawling', and acting as a deckhand, would be Sergeant Geoff Kane of the Royal Marines.

The crews of both vessels planned to fill their operations boxes with small arms of personal preference, ready for use in close engagement with the enemy. *Monique* and *Muguette* would each be equipped with four .50 calibre Brownings to give them heavier, subduing firepower. Mountings for these were already in place, fore and aft, indistinguishable at a distance – to non-fishermen – from the ancillary equipment serving the winches used to pay out and recover the fishing nets. Fresh lobsters, crabs and a range of fish, all caught off Tresco, would be placed on board in barrels of ice to add convincing authenticity to the assumed guise of the two boats. Once in international waters, both vessels would haul down their white ensigns and hoist first the Irish tricolour, then the French tricolour immediately prior to the seizure of the crabber.

Because of the delicate political nature of the operation, which involved a neutral country – and one with strong politico-emotional links to the US, maximum security would be maintained until the two boats were well out to sea. Then, operational radio contact would be conducted in French through 'Y' Service operators based at HMS Godolphin who were fluent in that language.

Enever had insisted on this as a necessary measure, bearing in mind that since De Valera's government had brought the Emergency Powers Act into play, Irish Signals Intelligence would be monitoring radio transmissions around their territory just like everyone else. He was particularly concerned that the radio message announcing the location of the seizure of the *Róisín Dubh*'s guests – and the weaponry intended for the IRA – was given in fluent French.

The last thing I need, dear boy, is an irate commissioner of the Garda Siochána* telephoning Admiral Hembury to bite his balls off because 'Perfidious Albion', yet again, has shown more crass insensitivity towards Ireland and her precarious neutrality.'

At 19.00 hours on the night before the operation, *Monique* and *Muguette* slipped their mooring warps at Braiden Rock and headed north by north-west for the Cobh of Cork.

*The Irish Police Service

An ominous reminder of the political delicacy of the operation, Cromwell's Castle loomed large and forbidding in the dark off their starboard beam as a stark symbol of England's savagery under the Protector against the people of Drogheda and Wexford.

With Tremayne and Willoughby-Brown in *Monique*'s small wheelhouse were Petty Officer Bill Irvine, the redoubtable coxswain, and Leading Yeoman of Signals 'Yorky' Rayner.

With a grin, Tremayne turned to Irvine: 'No singing of *The Sash* if you please, Cox'n, when we come within earshot of the Irish crabber. Remember – this is not July 12th!'

'Aye aye, sir. And I won't even shout 'No surrender!' sir, so I won't!'

Tremayne laughed as he saw the all too rare twinkle light up the dour Ulsterman's eyes – fixed, as always, on the sea ahead and the binnacle compass in front of him.

Clearing Shipman Head at the north end of Bryher, Tremayne ordered Rayner: 'Make to *Muguette*, Yeoman: '*Set course for Youghal Bay. Full speed ahead!*'.'

Emma woke with a start. She was freezing cold. The chill damp of the ground seemed to have penetrated her very bones and her limbs felt as stiff as boards. She took a second to come to and recollect where she was. A thin covering of morning frost lay like a white, gossamer shroud over the ground, undergrowth and trees alike. Grim reality hit her as she realised it wasn't the icy morning that had woken her from a fitful sleep, but shouts from within the forest. There seemed to be German soldiers everywhere. It was patently obvious who they were searching for – and hell-bent on finding.

Instinctively, she looked at her watch. It was 10.43 and she was shocked to see the time. She remembered the long awful night of fitful dozing and seeing three o'clock, then four o'clock on the luminous face of her watch in the darkness of the early dawn. Finally, completely drained, she had fallen into a deep sleep, punctuated by a succession of disconnected, terrifying nightmares. She had slept far later than she had intended. Sheer exhaustion – physical and emotional – had taken their toll on her energy, but not her resolve.

Slowly and silently, she eased herself round and checked that the pistol and partially used clip of ammunition were still in her coat pocket. She had just fourteen rounds in total against what, she guessed, must be upwards of a hundred well-armed troops. The sheer hopelessness of her situation threatened to immobilise her. With her hand shaking from cold and fear, she carefully removed the rubber-coated cyanide pill from her bag and slipped it into a pocket of the woollen cardigan she wore under her coat.

The guttural, shouted commands were coming closer. She felt sick with terror and indecision. Utter tiredness and the penetrating cold were numbing her brain. Should she break cover like a cornered hare and make a run for it? Should she lie low and pray that they didn't discover her? If she ran, she guessed that at least a dozen well-aimed shots would bring her down — but it would be a quick death. If she remained where she was, they surely *must* find her — sooner rather than later. They couldn't possibly miss her. Would she then have the courage to bite through the suicide pill's coating and into the cyanide? Could she, instead, put the pistol to her head and blow her brains out? The thought of either horrified her. For that moment, all she could bring her mind to focus on were Richard and their child. Once again, the self-pitying, useless question — 'How did I ever become involved in all this?' — welled up, threatening to destroy her concentration and will to survive.

Training, the very instinct to preserve life, and raw courage took over. 'For God's sake, girl, get a bloody grip. You are NOT going to give up and die! THINK!'

She looked around. Although the nearest troops must be, at the most, about a hundred yards away from her, she could not see them through the dense undergrowth — although she could hear them clearly enough, blundering through the thick forest. She vigorously rubbed her frozen limbs to get the circulation flowing again and, slowly, feeling came back into her legs. Quickly she leapt to her feet and moved to her right, away from the main body of searchers and in the only direction that seemed relatively free of Germans. Moving both as stealthily and as fast as she could at a crouching run, Emma made her way towards a small clearing that unexpectedly opened up ahead of her. Though it offered her no immediate cover, it gave her a chance to reorientate herself and try to get a mental fix on her customary cycle route back into the liberated zone.

In contrast to the noise elsewhere, the clearing was eerily quiet. No birds sang. There was no rustling in the undergrowth. 'Too damned quiet,' reflected Emma, her hand gripping the butt of the pistol in her pocket. Moving into the trees lining the glade, she dropped onto one knee, listening and keeping her mouth open in order to hear just that little bit more, as she had been taught by the commando instructor at Milton Hall.

She froze in terror as one hand grabbed her shoulder from behind and another stifled her shocked gasp.

'It's okay, Giselle, you're amongst friends, don't scream or shout!' She turned as the hands dropped away from her and, to her relief, found herself looking into the calm brown eyes of Armand, one of Philippe's men, who was kneeling on the ground behind her.

Out of sheer relief, Emma flung her arms around the large, bearded Breton and kissed him on the cheek. 'Am I glad to see you!'

'And, mon Dieu, we are so pleased to see you too, Giselle. We have been very concerned about you. The Boche are out in force, trying to get to you before we did. Did you know you are very famous? The radio announcements are full of the 'female terrorist' Giselle Trenet!' He paused to listen, cocking his ear to catch the slightest sound.

'There are about thirty of us around this glade and several more behind us. We've been out looking for you since two o'clock this morning, but this forested area extends west of here by at least another seven kilometres and north and south by a further three kilometres in places. It's been slow work in the dark.'

Armand rolled over and, half running and half crawling, disappeared off to Emma's right – only to re-emerge from the undergrowth minutes later with a beaming Philippe.

'Ha ha, mon petit choux*. So, you return to the fold! Thank heavens – you had us worried!'

Philippe shifted his Sten gun directly in front of him, automatically checking the safety catch and magazine and clearing an arc of fire through the bushes ahead of him, with a sweep of his giant hand.

'This forest is alive with the Boche. They have already searched this section and we followed after them, but there are more of the bastards behind us. They will shortly be coming this way again and, in minutes, will make contact with my rearguard – unless I shift them pretty damn quick and move the whole company to somewhere safer.'

'How many are you in total and how far back have you placed the rearguard?' asked Emma.

'Forty-one with you, Giselle. My ten rearguard are deployed about one hundred metres over there.'

Philippe waved his Sten gun in the direction of the heavily wooded area directly behind them.

---

*'*My little cabbage' – a term of endearment normally used for children*

'We are about four hundred metres to the right of the path you cycle along, but I fear that will be already covered by large ambush parties, as far along as the Germans may safely go without running into the bigger Resistance groups dominating no-man's-land. They will have secured your escape route from there on in. But, to reach them, we'll have to fight our way through possibly four or five times our number of Germans.'

Philippe slipped away to bring forward his well-concealed rearguard and to transfer the whole company towards Emma's escape cycle route. They had little or no food with them but took time to snatch a quick drink from their water bottles.

Within minutes, the group moved off, maintaining all-round defence, as four 'box' formations, each of ten men, to their new position close to the cycle track. Silently, Philippe, Emma and three of the company wormed their way forward to suss out the location of first ambush point.

'There! There it is, thirty metres ahead, concealed within that thicket just the other side of the cycle track. It's an MG Type 42 machine-gun post with four soldiers in it.'

Philippe pointed towards the ambush position with his unsheathed fighting knife, his voice the merest whisper.

'The bastards will have covered that one with another this side of the track and about another thirty metres further back. The second one, I'll wager, is itself protected by at least one more, probably another thirty metres to its rear and again located on the other side of the track.'

Philippe and his three colleagues conferred in rapid French for a couple of minutes before he turned back to Emma.

'Right, Giselle, we are going to wait until the Germans take a delayed break to eat, when their guard will be down for a while. Then we're going to crawl up to the first MG post and deal with them.' Meaningfully, he drew his hand across his throat. 'I have asked Jean-Marie to bring up two more silenced pistols. I have one with me and so does Armand.'

Moments later, the silenced pistols arrived and, bidding Emma to stay well hidden, the four crawled forward. Behind them another four, acting as a diversionary group, crept through the trees to place themselves close to the second MG ambush post. Half an hour later, the Germans decided to eat. The waiting was over.

In the Maquis group, one of the members – a fluent German speaker – called out to the second MG position from within the trees that a party of Resistance fighters was advancing on them through the forest to their rear.

As the second MG team swung their machine gun round and turned to face the oncoming threat, Philippe's group leapt across the path as one and shot the four soldiers manning the ambush with their silenced pistols. Within seconds it was over. Philippe slipped back into the woods, leaving his three Maquisards to man the first MG post – donning the dead Germans' helmets and uniform jackets to maintain the characteristic Wehrmacht profile to anyone looking at them from the woods or along the cycle track. He placed a further seven of his men within the trees to back up the three Maquisards occupying the first MG post and to cover their retreat when the time came to move.

Creeping through the undergrowth with another ten men to just below the second MG nest, he signalled his German speaker to give more news on the progress of the fictitious Maquisards. As the MG crew scoured the ground ahead of them, through binoculars or the sights of their machine gun, Philippe and three of his Communists leapt out of the trees, now to their unguarded rear, and carried out a copy-book slaughter using their silenced pistols. Exactly as before, they donned the helmets and uniform jackets of the dead MG crew. Their luck held and it seemed as if the uppermost MG crew, thirty yards or so ahead of them, had seen nothing untoward.

Likewise, Philippe left the second captured ambush post with a back-up of seven Maquisards deployed close to them among the trees. He then returned to where Emma and the remaining twenty of his men were hidden and brought them silently through the trees as far as the newly occupied second MG position.

To the surprise of the Maquisards occupying the second position, the field telephone rang. In the rush to seize the post, the attackers had failed to notice that the three MG posts were all interconnected by telephone. One of the Communists who had some elementary German attempted to answer the call. He failed to understand what was said to him and responded with what proved to be the wrong reply. The answer he received was a sustained burst of fire from the third MG42, which instantly killed one of his comrades and began shredding the sand-bagged protection around the ambush position.

The harsh, tearing sound of the MG42 shattered the silence of the forest, bringing an unexpected immediacy to the Resistance group's next actions

'Damn, damn!' cursed Philippe, 'that'll bring the rest of the Boche down around our ears.'

Directing the twenty Maquisards and Emma to move quickly through the trees and closer to the third German ambush position, he yelled at the remaining two of his men in the second MG post to return fire. This they gallantly did, but the Germans had their range and, within seconds, had killed both and blown apart the captured MG42, exploding the ammunition in the magazine holding the feed belt.

Shocked at the sudden carnage in the gun pit that his men had taken only minutes before, Philippe rallied the rest of his group as he prepared to neutralise the third MG ambush position. Creeping up to the line of trees edging the cycle path, five Maquisards hurled stick grenades, captured from the enemy in earlier operations, into the open-topped machine-gun emplacement. Screams of realisation and horror from the MG crew were followed almost immediately by a rapid succession of explosions as the grenades tore the position apart, killing those manning it and destroying the machine gun and its mounting.

The Maquisards rushed forward, but those who spilled out

onto the track were immediately cut down by a suspected, but largely forgotten, fourth ambush position less than thirty metres away – cleverly sited to cover any further movement along the track towards the enclave perimeter. Philippe reacted immediately, shouting to his men to withdraw back to the trees and into cover. His desperate order to retreat was too late. Nine of his men lay dead, or dying, along the track and three more were dead inside the machine-gun post. For an agonising moment, those already in the woods and witness to the sudden slaughter stopped, shocked, looking on in vain as their comrades fell in droves.

Taking everyone by surprise, it was Emma who broke the mood of dismay and rallied the faltering Resistance fighters, pistol in hand, yelling, 'A moi, en avant! En avant, Maquisards!'*

Before Philippe had time to regain command, Emma had redeployed the remainder of his men in all-round defence. Ordering five of them to cover her with automatic fire, she took two of the Maquisards' stick grenades and edged herself forward towards the last MG ambush position, which had inflicted such appalling casualties on the French.

Not just adrenaline, but the blood of the Highland Frasers, was coursing through her veins as screaming 'Claymore! Claymore!' – the ancient Gaelic battle cry – she hurled the two grenades into the sandbagged enclosure. The sudden total silence that followed the loud explosions was broken at once by an unearthly moan from inside the shattered MG position. As the moment of violent combat passed, Emma sank her

---

* *'To me, forward! Forward, Maquisards!'*

head in her hands, murmuring, 'Oh dear God, forgive me. Forgive me.'

Philippe came up and enfolded her in a bear-like hug, murmuring to her as he would to a distressed child. 'It's okay, Giselle. It's all over. Your brave act saved a lot of my men from further slaughter and, for that, I can never thank you enough. But, it's all okay now, mon petit choux.'

Still holding Emma as she broke down, sobbing, he nodded briefly to one of his men, indicating the still smoking MG nest. Quietly, the Maquisard moved across to the position and, using a silenced pistol, quickly ended the agony of the dying German soldier. The other two had died instantly. Gently moving Emma forward, Philippe signalled to his men to advance. The enclave defensive perimeter was now less than a hundred yards away but, drawn to the sound of gunfire, German troops could clearly be heard closing in on the Maquisards.

Hoarsely shouted commands gave urgency to the Germans' advance, confirming that they were moving in on Philippe's severely depleted party from behind and, more dangerously, from his left flank, seeking to cut off his retreat. Their intention to attack and annihilate the Maquisards was only too obvious by the speed with which they were now crashing through the undergrowth.

Heedless of any need for stealth or silence, their shouts and curses as they blundered through the woods indicated that it was only a matter of minutes before they were in amongst Philippe's men. What he still did not know was how many

Germans were lying in wait for them as they retreated up to – and through – the perimeter and into no-man's-land. Philippe urged his men on faster.

Suddenly, the sound of urgent shouted commands up ahead, followed by the flat thump of mortars being fired, brought Philippe's party to a halt.

'What the hell is that? Who the devil is in front of us?' Turning to his remaining senior NCO, Philippe whispered, 'Pierre, take two men and scout a –'

'They're ours! They're British!' Emma paused, laughing through her tears. 'And French, too!'

She turned to Philippe. A look of weary relief crossed her face and then slowly turned into a radiant smile. 'They must be the Jedburgh team with the FFI boys. Thank heavens!'

The crump of mortar bombs exploding behind them and across their left flank amongst the advancing Germans, confirmed Emma's joyful announcement.

Their relief was suddenly cut short as bullets began to tear into the Maquisards' ranks, followed by a salvo of stick grenades. Two were killed outright and three fell wounded – one severely.

'Get down! Get down! Take cover!' Philippe's hoarse voice betrayed his chagrin and anger as his group took more casualties, just as escape to safety had seemed to be within their grasp. He rapidly deployed his men to engage the advancing enemy, in view on what was now their right flank, as the French turned around and took up firing positions. Seconds later, more Germans began to emerge from the trees, firing as they advanced from what – moments ago – had been the Maquisards' rear.

Attacked from two angles and heavily outnumbered, it looked as if the near triumph of a few minutes ago had turned to disaster. Ammunition was running dangerously low and, between them, the Maquisards possessed only five grenades. Philippe checked his watch. It was 14.39. Unbelievably, they had been fighting on and off for over two hours.

Emma could not remember when she had last eaten. All that had passed her lips had been sips of water from Maquisard water bottles since she fled her office twenty-eight hours ago. She lay as close to the ground as she could, her fingers instinctively digging into the soil as if to scrape a safe haven for herself. With increasingly frequent bursts of aimed automatic fire, incoming rounds smashed through the trees and ripped into the undergrowth. Small branches, pieces of torn foliage, even the bark off trees began to shower Emma and those sheltering around her. An unnerving scream, followed by the most heart-rending moans – 'Maman, oh maman' – announced that someone close by had been hit, cut down by the withering fire. There was no let up in the German fire and no way of escape...

With still no news of Emma, Tremayne spent an agonising night in *Monique*'s crowded wheelhouse, though grateful for the company of his crew which helped him to concentrate on the task ahead. The only illumination that they allowed themselves was the glow of the light on the binnacle. At 04.30, with the Irish coastline less than twenty miles ahead but still invisible in the chill darkness of early dawn, Tremayne ordered both boat crews to be stood to at defence stations. Operations boxes were emptied of weapons as both officers and ratings selected the firearms of their choice – the reliable Lanchester, with its fifty-round magazine, emerging as a favourite among the British crew members.

All were dressed in indeterminate navy-blue working rig, sea boots and either Breton sailors' faded peaked caps, or knitted woolly hats – similar to the cap comforters worn by commandos but in black or dark blue instead of standard-issue khaki.

At 04.50, as the first streaks of grey began to lighten the sky, it was Leading Yeoman of Signals 'Yorky' Rayner who spotted the surfaced U-boat, attended by the dim outline of a smaller vessel with reefed sails. Tremayne and Willoughby-Brown began refocusing their night glasses to confirm the target about three miles ahead and to port.

'Yeoman, make to *Muguette*: '*Target ahead five thousand yards. Maintain seven knots. Follow the leader. Do not acknowledge*'.'

'Anyone out there, looking in this direction, would see Pierre's reply,' said Tremayne. 'We'll keep to our planned ruse of appearing as if we're returning home, Number One. But, just in case, have the crew stand by to whip the Brownings up onto their mountings.'

'Aye aye, sir.'

Turning to Irvine, he ordered, 'Slow ahead, both engines, Cox'n. Maintain seven knots. Steer six hundred yards to starboard of the U-boat and her consort. Head for Oyster Haven. We'll round the headland and lie up there and wait for the *Róisín Dubh*.'

'Aye aye, sir.'

'Number One, check the charts and navigate us in, please. We'll heave-to below Kinure with a clear view of anything coming in or out of Cork outer harbour.'

Tension mounted as the two fishing boats, Irish tricolours hoisted, slowly chugged by the U-boat and the crabber. Tremayne could feel the cold sweat running down his back as he gripped the foredeck guardrail, his right hand raised in what he hoped was a casual enough wave. He could imagine, all too easily, several pairs of inquisitive eyes sizing up his boat through binoculars, both on the U-boat's conning tower and from the stern of the bobbing Irish crabber. For a moment, he went even colder as he saw both the 37mm and 20mm guns, abaft the conning tower, traverse purposefully towards the *Monique*, the lead fishing boat.

Addressing those on deck as well as in the wheelhouse, Tremayne ordered, 'Wave to the bastards, everybody, but then keep going about your duties as fishermen.'

For a moment he waited, bracing himself for the fatal impact of the shells which, at point-blank range, would shred his fishing boats in an instant. Even survivors, he knew, would be executed – if not by the Germans then by the IRA – once they were discovered to be British. The Germans, on a covert operation, would be unlikely to show the Frenchmen any mercy.

As they continued sailing on at quarter revolutions towards the Irish coast, Tremayne heard a hoarse command carry across the gently swelling sea. For a second he froze, then relaxed as the U-boat's gun barrels slowly swung away, pointing out to sea once more.

'I think, sir, that frightful hat of yours did the trick,' grinned an equally relieved, but ever urbane, Willoughby-Brown. 'No one in their right minds, sir – not even an Irishman, much less a German – could possibly mistake you for anything other than some oik from the bogs!'

Tremayne exploded with laughter – the first time he had done so since the paralysing news of Emma's disappearance.

'Clearly, Number One, you have an assured future in Vaudeville and end-of-the-pier shows!'

The taciturn Irvine's studiously indifferent reaction to the ribbing in the wheelhouse conveyed just enough thinly veiled disapproval as he stood silently, hands on the boat's wheel and eyes set on the slowly emerging detail of the coast ahead. Rayner, previously more used to the formality of RN ships and 'stone frigates' – not Special Forces *boats* – took his lead from the dour Ulsterman and, rather too obviously, fixed his binoculars on the approaching coastline.

Just under twenty minutes later, *Monique* and *Muguette*, both riding the slowly rolling waves of the incoming surf tide and with Irish tricolours still hoisted, awaited the approach of the

Rósin Dubh and her lethal cargo. As Tremayne and Quilghini reviewed their plans, yet again, for the seizure of the Irish crabber, the two fishing boat crews chatted to each other, glad of the mugs of rum-laced kye in their hands.

Their temporary respite was rudely interrupted by an urgent call from Willoughby-Brown, standing for'ard of *Monique*'s wheelhouse.

'Here she comes, 'bout five miles out!'

'Thank you, Number One,' replied Tremayne. 'Put Vaudeville on hold. Stand by to move!'

Through binoculars, there was no mistaking the emerald green hull and white, ketch-rigged sails.

Tremayne ordered 'Both boats, line abreast. Half revolutions ahead!' and together, no more than fifty yards apart, *Monique* and *Muguette* moved out into the open sea, pointing their bows on a parallel course to that of the approaching Irish crabber. Through their binoculars, Tremayne and his first lieutenant could see that there appeared to be some interest in their sudden appearance, but their measured pace gave no intention of threat to those on board the *Róisin Dubh*. At this stage, the two fishing boats maintained what they hoped would be the impression of vessels which had dropped their catch, for fishmongers and restaurants around Kinsale and Cork, and were on their way back to fresh fishing grounds or to their home port, elsewhere along the south-west coast of Ireland.

The Irish crabber, running on her diesels with auxiliary sails, was making a steady seven or eight knots, Irvine announced.

She was closing slowly and was about half a mile ahead and slightly to port when Tremayne called to Willoughby-Brown who was standing on the foredeck: 'Right. Now, Number One!'

Willoughby-Brown waved briefly to Quilghini and both boats swung across the *Róisín Dubh*'s line of sail.

Abandoning all pretence of being lumbering fishing boats and swiftly accelerating to thirty-two knots, *Monique* and *Muguette* rapidly closed on the crabber, lining up one on each side of her.

'Action stations! Hoist the French tricolour!' yelled Tremayne. Seconds later, the flag of Ireland was quickly hauled down. Through their glasses, those in the wheelhouse could see a feverish eruption of responsive activity on the crabber's deck. Men in civilian clothes, some with ammunition bandoleers around their shoulders and chests, appeared as if from nowhere and began to line the crabber's bulwarks – rifles and sub-machine guns in their hands. Already, several were beginning to take aim at Tremayne's fishing boats.

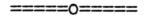

The Maquisards, pinned down by intense German fire and running out of ammunition, returned fire as best they could. Horrified, Emma could see that their position was fast becoming untenable. Though she recognised the uselessness of a pistol in a firefight of such intensity, firing aimed rounds

—albeit a limited few—at the Germans gave her the satisfaction that she was, at least, hitting back. She discarded her empty clip and pushed home the one containing her last six rounds.

As she checked the Walther's action, several bursts of automatic fire behind her announced the arrival of the three Jeds officers and more than thirty FFI fighters who were in among the trees where Philippe's Maquisards were desperately making what was in danger of becoming their last stand. Hurling grenades and using almost entirely automatic weapons, the relief force put down a devastating volume of fire, forcing the Germans to keep their heads down. In the dense forest, the stench of cordite hung heavily in the air and the noise was deafening. Tim wormed his way through the thick tangle of undergrowth to Emma, bringing with him two FFI NCOs.

'Bloody well done, Giselle! Thanks to you, the Keroman operation was a major success. We've never known such commitment from the Communists. I've already sent my report to SOE 'F' Section. I can't tell you how pleased they are.'

Squeezing off two short bursts from his Sten gun, he touched her shoulder.

'Time for you to exit, girl. Bernard here will guide you back to the rear. You've already done far more than your share.'

Emma protested, but Tim shook his head. 'Sorry, Emma —I think it's safe enough to call you that now—that's a direct order. Now, GO!'

More FFI moved up, loaded down with ammunition and grenades which they began to share out with Philippe's

Maquisards. Almost immediately, the renewed intensity of fire began to pin the Germans down. Using fire and movement tactics, the combined Resistance group then started their withdrawal, section by section, to prepared positions at the perimeter, where a further two hundred FFI men were dug in, covering the cycle track back into the liberated zone.

Emma, now armed with a fallen Maquisard's Sten gun, insisted on remaining at the fighters' defensive position at the edge of no-man's-land. She was determined to make sure that Philippe and the tragically few survivors of his Maquisards also reached the comparative safety of the FFI position before she agreed to be escorted back by the jubilant Resistance forces and the Jedburgh team to their HQ in liberated France. It was almost 19.00 hours before the Germans, who themselves had taken many casualties, called it a day and retreated back to the safety of 'Festung Lorient'.

'I'm bloody well starving! I am going to enjoy the best supper of my life,' she announced to the three Jedburgh officers – her beautiful face set in the broadest of smiles, 'after a long-overdue bath and, yes, gentlemen, the unashamed luxury of putting make-up on! Then I want to talk to my husband, if you will arrange that for me, please!'

The first shots from the *Róisín Dubh* struck *Monique*'s solid teak wheelhouse, doing little damage other than to gouge and scar the tough, age-seasoned timber and shatter one of the windows. Inside, ducking to avoid the jagged shards of flying glass, Irvine swore.

'Ye Fenian bastards!' he muttered under his breath.

Tremayne called to Rayner. 'Yeoman, make to *Muguette*: *'Tirez'.'* He spelled it out for the Chief Yeoman of Signals, concerned that the Irish and Germans saw an order given in correct French, and immediately nodded to the forrard gunner to fire a burst from the twin .50 calibre Brownings, calling, 'Just over the bastards' heads.'

Quilghini fired almost simultaneously; dramatically reducing *Róisín Dubh*'s fore and aft sails to shreds.

'Hmmm. Now *that's* what I call Gallic flair – a real *coup de théâtre!*' murmured Willoughby-Brown approvingly, checking the magazine on his Lanchester.

Aware that he was facing the undaunted fighting spirit of the Irish as more aimed rounds thudded into *Monique*, blasting out the remaining windows of her wheelhouse and moving her coxswain to even stronger expletives, Tremayne ordered another burst from the awesome Brownings.

'Remove the bastards' foremast!'

'Aye aye, sir.'

Within seconds, the heavy bullets – at a combined cyclical rate of fire of almost a thousand rounds per minute – splintered and tore through the wooden mast, bringing it crashing down among the IRA men and Germans on deck.

'Now their aftermast.'

It was a copy-book repeat of the destruction of the crabber's foremast.

Quilghini responded with a terrifying sustained sweep of .50 calibre, inches above the heads of those lining *Róisín Dubh*'s bulwarks.

With a thoroughly convincing and none too theatrical French accent, Tremayne yelled at the now somewhat subdued crabber crew through his loudhailer: 'We have no quarrel with the Irish. After all, my name is Jean-François O'Riordan, descendent of one of the 'Wild Geese' who fought for France against the common enemy. We want the Germans you have on board and the weapons they bring you. We are coming alongside to board you.'

As *Monique* and *Muguette* manoeuvred alongside the crabber to port and starboard, an Irish voice yelled, 'Remember Tom Barry, boys. Give it to the bastards! Erin Go Bragh*!'

A fusillade of shots rang out, with rounds ricocheting wildly off *Monique*'s steel winch and other equipment on deck. Ironically, it was O'Hanlon who was hit and fell to the deck, luckily not seriously wounded.

Concerned not to create casualties on the crabber's deck, Tremayne directed his Brownings, fore and aft, to empty their magazines into the crabber's wooden hull in the area of her engine compartment. The impact of the sustained firing was fearful. Within seconds, the timbers of *Róisín Dubh*'s elderly hull

---

* *'Ireland for ever!'*

began to fly apart, exposing her engine compartment.

'Empty your magazines into that bloody lot,' said Tremayne to both gunners, who were well protected by their weapons' shields. Following Tremayne's lead, Quilghini similarly poured sustained fire from his Brownings into the crabber's hull on her other quarter. After what must have seemed an eternity in hell for her crew, her diesel machinery disintegrated, with oil spewing all over the engine room and down the shattered hull sides into the sea.

'You've wrecked my boat, ye feckin' frogs. Come aboard and get yer feckin' Germans. My boys and I will be waitin' for ye.'

Seizing belaying pins as well as their small arms, the Irish crew gave no indication of a readiness to surrender.

Speaking little above a whisper to both gunners, Tremayne said, 'As close to their heads as you can, lads, but DON'T hit 'em.'

Volley after volley swept unnervingly close and the men on the crabber finally flung themselves down, seeking whatever cover they could. Tremayne, yelling, 'A moi! A l'attaque!'* led his and Quilghini's men onto *Róisín Dubh*'s deck. Using their weapons as clubs, they pitched into the crabber's crew until bloodied – but obviously still unbowed – the outnumbered Irish finally gave up.

The Germans were flushed out from below and lined up on deck. Dressed in civilian clothes, they refused to give their names, ranks and service numbers. In no mood to tolerate

---

* *'To me! Charge!'*

further delay, Tremayne nodded to Harberer, Lejeune and Duhamel and indicated the sea: 'Alors, la mer! Vite!'*

Shocked, the Germans were only too willingly thrown overboard by the three French ratings.

'Ye murtherin' frog bastards!'

Turning angrily on the Irish skipper who had just spoken, Tremayne, maintaining his French accent, snarled, 'Open your mouth once more, monsieur, and I'll put *you* into the sea!'

Still glaring menacingly into the Irishman's eyes, Tremayne pointed to the two Germans – one of whom was clearly in difficulty – and ordered the crabber's skipper, 'Now, throw them lifebelts. MOVE!'

Shocked by the dramatic turn of events and seeing their soaking comrades hauled out of the cold uninviting sea, the Germans were clearly not imbued with the same aggressive spirit as their Irish hosts. Questioned once more by Willoughby-Brown in fluent German, they admitted that they were members of a military mission, but refused to give away any more information.

With her crew under close guard, but with plenty of fight left in them, Tremayne ordered the *Róisín Dubh* to be searched. Quilghini and Harberer, Sten guns in hand, returned moments later and, speaking in French, confirmed a huge supply of explosives and weaponry on board.

Willoughby-Brown, on Tremayne's command, ordered the Germans to bring the arms, ammunition and boxes of hand grenades up onto the deck. The haul was enormous –

* *'The sea it is! Quickly!'*

enough to equip several IRA Brigades for a sustained campaign of murder and mayhem in mainland Britain.

'Throw them over the side!' ordered Willoughby-Brown.

As the Germans sullenly began to dump the rifles, machine pistols and boxes of ammunition into the sea, the skipper of the crabber yelled at Tremayne, 'Ye feckin' eejit, ye! Those were meant for the IRA.'

Tremayne, with the speed and flowing movement of a panther, stepped forward and – before the Irishman realised what was happening – put him in an arm lock and hurled him after the disappearing weapons.

'I told you to keep your damned mouth shut!' he yelled, as the man fell, arms flailing, into the sea.

'Sure, he'll drown, ye mad Frog bastard. He can't feckin' swim!' shouted one of the crew, coming up to Tremayne with his fists clenched.'

'Then throw him a line. You're wasting time you fool.'

As he spoke, Tremayne moved in closer to the man, his eyes cold with lethal intent.

Tremayne suddenly became aware that in the heated exchanges he was losing his adopted French accent and was in serious danger of giving the game away. So, for effect, he added, 'Vite, idiot, vite!' as the man backed off, muttering in impotent fury.

Dragged back out of the sea – choking, coughing up water and badly shaken – the enraged skipper glowered at Tremayne, who snarled, 'The defence of one's country is the prerogative and duty of the patriot. The murder of innocent civilians is the preserve of scum, monsieur.'

Willoughby-Brown searched the disconsolate Germans before herding them onto *Monique* and *Muguette*. Quilghini, while searching the crabber's wheelhouse and quarters, reappeared with a briefcase full of papers relating to the arms-running operation. He nodded to Tremayne to indicate that all below was now clear. Still covering the crabber's crew with their weapons, the British and French seamen threw the Irishmen's rifles, pistols and Tommy guns overboard and boarded their own vessels.

As the two fishing boats drew away, Tremayne called out to the *Róisin Dubh*'s fuming skipper,

'Au revoir, mon ami!'

He and Willoughby-Brown smiled wryly as his savage reply rang in their ears – 'Mon ami –mon feckin' arse.'

'Y' know, Number One, I'm glad we chose not to hustle that crabber out into international waters. Getting that skipper and his crew to stop engines and comply would have resulted in a bloodbath. That would have been far too high a price to pay with such brave men – ours *and* theirs.'

At 16.00 hours that same day, *Monique* and *Muguette* rendezvoused south-west of the Scillies with a Grimsby-class frigate – sister ship of Tremayne's 'first love', *HMS Fleetwood* – to transfer the now blindfolded prisoners for interrogation by SIS and SOE at RN Devonport.

Nodding to Irvine, Tremayne smiled – pleased with the

way the operation had gone – and said quietly, 'Right Cox'n, take us home if you please!'

Calling down the after companionway to Leading Seaman Pablo' Watkins who was below in the fishing boat's tiny galley, Tremayne shouted, 'Watkins, I think we could all do with a mug of that wondrous brew of yours.'

'An' the Frogs – beg pardon sir, I mean the French. Them too, sir?'

'Yes, Watkins – the Frogs too!'

'An' the Jerries, sir?'

'Giving them your torpedo propellant probably amounts to a war crime under the rules of the Geneva Convention, but yes – please do – and, in your defence, the first lieutenant and I will testify to your otherwise good character if you are so charged!'

''Aye aye, sir. Thank you, sir. That's a comfort to know!'

Tremayne grinned at Willoughby-Brown. 'That man is pure gold. His deadpan Brummie sense of humour just cracks me up!'

A little over an hour later, the two 'mystery boats' as they had become known to the locals on Tresco, passed through New Grimsby harbour in line astern, with *Monique* leading, and secured at Braiden Rock anchorage. Tremayne warmly thanked both boat crews for their part in the successful operation off Youghal Bay and made sure that O'Hanlon was safely transferred by harbour motor launch to the hospital on St Mary's. Now, duty done, Emma was once more uppermost on his mind as he raced up the rough-hewn rock steps to the path leading to HMS Godolphin.

Returning the salute of the sentry on the gate, Tremayne almost collided with Enever who had been delayed by a telephone call on his way to meet the returning boat crews.

'Richard, dear boy, am I glad to see you! We've picked up the news of your outstanding success on the blower from SIS. They and SOE can hardly contain themselves that everything's already done and dusted – and so successfully.'

Enever positively beamed, his half-moon spectacles perched on the end of his patrician nose.

'Radio Éireann is full of righteous indignation and accounts of piracy by the French in Irish territorial waters and the barbaric near drowning of unarmed Irish fishermen. Nowhere, of course, is there any mention in the reports of a clandestine German military mission – or the IRA!'

Enever was still vigorously pumping Tremayne's hand, when he said, 'Oh lord, Richard, I almost forgot. Someone's on the blower for you. Something about the stores you ordered just before you left for Ireland. They do sound a bit 'agitato' – better have a word with them.'

'Stores? I don't remember ordering any stores – other than checking on victualling for the operation. I suppose some bloody clerk with thumb up bum and mind in neutral and nothing better to do wants a signature in triplibloodycate. Please bear with me, John, while I sort the useless buggers out.'

Enever guided Tremayne to the phone, which was off the

hook in the small Signals Intelligence admin office.

Tremayne picked up the phone, furious that his return to base had been interrupted by some irksome bureauprat.

'Lieutenant Commander Tremayne speaking. What's all this nonsense about bloody stores?'

The voice at the other end, with a strong Glaswegian female accent, chided, 'Och my, sailor boy, and aren't *we* the uppity one?!'

Tremayne stopped, taken aback for a split second, before his face broke into a huge grin.

'EMMA! Darling Emma, thank God you're safe! Where are you?' he almost shouted, oblivious to the grins, matching his own, of the Wrens in the office. Neither did he see Enever's conspiratorial smile as the Senior Naval Intelligence Officer slipped away, bidding the Wrens follow him out into the corridor and down to the NAAFI canteen...

Fifteen

The Final Curtain

I n the heady days following their respective operations in the Lorient enclave and the waters off the Irish coast, Emma and Tremayne spent so much time talking to each other on the telephone. Each was conscious of the other's need to talk out their first-hand experiences exhaustively, in order to be able to re-enter their shared world again as husband and wife – and as parents.

Tremayne had been through extremes of doubt, terror and exhilaration many times during the last four years. In order to survive and retain his sanity, it had been necessary to develop a certain degree of 'case hardening' against the horrific trauma of war — especially the vicious immediacy of close-quarter battle. He recognised, however, that he would be forever grateful for knowing that he could never become accustomed to — or regard as normal — the deliberate slaughter of his fellow human beings. Though war, to Tremayne, was an obscene anathema, he had learned that there comes a time when freedom can only be won by fighting for it.

His major concern was how well Emma would be able to put into perspective — and come to terms with — the horror and brutality of her own actions in the successful fulfilment of her dangerously exposed role. Working with a Jedburgh team and members of the French Resistance, she had known, at first hand, the terrifying sense of isolation of being behind enemy lines.

This had been the first time that she had looked death in the face. Milton Hall apart, Emma had received minimal preparation for the terror of personal, one-to-one confront-ation, where she had had to defend her very life and brutally maim, or even kill, others in order to do so. Her previous experience in Signals Intelligence and SIS had neither trained her for the instant savagery of such kill-or-be-killed encounters nor for the disorientating din, horror and sudden shock of battle — especially a company-strength firefight at point-blank range.

Ten days after their return from operations, they were able to snatch one week's leave together in the Isles of Scilly. They roamed the islands by sail and on foot — talking, laughing and, above all, experiencing the healing power of love. Morag insisted on looking after Catriona for those few restorative days and nights. As ever, Aileen and Dick Oyler at the New Inn provided the secure haven that Tremayne and Emma needed as part of their re-entry to life – and to living in a world that would shortly be free of war.

The normality of Christmas leave came a few weeks later, in between more routine operations for both Tremayne and Emma as the Allied armies progressively brought long overdue liberty to much of Western Europe and the Soviet war machine continued to storm its way through Eastern Europe to the east German frontier. The shock of the Germans' Ardennes offensive and the temporary threat to the recently liberated port of Antwerp did not impinge directly on the role of the Tresco flotilla. Neither was Emma involved in Allied counter-measures to that unexpected setback. Her role, now back in SIS, increasingly focused on the liberation of Norway and Denmark, the recovery of Finland from Nazi clutches and the inevitable occupation of Germany, from the Rhine up to Schleswig Holstein and beyond.

In recognition of his outstanding achievements as flotilla commander, since receiving a Bar to his DSO and several mentions in despatches, Tremayne learned to his embarrassed delight that he was to be awarded the DSC. Enever clearly took great personal pleasure in confirming the decoration and also that of a Bar to Willoughby-Brown's DSO. What had so regularly impressed Tremayne in his relationship with Enever was the older man's genuine, uninhibited delight in others' successes – and consequent rewards. He seemed to be totally free of the envy or jealousy apparent in so many, who appear to die a little every time those they know succeed and thrive – particularly when they don't happen to be enjoying success to the same degree.

Tremayne had come to regard his service as a subordinate to Enever as the most fulfilling personal and professional experience of his life to date. He knew that with the liberation of Europe, the end of the war and the inevitable winding up of HMS Godolphin as an active naval base, he was going to face a major vacuum in his life that he would never quite be able to fill. His original intention had been to return, after demobilisation from the Navy, to pursue his studies in law in order to take silk and qualify as a barrister. After more than three years with the Tresco flotilla, he was no longer sure that this was what he really wanted. It was an issue that nagged him increasingly for a decision and resolution.

Emma's courage, tenacity and skills in bringing the Communist Maquisards so completely into the Jedburgh-led Resistance fold – together with her resourcefulness in coordinating so much of the operation in the U-boat pens at Keroman, had earned her the George Cross. She learned of the award of this coveted decoration from her very appreciative and enthusiastic SIS controller on her return from Christmas leave.

Like Tremayne, she suffered from impostor syndrome and

a genuine belief that 'given the time, the place and the opportunity, anyone would have done what I did'. In neither case did false modesty enter into it. Both saw themselves as being lucky enough to be where needed, at the right time, because of the very nature of the role that each had taken on. What really delighted Emma was to learn from her controller that she was also to be awarded the Legion d'Honneur, based upon the strongest of recommendations from Major Tim Galway and Philippe. When an overjoyed Enever learned of her awards, he ordered 'Splice the mainbrace' for the whole of the Intelligence Section at HMS Godolphin – secretarial staff included – to celebrate his former protégée's outstanding achievements with a double issue of the daily tot of rum. As he later admitted, some rather curiously worded memos and misspelt missives left the Intelligence office that afternoon.

Most of the Tresco flotilla's operations from New Year's Day 1945 until the German surrender on May 8th, were routine anti-U-boat sweeps in the Western Approaches. During what was a little over four months of patrolling by three boats, only one contact was made, which was sunk by depth charges by a fully recovered Hermann Fischer and his Camper and Nicholson MGB.

Tremayne was involved in one final operation with HMMTB 1510, accompanied by Fischer's Camper and Nicholson, which was to escort two Type 100 E-boats to RN Portsmouth that had evaded the Russians and escaped from the Baltic through the Kiel Canal. They had been part of a flotilla that had been harrying Soviet troop-carrying vessels and freighters in the Gulf of Finland.

From Brunsbüttel at the mouth of the Elbe and the western end of the Kiel Canal, they had made their way to the Kriegsmarine base at Cuxhaven. The RV, agreed with the Royal Navy, was off Spitzsand, three miles north of Cuxhaven on the edge of the Wattenmeer – the shallow, mysterious and often fog-bound waters around the coast of Schleswig Holstein.

As the British motor gun boat drew near to the sleek E-boats, looking even more sinister in the eerie dawn mist of the haunting Wattenmeer, Willoughby-Brown murmured,' This is just like something out of Erskine Childers' prophetic novel, *The Riddle of the Sands!* Any moment now, I half expect to see hordes of Prussians in landing barges emerging from the gloom to start rehearsing for their invasion of England!'

'Looking across at those two crews, I don't think that there's much fight left in them, Number One. They look completely exhausted.'

The enveloping mist added to the air of melancholy of the surrender. Easing alongside the nearer E-boat, Tremayne felt only compassion, rather than any sense of triumph, as he studied the pale, drawn faces numbly looking at him. Instead of the supreme self-confidence and arrogance that he had come across so often in his encounters with the E-boat arm of the Kriegsmarine, what he saw now was resignation and a dispirited acceptance of defeat.

Returning the nearest German boat captain's salute, Tremayne handed over the loudhailer to his first lieutenant who called out in fluent German: 'Good morning, gentlemen. We appreciate your punctuality. Set course for Portsmouth. Clear all weapons and torpedo tubes. Follow me please. Speed thirty knots.'

With Fischer bringing up the rear, the convoy set off in line astern, Tremayne's after Oerlikons and Fischer's for'ard six-pounder trained on the two E-boats. It was late evening when they drew into Portsmouth harbour. Still under the guns of the Tresco flotilla, the two E-boats secured near to *HMS Victory* – that enduring symbol of British naval power from a bygone era – and their crews marched off under escort into captivity.

The next day, Tremayne, Fischer and their crews celebrated their final successful operation of their war as the Tresco flotilla in an inevitably emotional evening at the New Inn.

'It's almost impossible to believe that it's now all over for us,' said Willoughby-Brown. 'For a time, we're going to feel quite lost when we break up and go our separate ways.'

Caught up in the more sombre mood of his words, the group maintained unusually low-key conversation for the rest of the evening. Each, in his own way, probably welcomed the end of the party and the excuse to retire to his cabin, to be alone with his mixed thoughts and feelings.

Major celebrations – a mixture of the joy of knowing that the war in Europe was at an end and the sadness at the break-up of so many close friendships – marked the official closure of HMS Godolphin and standing down of the Tresco flotilla. A very moving farewell parade, commanded by Admiral Hembury, was held on Godolphin's compact square and many officers and ratings alike – Tremayne especially – felt a lump in their throats as the ship's company marched off to *Heart of Oak* for the very last time.

Tremayne and Emma attended their award investitures at Buckingham Palace, while Emma proudly received her Legion d'Honneur at a special presentation in Lorient, two days after the German garrison surrendered to the French and Americans on May 9th 1945.

Richard Tremayne spent his very last day as flotilla commander talking through future career options with John Enever and David Willoughby-Brown who, over the years, had become his closest and most trusted friends. Saying farewell to them, his fellow boat captains and to those most memorable and enduring of all his crew members – Petty Officer Bill Irvine and Leading Seaman 'Pablo' Watkins – was, for Tremayne, the hardest part of the break-up of the Tresco flotilla. The islands – and stalwart friends like the Oylers – he knew he *would* see again – and regularly so. That was an earnest vow that he and Emma had made. Tresco and the other islands had become a fundamental and inseparable part of their lives – and love – together. They would forever remain so – of that, he was certain.

'Dear HMS Godolphin has officially closed down,' said Enever, 'but its location and crucial role will remain secret for as long as fifty years under the rulings of the Official Secrets Act, because we don't know if or when we might need to reactivate it again – possibly even in a different form. Always have a plan B in reserve, dear boy, but I think we both agree you should return to the law and take silk. But do, I beg you, remain active in the RNVR, gaining further promotion in due course. I know that you, David, intend to apply for a regular commission and make the Royal Navy your career and I wish you well in that. Unfortunately, with the way things are already shaping up in our relationship with the Russians, you never know when your unique services may be needed again. For all three of us, gentlemen, the cry is – watch this space!'

Enever affectionately shook hands with both Tremayne and Willoughby-Brown. 'My warmest, heartfelt thanks to both of you – I could not have wished for better, more delightful colleagues. Without you and the Tresco flotilla, maintaining the channel to freedom would have been a far more fraught and protracted affair. Somehow – and don't ask me how – I *know* that our paths are going to cross again – though perhaps not immediately. In the meantime, let's enjoy our hard-won peace, gentlemen. Good luck and Godspeed!'

Epilogue

2010

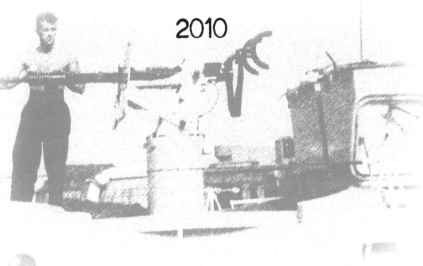

The crowds lining the High Street of Wootton Bassett, an attractive little market town in Wiltshire, were more than ten deep in places. Though the sun shone, the mood of the people was solemn and dignified – pain and compassion etched on so many of their faces. Conversation was maintained at the level of a respectful murmur. All too often in recent years, they had quietly arrived and lined up to pay their respects and bid a last farewell to a succession of British servicemen and women, killed on duty in Afghanistan.

Among the still gathering crowd were many elderly ex-servicemen and women. Their regimental badges adorned berets of various colours and their ties proudly reaffirmed the arm of service, regiment or unit proclaimed by their headgear. Many of these men and women were in their seventies and eighties and several, too, retained the permanent stamp of people who have seen active service and known the loss of friends and comrades in action. Most wore campaign medals and ribbons on their chests – testimony to their part in helping to shape history.

In a bright splash of colour there were the white-topped, red-banded caps and navy blue uniforms of a group of Royal Marines. Today, with its sadness and poignancy, was *their* day. They were welcoming home one of their own, brought back to RAF Lyneham, just a few miles away, earlier that morning. Their sense of 'family' was one of the strongest – they were 'Royals'.

Seated close to them in a wheelchair, to ease the tiredness of standing for long periods, was a distinguished looking, white-haired man in his early nineties, wearing medals, the DSO and Bar and the DSC among his campaign medals. By his side, her hand on his shoulder, stood a petite, elderly lady with strikingly clear blue eyes – a Royal Navy Tudor crown gold brooch pinned to her fashionably cut jacket. On the left breast of her jacket she wore the George Cross and Legion d'Honneur. Before they had set out from London to catch the Penzance helicopter to Tresco for their late spring holidays, they had been told by representatives of the British Legion about the repatriation of a Royal Marine, killed in action in Afghanistan.

Tremayne, remembering with deep affection Sergeant Geoff Kane, Corporal 'Blackie' Cotterell, Marine Weaver and the many other Royal Marines he had served and fought with all those years ago, had told Emma that he wanted to be there to see the young Royal come home.

'It is now one way I can respect and acknowledge, with humility, what he and others like him have given and show my gratitude for their sacrifice.'

They decided they would break their journey down to Cornwall and stay one night in Wiltshire. Their daughter Catriona, herself a former Lieutenant Commander, RN, had willingly acted as their chauffeuse. She now stood on his other side.

With the solemn tolling of the church bell, the crowd fell silent with just a few muffled sobs as the cortège slowly approached. As the hearse drew level – bearing the coffin draped in the Union Jack – Tremayne briefly bowed his head and quietly murmured, 'Once a Marine – always a Marine. God bless, Royal.' Emma, her hand still on her husband's shoulder and tears in her eyes, whispered, 'And once Navy – always Navy.'

Despite the deliberate quietness of their voices, their words had been heard by several of the young Royal Marines standing close by. When the hearse had passed, they immediately crowded round Tremayne, instantly creating an impromptu 'family' bond marked by warm, uninhibited spontaneity. Enthusiastically identifying the medals he wore, they plied him with questions, obviously keen to know much more about the clandestine naval unit, which was completely new information to them. One of the Marines suddenly spotted and recognised Emma's George Cross and – within seconds – she became part of the 'family'. Only when a Royal Marines colour sergeant appeared on the scene to lead them to their transport back to RAF Lyneham, did they reluctantly break off the animated conversation and leave. But they left knowing that they had met someone who believed in them and who would not easily forget their fallen colleague.

'Once again, it would seem, the price of keeping the channel of freedom open remains painfully high,' said Tremayne, 'but, even after all these years and our own experience, I continue to believe that dear-bought liberty is infinitely better than oppression.'

Taking his walking stick from Emma and rising stiffly from his wheelchair, he insisted on walking back to Catriona's car, which was parked close by. While a dignified air of quiet reflection remained in the town, the mood had slowly begun to lift from the intense grief of minutes ago to one of indelible gratitude and respect.

As Catriona opened the car door for him, Tremayne smiled, 'Set a course for Tresco. This time, we'll make sure we take you to Juliet's Garden on St Mary's for one of their unbelievably good lunches and raise a glass of their marvellous Conch y Toro rosé with the Willoughby-Browns! Take us home, Cox'n!'

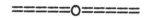

Glossary of naval and Royal Marine terms

=============================

Abaft	Nearer to the stern than…
Abwehr	German Military Intelligence
Acoustic torpedo	Torpedo which homes in on the sounds generated by its intended target
After	Behind or rear, eg the after (rear) deck
AFO	Admiralty Fleet Orders (the Royal Navy's operational 'Bible')
Aldis	Signalling lamp
Ammo	Ammunition
Andrew	Colloquial naval term for the Royal Navy
Battle ensign	A larger version of the normal naval ensign, flown in battle to aid recognition and identity
Beam	The side of a ship or boat, eg port (left) or starboard (right) beam
Bergen	Special Forces/commando name for a military rucksack
Bofors	A high-angle automatic gun of Swedish origin that fires 40mm shells
Bohemian Corporal	Derogatory term for Hitler, used by some aristocratic German officers who derided his

lowly Austrian origins and former military rank of corporal in the First World War.

Brew up	Burn fiercely then explode
Cable's length	Nautical unit of measure of 200 yards
Cockle (Mk I or Mk II)	Early Royal Marine term for Service two-man canoe
Compo	Composite tinned rations
Cox'n	Abbreviation of coxswain – the petty officer/rating who steers the boat
E-boat/ S-Boot	British and German terms for Kriegsmarine high-speed motor torpedo boat
Ensign	Naval flag usually indicating nationality/identity
FFI	Force Françaises de l'Intérieur – French Resistance fighters opposed to the Communist Resistance. Sometimes referred to as 'Fifi' by their rivals
Forrard/ for'ard	Forward, towards the bow of the ship or boat
Gun-layer	Crew member who feeds the weapon with ammunition
Guz	Naval slang for Plymouth/Devonport
Jack	Ship's flag, usually indicating nationality or naval slang for a sailor, eg 'Jolly Jack'
Kriegsmarine	German name for their navy under the Nazi regime
Kye	The Navy's own hot drinking chocolate
Lanchester	A well-engineered, but expensive sub-machine gun, which was favoured by the Royal Navy rather than by the other services

LMG	Light machine gun, ie section or squad machine gun
Make to...	The command to send a signal to someone
Maquis	Rural guerrilla groups of the French Resistance. Preferred to operate in the cover of forests and mountains
Maquisard	Member of the Maquis
MAS36	French military/gendarme sub-machine gun, 1936 vintage
MG42	German machine gun of 1942 vintage
MGB/MTB	Motor gun boat/motor torpedo boat
Milch cow/	
Milchkuh	German U-boat adapted as a supply vessel to other U-boats
Milice	A paramilitary police force set up in Vichy France to uphold the law, as interpreted by the Germans. Often as vicious as the Gestapo in putting down the Resistance, they were usually executed when caught by the Maquis
MP18/	
MP40	German machine pistols of 1918 and 1940 vintage
MT	Military motor transport section
NCO	Non-commissioned officer, eg petty officer, corporal or sergeant
Nelson slice	A very solid wedge of pastry and indeterminate fruit, topped with icing
Oerlikon	An automatic gun of Swiss origin that fires 20mm calibre shells

'O' Group	Orders Group – ie, a pre-operational briefing
OKM	Oberkommando Marine – Office of Chiefs of Staff of the German Navy
OSS	Office of Strategic Services – US equivalent of British SOE
Pompey	Naval slang for Portsmouth
Pongo	Naval derogatory term for a soldier
Pusser	Slang for purser, also used in the sense of 'officially' or 'properly' naval
Rate	Rank
Rating	Non-commissioned sailor
R-boats/ Raumboote	German inshore minesweepers and patrol boats
Royal	A Royal Marine term for one of their own – ie, a fellow Royal Marine
Schnorkel	A device developed by the Germans and Dutch, which allows submarines to 'breathe' while submerged
Sick bay	Temporary or local military/naval hospital
SIS	British Secret Intelligence Service (more recently, MI6)
Slip	The command to let go mooring lines and move off
SMG	Submachine gun
SNIO	Senior Naval Intelligence Officer
Snorker	Slang for sausage
SOE	Strategic Operations Executive – British wartime Intelligence Service

Sparks/
Sparker   The ship's radio operator

Stone frigate Naval shore establishment

'Swain   Alternative abbreviation for coxswain — often used
                 as a form of address

Sweep   Systematic search for enemy mines, vessels or other
                 targets

Three-badge
veteran   Rating with twelve or more years' service (a 'badge'
                 or arm stripe represents four years' service — hence
                 'three-badge' veteran for twelve years' naval
                 service)

Walther P38   The standard German military 9mm sidearm of
                 1938 vintage, which gradually replaced the famous
                 Luger pistol which dated from 1908

Wardroom   Room in a ship/shore establishment reserved for
                 commissioned officers

Yeoman of
Signals   The ship's signaller — often abbreviated to Yeo
                 when addressing the yeoman directly

=====O=====

Acknowledgements

==============================

The Channel to Freedom is the third volume of the fictionalised account of a Special Forces Unit that operated out of Tresco in the Isles of Scilly, making a vital contribution to the liberation of Europe during the Second World War.

I owe much to so many people for making this project become a reality.

First, for eleven of the most fulfilling and stimulating years of my professional life, I have enjoyed the rewarding enthusiasm and support of Thorogood Publishing's executive team. Always ready to listen and explore new ideas, they are a joy to collaborate with. My working relationship with Neil Thomas, Angela Spall and Elizabeth Hall is one which I value immensely.

In the Isles of Scilly, many people have generously given their time to answer my questions and provide helpful information, which has added historical authenticity and local context to the Tresco flotilla trilogy.

Those who have helped on Tresco include:

The ever-friendly and helpful folks of Radio Scilly, for publicising my work 'live' and on their excellent website with such enthusiasm.

The late Richard Barber, author of *The Last Piece of England* and former editor of *The Tresco Times*, who generously shared his own extensive research on Tresco's secret operations during the Second World War.

Robin Lawson, Manager of the New Inn Hotel, for his invaluable historical information about the role of the New Inn — and its integral shop — during the war. The New Inn features prominently throughout my trilogy.

Alasdair Moore, editor of the outstanding *Islander* journal, to whom I express my sincere thanks for his continued encouraging support.

Isobel Nelhams, whose sales of my books at Tresco Garden Centre allow me to continue to eat!

On St Martin's, I owe much to former postmistress Daphne Perkins and to Julia Walder, the present postmistress, for their enthusiastic assistance and willingness to answer my questions about the island and its role in the recent history of the Isles of Scilly.

To the late Sir Brooks Richards, author of *Secret Flotillas,* the HMSO definitive account of clandestine small boat operations between 1940 and 1944, I owe an inestimable debt for the time he kindly gave to answer my many questions during the initial research for my books. Being a spectator at Braiden Rock in July 2000 at the moving unveiling of the commemorative plaque to the Naval Special Forces based on Tresco during the war — and meeting Sir Brooks — was an unforgettable experience. It remains the driving force behind my books about the Tresco flotilla.

As a member of the Naval Club, Mayfair, I express my gratitude to Commander John Pritchard RN, the chief executive, and the Club journal, *WAVE.* This has regularly proved to be a source of relevant information on covert Coastal Forces operations during the Second World War and, especially, on the role of former RNVR officers.

Eight years of full-time and volunteer reserve service in first the Royal Navy (Intelligence) and secondly, the Royal Marines (Special Boat Service and Commando) have provided me with a rich source of personal experiences and material, upon which I have drawn extensively for all three volumes of the trilogy.

Three other Royal Navy contacts who have been extremely helpful are, firstly, Elizabeth Vaughan-Hughes for her kind permission to use a photograph of her late husband, Lieutenant Commander D M Vaughan-Hughes – former captain of the frigate, *HMS Fleetwood.*

Secondly, Keith Rayner, secretary of the HMS Fleetwood Association for his frequent invaluable help in so willingly providing naval data for my research.

Tremayne's love of *HMS Fleetwood*, I confess, is entirely autobiographical. During the war, she was heavily involved in Norwegian waters and in the Atlantic, when Tremayne would have known her. Within a day of joining her in December 1952, just before my twentieth birthday, I was hopelessly in love with her and the walls of my study are still covered in her portraits! After a frigate, serving with motor gun boats and two-man canoes felt like cheating on my first love – though they never failed to raise my adrenaline levels!

Thirdly, to Gray Young and Dr Dennis Mills … and my other former colleagues from the Joint Services School for Linguists, I express my unreserved gratitude.

I owe so much to Brenda, my wife, my best friend – and my canoeing companion – for her imaginative creativity, honed as a talented children's poet and author. I continue to learn so much from her about the challenging art of writing. Her ready combination of perceptive insight and a devastating sense of humour is the best antidote I know to my geriatric pomposity!

We first canoed together around the Scillies in 1959 as members of the Birmingham Canoe Club. Now in our seventies (and largely when the weather is warm and sunny!), we still go kayaking in the ever-changing waters between those enchanting islands…

Mike Williams